PRAISE F

"Daniel Judson is so much more than a crime-fiction novelist. He's a tattooed poet, a mad philosopher of the Apocalypse fascinated with exploring the darkest places in people's souls."

—*Chicago Tribune* on *The Water's Edge*

"Shamus winner Judson once again successfully mines Long Island's South Fork for glittering noir nuggets."

—*Publishers Weekly* on *The Violet Hour*

"A suspense masterpiece."

—Bookreporter.com on *The Violet Hour*

"Judson hits you with a 25,000-volt stun gun in chapter one and doesn't let up until the satisfying end."

—Alafair Burke, author of *212*, on *Voyeur*

"Judson is a thoroughly accomplished writer."

—*Kirkus Reviews* on *Voyeur*

"A searing, brooding look at the bleak side of the Hamptons . . . an intense novel."

—*South Florida Sun-Sentinel* on *The Darkest Place*

"Action packed. Loss and redemption rule in Shamus Award–winning Daniel Judson's third novel, set in Southampton nights so cold that they could cool off a reader sizzling in this summer's heat. It's noir on ice."

—*USA Today* on *The Darkest Place*

"This taut thriller is far from predictable, and its dark and mysterious plot suits Judson's understated writing style."

—*Publishers Weekly* on *The Poisoned Rose*

THE SHADOW AGENT

OTHER TITLES BY DANIEL JUDSON

The Agent Series

The Rogue Agent
The Temporary Agent

The Gin Palace Trilogy

The Poisoned Rose
The Bone Orchard
The Gin Palace

The Southampton Trilogy

The Darkest Place
The Water's Edge
Voyeur

Stand-Alone Titles

The Betrayer
Avenged
The Violet Hour

THE SHADOW AGENT

DANIEL JUDSON

This is a work of fiction. Names, characters, organizations, places, events, and incidents are either products of the author's imagination or are used fictitiously. Any resemblance to actual persons, living or dead, or actual events is purely coincidental.

Published by Thomas & Mercer, Seattle

www.apub.com

ISBN-13: 9781503959156
ISBN-10: 1503959155

Cover design by Rex Bonomelli

Printed in the United States of America

in memory of my mother, Mary B. Judson

Prologue

"I'm done running," Stella says. "And I'm done hiding. So let's not fight it anymore. Raveis wants you, always has, so he'll take me, too, if it means getting you. We'll learn what he has to teach, because no matter what we do or where we hide, the Benefactor will find us. So let's be ready for him when he does. Or better yet, let's save him the trouble and find him first. We'll bring them the Benefactor's head, and then we'll go somewhere and live our lives in peace. I'd rather die beside you than live without you. Maybe if we do this, we won't have to do either."

Tom looks at her but says nothing.

"So let's call Raveis now because there isn't a lot of time to waste. The Benefactor is out there, Tom, and you know it. He's out there, and he wants us—all of us—dead."

It is six a.m. when the vehicles arrive—a convoy of black SUVs sent by the Colonel and driven and protected by men Raveis has recruited and trained.

To Stella's eye, each and every one of these heavily armed men possesses the zeal of a true follower.

Hardened disciples of Sam Raveis, these men will not betray them.

And may God have mercy on them if they try.

By the time the vehicles depart again thirty minutes later, the Cahill estate on the eastern edge of Shelter Island is closed up. The SUV that Stella and Tom occupy is the last to leave the grounds.

She watches through the rear window as the gates are closed by the guards who will remain behind as caretakers.

The home that had once been full of life and light and healing is now silent and empty.

Abandoned, like so many of the places in which Stella has lived over these past years.

But what is behind them doesn't matter.

She tells herself this, believes it now more than ever.

What does matter is who is beside her and who is around the two of them.

Not just Raveis's armed men but the four women in the other vehicles whom Tom calls his sisters-in-arms.

Krista MacManus and Sarah Grunn and Valena Nakash and Sandy Montrose.

Stella is among warriors, but more than that, she is herself one now.

She is strong and will only get stronger.

Nothing is the same, nor will it ever be again.

Two days later, in an upper-floor room of a New York City hotel, Raveis lays out what it will mean for Tom and Stella to sign on.

"I won't train you together. As you know, I have multiple compounds, each set up to address a certain stage, so one of you will be at one while the other is at another. Tom will finish first, obviously, because of his military background, but also because of what he's already done for us. There's no point in teaching him what he clearly knows. I'm

thinking it will be three months, tops, for him, and possibly double that for Stella. And once Tom completes his training, he'll be put in the field immediately, which means I can't guarantee the two of you will be assigned together, at least not at first. We can't pull Tom off whatever he might be working on just so you two can have a reunion. Do you understand?"

Tom and Stella tell him that they do.

"Another thing you need to know up front is you won't see each other until after Stella graduates. No weekends off, no running away for a day or two to meet somewhere and screw. And during your training, your communications will be limited."

Stella asks, "How limited?"

"You'll have to surrender all devices, no exceptions, but we set up an email account for each of you to use. You'll have computer access for thirty minutes once a week."

"Why did you set up the accounts?"

Tom answers for him. "So communications can be monitored."

Raveis nods. "Everything is read, incoming and outgoing." He watches them before continuing. "It's a major commitment for someone to make, signing up for this, but it's also a costly investment for us. That's why we generally recruit ex-military with an emphasis on former Special Forces. That way we have reason to expect that our candidates will make it through to the end."

"I can handle it," Stella says.

"If I doubted that, I wouldn't be here." Raveis looks at Tom. "If you haven't already, I need you to fill her in on what she should expect."

"She knows," Tom says.

"And you're okay with it? With what she'll be subjected to. What will be done to her in the course of her training. My staff is currently all male, Tom. They won't go easy on her. They wouldn't be doing her any favors if they did."

"We both know what to expect."

"It's not just the training. It's the work." He looks at Stella. "We're a private-sector answer to the CIA's Special Activities Division. We do what the government can't legally do, and that sometimes means the blackest of black ops."

Stella says to him, "I know. I understand."

Nodding again, Raveis pauses as if to make up his mind. He is a man about whom Tom and Stella know little beyond that he works for the Colonel—a man about whom they know even less, including his actual name.

A link in a chain, Sam Raveis, among other things, oversees the training of the candidates selected by his many recruiters, one of whom was Tom's former commanding officer.

For eight years, James Carrington was both a father figure and a commander to Tom. But this man, who Tom knows better than anyone—the man who led Tom during his years as a Seabee—can no longer be counted on, leaving the future Tom deeply craves in the hands of those who are barely more than shadows.

If he had his way, he and Stella would be far from here, beholden to no one but each other, their survival the only cause they serve. But just as Tom is a means to the end that Raveis and the Colonel seek, those two men are the means to the end that Tom desires for Stella and himself.

"There are contracts to go through and sign," Raveis says. "But do me a favor and think about it for another twenty-four hours."

"We don't need another twenty-four hours," Stella says.

Raveis looks at Tom.

Tom nods. "We're ready."

Raveis tells them that he will send some men to take them to the airport in the morning. Among them will be an attorney, and the necessary papers will be signed in the car en route.

Then he wishes them luck and leaves.

A moment passes before Tom and Stella do anything more than look at each other.

They now have just eighteen hours together.

Later that night, Tom watches from the bed as Stella emerges from the shower.

The lights are off, and the only illumination is the glow of Midtown beyond the window.

Stepping to the desk, Stella drops her robe and reaches for her clothes—jeans and T-shirt and cardigan, sports bra and boy shorts and socks.

Next to the neatly piled clothing is her strand of pearls, which, along with her Kimber K6 .357 Magnum and several disposable smartphones, represents the extent of her personal belongings.

Tom asks her to stop. Stella does and faces him.

Her dark, long curls, uncombed and wet, frame her face. A year and a half of intense CrossFit training, all of it done alongside a much younger woman, has given her a body that is hard and lean.

The same amount of years spent running a Vermont breakfast-and-lunch diner—up before dawn, done just prior to sunset, in bed and asleep by nine—has kept her skin pale.

She smiles. "Is there something you need, sir?"

"You know."

Her smile widens. She reaches for the pearls and puts them on, adjusting the long strand till the knot hangs between her breasts. Then she lets her arms drop to her sides.

She was wearing those pearls the first time Tom saw her, when he decided on a whim to stop at a railcar diner in northwestern Connecticut.

And she had those pearls on again the first night they'd spent together.

He had warned Stella beforehand about the state of his flesh so as not to shock her. His torso bears the scars of war—a mix of fragment wounds and suture marks, all now healed, some faded but others not.

The contrast of her exquisite beauty, augmented by the pearls against her bare skin, had only cast a harsher light on the markers of violence that had been left on him.

If she had minded the sight of his scars, though, she'd hid it well.

He looks at her now as if he will never see her again, which is true, because the world they are about to enter changes a person—Tom has seen it and has done all he can to avoid joining that world for that very reason.

The Stella he will find when they are reunited will not be the Stella who is before him now, just as he will not be the man whose stare she is meeting.

Learning all the ways to kill—among the many other skills Sam Raveis and his trainers will share—is not something from which any person returns unaltered.

Stella says, "Shall I come back to bed?"

"In a minute."

His fascination with her naked body has always pleased her. After all, at forty-six, she is eleven years older than he. Reading his expression, though, tells her that his watching her is different from his usual act of admiration.

She takes a guess at what he is thinking.

"We have to believe that we will be together again," she says. "We can't go into this doubting that."

"I know."

But Tom's expression doesn't change, nor does the way he is looking at her.

A moment passes before Stella asks, "What else is on your mind?"

"Raveis said our limited communications will be monitored and that he can't guarantee when we'll see each other once you're done with

your training. I'm thinking that we should have a way of getting a message through to each other, just in case."

"In case of what?"

"We have to consider the possibility that the time will come when our interests no longer align with those of our employer. If that happens—either during our training or after—we'll need a way to safely communicate."

"What do you have in mind?"

"First, we keep our emails brief. Spend five minutes on them, tops. We'll use the rest of our allotted time for something else. Since they'll likely be monitoring our internet usage as well, we'll use that against them. We'll need to hide in a well-established pattern of traffic whatever it is we want to say to each other when the time comes."

Stella thinks about that, then says, "Okay, Tom, tell me what you need me to do."

PART ONE

One

She watched as the old man grew nearer to death.

For three weeks he had hung on, drifting in and out of consciousness, losing coherence with each day that passed, really just fading away from existence, breath by breath, before her eyes.

She'd been aware of his stubbornness her entire life, had learned that very trait from him, among many other things.

She was, after all, in countless ways *him*; at one point he'd been the only influence in her life.

His stubbornness was all he had toward the end; his strength and will gone, it was the sheer inflexibility of his dark heart that kept him going.

And that was what finally prompted her to act.

She made a phone call, then left the small cottage and traveled twenty miles down the mountain to Bariloche, where she acquired what she needed from his doctor.

As was the case with most residents of this remote Argentine city, the doctor was a German by birth who still spoke German and was likely not far from death himself, having arrived here in the same influx of European immigrants in the 1940s.

Situated in the foothills of the Andes, Bariloche was akin to an Austrian ski resort; its deepwater lake, surrounded by snowcapped mountains, was more Alpine than South American.

As she began the return trip up the treacherous mountain road, she hoped that in her absence the man who had raised her had passed. But upon her return to the cottage, she found that he was still living—still *barely* living—and so she had no choice but to follow through with her plan.

Of all the kills she'd taken part in, none had been in the name of mercy, which meant this was new territory.

But newness appealed to her, drove her in her personal life toward occasional recklessness—a counterbalance to the precision and precaution that her profession demanded.

A month shy of fifty-five, she'd been killing since she was twenty, though she had taken part in several of her grandfather's kills prior to coming of age and turning pro.

She'd been fifteen when he initiated her apprenticeship, bringing her along when he journeyed to Mexico City to assassinate a general whose campaign against drug cartels had become too successful.

A man traveling with his lovely and doting granddaughter had made for a good cover.

There wasn't a month that went by that she didn't dream of that journey, reliving in vivid detail the night she had first observed the act of one person killing another.

But she and her grandfather had drifted apart over the years. He hadn't aged well, becoming sick and feeble of both body and mind, and her busy schedule had kept her on the move and unable to make it back to the cottage, which because of its seclusion wasn't an easy journey.

She knew, though, that the inconvenience was an excuse and that it had been her choice to pull away from him for the sole reason of sparing herself from having to witness the inevitable degradation of the man to whom she owed everything.

The man who had once been everything.

Standing at the foot of his bed, she understood that it was time now—long past time—to end that degradation, and with it, her debt.

Turning off the lights, she pulled up a chair and sat, then injected him with a lethal dose of fentanyl and waited.

The cottage had been a place of refuge in her childhood, a destination for her and her father, who had also been devoted to the man who was now, finally, drawing his last breaths.

As his labored breathing grew more and more ragged, she knew that she would never again be required to make the journey to Bariloche and face the memories that the dark and cold rooms of this cottage evoked.

And as she observed his final, tortured exhalation, she knew, too, the immediate actions that were required of her now that Ernst Schmidt was at last dead.

The peacefulness that settled in the room was oddly discomforting.

The sounds of his struggling lungs silenced for good, there was nothing for her to hear but her own breathing.

She stood by his bed and said her goodbye.

First, she thanked him for all he'd done to make her what she was now, and then she apologized for the trouble she had been in her youth—the sullen child, the willful adolescent, the risk-taking adult.

Drugs, men, women, living beyond her means—everything she had done to herself then had been a source of pain for him, though she had sensed that he'd understood her rage.

He had, in fact, done everything in his power to cultivate it.

With her apology spoken, she left him and packed up her few things.

Of all his possessions, the only item she wanted for her own was kept in his small windowless office, hidden behind a false wall.

Passing through the secret door, she took one last look at his cherished belongings—mementos of the man he had been.

Black-and-white framed photographs, still clear after seven-plus decades without exposure to sunlight, showed Ernst Schmidt in his Hitler Youth uniform.

In some, he was posing alone; in others, he was among older SS officers.

A handsome teenage boy back then, he was tall and athletic and smiling, no hint yet of facial hair.

It was in the photographs of him taken during the final months of the war that he more resembled the man she'd known.

Older by a few years, he was at that time a veteran member of the *Werwolf*, the Nazi guerrilla outfit tasked with behind-the-lines skirmishes during the Allied invasion of Europe.

A year later, during those last, desperate months of the Third Reich, he had shifted exclusively to reprisal killings.

By then he had a beard and an animal's fierceness in his eyes, both of which seemed at odds with his still-young face, and he had participated in a campaign of atrocities—summary executions by firing squad, public hangings of town officials in village squares, burnings of countless homes and farms.

Tactics meant to instill terror in the towns that had been liberated by the Allies as they moved to encircle Berlin.

He'd first learned to hunt men as a *Werwolf*, and it was this skill that had caught the attention of the man who would later become his lifelong employer.

The same man for whom she worked.

The memento she wanted had nothing to do with her grandfather's politics, which she cared little about.

Profit was her cause, pleasure her religion.

The item hung on the wall above his desk, along with his collection of medals and ribbons. A strange place for a wedding photo, perhaps—or not, considering that in it he was wearing the uniform of which he had been so very proud, even at the end.

His bride—the grandmother she'd never met—was a beautiful woman. As a child, she would often sneak into this sanctum just to stare at that radiant face and compare it with her own.

Despite having the same curled blonde hair and prized Aryan features—blue eyes, high cheekbones, full lips, broad face—she had always felt that she did not compare and never would.

In moments of happiness—flirting with men to lure them either to their deaths or, briefly, into her bed—her smile did not live up to that of the woman grasping the arm of the uniformed man.

She was as drawn to that photo now as she had been as a child. Taking it from the wall as a reminder of the only brightness in her childhood, she turned her attention to the last detail that needed tending before she was free to leave.

The gasoline required was stored in gallon-size containers in the small shed behind the cottage.

Six gallons total, more than enough to do the job.

Carrying them two at a time into the cottage, she proceeded to spread the accelerant in every room—the greatest concentration of it in his hidden office, the next greatest around his deathbed.

Then she stood at the front door and took one final look around.

She was alone in the world at last—no family, her only human contact reduced to business associates and those necessary in her fervent pursuit of pleasure.

She had waited a long time for this day, for the moment when there would no longer be anyone close enough to judge her, no one to ask anything of her, no one to whom she owed anything or any part of herself.

She lit a match, tossed it toward the center of the room, turned, and ran.

By the time she was in her car and driving away, the cottage was engulfed in flames that reached fifty feet into the clear morning air before diminishing into twisting ribbons of black smoke.

She reached Montreal by the following evening, and shortly after ten the next morning, the FedEx package arrived.

The cell phone it contained, once she had powered the device up, received a single message summoning her to meet her employer in New York City.

Having been away from her beloved apartment for three weeks, she regretted that it would be necessary to seal the place up again, especially since what she found most enjoyable about where she lived was the breeze that came in off the Saint Lawrence River and the way it caused the long white curtains hanging at her open windows to swell and flutter like happy ghosts.

The fact that it was an early-autumn breeze, her favorite, only deepened her sense of regret.

But the place would be here when she was done, and there were more than enough days of fall weather ahead.

And anyway, maybe what she really needed to do was work.

Two hours after receiving the directive, she had closed up her apartment, packed, and was en route to meet with the Benefactor.

Depending on how long Customs questioned her at the border, it should take roughly seven hours for her to reach New York.

A long drive during which she would have plenty of time to think about, among other things, what she had just done.

He called her what her grandfather had called her—Esa.

She addressed him by his title, the way everyone did—the Benefactor.

She knew, however, who the Benefactor really was.

Pascal Henkel, born in Munich in 1950.

She knew, too, what even fewer did—the story of his origin.

Henkel had been in his early twenties when she first met him more than forty years ago. Her grandfather had seen in that young man something that he believed this failing world needed. And the young man had seen in her grandfather a man whom he could make good use of.

In the years that followed, Henkel had been one of the handful of visitors to make the arduous journey to the isolated cottage.

A pilgrimage, of sorts, for the dark-souled.

Henkel had not only made that trek but also repeated it often.

He would never stay for more than a few days at a time, but he and her grandfather would barely sleep during those visits, spending their time drinking buttered *Kaffee* and talking.

She'd sometimes listen to her grandfather retell his war stories, which, once the *Kaffee* was replaced with schnapps, would lead to lectures on the history of terrorism and the virtues of asymmetric warfare.

His hatred for Jews did not prevent him from acknowledging the brilliance of their victory in the Six-Day War.

He despised Communists, yet that did not stop him from recognizing the significance of the defeat of the United States in Vietnam.

Nor did his contempt for Muslims blind him to the importance of the Soviet defeat in Afghanistan.

In all coming wars, he had predicted, the powerful would inevitably lose to the insurgent.

The days of fronts and armies and occupations were waning, and the reign of terrorism—death by a thousand cuts—was upon us.

Those lessons weren't lost on Esa, either, and so she had chosen her profession with that understanding in mind.

Really, though, what other profession could she have chosen, having grown up as she had in the home of a former *Werwolf* who had been visited almost exclusively by the kind of men who were drawn to such a person?

She remembered every one of the young Henkel's visits, remembered being fascinated by the handsome young man—the elite but disillusioned soldier—sitting at her grandfather's breakfast table.

Though she and Henkel had barely interacted, speaking for the most part only when she brought meals to the table, he had always been kind to her.

And when Henkel rose to his position of power and became known as the Benefactor, he had repaid his debt to her grandfather by first employing him and then, once she was grown, Esa.

In his later years, however, her grandfather had warned her never to fully trust the man he'd helped create.

The monster the world very much needed.

He'd skin you alive if doing so suited his needs, the old man would say. *And he'd look you dead in the eyes as he did it.*

Esa kept that in mind, always.

It was past midnight, and the East River State Park was empty.

The Benefactor was standing with his longtime bodyguard, Karl.

Both men were well dressed—dark overcoats, tailored suits beneath, Italian leather shoes. But that was where their similarities ended.

In his midsixties now, the Benefactor had gray hair and the kind of clean-shaven, taut face that indicated wealth and pampering. Tall and athletically built, his menace came more from the power he wielded than from the physical strength he clearly still possessed.

Once a soldier, always a soldier.

Karl, on the other hand, was a brute somewhere in his thirties, stoic, and always staring, his weightlifter's build and the violence it promised a constant, overt threat.

He seemed to stand with a slight forward lean, as if anticipating the order to pounce, eager to do the work for which he was made.

Usually Karl remained several feet behind the Benefactor, but tonight he was a few steps ahead, placing himself between his protectee and the woman his protectee had beckoned.

Esa noticed two other men standing fifty feet back—far enough to be out of earshot, but close enough to cross the distance in a matter of seconds.

These men were dressed in jeans and leather jackets—a plainclothes protection detail, and likely not the only such detail in the vicinity.

Their presence, along with Karl's unusual placement, told Esa that something had changed.

"I was sorry to hear about your grandfather," the Benefactor said.

"News travels fast."

"It does, as it should when it's as important as the passing of a great man. He had a vision. You and I both owe him a great deal."

Esa nodded, glanced at the bodyguards before looking back at the Benefactor. "What's the job?"

The Benefactor paused. "A deep-cover operative we need terminated is about to be drawn out into the open. I will not lie to you, Esa. Everyone we have sent to take him out so far has been killed, the Algerian included. Since our most recent effort, however, this person has become even more dangerous. Whatever resources you require will be provided. Your budget is unlimited, but your time is not. Our window of opportunity is narrow, and it is unlikely we will get another chance like this anytime soon, so you must not fail."

"How reliable is your intelligence?"

"We have operatives on the inside at many levels. This comes from a source high up. Your target will likely have a security detail, so you'll need to assemble a team. You may staff it as you see fit, but I suggest you keep it small. A four-man fire team should be sufficient."

Esa nodded. "How much time do I have to prepare?"

"We won't know the exact timetable till morning, but the target should be departing for a meeting at some point the following evening. All this is contingent, of course, on his taking the bait, but I have every confidence that he will." The Benefactor paused. "An associate with a shared interest in this matter wants a representative of his inserted into your team. I apologize for this, but it is unavoidable. The good news is you have worked with him before."

"Who is he?"

"An American named Walker."

Esa nodded. In the fraternity of assassins, having killed someone together was as close to a bond of trust as could be found.

"Yes, I know him," she said.

"A hotel room has been booked for you, and a complete dossier on the target and his known associates is waiting there. The specific details of the operation—times, location, route, size of his security—will be forwarded to you as they become available."

"May I ask who the subject is?"

When the Benefactor did not offer an answer, it was yet another indication that something had changed.

Esa took another look at the men on the periphery.

She recognized a war footing when she saw one. "Anything else I need to know?"

"Your target is not someone to be underestimated. I can't stress that too strongly. And neither are those with whom he associates. A Tier 1 security detail will no doubt be assigned to him, but it's those he calls friends who should be your real concern. Two kinds of people are drawn to this business: those seeking to profit and those driven by ideology. I have always found the latter to be more dangerous. Your grandfather was the latter, I am the latter. Our target and his friends seem to be that as well."

The Benefactor watched her before continuing. "Kill him, Esa, and anyone who gets in your way. What we do—our continued success, everything we've striven for these past three decades—is dependent on the elimination of this threat. Do you understand?"

"I do," Esa said.

The Benefactor extended a gloved hand. "Good luck."

Esa took his hand, matching his powerful grip as best as she could.

The boutique hotel was located on the Lower East Side.

Esa arrived at two in the morning; picked up the key that had been left for her at the front desk; rode the small, cage-like elevator to the fifth floor; and let herself into the room that overlooked Orchard Street.

Using a burner phone to send and receive a series of coded texts, she worked to find the two men she hoped would fill out her team.

It took time, but the men who topped her list—the McQueen twins—were available and could arrive in New York by dawn.

The twins were handsome, Irish by birth but raised and educated in Paris. Esa had first worked with them four years ago when together, they had comprised one-half of a six-man team sent to kill a journalist in Johannesburg.

She and the McQueen twins had celebrated their success with too much grappa, and in the morning she'd awakened in a hotel bed with both men.

In the years that followed, they had worked together twice more, ending both collaborations with a similar celebration, each encounter leaving her fantasizing about the next time.

She'd be lying to herself if she didn't admit that she was hoping for a variation of that routine.

With the team set, she sat at the desk and opened the dossier, which contained psychological write-ups of the target and his compatriots, as well as numerous after-action reports that the target had written following various operations.

She was interested in the reports concerning the Algerian.

If he had screwed up in some way, she was determined not to repeat his errors.

But what she wanted to see before diving in to her reading were the photographs.

The first one she came across was of a young man in his navy uniform.

Barely more than twenty years old, he had dark hair, a handsome enough face, and eyes that stared intently—not unlike Karl's eyes, she noted.

The next photograph was clearly a surveillance photograph of that same man, though older this time—midthirties, she estimated.

The man was standing at the edge of a body of water, and a woman was facing him, the two in an intense discussion.

It was night, and in the background a well-kept yard sloped upward to the back porch of a large home, its windows lit.

Beneath that photo two names were printed in bold letters:

SEXTON, TOM.

QUIRK, STELLA.

Beneath that, LOCATION: THE CAHILL ESTATE, SHELTER ISLAND, NEW YORK.

Esa noticed right away that Quirk appeared to be significantly older than Sexton, maybe in her midforties.

It crossed Esa's mind that this particular fact may have figured heavily into the Benefactor's decision to select her for this mission.

Preferences were weaknesses, and she'd made a career out of exploiting the weaknesses of men.

There was always the chance that the job would come down to her and her subject face-to-face, and should that prove to be the case, any resemblance to the woman he loved could give her the edge.

Quirk's hair was thick and curled, like her own.

Achieving the exact shade of black wouldn't be a problem.

The next photo showed two women seated together on the porch that had been in the background of the photograph of Sexton and Quirk.

One was blonde and professional-looking, in her thirties; the other was younger, tattooed, and edgy.

They were alone, holding hands.

GRUNN, SARAH.

MACMANUS, KRISTA.

Other photos showed a series of known associates, all of whom were identified by the same bold print along each photo's bottom edge.

CAHILL, CHARLIE.

MONTROSE, SANDY (WHEREABOUTS UNKNOWN).

A man in his fifties—CARRINGTON, JAMES.

And another man, maybe a few years older—HAMMERTON, JOHN (WHEREABOUTS UNKNOWN).

Four more photos remained. One was of the security detail that would be escorting their target, and of the three men in that photo, only the leader was named—LYMAN (SEAL).

Another photo was of a woman in her midthirties—DURAND, SARAH. She was listed as support staff. The third was of another woman, TORRES, GINA, and a man, GARRICK, ANDREW. They were listed as Sexton's close-protection team.

The final photograph in the file was an oddity—a printout of a selfie taken by Quirk as she stood in front of a free-standing oval mirror, her cell phone held off to one side in an effort to capture her full reflection from head to toe.

As Esa had done with the photograph of her grandmother, she compared herself to this subject.

She saw confidence in the woman wearing a white Oxford shirt, a string of knotted pearls, and nothing else.

The shirt was unbuttoned and parted, showing her breasts and flat stomach and hips, as well as the dark strip of pubic hair between them.

A single word was printed on the photo.

INTERCEPTED.

The abundance of material—easily the most complete packet she'd ever received—supported the Benefactor's claim that this was a critical job.

It also confirmed that the source of all this material was someone with access to personnel files and sensitive logistics.

When she was done studying the photo of Quirk, Esa placed it with the others, then reached for the dossier and began reading.

Esa and the McQueen brothers met at a diner to await their instructions.

It was just after dawn when the text came in.

The exact time and location of the target's departure was included in the text as well as the location of the meeting.

A second text instructed Esa at precisely what point in the target's journey she and her team were to strike.

That text also included an unexpected command that altered the mission.

Secure item and deliver.

An all-out kill mission was one thing, but a kill-and-retrieve mission was something else entirely. It narrowed the options, eliminating outright the possibility of striking from a distance and then fleeing, which was any assassin's first choice.

A long-range kill was still in the mix, of course, but that would mean whatever distance there was between her team and their target would have to be traversed, after which the body of their target would have to be thoroughly searched.

Even in the best-case scenario, these were time-consuming actions. More than that, the failure to cross the distance meant the inability to search and retrieve.

It was better, then, to kill up close and eliminate the chance of having success in one part of the job but complete failure in the other.

This complication wasn't something Esa couldn't handle, though.

She'd done such work many times before—killed men and women, standing near them or, in some cases, lying beside them as they died, after which she'd seized what she had been sent to obtain and made her escape.

In all those missions, the objective was something specific, so she composed a follow-up text requesting a description of the item.

But before she could send it, another text came through.

Flash drive.

Esa shared the updated information with the brothers, then shut down the phone and pocketed it.

The schedule the Benefactor had established meant that she and her team had fourteen hours to prepare.

Driving to New Jersey to select the weaponry and obtain a vehicle would take six hours at most, leaving them eight hours of free time.

There was, she saw, no reason to wait till after the job to celebrate.

Two

In a Brooklyn safe house, Tom Sexton sat up and moved to the edge of his bed.

It was a strange bed, but he was used to that.

He hadn't slept in the same place twice since the completion of his training three months ago.

Since he was even more of a threat to the Benefactor than he had been before, and therefore more of a target, it was better for all concerned if he kept moving, grabbing whatever rest he could in the places where no one would think to look.

Should someone come looking for him, however, and should the worst then occur, his occupying these forgotten neighborhoods meant that collateral damage would be limited. An unseen escape after an attack was also at least within the realm of possibility, since witnesses would be few to none and security cameras unlikely.

Deep in the shadows now, deeper certainly than he'd gone before or had ever thought possible, Tom was a man in hiding—a man waiting for a chance at justice.

Or maybe it wasn't justice at all, but vengeance. Maybe there wasn't a difference. He'd come to consider that justice might simply be an illusion constructed to make acceptable the deepest of human impulses: the desire to punish those who have wronged us.

And be certain they could never wrong us again.

When he had first arrived at this safe house—a long-abandoned seven-story hotel—he'd immediately thought of his father's last night alive.

Though he hadn't witnessed the events, Tom had heard enough to have a clear idea of what had transpired.

His father had lured the four killers for hire to a hotel not unlike this one. It had taken George Sexton two years to track the team down and arrange the meeting, under the pretense that he was looking to hire them.

But they had killed his wife and daughter in his home, and since that night he'd given up everything except his drive for revenge.

Tom often wondered what his father had seen when he'd finally stood face-to-face with these men.

After a long search—a costly search that all but bankrupted him—there they'd been before him, within reach.

At some point someone had acted—either his father had made his move or one of the assassins had beaten him to it.

In the resulting struggle, his father had killed three before the fourth had gotten him.

The report filed by the medical examiner made clear the violence of the encounter, which had descended into vicious hand to hand.

Eyes gouged, windpipes crushed, ears half-torn.

Tom had been in such life-or-death struggles, so he knew full well the horror of them.

The cause of his father's death had been listed as strangulation, but Tom did his best to turn his mind away from that fact.

Being in his own small room with nothing to occupy him but memory and imagination, it was impossible to keep his tired mind from wandering yet again to what he both knew and didn't know.

What he was sure of was that more sleep wasn't coming, so he looked toward the room's only window, the view beyond which was the brick wall on the other side of a narrow alleyway.

But if he couldn't see out, then no one could see in.

And anyway, he wasn't here for the view, having long ago shut himself down to any and all pleasures. Still, he allowed himself to indulge in the memories of his last days with Stella.

Those final, precious hours he'd spent beside her, the things they had said, the sight and feel and smell of her—these were his only refuge from his current life as an operator awaiting an assignment.

Once he'd gotten all that he could from his memories, Tom cleared his thoughts.

There were dangers in his line of work, so he needed to remain alert.

Thinking about Stella for too long always led him to wonder what stage of training she was in, and by his calculations, she was possibly in her final weeks now; if that was true, it meant she was currently in the hands of men tasked with pushing her to the point of breaking.

It was during the last weeks that candidates were instructed in survival, evasion, resistance, and escape—SERE training, a grueling indoctrination that, among other things, included simulating as realistically as possible the treatment one should expect upon being captured by an enemy.

Brutal confinement, forced nudity, enhanced interrogation techniques.

Degradations and deprivations—firsthand experience of these was the only way to prepare the human mind and body for the anguish one human was capable of inflicting on another.

But Tom didn't want to think of Stella in the midst of the collection of ordeals that Raveis's men called training.

She would endure; Tom knew this, trusted this. And she would be made stronger by it, just as all who had come before her had been.

But she would also be changed by those events, just as Tom had been changed by them, exactly as he had once predicted.

Of course, acknowledging that change was to think about what would cause it, so Tom sought out something else to think about in the remaining hours before light.

As hard as he tried, though, nothing came to mind, because there was, really, nothing but Stella and the drive for vengeance and the freedom that came with it.

But he caught a break after a few moments—one of the three burner phones resting on the table by the strange bed buzzed.

Picking up the device, he turned it faceup and glanced at the text message.

Gather your team, location echo.

Three

The hotel had been shuttered nearly a decade ago.

In that time, the decay that had likely begun while it was still in business had only accelerated.

Wallpaper peeling, floorboards rotting, ceilings water damaged.

Tom and the two members of his close-protection team had taken three of the more habitable rooms on the top floor. Within minutes of Tom's notification, they had packed up their gear and were on their way out.

No member carried more than what a medium-size backpack could hold, nor was any evidence of their presence ever left behind.

Garrick took point as they headed down the six flights of stairs, Tom behind him, and Torres behind Tom.

In his late thirties, Garrick was a few years older than Tom. He was larger, too—taller, with a solid torso and thick limbs. Energetic, even when he was at rest, he seemed always ready to burst through any physical obstacle that might be put in his way.

As a rule, each teammate shared as little personal information as possible, but Tom knew that Garrick, prior to signing on with Raveis, had been army infantry, served three tours of duty, one of which had delivered him to the same hellish province in Afghanistan where Tom had served his final months.

Tom's impression was that Garrick was dependable, coolheaded, and intelligent.

The presence of a gold wedding band on Garrick's left hand was, in fact, the only thing Tom didn't like about the man, but there was nothing that could be done about that.

No one was without some loved one somewhere.

More than that, Tom knew too well that men with nothing to lose tended to act in accordance with that belief, sometimes bravely, though often enough foolishly, and the last thing he wanted was someone on his team with the potential for the latter.

Perhaps having sensed Tom's concerns, Garrick had made an offer during his final interview.

You keep me alive, and I'll keep you alive.

The third team member, Torres, was thirty, tops. Only recently, Raveis had begun recruiting candidates from law enforcement, and Torres was one of the first of that class of graduates.

Based on the little he knew about her, Tom had been reluctant to choose her until Raveis had provided him with her records and requested that Tom look them over before reaching any decision.

You'd be lucky to have her, Raveis had said.

By the time Tom was halfway through her academic records, he realized he'd be a fool not to want her.

Her police academy records had only deepened his conviction.

Torres had risen fast during her eight years in the NYPD, her final promotion placing her within the elite Critical Response Command—the first line of defense against a terror-related attack. But there was more than her bona fides that had intrigued Tom. Having been born and raised in New York City, she knew her way around the five boroughs, and the idea of a local who could serve as a scout had its appeal.

The absence of any hint of a Bronx accent told Tom that she had both the desire and the ability for reinvention, which of course made him think of Stella, who had reinvented herself more than once.

It was her very reinvention that had saved Tom's life.

So having someone around who reminded him of the reason why he had committed to this world of private-sector special operations seemed like the thing to do.

For two months, Tom and Garrick and Torres had lived and worked together, moving from safe house to safe house, picking up the occasional close-protection assignment tossed their way by Raveis, mainly to keep them sharp while they waited for something more substantial.

As a rule, Tom didn't allow himself to give in to impatience, because haste was the enemy, worse even than fear.

More than a rule, his refusal to give in to impatience was deep within his nature.

But the sooner he got started—and his real work began—the sooner he and Stella would be free from all this.

Free of the man who employed them, and of the man who wanted them dead.

Perhaps this predawn order to gather and meet meant today was that day.

Exiting the hotel, the team started toward the SUV parked halfway down the block. The street was empty, the October morning rainy.

The team moved in formation, each member actively covering predetermined directions.

Front, rear, left, right, and points overhead.

Quick, expert, but also as covert as possible.

Knickerbocker Avenue was an isolated street in the Brooklyn neighborhood of East Williamsburg, but even places such as this one weren't undiscoverable by those charged with capturing or killing one or more of the Colonel's private contractors.

Tom himself had been at the top of the Benefactor's kill list for years without even knowing it.

He knew it now, though, and knew it well.

After reaching the SUV, the team placed their gear packs into the rear compartment before making their way around the vehicle and climbing in—Torres behind the wheel, Garrick in the front passenger seat, Tom in the seat directly behind Torres.

As he buckled in, Tom asked, "Time?"

Torres started the engine and shifted into drive. "This early there shouldn't be any traffic. We'll be there in twenty."

Tom nodded, focusing on what was outside the window to his left.

He would cover the driver's side while Garrick covered the passenger side.

Torres would keep a forward watch while frequently checking the rearview mirror.

Precautions, alertness, keeping to the shadows—this was the way they lived now, existing like the occupants of a city under siege.

Riding in silence, they crossed the East River, then headed north on the FDR Drive.

Echo was the code name for a Raveis-owned multistory parking garage on Manhattan's Upper East Side.

Tom had been there before—had, in fact, first encountered Raveis there—so he knew all the reasons why it was considered a secure meeting place.

He had also killed there, fighting shoulder to shoulder with Charlie Cahill, and so the idea of returning put Tom on his toes to an even greater degree.

Torres steered the SUV onto Seventy-Second Street, then turned into the garage entrance and headed down the first of the two steep ramps that would bring them to the lowest level, a subbasement where no cell phone signal could reach and even the loudest of sounds would be muffled.

As they reached the bottom of the second ramp, Tom saw three vehicles parked in the farthest, darkest corner: a Lincoln Town Car, a Ford panel van, and a BMW K1200R motorcycle.

All the vehicles were painted some variation of black—glossy, flat, matte. Their surfaces glistened from the rain.

Of the two people visible to Tom, he recognized just one.

Sam Raveis.

The second person, dressed in wet-weather motorcycle gear, was a woman. One of the first things Tom noted was that she was taller than Raveis by at least two inches.

She studied Tom closely as he exited the SUV alone and started walking toward them. Twenty feet short, he stopped.

From where he stood he could see the front of the panel van.

The two men inside were the kind of men in whose company Sam Raveis always traveled—dark-suited professionals with neatly trimmed hair and clean-shaven faces, men who were meant to appear anonymous while also standing out as members of a security detail.

Though Tom had recently served as a close-protection agent, the type of mission for which he'd specifically trained was deep-cover recon, so unlike Raveis's men, he had let his hair grow long over these past months and was sporting a full beard.

He was dressed now in the manner in which he always was: faded jeans, dark T-shirt, untucked work shirt over that to conceal his side-arm, and a billed operator's cap to obscure his face. The weather today required a light black raincoat.

Even before he'd been sent to Raveis's compounds and taught the art of tradecraft, Tom had learned that men who looked as he did now—unkempt, rough, maybe even a little dangerous—were disregarded by most, sometimes even actively ignored.

Moving unseen was more than his job.

It was what would keep him alive.

Tom glanced at the license plate of the motorcycle, committing it to memory, then did the same for the panel van.

Then he looked back at Raveis and the tall woman beside him.

The four-pocket leather field jacket she wore did little to hide her athletic build. Her dark hair hung straight, ending in a blunt cut just below her chin.

A full-face helmet was resting on the seat of the BMW, and Tom concluded that with the helmet and motorcycle gear on, it would be difficult for any observer to recognize that the rider speeding past was a woman.

The helmet would also mask her face, rendering more or less useless the web of security cameras that covered almost the entire city—at least when it came to leaving a definitive record of her presence.

Tom briefly imagined the freedom that would come with moving about with such anonymity.

Thinking about freedom—any kind of freedom—served only to remind him yet again of the life that awaited Stella and him: a home where no one could find them, no need to use fake names, no reason to look over their shoulders during the day or listen for footsteps at night.

The woman continued to stare at Tom, sizing him up. Tom simply stared back.

Raveis broke the standoff. Nodding toward the sedan, he said, “C’mon, Tom. You know the drill. Get in. We’ve got a lot to cover.”

Four

The Town Car began to move, but that didn't surprise Tom.

Meeting in a stationary vehicle parked in a concrete garage was one way to increase privacy, but putting that vehicle into motion offered an added level of protection against eavesdropping.

It also put Tom in the position of being a passenger along for the ride—and at the driver's mercy.

But just as the men in the black panel van would follow Raveis's Town Car, Tom's team would follow the van.

A minor consolation, but he would take what he could get.

Raveis and the tall woman had taken the seats facing forward, leaving Tom the seat that faced them.

This meant he would have his back to the driver, but before Tom could say anything about that, Raveis pressed a button on the door-mounted console and raised the opaque privacy screen.

With the windows already closed, the rear compartment of the Town Car was now sealed as tight as a tomb.

The vehicle exited the parking garage before proceeding east on Seventy-Second Street. Tom watched through the heavily tinted rear window as the two vehicles fell into formation behind them.

Raveis gestured to the woman. "This is Slattery. Since it's her meeting, she's going to start things off."

"It's good to finally meet you, Tom," Slattery said.

Her voice was low and steady, her manner reserved and professional to the point of being abrupt.

She spoke with an accent—or rather a mix of them—that caught Tom's attention right away.

There was a hint of southern lilt, with long midwestern vowels, but added to that was a slight Texas twang.

A stew generally indicative of someone who had moved around the country frequently as a child.

Tom had only ever encountered that mix in people whose parents had been career military.

He glanced at her hands for rings—school ring, wedding band, engagement ring, anything that might tell him something more about who she was.

Slattery's fingers were bare, and they were also long. Her hands were slender, yet large for a woman.

The last woman Raveis had introduced to Tom in a manner similar to this one had ended up trying to kill him.

Tom looked her in the eye, nodded, and replied that it was good to meet her as well.

Formalities complete, Slattery began. "I understand that Sarah Grunn is a close friend of yours."

"Yes."

"More than friends, no?"

Tom wasn't sure how to respond to that, but before he could say anything, Slattery clarified. "She's family to you. Like a sister."

Tom nodded.

"How did you meet her?" Slattery said.

"She led a team that was assigned to provide force protection outside my residence."

"This was the restaurant you lived above. Up in Vermont."

"It wasn't my restaurant."

"Your girlfriend owned it. Stella Quirk."

"That's technically correct, yes."

"Why 'technically'?"

Raveis said, "Tom strives to be at least accurate if not brutally honest. Back then he was separated from us—lying low, using assumed identities, false documentation, the whole thing. Stella had used her dead mother's identity to buy the business."

Slattery nodded. Tom got the sense that this information mattered to her. Then she said, "You had taken in the teenage daughter of a former Syrian intelligence officer who at the time was working for us, correct?"

"I was asked to, yes. By the Colonel."

"And later that night you came under attack. Ten heavily armed men led by an Algerian assassin affiliated with the Benefactor."

"I'm sure Raveis has reports on all this somewhere."

"He does, and I've read them. You provided overwatch during the attack," Slattery said.

"Yes."

"During all that, how did Grunn perform?"

"I only witnessed the initial attack, but from what I saw, she was Tier 1."

"But both men on her team were eventually killed."

"Like I said, I only witnessed the initial attack."

Slattery nodded. "Grunn's troubles didn't end with the loss of her men, though, did they? She was captured by the Algerian, roughed up by one of his men before being used as a hostage to draw you out. A knife was held to her throat."

"I don't hear a question."

"You witnessed that part, correct?"

"Yes."

"Describe it to me."

"I had remained behind to cover Stella's escape with Valena."

"The Syrian girl."

"Yes. The Algerian wanted to know where Stella was taking her. He said if I told him, Grunn would die quickly. If I didn't, he'd have her throat opened and she'd drown in her own blood."

Tom recalled the fear he'd seen in Grunn's eyes.

He recalled, too, her moving her head from side to side, indicating that Tom wasn't to tell the Algerian what he wanted to know.

It was a small but unmistakable gesture of defiance.

"Was she shaken by that experience?" Slattery said. "Losing her men, being roughed up by the Algerian, facing a particularly gruesome execution?"

"Who wouldn't be?"

"A direct answer, please."

"We were all shaken by it."

"How were you able to get out of that situation alive?"

Tom hesitated, then said, "Unknown to Stella and me, a deep-cover close-protection agent had been assigned to us."

"Krista MacManus."

"Yes. She worked as our line cook, had been with us for a year and a half." Tom paused. "She intervened."

"But the Algerian got away."

"Correct."

"And Grunn was the one who ultimately killed him. Two days later, at a safe house in Connecticut."

"I didn't witness that, either."

"According to her after-action report, she was grabbed again, this time by the Algerian himself. He held a pistol to her head."

"Like I said, I wasn't there," Tom said.

"After the Algerian was killed, all of you—Grunn, MacManus, Valena, you and your girlfriend, and a childhood friend of Cahill's named Sandy Montrose—shared some downtime together at the Cahill estate on Shelter Island. Was that the last time you saw Grunn?"

"It was."

"No contact at all after that. Emails, texts, phone calls."

"None."

Raveis said, "Tom signed up shortly after leaving Shelter Island, was at my camps for just over three months, has been a standby asset in the field since."

Again, Slattery nodded as if to give what Raveis had said due deference before asking Tom, "Do you know where she went after you left the estate?"

"She and Krista were headed to where Krista had been raised. A farm in northern Vermont. The two of them were to provide close protection to Valena until she enrolled at Taft."

"You were aware that Sarah Grunn and Krista MacManus had entered into a romantic relationship, yes?"

"I was. Is that a problem?"

"Everything we know about Grunn's history indicates that she was strictly heterosexual."

"Why would that matter?"

"Because while a sudden switch of sexual preference might be the realization of one's true nature brought on by a life-or-death experience, it could also be something else. Nothing wrong with a preference, mind you, it's just the suddenness of the change, and so soon after a bad episode in the field, that is a reason for concern."

"Are you her shrink?"

"I'm a lot of things."

Tom looked at Raveis. "What's going on?"

Slattery was about to answer, but Raveis raised his hand—a small gesture, but it stopped her.

Raveis took a breath, let it out, then said, "Six weeks ago, Tom, Grunn came back to work for us, said she was eager to get back into the field. After a requisite reevaluation, she was cleared and given an assignment, which she completed, then was given another, which she also completed, no problems whatsoever. Everything seemed fine; a valued operator was back where we needed her. But then three days ago she disappeared. Her teammates found her bed empty one morning, all her gear gone. The only item she'd left behind was a cell phone. There was no sign of a struggle, no data on the cell phone, nothing."

"What was the assignment she was on when she disappeared?"

Slattery and Raveis glanced at each other. Raveis bowed his head, and Slattery said to Tom, "Grunn was part of a team tasked with hunting down your former commanding officer."

Carrington.

"A kill squad," Tom said.

Raveis replied, "Yes. One of several we have on active status."

"Interest in that kind of work doesn't sound like Grunn. Not the one I knew."

"Which is our concern as well," Slattery said. "It's possible that her run-in with the Algerian and his men caused a trauma that either she was able to conceal during her reevaluation or that didn't manifest until some point after."

"Her sudden request for reassignment from protection to special activities didn't set off any alarms?"

"It was seen at the time as her simply wanting more skin in the game. That can happen to someone who goes through what she had."

"Also, she knew Carrington," Raveis added. "He had recruited her, they'd obviously met on several occasions during that process, and there was always the chance their connection would prove useful at some point. As you well know, a familiar face can come in handy at times."

When Tom had first met Raveis three years ago—in a furtive meeting nearly identical to this one—he'd been asked to help find a former recon marine he had served with during his time as a navy Seabee.

That recon marine was Charlie Cahill.

When Raveis had asked for Tom's help bringing Cahill in, the fact that Tom was unlikely to be instantly killed by the man whose team

Tom had once saved, and who himself had saved Tom's life, was stated as the reason for his having been chosen for the mission.

It fit, then, that Raveis would want someone who'd had prior contact with Carrington on the team actively hunting him.

A friendly face was often the best disguise.

Tom said to Slattery, "You interviewed Grunn's teammates, right? The people she was with before disappearing. What did they say about her frame of mind? Was she moody, prone to angry outbursts, anything like that?"

"None of them had met her previously, so they weren't in a position to identify any change in behavior, but the consensus was that while she did her job well, she was quiet and kept to herself during her downtime."

Raveis added, "You know, pretty much everything anyone says about a neighbor who snaps and goes on a rampage."

"Has anyone talked to Krista?"

"I did, an hour ago. She says they were estranged. Their breakup was what sent Grunn back to us."

"And did she say anything about Grunn's state of mind?"

"She didn't want to come out and say it, but I got the impression there were concerns."

Slattery reached inside her field jacket and removed a smartphone. Thumbing the display, she said, "This is the phone Grunn left behind. Shortly after her teammates handed it over to us, a message came through from a blocked number stating that the phone was to be kept powered up and that further instructions would be forthcoming. Two theories emerged right away. One is that Grunn was somehow coerced into leaving her post. Since her teammates were nearby and would have heard sounds of a struggle, coercion seems more likely than abduction. The second theory is that she left willingly."

Tom understood the implication. "Grunn wouldn't turn."

"That's what you used to think about Carrington," Raveis said. "Last I knew that's what you still thought."

Tom didn't respond.

Slattery ceased thumb-swiping, then turned the phone and held it for Tom to see. "This text came through just a few hours ago."

On the display was a series of digits.

41 20 40.7

73 04 42.9

"I'm told you have a memory for numbers," Slattery said. "One look at a series of numbers and you've memorized it. Have you ever seen those sequences before?"

"No. But they look like map coordinates to me."

"Exactly," Raveis said. "The first set is degree, minutes, and seconds north, the second is degree, minutes, and seconds west."

Tom saw in his mind the coordinates as they would be written out: 41◦ 20'40.7" N, 73◦ 04'42.9" W.

Slattery swiped the display one more time before holding the phone for Tom to again see. "This text came through right after."

Tom read what was on the screen.

A two-word missive written in all-capital letters.

SEND TOM

Five

Raveis said, "The coordinates mark a location in a city called Ansonia. That's up in Connecticut. I was wondering if perhaps you knew it from your travels."

Tom had wandered the Northeast during the five years that followed his discharge from the navy.

He'd been all of twenty-seven years old when he began that aimless journey, had worked when he needed to, sometimes living out of his pickup, sometimes finding an apartment, spending his nights either way reading and waiting for the scars on his torso to heal and fade.

They had all healed over time, but few had faded.

Every step he'd taken during those years had served to bring him one step closer to his chance meeting with Stella.

"It's off Route 8," Tom said. "In the Naugatuck Valley, I think."

Raveis pressed, "So you know it."

"I know of it. I've driven past it, but I never stopped there."

Slattery said, "It's your classic failed New England industrial city. Not particularly pretty—or big, for that matter. Main Street is all of five blocks long. Scattered throughout those blocks are several shuttered factories, all currently vacant and in decay. These coordinates put you in the exact center of one of those factories."

Tom said to Raveis, "It's not one of your safe houses."

"It's not. Records indicate that it was purchased just prior to the real estate crash back in '08 by a group of developers intending to convert it into a retail space with luxury condos above. But no work has been done since. And it hasn't changed hands."

"We dispatched a recon team right away," Slattery said. "The building is five stories tall, and there are no adjoining structures, so there's no way of approaching it without being seen by anyone positioned inside. And the buildings on the nearby blocks offer numerous vantage points that could serve as roosts for spotters. Or, for that matter, shooters. The building has multiple points of entrance and egress, as does the city itself. And the Metro-North train station is one block west."

"I'm guessing that fact is relevant."

"Those first texts were followed by another that simply said, 'zero dark,' which is, of course, the designation for midnight. That text was followed by yet another, this one instructing that you are to arrive by train."

Raveis said, "The last train from Grand Central to New Haven leaves at 9:39. Then there's a connection at Bridgeport that arrives in Ansonia at 11:44. An 11:44 arrival would give you more than enough time to walk one block west to the factory."

"The sender knows I'm in New York," Tom said.

"That crossed my mind, too. Again, you and Grunn have had no contact. You're sure of that."

"Yes."

"And you've had no contact with Krista MacManus or Valena?" Slattery said.

Tom shook his head. "No one knows where I am."

"What about Stella. Does she know where you are?"

"No."

Slattery watched Tom.

Raveis said to her, "Their emails are clean."

Tom asked, "Were there any other instructions?"

Slattery answered, "You're to come alone. No security detail. We have to assume that whoever is behind this will likely already be monitoring the area around the factory, so we can't risk putting a watch team in place between now and midnight. We considered placing a quick-response force somewhere beyond the five-block perimeter of downtown, but the layout of those surrounding streets, combined with the time of night, means any vehicle we attempt to send in would easily come under scrutiny. With all the shops and businesses closed up except for one or two bars, there simply wouldn't be enough traffic to hide in." She paused. "Whoever picked this place knew what he was doing."

"I think we all know who that person is," Tom said.

Raveis and Slattery studied him.

"You believe it's Carrington reaching out to you," she said finally.

"Yes."

"What makes you think that?"

"I've been down this road with him before. A few times."

Raveis said to Slattery, "Carrington has a fondness for elaborate codes and extensive precautions. He was our only means of contacting Tom for a while." He shifted his attention to Tom. "I understand your loyalty to him; I know what he means to you, but he's not the man you think he is. Maybe he never was."

"It seems a long way to go just to kill me."

"Maybe, maybe not. But he wants you there for some reason, and I honestly can't think of one that I like."

Slattery said, "We shouldn't discount the possibility of this being an attempt to capture you, Tom, with two people you care about being used as the bait."

"I don't think it's that."

"Why not?"

"There were no threats on Grunn's life, right? No hostile overtones at all, no dire consequences if I chose not to go. If he really needed me to go there—if assets were in place or he was selling me out to the Benefactor—then he'd make it so I couldn't say no. Like you said, Grunn is family. How could I do nothing if her life were in danger? Also, the instructions didn't say anything about my going there unarmed. If he or someone else were luring me into a trap, I tend to think they'd specify that."

"A sidearm doesn't do much good against a sniper in a fixed position," Raveis said.

Slattery added, "And what if he didn't know he was leading you into a trap? It's also possible that he could have been given no choice but to do it."

"This is an invitation, not a demand," Tom said. "It's as polite an invitation as circumstances allow. Carrington wants a meeting with me. He wants to tell me something."

Slattery asked, "Then why didn't he identify himself?"

"Because he knew he wouldn't have to. He knew I'd know. He knew you'd know. You both knew it when you texted me."

"We weren't sure what to think," Raveis said.

No one spoke for a moment.

"It's Carrington," Tom said. "Everything about this, everything I know about him, tells me that."

"So you're going," Slattery said. "You're in."

Tom looked at her. "Yes."

Raveis waited a moment, then gestured to Slattery, who reached for a small backpack by her feet.

She picked it up and handed it to Tom.

"A Kevlar vest is inside," Raveis said. "Obviously, it won't protect you from head shots or intermediate-caliber rifle rounds, but do me a favor and wear it anyway. There's no point in wiring you or giving you a recording device to carry. Even at his most drunk, Carrington is too smart to let himself get caught on tape. There is a tracking device in the pack, though. It'll fit in your pocket and is accurate up to three feet. It will guide my team to wherever you are."

"Your team?"

"I'm calling an audible here, Tom. The instructions said for you to come alone, but they didn't say anything about you traveling alone. I want your team with you on the train, tailing you from a safe distance. I want eyes on you for as long as possible, and I want your people in communication with mine at all times. The next stop after Ansonia is a town called Seymour. It'll take the train about seven minutes to get there. I'll have my own quick-response force waiting to link up with your team there. Once they do, it shouldn't take more than ten minutes for them to double back to where you are."

Raveis paused. It seemed to Tom that the man had stopped himself from saying something.

Tom had never known Raveis to do anything other than speak his mind.

"What are you thinking?" Tom said.

"Carrington is the reason a lot of good people are dead. He's how the Algerian found you and Stella. The Colonel is convinced of that, and so am I. So if Carrington *is* the one waiting for you up there, why would Grunn willingly help him? If the Algerian hadn't found you, Grunn wouldn't have suffered the way she did. Her team wouldn't have been killed. She wouldn't have had a knife held to her throat. And let's not forget that upon her return to us she volunteered for Carrington's kill squad. So if she is helping him now, if she has left us and gone to him willingly, then why the sudden change of heart? And how did he get to her to begin with? She was in the field, as well hidden as you are."

Tom had no answers, so he offered none.

Raveis said, "I learned a long time ago not to tell you what to do, and I know you being the one to kill Carrington tonight is too much to ask, but this is an opportunity I can't pass up. When you get off the train, you'll have roughly seventeen minutes before my people get there. And I don't need to tell you what their orders will be when they do. That's seventeen minutes we won't have eyes on you, so you'll be on your own. You see anything you don't like, you *think* you see something you don't like, abort your mission and get to a public place, and wait there for my team to find you."

"Copy," Tom said.

But Raveis wasn't done. "Carrington knows you better than anyone, and he'll say or do whatever it takes to try to turn you against us. You need to remember that. You need to view everything he tells you with a hefty amount of skepticism. If you can't do that, Tom, I'm calling this off right now."

"Don't worry about me," Tom said.

"That's what I'm paid to do."

"And what about Grunn?"

Slattery said, "I look at what she has done, and I see collusion. Maybe even conspiracy."

"Yeah, well, things aren't always how they look."

Raveis smiled. "I sure hope you're on my side if I'm ever falsely accused."

Tom said nothing.

"It's your op," Raveis answered. "Grunn is your call to make. You understand what I mean by that, right?"

Tom nodded. "Yes."

"Keep Carrington talking. It shouldn't be difficult if, like you say, he's there to tell you something. Find out what he's been up to these past few months, everything and anything you can, then get out of the way and let my people do their job. When it's over, they'll bring you and your team back to me for debriefing. Grunn, too, if you're able to bring her in, which I hope for your sake you are. Any questions?"

"If you want to know what he knows, why not take him alive?"

Raveis shook his head. "That call has been made, Tom. Those are my orders. James Carrington dies tonight."

Again, Tom remained silent.

"Anything else?"

Tom shook his head.

Raveis reached for the console and lowered the privacy screen by a few inches.

He said to the driver, "Take us back."

Six

Upon their return to the hotel just before eight a.m., Torres, Garrick, and Tom gathered in the small bar off the lobby to fieldstrip and clean their respective weapons.

The room quickly filled with the pine-like scent of Ballistol, the combined solvent and lubricant that Garrick had recommended to the team and Tom now preferred.

Tom's sidearm was a Heckler & Koch 45c Tactical—a polymer-framed compact chambered in .45 ACP and equipped with a suppressor-ready extended barrel.

Torres's pistol was a Glock 19, Garrick's a Beretta 92, both chambered in 9 mil.

Garrick also carried a commando-length Daniel Defense AR-15 fitted with an EOTech holographic sight. When disassembled into two pieces—one being the upper receiver and barrel, the other being the lower receiver and stock, the disconnecting of which required the removal of just two pins—the weapon fit easily into a backpack.

Known for frequently practicing reassembly of his AR to the point of obsession, Garrick could have the weapon out of the pack and hot in less than ten seconds.

They worked on their gear in silence. Tom had briefed his team during the ride back, so there wasn't much to talk about, but it was more than just that. Torres and Garrick sensed the mind frame of their leader and deferred to it, as members of a close-knit team would.

Spending every minute of every day together for months did that.

When they were done cleaning, and their weapons were reassembled and loaded, they took turns washing up in the bar sink; then, still saying little, they returned to their rooms on the top floor to rest for the long night ahead.

Tom was stretched out again on the bed he had slept in the night before, but it was no less strange to him today than it had been then.

He had hours to wait before it would be time to leave, and nothing to do but think.

So he did just that.

He recalled the first time he had met James Carrington and the truth he'd only recently learned about that day.

Tom had been led to believe his assignment right out of basic training to Carrington's Seabee Engineer Reconnaissance Team had been merit based, but in fact, it was the first of many acts taken on his behalf by a man he wouldn't meet for another fifteen years.

The man he knew only as the Colonel.

A man who, unbeknownst to Tom till recently, had recruited Tom's father, a civil engineer with clients that included foreign governments, for clandestine work.

It was that work that had caught the attention of the Benefactor, resulting in the murder of George Sexton's wife and daughter.

The night his family had been attacked at home, Tom's father had been away on a last-minute business trip, and Tom had been off at military school in upstate New York.

Two years later George Sexton had met his death while hunting those four men, after which the Colonel had recognized Tom's potential value.

Who better to one day kill the man the Colonel had devoted his life to fighting than the son of one of his victims?

And so a long chess game had begun.

His father's death had left Tom with nowhere to go, so he'd enlisted in the navy, as Sexton men had done for generations, with his eye on joining the Seabees—the construction battalion.

He had wanted to learn to build things.

When the Colonel had gotten word about what Tom had done, he had contacted a navy captain named James Carrington, who promptly traveled to Gulfport, Mississippi, to meet with Tom under the guise of looking for the right kind of man for his team.

From that moment on, Carrington had barely let Tom out of his sight.

For eight years, Tom had served alongside Carrington, but a month prior to Tom's discharge, Carrington had abruptly resigned his commission to pursue private-sector work.

It wasn't long after Tom's discharge that Carrington had arranged a meeting in New York, during which he offered Tom a lucrative contract as a private military contractor.

But Tom passed on the offer because he'd had enough of military life. He wanted motion, as in freedom of movement, and to, among other things, set his own bedtime.

Carrington had honored Tom's decision to wander, though not without first establishing a secret protocol through which they could contact each other, should either of them need to.

I might need your help, Carrington had said. *Or you might need mine.*

And so Tom had disappeared and begun drifting, always staying near the places he knew well—Vermont, where he had been raised in a town called Smithton; Troy, New York, where he had gone to military school; and New Haven, Connecticut, where he had spent one year at Yale.

He'd never actually visited any of those towns—Smithton, Troy, New Haven—but he'd remained within a few hours' drive of at least one of them.

He'd never understood why he had done that, but he didn't bother to think too much about it.

Like an animal, he was living by his instincts.

But that day finally did come when Tom's help was needed, and Carrington had reached out. And exactly as the Colonel had intended, the son of George Sexton was waiting and ready to do his part to take on the man who had ripped his family from him.

Under direct orders, Carrington had been unable to reveal the truth to Tom—the real reason why he'd found and recruited Tom that long-ago day as well as the connection between George Sexton and the Colonel.

He'd also kept secret the long-standing friendship between George Sexton and Sam Raveis.

For fifteen years, the Colonel and Raveis had been aware of Tom, though Tom had never even heard of either of them.

More than just aware, they had played an active part in guiding him onto the long and winding path that would ultimately lead him to Stella.

One alteration in that course, and Tom would have never met her, and without her, what would he have to fight for?

Without her, he would simply be a man seeking revenge.

The same act of madness that had gotten his father killed.

Tom heard knocking on his door.

The gentle rapping of a single knuckle told him who it was.

He sat up, moved to the edge of the bed, and checked his watch.

He had been daydreaming, awake but drifting.

"Come in," he said.

Torres swung the door open but remained in the doorway. "It's almost time to go."

Tom nodded. "Thanks. I'll be right down."

"How are you doing?"

"I'm good."

Torres lingered. Tom noticed she had an iPad in her hand.

"What's on your mind?" he said.

"I asked a friend to find the blueprints of that factory where your meeting is supposed to take place. I thought maybe I could determine all the exits for you, in case you needed them. He emailed the blueprints to me; I've looked them over, and I see a problem."

"What?"

She stepped to the bed, handing him the tablet. Remaining seated, Tom looked at what was on the display.

He could smell her perfume—just a hint of it. The only feminine presence in his life these days came from her.

Torres said, "As you can see, the factory is actually four connected wings situated around a center courtyard. The coordinates your old CO provided, they don't just put you inside the factory, they put you in the dead center of that courtyard. The factory is almost a block long, which means there are rows of windows, eighteen feet by eighteen feet, overlooking that open space. Five stories of them, and from all sides." She paused. "You see what I see, right? Because to my eye, that's a kill box."

Tom studied the blueprints for a moment more before handing the device back to Torres. "What would be your recommendation?"

"Don't go. And I don't mean stay out of that kill box once you're there. I mean don't go at all."

Tom had made a point of being the kind of leader who encouraged those with whom he worked to speak their minds, so he waited for her to elaborate.

"I'm concerned your judgment is clouded," Torres said. "I know what Carrington means to you. And I know you don't agree with the kill order."

"You were law enforcement. It doesn't bother you that he was essentially convicted without a trial?"

"Of course it does. But we're playing by a different set of rules. That's what we signed up for. It's the only way we're going to win."

Tom nodded, took a breath, let it out, then said, "I'll be fine."

If Torres was disappointed that he'd dismissed her concerns, she didn't show it.

He had never seen her lose the beat in any of the situations they'd been in so far.

"We should get going," Tom said.

"We'll be with you the whole way there, boss. Garrick and me. And we'll get to you as fast as we can once we join up with Raveis's team. So just don't do anything foolish in between, okay? For seventeen minutes, just be that supersmart guy we know you are. Deal?"

Tom nodded.

Torres lingered a moment, looking down at Tom, then turned and headed toward the door. Tom spoke, and she stopped, looking back at him.

"You still have friends in law enforcement, right?"

"Yes."

"Anyone you trust?"

"Yes."

"I want you to pay that person a visit. First thing tomorrow."

"Sure. Why?"

"I need some plates run. Write this down."

Torres removed a small Moleskine notebook and pen from her back jeans pocket. Tom recited a series of numbers and letters.

"Whose plates?"

"Slattery's. I want you and your friend to find out everything you can. No calls between the two of you, no emails, no texts. Do everything in person, okay?"

"Yeah. Anything in particular you want to know about her?"

Tom shrugged. "She knows a lot about me. It seems only fair I know something about her."

Torres returned the notebook and pen to her back pocket.

"And keep this within the team," Tom said.

Torres nodded. "What are you thinking?"

"I'm just being supersmart."

She smiled. "You know, you really shouldn't lie to a member of your team. It's bad for morale."

"I'll meet you guys in the lobby," Tom said.

Torres turned and left.

Tom waited a moment before reaching for his HK.

Completing a brass check—pulling back the slide just far enough to eye the cartridge in the chamber—he stood and took one more look around the small room, then gathered his things and left.

It was eight thirty when they exited the hotel.

The rain had stopped, but there was a mist in the October air. A breeze was blowing steadily, though every now and then it gusted hard and loud.

It was the kind of early-autumn night that gave the first hints of the coming winter.

Torres drove, with Garrick in the passenger seat, a backpack on the floor between his feet.

After opening the pack, he removed the two pieces of his carbine and assembled them, attaching the front pivot pin first and then locking the two halves of the receiver together with the takedown pin.

Pulling back and releasing the charging handle to confirm that the weapon was in working order, Garrick then inserted a thirty-round magazine into the magwell, cycled the carrier bolt again to chamber a round, and engaged the thumb safety.

He was ready and scanning their surroundings before the SUV had traveled a half block.

By 9:35 they had taken seats on the train—Tom by the front of a car; Garrick six seats behind him, the disassembled carbine in his backpack; and Torres across the aisle from him.

Tom looked at the passengers, those already seated and those still boarding, making a quick study of every face visible to him. He also made a point of seeking out the faces he couldn't see, watching them as casually as possible till those looking away turned in his direction or those staring down at devices finally lifted their heads.

By the time the doors were closed and the train was moving, Tom had gotten a good enough look at nearly every passenger in the car.

The last faces he glanced at were Torres's and Garrick's. Torres was watching the passengers, but Garrick's eyes were fixed on him.

Tom recalled what Garrick had said during his final job interview.

You keep me alive, and I'll keep you alive.

Turning forward, Tom settled in for the trip. Within minutes, the train exited the darkness of the terminal's long underground tunnel and proceeded to pick up speed.

It was raining again by the time they approached the first stop—125th Street.

Tom remembered the journey into the city that he and Stella had taken together two years ago. To keep her from the certain danger he was heading into, he had exited the train at this very stop, slipping through the doors at the last possible second, leaving her behind and in the care of a man named Hammerton—one of the few men Tom knew he could trust.

This was the night of Tom's first kill, and he was remembering that, too, as the train came to a stop at the Harlem platform.

Two passengers had risen and stepped toward the doors. After a brief delay, the doors opened, and those passengers exited.

Tom watched as three people entered the car and sought out seats. Not one of them looked at him or took a seat anywhere near him.

As he was watching them, he sensed someone in motion behind him.

A person two seats back had risen and was moving quickly up the aisle.

As the person reached Tom, he saw that it was a woman.

But he couldn't see her face.

Dressed in jeans, boots, and a white Oxford shirt, a leather jacket over that, she had dark hair that was as closely cropped as a soldier's.

As she hurried past Tom toward the still-open doors, she dropped something onto the empty seat beside him.

It was a small plastic bag, and by the way it landed, it was obvious that it contained something with a degree of weight to it.

The woman didn't once look down at Tom, simply continued toward the doors at the same brisk pace. She moved through them and onto the elevated platform just as the doors closed.

Tom looked for her as the train pulled out, spotting her as she was making her way toward the stairs that led down to 125th Street.

She turned and began down the stairs, and at last her face was visible.

He recognized her.

Her name was Durand, and two years ago she had been one of Raveis's drivers, assigned to a woman named Alexa Savelle—an NSA analyst who Raveis had enlisted to help find Charlie Cahill.

Tom had saved both Savelle and Durand when the vehicle they were in came under attack from a Chechen hit team.

They had barely escaped with their lives.

Watching Durand as she descended the stairs, Tom noted that she raised her eyes just long enough to look at him before casting her gaze downward again.

And then the train pulled away, and she was gone from his sight.

Tom glanced back at Torres and Garrick to get a read on his teammates. There was nothing about Garrick's manner that indicated he had observed the woman making the discreet drop.

But Torres was looking at Tom in a way that told him she had seen it.

Turning forward again, Tom opened the plastic bag and saw exactly what he was expecting to see—a smartphone.

He took it out and powered it up, watching the display and waiting.

The train was crossing over the Harlem River when the first of several text messages came through.

At 11:12 p.m., the New Haven–bound train pulled into the Bridgeport station.

It was here that passengers traveling north were required to exit and wait for the train that would take them up the Waterbury line.

That train was due to arrive at 11:17.

The Bridgeport platform was elevated and open, making it a security risk.

Tom was out of New York, and out in the open with the sprawling city below, offering any potential assassin multiple avenues of both approach and escape.

I'd consider taking you out there, Torres had said back at the hotel.

For the five minutes that the team needed to wait, Torres and Garrick would maintain their distance while keeping their eyes on Tom, as well as on the dozen or so passengers standing near him.

They were only a minute into that wait when a male in his late twenties appeared on the empty platform across the tracks.

He was dressed in work boots, jeans, and a flannel barn coat.

Standing still, with his hands in the pockets of his coat, he simply watched the people across from him, studying each person one by one.

The only person he never looked at was Tom.

His presence caused Torres to slowly and casually move through the small crowd of people till she was within only a few feet of Tom.

As she did that, Garrick took off his backpack and set it at his feet.

Tom noted that the man in the barn coat paid little attention to Torres and Garrick as well.

It was when the train finally appeared on the long, curving track to the west that the phone in Tom's pocket vibrated, indicating the arrival of another text.

But he didn't dare look at it.

Only when he was on board, and his team had settled into their seats several rows behind him, did Tom remove the phone and open the message.

It was a photograph of a glass door embedded with security mesh, below which were two words.

ENTER HERE.

He pocketed the phone as the train lurched forward.

Seven

Tom was one of three people to disembark at the Ansonia station.

The other two passengers were females, both in their twenties. One headed for a row of parked cars directly in front of the station, the other walked south toward a municipal parking lot that was empty save for a few vehicles.

With the countdown running and no time to waste, Tom proceeded to follow the instructions he had received via the drop phone.

The northwestern corner of the factory was visible at the top of a short incline one block to the east. Tom started up a narrow one-way street toward it, turned right onto Main Street and followed that for one block south, then turned left onto Kingston Avenue and crested one more incline before finally reaching East Main.

That brief journey had been completed in a little over a minute.

As he had covered that ground, he'd noted that Slattery's assessment of this city was accurate—the streets were so empty that any watch team, either parked or patrolling in an unmarked vehicle, would have been easily spotted by a knowledgeable party on the lookout.

He had noted, too, the absence of street cameras mounted on the traffic lights or lampposts.

The stores were closed, and of the three restaurants he had passed, only one was open, though by the sparse few souls inside it was likely that it, too, would be shutting down for the night soon.

Tom also noticed that Raveis's assessment had been correct as well: there were countless fixed positions in which a shooter could roost unseen.

Apartments and office spaces above the businesses lining the streets; another seemingly closed-down factory to the north, its brick face a checkerboard of windows; a four-story storage facility farther to the east—from any of these, someone with even marginal abilities would be able to easily zero a target moving at a walking pace.

The condition of the factory was pretty much what Tom had anticipated. Each of the five floors had large multipane windows, more than half of which were shattered, and those that had yet to be broken had been painted over with a thick coat of whitewash. The fact that the paint was both faded and peeling was an indication that this had been done long ago.

Some of the doors he had passed on his way to the building's southeast corner had been covered with sheets of bare plywood, while others had heavy padlocked chains wound through their pull-handles.

Tom's destination was the door he'd been sent a photo of—the only entrance he had seen that hadn't been sealed in any manner.

Pausing first to check his surroundings, he removed a pair of Mechanix gloves from his raincoat pocket and put them on as he approached the door.

He gave the handle a test pull to make sure the door was unlocked before pulling it open just enough for him to quietly and quickly slip through.

The numerous broken windows made the football-field-size interior space nearly as bright as the city streets outside.

Still, there were four corners of utter blackness in the open floor plan that Tom's eyes immediately went to and searched.

Though he sensed that he was alone, he remained ready to immediately begin the well-drilled process of drawing his sidearm from concealment while moving.

The next steps Tom was to take were simple—upon entering, he was to cross diagonally to the door leading to the open courtyard. He did that, and taking Torres's concerns into account, he looked through that door's cracked window and determined that the area beyond it was clear.

Right away he saw the item that was waiting for him.

On the cracked concrete floor, through which grass and weeds had grown, was a hard plastic case roughly twelve inches wide, fourteen inches long, and only a few inches deep.

Tom opened the door and entered the courtyard, pausing a moment before starting toward its center, where the case had been placed.

Looking up, he scanned the four floors of windows above him. Unlike the others, these large windows were all made of single sheets of glass, though some of them, too, were broken.

Tom saw no one in any of these windows, broken or intact.

The cement floor of the courtyard was blanketed with shattered glass—a mix of shards and smaller cube-shaped bits.

There was no avoiding the sound that was made as that glass was ground beneath the rubber soles of his tactical boots.

Reaching the case, Tom crouched down and located its four-digit combination lock.

Combo is the alphanumeric version of your given name, the final text had informed him.

The alphanumeric value of T-H-O-M, the first four letters in Thomas, would have been 8-4-6-6.

But Tom was short for Tomas, not Thomas, and only a handful of people knew that.

He spun the chrome-plated dials to 8-6-6-2—T-O-M-A—then moved the lock's release button to one side with his thumb.

The two lever-locking latches sprang up, and Tom opened the case.

Inside was a tablet. Tom removed it and stood, taking another look up at the dozens of windows above him.

The tablet in his hand emitted a chiming sound. Looking at the display, he saw an alert indicating an incoming video chat.

Tom could accept the call or deny it. He accepted it, and a chat window opened on the display.

Framed within that window was the face of James Carrington.

Like Tom, Carrington had a full beard and long hair—a far cry from the well-groomed navy captain Tom had served under for eight years.

Carrington's face filled the borders of the video chat window, which meant he was holding his device close. Tom suspected that this was intentional, to prevent him from seeing whatever was behind Carrington, which could give away his former CO's location.

"It's good to see you, Tom," Carrington said.

"Where are you, sir?"

"Not too far away. You're a hard man to reach these days."

"Is Grunn okay?"

"She's not in danger—well, no more so than any of us are."

"I'd like to see her."

"If you're lucky, you won't, not for a while, anyway."

"What does that mean?"

"First things first, Tom, okay? I know it's a lot to ask, but I'm going to need you to trust me right now. I'm thinking you owe me at least that much."

"Telling me why I'm here might help get me there."

"We don't have a lot of time. I'm guessing, what, ten minutes? Raveis has men waiting for your team at the next station, right? Seven minutes for the train to get there, another ten minutes or so for them to drive back here, taking into account the two traffic lights and the forty-mile-an-hour speed limit. It took you close to five minutes to get to where you are now, so that leaves ten, give or take." Carrington paused. "That's the plan, right? You keep me talking till they get here. And if you hadn't already killed me by then, they would."

"That was the plan, yes."

"Raveis's trainers, they can change a person. I've seen it, first-hand. Have they changed you? Are you here to kill me, Tom?"

"We're wasting time," Tom said. "My guess is you're in this building somewhere. So why don't you tell me where, so we can talk face-to-face."

"One step at a time. C'mon up to the third floor. Bring the tablet with you, but do me a favor and leave behind the tracking device Raveis gave you. We're detecting a signal."

Tom took note of the plural pronoun. "Where should I leave it?"

"Where you're standing is good."

Tom ended the video chat, then removed the device from his pocket and laid it on top of the container before exiting the courtyard.

Glancing at his watch as he climbed the stairs, he determined that another minute had passed.

Only nine remained.

He reached the third floor, saw that it was empty—saw, too, the same shadowed corners at its far ends.

He'd barely taken a few steps into the vast, echoing workspace when the drop phone in his pocket chimed.

Tom glanced at the number on the display before accepting the call.

Carrington's voice said, "Walk over to the fourth window from the right."

There was a row of ten windows ahead. The fourth from the right was one of the many broken ones.

As Tom reached the window, Carrington said, "I'm straight across."

On the other side of the courtyard, in the frame of a similarly broken window maybe fifty feet away, stood James Carrington.

Eight

Carrington was casually dressed—boots and jeans, work shirt with a black denim jacket over it.

Despite the distance separating them, Tom recognized a change in Carrington's build.

He was bigger than Tom had ever seen him be, obviously fitter, and Tom understood that he was looking at a man who took his survival seriously.

Tom and Stella had done the same during their time in Vermont, conditioning themselves so they would be ready for the day when they might be required to stay and fight or grab what they could and run.

In the end, both eventualities had occurred.

For a year and a half, though, they had lived peacefully, safe within assumed identities that Carrington had helped them establish.

Looking at him now, Tom wondered whether Carrington's devotion to the art of surviving had extended to include finding what it took to remain sober.

Intoxication wasn't conducive to stealth, among other things.

Tom slipped the tablet into his raincoat pocket and spoke into the phone. "So now what, skipper?"

"I was surprised when I learned that you and Stella had signed on full-time. That's quite a change of heart. I get it, though. You had no choice; the Benefactor wants you dead and has for a long time. When a powerful enemy wants to end you, you need to surround yourself with powerful friends. I get that, too."

"That was Durand on the train. She and Grunn are with you."

"Yes."

"You recruited them, got them to turn on the Colonel."

"No one has turned, Tom. And Grunn and Durand are with me because they want to help."

"Help with what?"

"Showing you the truth." Carrington paused. "I won't waste our time by telling you that everything I'm accused of—and that every piece of evidence they have against me—is a lie. That doesn't matter. It's too late for me—I'm a dead man sooner or later—but it's not too late for you. For you and Stella. That's what I've brought you here to tell you. That's why Grunn and Durand are with me. They've both been through hell, but they each owe you their lives, and they're ready to pay that debt."

"Pay it how?"

"We won't have time for everything. First, though, Raveis is going to want to know what it is I've told you, so just tell him exactly what he wants to hear. Tell him I pleaded my innocence, begged you to talk to the Colonel on my behalf, that kind of thing. Tell him I was fall-down drunk. That'd be an easy sell, because to him that's all I am, a pathetic drunk." Carrington paused again. "I find it interesting that Raveis didn't have his quick-response team waiting at the station before this one, as opposed to the one after it. His people could have been a minute or two behind you instead of fifteen. It seems that he wants us to have this time to talk."

"Why would he want that?"

"My guess is he wants to know what's so important that I'd go through the trouble of dragging you all the way up here. He talks big about sending a message by having me executed, that it's the only kind of justice the world we operate in allows, but the truth is he's afraid of me."

"Why is he afraid of you?"

"Because for the past few months I've been looking for someone, and I've finally found him."

"Who?"

"You need to trust me, Tom. You need to meet with this person. You need to hear what he has to say, hear it from him. He's somewhere safe—for now, at least. He's been in hiding from them, too, and for a lot longer than I have."

"Who?"

"You think your father was acting as a rogue agent when he hunted down the men who killed your mother and sister. That's what I thought, too, because that's what I've always been told. But it never made sense to me that your father would walk into that situation alone. Just him and four killers for hire in a tiny hotel room. I mean, he'd have to be crazy to do that, right? And we've been told that, too—that he was out of his mind with grief, blinded by his desire for revenge. It seems, however, that's not the whole truth. He didn't go to that hotel alone. Someone was with him, there to provide backup if he needed it, but also to set up and monitor the surveillance."

"What surveillance?"

"Audio and video. Right there in that hotel room."

"You've seen it."

Carrington nodded.

He gave Tom a moment to process this before speaking.

"You should know, Tom, that there's a chance that Raveis already knows what I know and sees our meeting as a way of gauging your loyalty by what you'll tell him and what you won't. If you do decide to lie to him—if you choose to trust me over him—and he knows what I'm up to, then you're screwed. He's a fucker, Tom. It's his nature and it's his profession. Don't put anything past him."

Tom remembered Raveis's warning about Carrington saying and doing whatever he needed to say or do to get to Tom.

But Raveis's warning about Carrington's ability to manipulate Tom could also be said about Raveis.

He would do or say whatever was necessary to get Tom to remain in his employ.

After all, he'd done and said a lot to get Tom to join up in the first place.

Tom asked, "Is Raveis the one who framed you?"

"I can't prove that, but it's possible. What I am certain of is that there's a shadow agent inside the organization. High up, too. The problem with finding out who it is, is that everyone takes orders from someone, even the Colonel. The men who run him are some of the most powerful men in the world. And men in power, they tend to do whatever it takes to keep their power. Or to get more." Carrington paused again. "Anyway, Tom, this isn't about me. I made my deal with the devil. I deserve what I get. This is about you, and the people you care about. This is about the shitstorm you and they are in because of me."

"How would I find your friend?"

"On the next floor up, to the right of the door, you'll see a fresh hole in the wall. Reach down through it till you feel a small leather bag. Everything you need is on a flash drive inside that bag. If you are going to do this, you can't give Raveis any reason to doubt you. You'll need to go back, debrief him, tell him what I told you to tell him, and continue to do your job. Then find a chance to get away as soon as you can. I know it won't be easy—Raveis has you on a tight leash—but you need to make it happen. The man you need to talk to is in New York, and the meeting shouldn't take long, so you're looking at an hour, tops. There is a set of instructions on the flash drive—how to contact him, what to do once you do. Follow those instructions to the letter, because they're as much about your safety as his. And you'll have to keep your team in the dark. You need to be very careful from now on who you trust."

"How do I reach you if I need to?"

"You don't. This is it for us, this was our one shot. I was never here, Tom. We talked, but via devices, not face-to-face. That's what Raveis's team needs to think when they get here. That's the only way my people and I can make a clean getaway. Understand?"

"The data on the tablet and phone will prove we were in the same building when we talked."

"Both devices are infected with a virus. I'll activate it remotely. All the intel they contain will be scrubbed."

Tom thought about that. "You've covered everything, haven't you?"

"That's the thing about living in hiding; you have a lot of time to think. But you know all about that, don't you?"

Tom nodded.

"This isn't the life I wanted for you," Carrington said. "I'm sorry I got you involved with these people. We'll call this my atonement, okay?"

Before Tom could reply, a faint chiming sound came from one of Carrington's pockets.

It echoed in the chasm between them.

Carrington reached in, pulled out a smartphone, and glanced at the display.

"They're almost here." He returned the phone to his pocket. "There's something else in that bag upstairs. In case you have any doubts, it should help convince you that I'm not full of shit. I want you to know that I haven't had a drink since Vermont. And I don't plan on having one anytime soon. It seems that my instinct for self-preservation is stronger than my tendency toward self-destruction. Imagine that, right? Worse comes to worst, at least I won't die a drunken traitor in your eyes."

Tom heard the sound of a vehicle pulling up outside.

"They made good time," Carrington said. "They must really want me dead."

The vehicle rolled to a stop. Car doors opened and closed.

"Stay safe, Tom. Be careful who you trust. And for now, everyone needs to stay where they are. Do you understand?"

Carrington knew, of course, that Tom's first impulse would be to find Stella and pull her out of training so he could put her somewhere safe.

That impulse was strong in Tom right now, and it would take everything he had to fight it.

But he nodded and said, "I understand."

"She's safest where she is—for now, anyway. I know it must drive you crazy to think about what she's being put through. Like I said, living in hiding gives you a lot of time to think."

A door downstairs opened, and several sets of footsteps were audible from three floors below.

Tom turned his head toward the sound, held it there for two seconds, then looked again across the courtyard.

Carrington was gone.

He listened to the sound of pounding footsteps, realized right away that it was two sets of boots he was hearing—one coming from Carrington's floor and the other from the floor directly above him.

By the heaviness of that second set of boots, Tom concluded that Carrington's bodyguard was a man.

Both men now were running for their lives.

Within seconds, both sets of footfalls had faded, and Tom broke into a sprint for the stairs.

Nine

He pocketed the phone as he made his way up to the fourth floor.

Stepping through the door, Tom began a visual search of the wall to the right, just as Carrington had instructed.

Twenty feet away, at about waist height, was a boot-size hole.

Broken bits of plaster and white dust on the plank floor directly below it indicated that someone had kicked this opening in the wall recently.

Tom hurried to the hole, reached in, and extended his arm down till he touched the leather bag. Grabbing it by the handle, he pulled it up and through, then dropped to one knee and laid the bag on the floor, unzipping it.

Inside was a gallon-size Ziploc bag, the flash drive held to it by a piece of tape. Tom tore the drive free and pocketed it before picking up the Ziploc.

The weight of it was instantly familiar, and yet what it contained was the last thing he was expecting to see.

It was pistol—a 1911, but not just any 1911.

This one had all the features of a World War II–era government model Colt 1911A1—Parkerite finish, short trigger, spur hammer, GI-style sights, and an arched mainspring housing with lanyard loop.

For a moment Tom was perplexed, but all it took was one glance at the serial number located on the right side of the frame and above the trigger for him to realize the implications.

Stella had given this very 1911 to Tom two years ago when he was in need of an untraceable weapon.

Her father, who as a young marine had survived the horrors of the Chosin Reservoir, had brought the Colt back with him from Korea and handed it down to her as one of his most prized possessions.

There was, then, no paperwork connecting her, or anyone, to this relic.

Tom had used the Colt for his first kill, and several days after that, the Colonel had personally assured him that the weapon had been destroyed and therefore could never be used to link him to that operation.

Disposing of it, per the Colonel's orders, was just one of several steps that had been taken to keep Tom in the clear.

The presence of this weapon, sealed in a Ziploc bag with a magazine inserted into the grip, raised the possibility that his fingerprints and residual DNA remained not only on the weapon but also on the mag and however many rounds it still held.

But it was more than just that.

There was every reason to believe that any and all trace evidence had been *intentionally* preserved, and there could be only one reason for that.

Tom didn't have time for any of the questions that rushed to mind.

His first instinct was to destroy this weapon once and for all, but he didn't have the means to do that now, so his only option was to find a way to dispose of it that would ensure he'd be rid of it for good.

He considered concealing it on his person and taking it with him; any of the numerous bodies of water that surrounded New York would serve as a suitable depository.

But the risk of the weapon being discovered on his person before he could do that was too great.

His only choice was to stash it here and come back for it another time.

Returning the Ziploc to the leather bag, he rose to his feet and stuffed the bag back in through the hole in the wall, lowering it till it came to rest on the crossbeam nearly three feet below.

Then he hurried to one of the broken windows that overlooked the courtyard, reaching it just as the first of Raveis's men appeared below, guided by the tracking device to the spot where Tom had been told to drop it.

Raveis's point man entered the courtyard with his carbine shouldered, his body squared behind it. He moved with a soldier's glide, hunched forward slightly, and scanned the confined space through his sights, his finger inside the trigger guard.

A second man appeared right behind him.

It was Garrick, his commando-length AR also shouldered and raised. The first man stepped to the right upon entering, and Garrick moved to the left, both men skirting close to a wall as they pressed forward.

With neither man yet aware of him lurking three floors above, Tom took this moment to check on the drop phone.

Its display was lit but didn't remain so for long.

Flickering once, then again, the screen went blank as the virus-infected phone died in his hand.

Raveis's man and Garrick had reached the empty case on the floor. They were looking down at the tracking device when Tom spoke.

"Up here."

Both men looked up.

Raveis's man said, "Where is he?"

His words sounded more like a demand than a question.

Tom understood the reason for the man's tone—he and his teammates had raced here to kill a traitor, and even for the kind of men who Raveis handpicked for his own detail, the idea of being seconds away from a cold-blooded execution had to have an effect.

Tom removed the tablet from his coat pocket and held it for the man to see. "He wasn't here."

The remainder of the kill team—two more men—entered, Torres with them.

"We need to get moving," Tom said. "Raveis will want my report."

Ten

The vehicle was a GMC Yukon XL Denali—an eight-seat luxury-trimmed SUV with a 6.2-liter, 420-horsepower, V8 engine that generated 460 ft-lbs of torque.

Tom was in a center-row seat, passenger side, and one of Raveis's men was beside him.

The driver was the point man who Tom had spoken with in the courtyard. In his midthirties, this man had short-cropped dark hair and a few days' growth of stubble on his face, so he was likely one of the suited and well-groomed men who Raveis always kept around him, only playing an undercover role tonight.

Tom took note of the fact that the man had to have known about this job in advance, otherwise he'd be more clean-shaven; unless, of course, he was a very recent hire or had come back to work after a few days off.

Either way, the man had the same bearing that all the men who surrounded Raveis had—that mix of athleticism, intelligence, and an alpha-male intensity that bordered on menace.

These traits weren't exclusive to former Special Forces operators—the pool of talent from which Raveis handpicked candidates for his private-security detail—but Tom had yet to cross paths with anyone from that rarefied world who didn't possess those three specific traits, and in abundance.

These consistent qualities, combined with the obvious devotion these men had to Raveis, were what led Stella to refer to them as zealots.

Tom did not disagree with that assessment.

In the front passenger seat was Garrick, and the third member of the driver's team was seated on the bank seat in the far back compartment, Torres to his right.

Tom noted that when the driver's eyes weren't watching the road ahead, they were looking into the rearview mirror, sometimes at Tom, though more often scanning through the heavily tinted rear window for any indication of a tail.

The SUV, guided by the onboard GPS, moved through the streets of Ansonia toward the highway.

Tom studied the traffic lights and streetlamps and telephone poles as they passed but saw no surveillance cameras mounted on any of them.

And after just a few turns, the SUV was entering Route 8, which would take them south to I-95, and from there straight into New York.

Tom realized that the entire meeting had been carefully choreographed, everything planned down to the minute, including the time needed for Tom to make it to the fourth floor and recover the items Carrington had left for him.

The use of cell phones guaranteed that no one would hear Carrington's side of the conversation, should Tom have arrived wired or carried with him some kind of recording device.

The abundant broken windows were likely to render ineffective any laser-assisted listening device, had Raveis dared to send a surveillance team that managed to embed itself unseen by Carrington's spotters.

The short notice, along with the assumption that Carrington would have the designated location watched, prevented the planting of a bug inside the factory, as did the size of the factory itself, which would have required an unknowable number of devices.

Tom doubted that he could have matched this level of tradecraft on his best day.

More than that, it caused him to see his former CO—the person who had been in his life the longest—in a new light.

He was dwelling on that when the driver spoke.

The man's eyes were on the rearview mirror, focused not on Tom but rather on something in the distance behind them.

"Eyes up," he announced. "We may have picked up a tail."

The man next to Tom responded immediately by turning his head, as did the man in the far back seat.

Tom glanced over his left shoulder and looked past Torres toward the rear window.

He spotted the headlights of a vehicle in the passing lane, roughly one hundred feet back and approaching quickly.

There were other sets of headlights behind that vehicle, three by Tom's count, but those were farther away and appeared to be maintaining both their relative distance and rate of speed.

This highway was well lit, more so than most, and Tom could easily see that the set of headlights closing in on them belonged to a beat-up white Ford Bronco.

As the vehicle drew nearer, Tom sought its driver, but every time the Bronco passed under one of the many overhead floodlights, a rolling glare was cast upon the windshield, blocking his view.

When the vehicle was between the highway lights—for thirty seconds, max—all that could be seen of the interior was the vague silhouette of a single head.

"It's been behind us since right before we got on the highway," the driver noted.

Torres said, "Tap the brakes, let it pass."

"We're almost at the exit for the Merritt Parkway. I'll get off there, see if it follows."

"It would be better to stay on this highway," Tom offered.

The man next to Tom asked why.

"Because there are a couple of stretches of no-man's-land on the Merritt," Tom answered. "If we're worried about a tail, then this road is better. It's well lit and wide, and the state police patrol it regularly. The Merritt is only two lanes and winds through some wooded areas. A tail will stand out more on the highway, but it could close easier on the Merritt."

The driver ignored Tom and maintained his current speed.

The Bronco continued to close.

Maybe fifty feet now.

Looking forward, Tom saw the southbound exit for the Merritt up ahead. He glanced down at the speedometer. The Denali had been doing seventy-five, but within a matter of a few seconds, its speed had increased to eighty.

"You don't want to get pulled over with select-fire weapons in your vehicle," Torres said.

The man next to Tom said, "We're credentialed."

"Which the state troopers will take their time confirming," Torres replied. "While all of us sit on the side of the road with our hands zip-tied behind our backs. We don't have time for that." Looking forward again, she said to the driver, "Slow down."

The man next to Tom said, "He's the leader."

"Good for him." Torres leaned forward slightly and spoke to the driver. "The main highways are better. Tom's right. Route 8 to I-95 is the way to go."

The Bronco was beside the Denali now. The man next to Tom unfastened his seat belt and turned his torso so he was facing his door—a better position from which to fire if it came to that. He was holding the grip of his carbine with his right hand, and his left hand was hovering above the window control, ready to lower the glass at a moment's notice.

Tom noted this man had positioned the selector switch to automatic fire.

The man in the back said, "Hey, maybe it's just O. J. Simpson. He's out, right? Maybe he bought a used Bronco for old time's sake."

The leader told him to stay focused.

Tom studied the white Bronco, straining to see the driver's face, but the dashboard lights were too dim for him to make out any details.

He had seen, though, that the driver was wearing a cap, its long bill pulled low—an odd choice for someone driving at night, even on a highway with as many frequent overhead lights as this one.

Tom determined that the Bronco was pulling ahead, working to pass them, but before he could communicate that, the Denali veered suddenly to the right, making the exit at the last possible moment.

As the two vehicles diverged, the Bronco increased its speed.

More than that, it changed lanes, moving through the center and into the far right lane.

Racing for the next available exit.

The Denali followed the exit ramp's sharp curve, and the Bronco was gone from sight.

The man beside Tom announced, "I saw the driver bring up a cell phone. I saw the display light up. He was making a call."

The driver addressed his men. "Keep a lookout."

Silence filled the interior again. Within a few minutes, the Denali had crossed into a light rain.

The Merritt Parkway's four lanes were divided into two northeast-bound and two southwest-bound lanes.

At certain points a concrete barrier set upon a narrow median of grass separated them, and at other points there was a small barrier fence made of steel posts and wooden planks.

In either case, there would be little room for evasive action, should it become necessary.

Since the Merritt was a winding road, with many crests and sudden dips, anyone seeking to come up behind the Denali unseen could do so easily enough.

Tom remained keenly aware of this as he watched several exits come and go.

It was as the Denali was approaching the first no-man's-land—a stretch of a few miles that ran through a secluded wooded area, the terrain of which caused the two-lane road to crest several rises and follow numerous bends—that the man behind Tom spoke.

"Headlights," he said.

Eleven

The driver glanced in the rearview mirror. "It's only been a few minutes. Could he have doubled back and gotten behind us that quickly?"

No one answered.

The man beside Tom was looking back as well. "They're sedan lights. You can tell by the height relative to the road."

A moment of silence fell, all eyes but Tom's on the vehicle behind them.

He was watching the eyes of the driver, who was splitting his attention between the road ahead and the rearview mirror.

Tom said to him, "You have plenty of eyes on the headlights. Pay attention to the road."

The driver locked eyes with him briefly, then grudgingly looked ahead.

"It's keeping its distance," the man in the back observed.

The driver asked, "Is it just the one vehicle?"

"As far as I can tell."

Garrick reached for his backpack, opened it, and removed the two halves of his AR-15.

Within seconds he had them assembled, then slapped in a mag and pulled and released the charging handle to chamber a round.

He turned to look back at Tom, was about to say something to him when a flash of white light filled the SUV's interior.

At first Tom thought it was lightning, but the sound that struck his ears immediately after it was no thunderclap.

It was the sound of an explosion coming from beneath the SUV, and it triggered a deafening, steady ringing deep in Tom's ears.

He felt a wave of supercompressed air hit him, moving both through him and past him at the same instant, pressing the air from his lungs and causing his mind to reel like a gyroscope.

Despite the sudden confusion that gripped him and the sickening wave of nausea that spread through him as his organs vibrated, Tom sensed the nose of the Denali dropping downward and knew that at least one of its front tires had been torn away by the blast of some kind of attached explosive device.

The front bumper made contact with the pavement, and the friction it encountered provided a pivot point that transformed the vehicle's forward motion into a sudden, violent spin.

The Denali turned counterclockwise several times, but the spin stopped as the vehicle traversed the shoulder and headed off the road backward at a high rate of speed.

For a second the SUV was crossing uneven terrain, shaking its occupants, and then the rough ride ended almost as instantly as it had begun, though this wasn't because the vehicle had come to a rest but rather because it had gone airborne.

A strange lull of several seconds of near-weightlessness ended as the Denali found ground again and began to crash through brush and trees as it descended at a steep angle into a deep roadside ditch.

The contents of the SUV that weren't strapped in took flight—carbines were ripped from hands; weapon cases, steel ammo cans, and backpacks were flung first into the air, then in near unison slammed against the ceiling once the vehicle was upside down, only to be flung into the air again as the roll continued.

The man beside Tom, who had unfastened his seat belt just prior to the crash, fared no better.

He was being thrown around the interior like a rag doll.

His faculties assaulted to the point of overload, Tom sensed that he was on the verge of losing consciousness.

Still, he managed somehow to observe tree limbs puncturing windows, and from the corner of his eye he kept track of the man beside him being tossed around by each successive rollover.

Then, without warning, that man was ejected from the vehicle.

To Tom, it looked less like he had been thrown through the broken window beside him and more like he had been pulled out by some unseen force.

Just like that the man was gone, and Tom blacked out.

Twelve

Tom woke to the smell of rain, a cold mist on his face.

Opening his eyes, he saw only darkness, but then the silhouette of his own hands hanging in front of him eventually came into focus.

The only source of illumination inside the cabin was the faint glow of the still-running dashboard lights.

It took a moment for Tom to realize that he was upside down, and then another before he could even think of what to do about that.

The first action he took was to reach up for the pocket that contained his folding knife. Withdrawing it and opening it with one hand, he carefully cut himself free of his seat belt—the shoulder strap first, then the lap belt.

He placed his left elbow against the ceiling below him to soften his fall, but the instant the serrated blade severed the nylon fabric of the second belt, he dropped fast, landing awkwardly on his left shoulder before rolling over so that he was on his hands and knees.

As far as he could tell, the only pain that registered was from the broken bits of glass digging into his bare hands, but that didn't necessarily mean there weren't other injuries.

The important thing right now was that he was able to move his limbs.

Whatever it was that had motivated him to get this far, however, was suddenly gone, and he lingered dumbfounded amid the wreckage surrounding him.

It was only at this point that he became aware again of the ringing deep within his ears. As loud as an alarm, it dominated his limited consciousness.

Like a mythical sea siren, it seemed to pull him farther off course.

He didn't know how long he'd been stunned into inaction before he'd finally managed to lift his head to look for the other occupants of the SUV, but it struck him that it had taken a while. Glancing toward the back of the vehicle, he saw that the man seated behind him had been impaled by a tree branch that had pierced first the rear window and then the back of the seat into which he was strapped.

The blunt end of the severed branch, a half inch in diameter, protruded from the center of his chest.

From Tom's position he couldn't see the dead man's face, not that he needed to or wanted to, because the shockingly mangled torso was confirmation enough that he was dead.

Beside that man, hanging upside down and limp, was Torres.

Tom said her name several times, feebly, but received no reply.

A fast glance at her rising and falling stomach, though, told him that she was alive.

Turning toward the front of the vehicle, he expected to find the driver and Garrick suspended upside down as well, but only seeing the driver caused him to fear that Garrick had been ejected during the rollover as well.

A rush of panic raced through him, and yet he still couldn't move any faster, nor could he perceive his surroundings without experiencing significant lag time between comprehension and action.

If anything, the space between perception and deed was getting longer.

But out of this chaos came the words he'd relied on often in times of desperate need—the words of his former skipper, James Carrington.

The only way out is through.

All Tom could count on now was his will to survive, and there was clarity enough in that.

He forced himself to determine the best way out—the window nearest to him—before pulling himself across the field of broken bits of glass toward Torres.

He'd only begun to move when he heard a single muffled *crack*, followed after a beat by several more.

Even in his condition—his hearing severely damaged and his mind spinning—he was able to identify those distant-sounding snaps as small-arms fire.

More than the sound itself, it was the pattern that served to inform Tom.

Tentative at first before opening up.

Bam . . . bam bam . . . bam bam bam bam bam . . .

What was also obvious to him was that more than one weapon was involved.

Looking toward the source of the sounds, he spotted several muzzle flashes, and this was what told him how many shooters there were.

Three—or at least three were currently firing.

The flashes also told him that each shooter was armed with an automatic rifle, though which variant Tom could not yet tell.

Any hope of surviving was dependent on determinations such as this.

Any and all advantages needed to be assessed.

Tom looked up through the path of torn-up woods to the point where the Denali had first taken flight, and parked on that section of the shoulder was a sedan, its running lights on and doors open.

All four doors.

The three shooters, roughly halfway down the steep bank, were firing at something several feet to the right of the overturned Denali.

Looking in that direction, Tom saw a figure crouched behind a large, half-buried rock.

Laying down the suppressing fire that had stalled the advance of the three armed men, the figure was holding a commando-length AR-15.

It was Garrick, his head and face bloodied.

Adrenaline cleared Tom's mind, and he knew what he needed to do.

And that he needed to do it quickly.

The driver suspended upside down in his seat was closest, so Tom cut him free first.

Crashing down onto the ceiling returned the man to consciousness.

"We're under attack," Tom told him.

Hearing those words, the driver was instantly, fully awake.

Tom would have expected no less from one of Raveis's best.

The two men briefly locked eyes before Tom turned and began to crawl across the glass toward Torres.

As he did this, the driver searched through the clutter of gear for his own carbine.

Tom reached Torres, but positioned as he was—on his right side with his arms stretched forward—there was little he could do to soften her landing once she'd been cut free.

And he knew enough about first aid to know that moving her at all would be dangerous, never mind letting her take a fall like that.

But he had no other choice.

The last overturned vehicle he had occupied had been set on fire by Chechen gang members—thugs passing themselves off as assassins and doing a poor job of it.

Tom had since lived with the threat of reprisal by surviving gang brothers, and there was the chance, however slim, that they were behind this attack.

If so, he had to get Torres out, and fast.

Tom cut through the shoulder strap, then the lap belt, and she fell like deadweight to the ceiling, landing hard. The impact, however, did not cause her to instantly regain consciousness, as it had for the driver.

She was still out cold.

Grabbing her by the collar of her jacket, Tom dragged her with him as he pulled himself by one arm toward his window.

The team leader was straining to reach into the space directly behind the driver's seat, where his M4 carbine lay amid a pile of ammo cans and backpacks.

After a few seconds, he finally grasped the weapon by its muzzle with his fingers and pulled it toward him.

Seizing it with two hands, he crawled to the driver's door window and wormed his way through it just enough to get his head outside.

The carbine came through next.

Lying on one shoulder, he flipped the selector switch to full auto, took aim up the bank, and joined the firefight.

Thirteen

Though Garrick had stalled the shooters' approach, it was the fact that a second man was now firing precise shots from a fixed position that caused the three attackers to scurry for cover.

Two dropped to prone positions behind outcropping rocks, and the third darted behind an intact tree on the edge of the path that had been created by the crashing Denali.

This brief interruption in their attackers' fire allowed Garrick to rise above the top of the rock, shoulder his AR, and seek out actual targets.

Seeing his chance, Tom scrambled out through the window and onto the rain-soaked ground. Once clear, he reached in for Torres and pulled her through.

Despite the return fire from his teammates, at least one of the shooters had spotted Tom and proceeded to take shots at him.

Tom heard the whizzing sounds from the near misses, and snaps from those rounds that were passing closer.

One of the attackers targeted the front of the Denali, taking out one headlight, then the other.

But these shots weren't coming from the three on the slope.

A fourth shooter, positioned as overwatch at the top of the bank by the waiting sedan, had joined in.

And he was now targeting Tom, menacing him as he dragged Torres toward the back of the vehicle.

A handful of backward strides was all it took for Tom to get there, and yet for each stride he made, a round was fired.

Despite his haste, Tom took note of the report from that weapon, observing that it was significantly louder than the other weapons being fired.

This indicated that the rifle trained on him was chambered in a caliber larger than 5.56—likely .308.

The rapidity of the shots meant the rifle being used wasn't a bolt-action variant but rather a semiautomatic, and a semiautomatic chambered in .308 wasn't the weapon of choice of a skilled sniper.

It was, however, the rifle favored by a DM—the designated marksman of a Special Forces squad.

The more Tom gleaned about his opponents—equipment indicated background, and background indicated level of training—the better he could fight them.

Reaching the rear quarter panel of the Denali, Tom attempted to pull Torres around the corner and behind the vehicle where there was cover, but he stumbled and fell backward into the mud.

Nonetheless, he held on to Torres and, seated, scrambled to pull them both the rest of the way.

Once safely out of the line of fire, he laid her out on the uneven ground and began to skim her head with his fingertips, checking her scalp for lacerations and contusions.

All he found was a good-size egg rising under the skin above the parietal bone on the left side of her skull.

Then he did the same with her neck, examining it carefully before moving to her arms, torso, and finally her legs, sweeping briskly downward with his palms as he searched for indications of serious injury.

Finding none, he leaned over her so his face hovered above hers, then placed one hand on her shoulder and jostled her as he repeated her name, doing this till her eyelids began to flutter.

It took several seconds, but finally her eyes opened. After another few seconds, Tom saw cognition in them.

"We need you," he said.

Torres nodded, her eyes on his, but then she heard the sudden burst of gunfire and turned her head sharply toward it.

Reflexively, she reached for the pistol holstered at her appendix.

"We're going to need more than that," Tom said.

The broken branch that had impaled the man who'd been seated next to Torres was jutting out through the back window.

Tom maneuvered around it in order to crawl into the rear compartment.

The man's carbine was still held securely to his torso by a sturdy nylon sling. Tom found the quick-detachment mount located on the buttstock, released it, and pulled the carbine clear of the dead body.

Crawling out backward with the weapon, he knelt beside Torres and handed the M4 off to her, then reached back for his HK, only to find, to his alarm, that his Kydex holster was empty.

Tom began a visual search of his recent footsteps, but he stopped when Torres removed her Glock 19 from its holster and held it for him to take. The trigger was forward, indicating that a round was already chambered.

"You'll need this," she said.

He took the pistol, released the mag to check that it was fully loaded, then reinserted it and carefully slid the pistol into the pocket of his raincoat. He helped Torres sit up, positioning her at the rear right corner of the SUV.

Once she was set, he opened her jacket and removed the two backup magazines from their carrier on her left hip.

As he did this, she eased back the M4's charging handle far enough to confirm that a round was chambered.

"Give me forward suppressing fire," Tom said. "Once I'm with Garrick, watch me, and when I go right, you go left, understand?"

Torres nodded, though her apprehension was clear.

"We can do this," Tom said.

She nodded again.

Still kneeling, Tom leaned down and looked through the Denali's rear window to the front cabin.

He said to the driver, "Hey."

The man ceased firing and turned his head.

"What's your name?" Tom whispered.

"Lyman."

"Watch Torres. When she moves, cover her."

Lyman nodded, turned forward again, and resumed his selective return fire.

Tom moved in a crouch around Torres to the very edge of the rear quarter panel.

He looked at her again, waited for her to nod, and then bolted out into the open.

The instant that Tom had vacated the corner, Torres leaned around it just enough to point the M4 up the bank.

She laid down covering fire, and another fighter had been added to the mix.

Tom scrambled over the rain-softened ground toward Garrick. It was a short sprint, but the shooter by the sedan had gotten off three shots in the few seconds that Tom was exposed.

The fact that this person was firing into a darkened and heavily wooded area from an elevated position put him at a disadvantage, but that wouldn't last forever.

It was only a matter of time before the shooter figured out the angle and made the necessary corrections to his aim.

And sooner or later his eyes would adapt to the low light.

At that point, Tom would have only the denseness of the woods working in his favor.

Tom reached the rock and dropped beside his teammate.

"We need to move," Garrick said.

"I'm on it."

"A four-on-four firefight is a stalemate unless we move."

"I know. I'm going right, Torres is going left. There's an asshole at the top of a bank that's trying to zero me. Keep him down, at least."

"Copy."

Tom removed the Glock from his raincoat pocket and braced himself against the rock, waiting for Garrick to signal that he was ready.

When Garrick did, Tom broke into another mad dash out into the open, heading for a tree ten feet away.

It wasn't the nearest tree, but it was the only one that Tom could see with a trunk thick enough to conceal him.

As Tom made his move, Garrick rose above the rock and opened up with his AR.

A skilled shooter could work the trigger of a finely tuned AR-15 fast enough to make the semiautomatic rifle fire nearly as rapidly as a fully automatic variant.

Garrick was clearly such a shooter.

As Tom made his run to the right, he had to trust that Torres had observed him and was making her run to the left.

If the two of them worked their way tree by tree to a flanking position, they could apply enough pressure on their attackers to force them to displace—into clear view of those near the Denali.

In the darkness of these woods, however, Tom and Torres would almost immediately lose visual contact, so they each would be maneuvering at their own pace.

There was no way to guarantee that they would reach their objective at the same moment, but there were many more steps that needed to be taken before they got to that point.

There was any number of things that could still go wrong with Tom's plan.

Safely behind his first tree, Tom was searching for his next cover position when he sensed movement nearby.

Something rose from the ground just twenty feet up the bank from him.

That motion was accompanied by heavy breathing, as well as the sounds of clothes rustling and twigs snapping.

It wasn't till Tom saw a human figure standing upright that he finally understood what was happening.

The man who had been ejected from the Denali during the rollover had survived, though barely. His head was bleeding—the thick layer of blood covering his face glistened black in the darkness—and the left sleeve of his jacket was torn to shreds, his bare arm hanging limp at his side.

Even in the low light, Tom could see that his left arm was connected only by tendons and tissue.

Secured to his torso by its duty sling was his M4, which he gripped with his right hand. Oblivious to Tom's presence, the badly injured man raised his weapon and lurched awkwardly toward the three shooters on the steep bank.

He was standing straight-backed as he moved—nothing close to the shooter's hunch and soldier's glide he had displayed back in the factory.

Tom had no choice but to abandon his cover and attempt to reach Lyman's teammate as quietly and quickly as possible.

He made his move, rushing toward the stunned man, but it was too late.

The man opened fire, and Tom was caught out in the open as everything went to hell.

Fourteen

The injured man's aim was nonspecific, and his weapon, which he'd set to automatic fire prior to the crash, muzzle-jumped by at least forty-five degrees during the first prolonged burst of 5.56.

Despite having an unobstructed view of the three enemy fighters, he hadn't managed to hit one of them.

All he had accomplished, in fact, was to give away his presence as well as Tom's.

The three shooters pivoted to return his fire, and Tom barely had enough time to hit the ground.

Undaunted by the imminent danger—or more likely unaware of it—the stunned man lowered his carbine till it was roughly level, then let go with another burst of automatic fire.

The muzzle climbed again, his wild shots missing, but those returning his fire did so with more precision.

The stunned man's carrier vest took several rounds, the impact of which he did not seem to register, thanks to the vest's steel chest plate.

The last few shots of the return burst, however, were head shots—one creased the side of his neck, causing him to grunt. Another grazed his ear.

A third struck him square in the forehead, dropping him dead in front of Tom.

Within seconds, the shooters had turned their attention back to Garrick and Lyman, who were doing their part by keeping the pressure on.

No longer under fire, Tom elbow-crawled the remaining few feet to the fallen man, found the quick-detachment mount located at the castle ring of his carbine, pressed it to release one end of the sling, and then pulled the weapon free.

Placing the Glock on the ground, Tom sought out the man's spare magazines—a mistake, he realized too late, because the shooter at the top of the bank had resumed his harassing fire before Tom could locate what he was seeking.

Having repositioned himself so that he was out of Garrick's line of fire, the shooter was now directly above Tom.

This fresh fire drove Tom to abandon his search for the backup mags, and in his scramble for cover, he'd also been forced to leave the Glock where he'd laid it down.

Returning to the temporary safety of his tree, Tom lay on his side and released the magazine from the carbine. A narrow aperture running down the side panel allowed for a fast ammo count.

Out of the thirty rounds this mag was capable of holding, ten remained.

Not a lot.

Reinserting the mag, Tom thumbed the selector switch from full-auto to semiautomatic.

He needed to make every round count.

Rising to a kneeling position and facing the bank, he leaned his right shoulder against the trunk for greater stability. The M4 was equipped with a Trijicon ACOG optic, which featured an illuminated red chevron reticle and bullet-drop compensator with a 4x32 magnification.

During his firearms training at Raveis's compound in rural Tennessee, Tom had handled a large variety of weapons, along with nearly every optic imaginable—the ACOG included.

He also understood that he needed to sight the shooter farthest from him first, because that would be the more difficult shot to make.

Once that initial target was taken out, the ones nearer to him, who would be alerted to his presence by his fire, could be acquired more quickly.

The man he now had in his field of view was also the one closest to Torres, who was out there somewhere, exposed as she moved from cover to cover.

Getting his entire team out alive—as well as what remained of Raveis's men—was all that mattered to Tom.

The near-complete darkness made his target all but invisible—except for the instant the man fired his weapon and the flash from its muzzle showed his face perfectly.

It took only two such flashes for Tom to know he had the man zeroed.

Those milliseconds of bright light were also enough for Tom to continue to gather essential information.

This man was wearing a tactical vest, and his carbine was a CZ 805 Bren, which was a European weapon.

In Tom's experience, most private-sector operators with military experience opted for the platform on which they had put in the most time—the weapon they had trained on and carried with them during deployments.

A European weapon more often than not meant a European shooter.

What really mattered to Tom at this instant, though, was that this man was without a helmet, and this made what Tom needed to do considerably easier.

Holding the reticle on the exact spot of darkness where he had last seen the man's bare head, Tom waited with his finger inside the trigger guard for a third muzzle flash to confirm his aim.

The instant that flash came, Tom pressed the trigger, holding it back till the weapon's minor recoil settled down and the reticle returned to its target, at which point he eased the trigger forward just enough for it to reset with a *click*, then pressed it straight back again.

This process took less than one second to complete, and in that time two rounds had been sent downrange, one behind the other.

The orange light from the man's final shot lasted just long enough for Tom to witness the effects of a pair of intermediate-caliber, high-velocity rounds on an unprotected human skull.

Tom didn't linger on that kill, however, because he had just announced his location and needed to displace.

Though the tree he'd been leaning against protected him from the shooter above, it offered no cover from the two who remained on the bank, one of whom had immediately turned back toward Tom and opened up.

Tom bolted, continuing his rightward sweep, moving past smaller trees as he sought out one large enough to shield him.

In the air around him, rounds buzzed like hornets.

Tom needed to negate the advantage the shooter on the road had gained by repositioning, but he also needed to protect himself from the two remaining attackers on the slope, and the only way to do that was to cross enough distance to achieve an angle that would allow one obstacle to block all attackers.

The problem, though, was that the deeper he ventured into the woods, the farther he got from his team by the Denali, and the farther he got from them, the more he was cut off.

Tom reached a tree that suited his needs and got down low behind it.

Instantly, the fire from the bank ceased, though the sounds of shooting from that direction continued.

Garrick and Lyman were once again drawing the fire of the two entrenched attackers.

Tom peered around the tree, but the dozens of saplings between him and the fighting obscured his view. Even muzzle flashes were lost. Moving to the other side of the tree, he scanned the top of the crest, looking for that shooter but seeing no sign of him.

A moment of odd stillness passed while he waited and watched.

It wasn't until the familiar report of the heavier-caliber rifle reached Tom's ears that he was able to locate his tormentor—but the sound wasn't coming from above, and Tom knew right away that the man had given up hunting Tom and had returned to the clearing that the Denali had created.

He was now providing overwatch to his two remaining teammates.

Rising to his feet, Tom began to make his way back toward the firefight, but instead of following a straight return path, he pursued a wide circle, taking a few steps up the steep incline for every forward step he took.

The sooner the shooter in the overwatch position was taken out, the better.

Fifteen

Crouched low, Tom wove at a steady pace around the trees, careful of the uneven terrain and ever aware of the fact that he could barely see the ground at his feet.

As he moved through the crowd of saplings and drew closer to the cleared bank, he began to spot muzzle flashes again.

Closer still, and he could make out the shape of the Denali and the half-buried rock near it.

The bright-orange flashes from those two places told him that Garrick and Lyman were still doing their part.

But in battle the tide can turn all too quickly, and the advantage of holding a position can easily pivot into the disadvantage of finding oneself pinned down.

With that in mind, Tom pressed on, continuing to circle up the bank. As he neared the top, he slowed dramatically to minimize the sounds he was making as he moved through what was essentially a web of narrow, leafy branches.

When the crest was just a few feet away, he got down onto his belly and, cradling the carbine in his elbows, crawled up to the pavement's edge, facing the parkway.

There to his left was the shooter, in the kneeling position.

The night sky was overcast, so there was no moon or starlight, and no streetlight was visible due to the winding nature of the road, but the engine of the waiting sedan had been left on, and its amber-colored running lights provided exactly the level of illumination Tom needed.

This shooter's dress and gear were nearly identical to those of the man Tom had viewed through the ACOG, but the weapon this man was shouldering was an M14.

Among those in the US military who opted for the higher-powered M14 were Marine Corps Force Reconnaissance sharpshooters, and the last man who had tried to kill Tom—and everyone he cared about—had been a former recon marine named Ballentine.

Tom had put a bullet into Ballentine's head, but the possibility of yet another highly skilled operator hunting him—someone, perhaps, with whom he and Cahill had once served—sent a chill down his back.

Moving slowly, Tom rolled onto his right shoulder and placed the stock of the M4 between his pecs, then straightened his right leg while extending his left leg forward, resting his left foot on the pavement.

Even the relatively light recoil from the 5.56 round could destabilize a shooter in an off-balance position, and Tom's extended left leg provided just enough counterweight to give him the stability needed to take fast and accurate follow-up shots.

Raising the M4 so that its stock was at the center of his chest meant that the distance between Tom's eye and the optic would be greater than usual, but this wasn't a problem with the ACOG; Tom could see clearly both the bright-red reticle at the scope's center and his magnified target twenty feet away.

His index finger was outside the trigger guard as he adjusted his aim till the reticle was placed directly over the man's left temple.

Then he eased his finger inside the guard and hovered it just above the trigger.

Those movements affected his aim, but only slightly, and within a second he had the reticle back on target.

Tom was exhaling lightly through pursed lips when the shooter's M14 emptied, and in a well-rehearsed movement the man immediately dropped down to the prone position so he would have some concealment as he reloaded.

In doing so, he disappeared from Tom's view.

It took only a minor adjustment for Tom to find him again, but the man had already ejected the spent twenty-round mag and was pulling a fresh one from a pouch on his vest.

His moves were fast and efficient.

It was then, as the man was inserting the mag, that he saw Tom.

There was time enough for a moment of cognition—and for the man to release the bolt, chambering a round—before Tom pressed the trigger once, let it reset as he had done before, and pressed it again.

Rising to his feet, he moved forward in a low crouch, his carbine trained on the downed man.

Tom grabbed the weapon, laying the M4 on the pavement and completing a quick brass check before shouldering the M14.

His view of the two remaining attackers was unobstructed, and he aimed at the one to his right, directly in front of Lyman's position.

The M14 was equipped with a Leupold 10x40 mm scope, and within seconds Tom had the etched crosshairs on the prone man's back.

Six feet to that man's left was the other shooter, lined up with the rock Garrick was using for cover.

Tom shifted the scope in that direction and saw something he wasn't expecting to see.

That shooter was a woman.

A woman with dark, loosely curled hair.

Just like Stella's.

Tom hesitated, but only for an instant, because he caught a flash out of the corner of his right eye.

He swung the M14 in that direction in time to see that Torres had completed her flanking maneuver and was just twenty feet from the remaining male shooter.

The flash had been the quick burst she had unleashed at the surprised man.

Tom swung the M14 back to the woman, reaching her just as she was turning to open fire on Torres.

If he killed her, any valuable intel she possessed would die with her.

Who had sent her team? How had they known where to find them? Why an assault-style attack at all, and why after his meeting, when they could have easily—and more quietly—taken out Tom as he had walked alone from the train station?

Tom needed to know all that she knew, that was true.

But he had to do something, and he had to do it fast.

When the woman's weapon came into his view as she was taking aim at Torres, Tom placed the crosshairs on the heart of her weapon, between the box magazine below the receiver and the optic directly above it.

Then he made a last-second correction, intuitively adjusting for his elevated angle, and fired.

The .308 round struck a fraction of an inch below the bolt, piercing the weapon clean through and destroying it before the woman was able to fire.

Fragments of the bullet's jacket shattered, scattering thin shavings of brass into her face as the impact of the round sent the weapon flying out of her hands.

If the woman hadn't been stationary, and had Tom been under fire, there was no way he would have made that shot.

The remaining gunfire from his team ceased.

With no time to waste, he made his way down the bank, reaching the woman just a few seconds after Torres.

Torres rolled her over as Tom trained the rifle on her.

The woman, her face bloodied by superficial abrasions, was stunned but alive. Torres knelt and searched her for weapons.

"We're taking her with us," Tom said. "We need to get out of here now."

Torres found a nine-mil SIG Sauer 238 and stiletto switchblade, both of which she pocketed.

She and Tom were getting the woman to her feet when Lyman called, "Sexton."

Though Tom barely knew the man, he nonetheless identified something in his tone—something grave.

Lyman was standing by the half-buried rock.

Tom hurried the rest of the way down the bank toward it, but a part of him already knew what he was going to find there.

Reaching the rock, he looked over it and down at Garrick's body lying lifeless in the mud.

He'd been killed by a head shot, and the condition of his skull told Tom what weapon had inflicted the instantly fatal wound.

It wasn't the .308 he was holding.

Lyman nodded toward the woman beside Torres. "She got him."

Tom said nothing, simply looked down at the man who had promised to keep him alive if Tom did the same.

Garrick had died keeping the promise that Tom couldn't.

"I'll carry him out," Lyman said.

Tom shook his head. "He stays here."

"We don't leave anyone behind, dead or alive."

"There's no time. He'll just slow us down. We've pressed our luck as it is."

"I have a man in the SUV."

"Same goes for him."

"It's my op, I'm team leader."

Turning, Tom handed Lyman the M14 and said, "Good for you."

Torres was beside the woman, keeping her on her feet. As Tom approached them, the woman lifted her head and looked at him.

Tom locked eyes with her as he closed the distance, each step he took faster than the one before. A look of concern crossed Torres's eyes, but when Tom reached the woman, he simply bent at the waist and placed his right shoulder into her pelvis, then straightened his back, hoisting her off the ground and into a fireman's carry.

"Let's go," he ordered.

Torres pointed out that they didn't have a vehicle.

"We'll take theirs."

Lyman said, "It may have a tracking device."

"We have to risk it. Torres, contact Raveis, have him send transportation. We'll get as far away as we can, then ditch the vehicle and wait."

Tom started up the steep bank. Torres followed him, Lyman behind her.

He and his team were twenty feet from the crest when the whooshing sound of a fast-approaching vehicle caused them to stop.

The unknown vehicle decelerated.

There were no good scenarios here—a late-night traveler playing good Samaritan was a potential witness, and law enforcement would cause both complications and delays they could not afford.

Those two were the better options, the third and worst being that this was backup for the hit squad that had attacked them.

Torres moved up and took position beside Tom, her carbine held ready. Lyman did the same.

The vehicle rolled to a stop behind the waiting sedan, its headlights eliminating the roadside darkness that Tom had been counting on.

A single door opened, and this sound was followed by audible footsteps on pavement.

Moving fast but also lightly.

Someone was checking the sedan first, confirming that it was empty.

Torres and Lyman shouldered their weapons, their points of aim converging on the same six-foot-wide space at the top of the bank.

There were no more sounds for a moment, nothing to tell them what was going on, but then finally out of the darkness came a voice.

A female voice, calling Tom's name.

He recognized it immediately.

Sixteen

Tom replied, "Grunn!"

A stoic by both nature and philosophy, Tom was a little surprised by the excitement in his own voice.

Grunn appeared at the top of the bank, her pistol held ready in a two-handed grip, its muzzle pointed safely at the ground. Peering down at Tom and quickly assessing the situation, she muttered, "Shit," and holstered her weapon as she stepped to the edge.

Torres, reading her leader, lowered her weapon first, followed by Lyman.

Grunn held out one hand for Tom. "C'mon."

Tom continued the rest of the way up the bank, his legs nearly drained, Grunn straining to grab him by the shoulder. Even before he was all the way up, he sought out Grunn's vehicle parked behind the sedan.

It was the white Ford Bronco.

Reaching the pavement, Tom headed toward the vehicle. Grunn moved around so she was ahead of him, ran to the back of the Bronco, and swung open the rear gate.

She asked if the person he was carrying was wounded.

Tom shook his head. "Prisoner."

He bent forward and sat the woman on the rear bumper, then took a step back as Grunn grabbed the woman, as much to restrain her as to hold her up.

Torres rushed in and raised her carbine, aiming it point-blank at the woman's face.

The message she was sending to their captive was clear.

"Search her again," Tom ordered. "Make sure you got everything, then put her inside."

He walked to Lyman, who was standing over the sharpshooter Tom had shot.

"We'll need to identify him," Tom said.

He removed his smartphone and activated the camera, taking a photograph of the man's face.

"We're going to need more than a picture," Lyman said.

Tom understood what he meant. "Make it quick."

Removing a folding knife that was clipped to his vest, Lyman released the spring-assisted blade.

Tom stepped around to the nose of the Bronco, glancing at the sedan's rear license plate as he went, committing the sequence of letters and numbers to memory.

Then he got in behind the wheel.

Torres was in the back compartment with the woman, the two seated face-to-face.

Tom asked her if she had found anything in the second search of the woman's pockets.

"Nothing more," Torres said. "Maybe there's something in their vehicle."

Tom doubted it, and anyway, there wasn't time to conduct a search.

Grunn swung the rear gate closed, then hurried into the back seat, where she sat sideways so she was facing the captive.

Her sidearm, a nine-mil commander-size 1911, was out and aimed at the side of the woman's head.

The last to enter the vehicle was Lyman, his opened knife in one hand and a severed index finger in the other.

Grunn picked an empty takeout cup off the floor, peeled off its lid, and handed the cup to Lyman. He dropped the finger inside, then replaced the lid. Closing the knife, he returned it to his vest as he pulled the passenger door shut.

Tom shifted into gear and steered around the sedan, getting the aged Bronco up to highway speed as fast as he could.

He glanced at the rearview mirror for any indication of a tail.

But he was also studying Grunn.

Knowing where to look, he could make out the faint scars that had resulted from the beating she had taken at the hands of the Algerian's men.

What wasn't clear by looking at his friend was her current state of mind—what internal scars she might be carrying.

The fact that Grunn did not appear damaged or broken didn't necessarily mean anything.

One of the many skills learned by those trained under Raveis was the art of masking one's true self.

Lyman had turned in his seat and was looking at Grunn as well. "I take it she's a friend of yours," he said to Tom.

Tom nodded.

Lyman started asking Grunn questions—why was she following them, what the fuck was she doing passing them the way she did—but Tom put a stop to that right away.

"No one talks," he said.

He was looking at the rearview mirror again, though this time his attention was fixed on the woman in the back compartment.

Lyman looked at her, too, before turning forward.

"She may have a tracking device on her," he said to Tom.

Tom nodded. "We have to risk it." He looked at Grunn. "Is there a place near here?"

"Yes. You're heading in the right direction."

"We should get off the Merritt as soon as we can."

"It's just two more exits, then I can get us where we're going by side streets."

"If you have people waiting there, let them know what's coming their way."

"Durand is already there," Grunn said. She began composing a text on her cell phone.

Tom looked at Torres, who was mud covered and bloodied. He studied her for a moment, then said, "You did good."

She nodded, but Tom noted a faraway stare in her eyes.

He'd seen that exact look in the eyes of many who had faced the choice of killing or being killed.

Man, woman, soldier, sailor, marine—Tom had yet to meet anyone who was spared the shock that comes with the first kill.

Not even Raveis could train away that.

Tom focused on the woman seated across from Torres.

As if sensing his attention, she turned her head and returned his long stare. The blood flowing from the shallow cuts had caused her thick black curls to cling to her face, but this did not conceal her, nor did it prevent Tom from seeing the most obvious thing about her.

She was older than he, probably in her fifties.

Even more than before, he couldn't look at her and not think of Stella.

He had no way of knowing if this was intentional, but if it were, it meant that whoever had sent this woman had anticipated Tom's reaction to the sight of her.

Perhaps her employer had hopes of triggering the very hesitation Tom had experienced, or something more basic than that, a moment of fear.

If this woman was experiencing fear of her own—or any other primal human emotion—she was hiding it well.

Though her face was expressionless, there was something in her eyes that caught Tom's attention.

Cold determination.

And now he had no doubt that he was who she had been sent to kill.

He said to Grunn, "Find something to secure her hands, and cover her head."

Grunn found a baggie of large zip-ties in a small toolkit and handed it to Torres, who used several of the ties to bind the woman's wrists together.

A drawstring nylon pouch that had contained a pair of jumper cables made an adequate hood.

The woman remained passive, her eyes on Tom until the hood was finally over her head.

After that, no one said a word.

It would take roughly ten minutes for the Bronco to reach the exit. As Tom drove, his passengers each chose a direction and searched it for any indication of an ambush.

Eventually, Tom glanced at his own reflection in the mirror and spotted a cut on his forehead that he hadn't been aware of.

Caked mud had served as a clotting agent, but not before a trail of blood had covered the left side of his face.

The rendezvous point was an out-of-business cab company in Bridgeport, only a few blocks from the elevated platform where Tom, Torres, and Garrick had waited for the train to Ansonia.

The building was small, just an office connected to a two-bay garage. Its windows were boarded over and dark; the lot on which it stood—barely a quarter acre—was surrounded by a rusted chain-link fence topped with a single coiled strand of razor wire.

It occurred to Tom that Carrington's operation was larger than he had first thought.

This wasn't simply the case of a man teaming up with the two women who owed Tom their lives.

More than that, Carrington's tradecraft was even greater than Tom had recognized back in that factory, when every minute had been accounted for, every act by Raveis anticipated.

Now he knew that the real reason he'd been lured to that out-of-the-way place was so that Grunn could follow him as he exited and ensure that he got back to the city in one piece.

What had Carrington said when Tom had stated that he wanted to see Grunn?

If you're lucky, you won't, not for a while, anyway.

Tom's appreciation for his former CO increased even more when he spotted a familiar figure waiting by the gate to the fenced-in lot.

It was the man in the barn coat from the train platform.

The man swung the gate open, letting the Bronco enter, and then closed it again, securing it with a heavy chain and a padlock.

One of the two garage doors was opened.

Standing ready to pull it closed was Durand.

She and Tom looked at each other as he steered inside.

Durand waited for the man in the barn coat to follow the Bronco into the garage before pulling the metal door down.

In the next bay over, a Chevy Blazer was parked.

Like the Bronco, it had seen better days.

Looking at it, Tom understood his next move.

He checked his pocket to confirm that the flash drive was still there.

It was, and intact.

PART TWO

Seventeen

Grunn was in charge, giving the orders.

She called the man in the barn coat Rickerson. He hurried to the Bronco's tailgate, Durand right behind him.

Rickerson opened the gate and grabbed the hooded woman, pulling her out roughly and standing her up.

He held her by the back of the hood as though she were an animal he was grabbing by the scruff. Durand removed a handheld GPS tracker detector from the pocket of her leather jacket and held it an inch from the woman, moving it down the front of her body from head to toe, then up her back from heel to head.

"No signal," Durand announced.

Tom said to Grunn, "Is there another location your people can take her to? Somewhere more out of the way."

"Yes. We have a few to choose from, just in case."

"Don't tell me where. Have Durand and Rickerson take her there. Torres and Lyman should go with them."

Lyman said, "My orders were to bring you back to Raveis."

"Change of plans."

"Not for me."

Tom waved for Lyman and Grunn to follow him, then led them to the other side of the bay, out of earshot of the others—the woman in particular.

Tom said to Grunn, "You were outside the factory, correct? Waiting for us to leave."

"Yes."

"Was the SUV in your line of sight the entire time?"

"Yes."

"Did you see anyone go near it?"

"No."

"You're certain."

"Of course."

Tom turned to Lyman. "If Grunn, here, was watching your vehicle while we were inside the factory and no one went near it, then the device that took out your front tire had to have been attached before you left New York. Who else but someone on the inside could have done that? Someone who knew where you were going and what vehicle you were taking?"

It took Lyman a moment to respond. "If you suspect Raveis, I can give you five reasons why that's bullshit."

"You want to go back and find out the hard way, be my guest. But not with Torres, and not with my prisoner." Tom paused. "Whoever did this was willing to sacrifice you and your men. Until we've started ruling people out, you might want to reconsider reporting in."

Lyman fell silent.

Tom turned to Grunn. "Tell your team to take the Blazer and bring everyone to a safe house. When I'm ready, I'll text Torres, and she can let me know where they are." He turned back to Lyman. "In the meantime, we need to know what the woman knows. Get her ready but don't ask her any questions until I'm there. Understand?"

"I know what to do," Lyman said.

"Go and get everyone ready."

Lyman stepped back to the Bronco and began issuing orders, leaving Tom and Grunn alone.

Tom spoke softly. "What happened back there on the highway?"

"I picked up a tail, wasn't sure if it was following me or just behind me as I was following you. If I got ahead of you, I'd know who they were tailing. I didn't mean for you to get onto the Merritt." She paused. "Things might have gone differently if you'd stayed on the main highway."

"Don't dwell on it," Tom said. "For all we know, crashing down into that ravine might have saved us. Otherwise, they could have killed us right away." He looked around the garage. "This place, these vehicles, the safe houses you have access to, it all costs money. Either Carrington is wealthier than I thought he was or someone with resources is helping him."

"He has never mentioned anyone else."

"Are you three the extent of his team?"

"As far as I know, yes—aside from a bodyguard who is always with him."

Tom remembered the second set of footsteps he'd heard as Carrington was exiting the factory.

He also remembered the drop phone going dead in his hand.

"Can you contact Carrington?"

"No. Every time I hear from him, he uses a different phone. I have no way of reaching him."

"Raveis said you were back in the field, on deep cover. How did Carrington find you to recruit you?"

"He came to me while I was at Krista's farm. About a month after we got there."

"Carrington recruited her," Tom said. "So he knew where she came from."

"Exactly."

"So Krista knows about this."

"Yes."

"The breakup was cover."

"Yes."

"So that whole thing with you requesting to be assigned to Carrington's kill squad, that was all part of the plan."

"Yes. That way I could tip him off in case they closed in on him before he could find who he was looking for and get to you."

"And the odd behavior your teammates reported, all that was an act, too."

"Carrington wanted to make sure you couldn't say no, but that was more to manipulate Raveis than you. It was important that Raveis didn't doubt you for a second, both before you went and after you got back."

Tom thought about that, then said, "You took a terrible risk. I don't mean just coming back to work like you did. Trusting Carrington was a huge gamble."

"I know. When he showed up at the farm, I almost killed him right there."

"What stopped you?"

"You would have wanted to hear him out. So I decided to do what you'd do."

Tom nodded in appreciation.

"If Carrington is right, Tom, if there is a shadow agent high up in the organization, and if the lives of everyone you and I care about are in danger, then how could I not want to help him reach out to you? And considering what just happened, I'd say the 'if' has been removed from that equation. Now it's a matter of finding the 'who.' And then killing that motherfucker."

Tom heard vehicle doors being closed.

The transfer of the prisoner from the Bronco to the Blazer had been completed.

Lyman was inside and seated next to the woman. Rickerson, Torres, and Durand were standing by outside the vehicle, watching Tom and Grunn.

Tom said to her, "Are there any tracking devices on either of those vehicles?"

"No."

"You're positive?"

"Yes, we sweep them daily."

"Good. I'll need the Bronco."

"Yeah, of course. But where are you going?"

"To see a friend of ours."

He could tell by Grunn's reaction that she had a good idea which friend he was talking about.

After all, Tom only had a few.

And there were fewer still whom he'd seek out in a time of need.

"No one knows where he is."

"I do."

"I'll go with you. Safety in numbers."

"No, I have something else for you to do."

"What?"

"I need you to deliver a message for me. I'm guessing the next train into the city isn't till dawn, but you should be able to find a cab near the station that will take you in. Once you're there, grab another cab and have it take you to 166 Delancey Street."

"What's at 166 Delancey Street?"

Tom looked toward the vehicle. Torres, Durand, and Rickerson were still watching him.

He shifted his position, putting Grunn between the team and him, then mouthed a single word.

Hammerton.

Grunn nodded. "What's the message?"

"That I need him to stay out of this."

"You really think he'll listen to me?"

"It's your job to make sure he does. Get him to Shelter Island, drag him out there if that's what it takes."

"Then what?"

"Wait there with him till you hear from me."

"And if we don't?"

Tom didn't respond.

"I can do more than babysit, Tom. Let me come with you, let me help you. I didn't come this far just to sit out the rest of the game."

"This is what I need from you, Grunn. Please. And anyway, if things go bad, that's where a lot of us will be heading. It'll be good to have you already there."

She looked at him, then nodded and said, "Do you need anything other than the vehicle?"

"Tell Torres that once they reach their destination I need her to take a photo of our prisoner and text it to me. And I'd given her a job to do before we left New York, but I want her to hold off for now, stay put till I get back to them."

"I'll tell her."

"Someone should stay behind and keep an eye on this place. If we need to come back to it, we'll want to know it wasn't compromised."

"It's Rickerson's safe house. He'll stay. Anything else?"

Tom's clothes were caked with cold mud, and he was without a sidearm, but he would be able to take care of both problems where he was going.

He would also have access to a computer there, which he needed to view the contents of the flash drive in his pocket.

"No," he said. "Thanks, Sarah. For everything."

She smiled warmly.

Tom remembered the time they had all spent together at the Cahill compound.

He and Stella, Grunn and Krista, Cahill and Sandy Montrose, and Valena Nakash.

Each had been wounded in one way or another, but more than just the initial recovery from their respective injuries had occurred in the week they'd stayed there.

Tom had found himself, suddenly, to be a part of a family.

He'd lost his first family to violence, but it was the collective act of finally ending the Algerian that had deepened this newly found bond during their stay at Shelter Island.

There were moments during that week, in fact, when Tom entertained fleeting thoughts of never leaving—an odd thought for a wanderer like him.

But the outside world had come crashing back in when Raveis and the Colonel had visited, bearing the news of James Carrington's betrayal.

After that, there was no staying put, and no safety to be found in numbers.

The only choice left was for that family to scatter.

The same choice Tom faced now.

All he wanted from those he cared about was for them to run and hide and stay out of harm's way.

As long as he remained the target, they would be safe.

And as long as he kept moving, maybe he could do what needed to be done.

"I'll see you," Tom said to Grunn.

"Good luck, Tom."

He nodded. "You, too."

Tom was the first to leave, backing the Bronco out of the garage and turning around in the small lot while Rickerson unlocked and opened the gate.

Driving away, Tom looked into the rearview mirror and watched as the Blazer pulled out, too, with Torres behind the wheel.

Durand followed on foot as the Blazer cleared the gate and came to a stop on the street. Grunn was walking beside her and talking, likely telling her to relay to Torres what it was Tom wanted her to do.

Then Durand climbed into the vehicle as Rickerson locked the gate and returned to the building.

The last Tom saw of the group, Grunn was walking toward the train station three blocks away, and the Blazer was heading in the direction of the on-ramp to I-95 south.

Tom's route was a different one—up Route 8 north to a town called Thomaston. There he would get off the highway and follow familiar roads to Litchfield, after which it was a straight run up through Goshen and Sharon to Route 7, a winding ride that would take him past farms that predated the American Revolution.

For Tom, this journey into the past was more than just scenic.

Eighteen

His destination was the small town of Canaan, in the northwest corner of Connecticut.

It was here that Tom had first met Stella.

He had wandered into town on a cold spring day, spotted the old railcar diner, and, being a history buff, stopped there for an early lunch.

Stella was waiting tables.

One look at her, and he'd decided to stick around for a few days.

After a few days of quiet recon, he had finally offered to buy her dinner.

It wasn't long before she asked him to move into her apartment, located above a building she owned on Main Street.

It was the last of the multiple real estate holdings she'd once had—the only one she hadn't lost during the recession.

Heading back to that town now, Tom couldn't help but think of the life he and Stella had built together—the two of them working hard to pay the bills, spending their precious time off together, indulging in the luxury of Friday night takeout.

To each, all that mattered was being with the other.

More than that, the bad luck that they had endured prior to their meeting had started suddenly to look a little more like good fortune.

Without that series of setbacks and struggles, they never would have crossed paths.

It was this life that had been disrupted by Tom's first encounter with Raveis and the Colonel, via Carrington. Another op for the Colonel a year and a half later had the same effect on the new life that Tom and Stella had built in Vermont.

A second life, a hard life, but one that they'd hoped was theirs to live in peace.

It was that second op that revealed a dangerous truth—that Tom was considered a high-value target by a man known only as the Benefactor, and had been for all of his adult life.

For Tom and Stella, outsiders up to that point, the only safe place for them was deep inside the Colonel's organization.

Their only hope for survival was to learn all that Raveis and his men had to teach.

But the sanctuary they had sought was a false one, Tom saw that now.

If he could come under attack while waiting in deep cover for his work to begin, then how safe was Stella?

Wherever she was, whatever was being done to her at this moment in the name of training, she was in danger.

Ten minutes after leaving Bridgeport, Tom was passing the exit for the Merritt.

Five minutes after that he was passing Ansonia.

From the elevated highway he could see down into the valley floor the city occupied, and for an instant he glimpsed the factory where he'd hidden the Colt.

He considered exiting the highway, making his way to the factory, and retrieving the weapon, but he decided against it.

There were no bodies of water deep enough between here and Canaan for him to dispose of it.

And anyway, his destination was still an hour away, and time wasn't on his side.

He didn't dare speed, but he pushed the sixty-five-mile-an-hour limit whenever he could, his eyes always scanning ahead for state police cruisers lying in wait on the side of the road.

It was almost two a.m. by the time he reached Thomaston, which meant he would reach Canaan at quarter to three.

The moment he exited the highway, he pulled over and removed his burner phone from his pocket, manually entered a phone number from memory, then composed a brief, coded text and sent it off.

The reply came through less than a minute later.

He was already driving again when he sent his response, which included the photo he'd taken of the man he had killed—the designated marksman armed with an M14.

The text also included a request to submit that photo for facial recognition.

Canaan was as he remembered it, though he really hadn't expected it to change.

Towns like that didn't.

He passed the railcar diner, turned right at the light. A half block down on the left, just prior to the second-run movie theater, was Stella's building.

The storefront windows were covered with sheets of brown paper held in place by masking tape, but the windows of the apartment above were open to the cool night air.

They were also lit.

Tom pulled into the narrow alley between the building and the theater, steered around to the small back lot, and parked.

He had once parked there every night for six months.

There were two vehicles there now, both with New York state plates—a Ford Mustang 5000 and a Ford Ranger. Neither vehicle was less than ten years old.

Walking through the alley to the street, he remembered those nights he'd come home, spent from work but eager for his shower and his time with Stella.

Mere hours before sleep took them both.

He surveyed the empty Main Street as he walked to the door, pausing when the phone in his pocket vibrated.

Removing it, he glanced at the display and saw the photo he'd been waiting for.

It showed the woman with the dark hair, wide face, and high cheekbones who was now their captive looking straight into the camera.

She still had the look of determination Tom had seen as they'd fled the scene of the crash in the Bronco.

The photo was an indication that Torres and the others had arrived at the safe house, its location still unknown to Tom.

And that soon Lyman would begin the process of "softening" their captive in preparation for interrogation.

Putting that out of his mind, Tom slipped inside the building and started climbing the narrow stairs. He was midway up when the apartment door at the top opened and Charlie Cahill appeared.

Sandy Montrose was standing behind him.

Tom strode to the last step, greeted his friends, and entered his erstwhile home.

Nineteen

The quick shower and change of clothes were restorative, and a cup of coffee was waiting for Tom on the kitchen table when he walked in.

Sandy was leaning against the counter, a mug in her hand.

Tom noted a bottle of Irish whiskey, its cap removed, on the countertop beside her.

In the sink were Tom's boots, which had been cleaned of mud. Next to the sink was a carving knife.

Sandy handed the boots to Tom. "Charlie's clothes fit you okay enough, but we don't have any shoes in your size, so I sliced up the soles of your boots a little bit, in case you left usable footprints back in the mud."

Tom sat down at the table and glanced at the bottom of his boots, both of which had several crude star patterns cut into the hard rubber tread. He thanked her, then pulled the boots on one at a time.

Though the attack had occurred less than three hours ago, Tom felt as if time were slipping away.

Driving to Canaan, then briefing Cahill and Sandy on everything that had happened, followed by the necessary shower—every minute counted, and he'd lost so many minutes already.

"Where's Cahill?"

"Downstairs."

Tom had emptied his pockets prior to the shower, placing the few items they'd contained on the table.

He'd had with him his cell phone, pocketknife, wallet, Surefire penlight, and the flash drive Carrington had given him. Attached to his rigger's belt had been the Kydex holster for his HK45c and the double-mag carrier containing his two backup mags.

Looking at the pile of items now, Tom saw that everything was present except the flash drive and cell phone.

Sandy saw him studying his belongings.

"Cahill has the cell phone and the flash drive," she explained. "Once I check you out, you can go down and talk to him."

She turned and opened a cupboard above the kitchen counter, removing from it a leather doctor's bag, then stepped to the table and pulled out the chair next to Tom's.

"I'm fine," Tom said.

"You were in a car crash and a gunfight, Tom." She placed the bag on the table. "Anyway, I have my orders."

Tom finished tying his boots as Sandy readied a blood pressure cuff and stethoscope. Her eyes went to the cut on his forehead.

"Any dizziness, nausea, vomiting?"

"No."

"Blurred vision, ringing in your ears?"

"No," Tom lied.

His ears rang, but he was confident that was from him being exposed to small-arms fire without the benefit of hearing protection.

And anyway, if it were something more than that, he didn't want to know.

"That Kevlar vest you're wearing under your shirt, did it take any shots?"

Tom shook his head. "No."

"So just the cut on your forehead, then."

"Yes."

"Do you remember when your last tetanus shot was?"

"I don't."

"I'm guessing probably back when you were on active duty."

"That sounds right."

As she worked on Tom, first checking his vital signs and then tending to the cut on his head, he was keenly aware of the fact that he was in the presence of someone who had just months ago suffered a tremendous loss.

Her husband, Kevin, a veterinarian, had been shot dead in front of her as they were both rushing to lend aid to whom they had believed at the time to be a comrade in need.

After that Sandy had been used as a human shield by the man who had gunned down her husband as he attempted to kill others, Stella among them.

Tom hadn't witnessed that event, only heard about it from those who had been there.

But the horror was something he knew full well.

This made Sandy Montrose the very personification of the pain he sought to avoid—now and always.

She also reminded him of another terrible fact: Garrick's wife, too, was now a widow and likely didn't even know it yet.

Sandy prepared a syringe, then injected Tom's left shoulder.

"I can make you some food," she said.

Tom shook his head. "No, thanks."

She was watching him closely, studying his eyes. "How long since you last slept, Tom?"

He lied again. "Not too long."

"Seventy-two hours with no sleep is pretty much all the brain can handle. After that, cognitive function decays dramatically. So does reaction time. And it only gets worse from there."

Tom was nearly twenty-four hours into that countdown, but he couldn't think about that now.

Again, he assured her that he was fine.

"You and Charlie are cut from the same cloth," she said. "Why is it you Type A personalities refuse to listen to your doctor?"

Tom half smiled at the joke but said nothing. He could smell the whiskey on her breath now.

Sandy had first met Cahill when they were both teenagers—he a troubled prep-school student, she the daughter of the school's resident physician, a man who would become Cahill's mentor.

The man who single-handedly had set him on his life's course.

Dartmouth, enlistment in the marines, three tours of duty before joining Force Reconnaissance, the corps' elite special operations unit.

Upon his medical discharge for grave wounds sustained on the night he'd saved Tom's life, Cahill had been recruited by James Carrington into the Colonel's private-sector Special Activities Division—a non-governmental equivalent to the CIA's black ops group.

Cahill and Sandy had remained close friends during that time, and her family farm in Connecticut, a mile from the prep school where they had met, had become his own personal Alamo.

After the murder of Sandy's husband, she and Cahill had needed somewhere to go where no one would look for them.

Stella's building, its upside-down mortgage having been paid in full by the Colonel and his associates, seemed a good place for them to stay and regroup.

Unused and tucked away in this out-of-the-way town, it would serve as Cahill's second secret Alamo.

Despite Tom's state of mind—his urgent desire to set his plan into action—he took a moment to ask Sandy if she liked living here.

She smiled politely. "It's a quiet little town you've got, I'll give you that much."

"Yeah. There's peace in boredom, though, don't you think?"

"I guess."

"Stella and I loved it here. We had a routine. Every moment we got to spend together was gold, you know. There are times I wish we'd never left."

Sandy nodded. Her eyes were locked with Tom's, and there was no avoiding the sorrow they held.

"We're all set here," she said finally. "Charlie's waiting for you."

She stood, returned her gear to the med bag, then gathered up the bandage wrappers and tossed them into the trash.

Walking into the hallway that separated the kitchen from the bedroom, she turned in to the bathroom and closed the door.

With the hall now empty, Tom could see into the bedroom, where the only bed in the small apartment was located.

By the way the blankets had been left, he knew that two people had been occupying that bed, likely rousted out of a sound sleep when his emergency text had come in.

Suddenly he felt as though he were invading his friends' privacy, so he turned away and began to gather his things from the table.

Leaving the coffee, he headed downstairs.

The ground floor appeared to be in the early stages of renovation.

Scattered about the empty space were stacks of two-by-fours, piles of paper-wrapped Sheetrock, several pallets of floor tiles, and rolls of electrical wire.

A partially constructed wall frame was laid out on the floor.

Farther into the room were a table saw and a pair of sawhorses.

Having been a Seabee—construction battalion—Tom could recognize an amateur's work space when he saw one, and this had all the markings of that.

In the middle of the room was an antique desk—a partner's desk, large enough for two individuals to sit at and work facing each other.

Stella had told Tom that she believed the desk had been in the building since it was first constructed in the late 1800s.

On that desk were a laptop computer and router.

The computer's display showed what looked to Tom to be a secure messaging program.

A chain of incoming and outgoing messages was visible, though Tom wasn't close enough to read any of them.

Cahill was nowhere to be seen at first, but then Tom heard footsteps coming up the basement stairs.

He looked at the door and waited.

Cahill appeared, carrying a messenger bag. Black and compact, it was made out of thick ballistic nylon.

He walked to the desk and laid the bag upon it.

Tom said, "Doing some renovating, I see."

Cahill looked around the unfinished space. "I was thinking maybe Sandy could set up a private practice here. Anyway, it gives us something to do."

"How is she doing?"

"She has good days and bad."

"It's a long road."

Cahill nodded, said nothing.

Two years ago, the woman Cahill loved had been killed by a Chechen hit squad, shot in the chest at point-blank range in front of him.

It seemed to Tom that Cahill and Sandy were members of a terrible club, one to which no one would want to—nor should ever have to—belong.

Though Tom had lost loved ones, he hadn't witnessed their murders like Cahill and Sandy had.

He was grateful for small mercies.

Cahill checked the laptop display for any new messages.

"What have you got for me?" Tom said.

Cahill minimized the chat window and maximized another one.

On the screen now was the photograph Tom had taken of the sharp-shooter he'd shot, placed side by side with what appeared to be a boot-camp graduation photo of the same man.

"Facial recognition got a hit," Cahill said. "I'm running the woman's photo through now."

Tom stepped closer to the desk.

Next to the laptop were his cell phone and the flash drive.

Tom asked, "So who was he?"

Twenty

"His name was Walker," Cahill answered. "Born and raised in Dayton, Ohio, enlisted in the army straight out of high school. The guy was a paratrooper, Tom, served in the 82nd Airborne, but he was stripped of his jump wings and was facing a bad-behavior discharge after assaulting a medic who happened to be an immigrant from El Salvador. At the last minute, though, Walker's discharge was averted when a general stepped in and handpicked him to be his personal driver. Walker spent the next three years stationed in Germany, but he was eventually court-martialed for another racially motivated assault. Our true natures always win out, right? After his discharge he went back to Ohio, worked a series of shit jobs, had a couple of minor run-ins with local law enforcement, then eventually fell off the radar entirely. But before he did, he managed to leave one hell of an online footprint."

"What kind of footprint?" Tom asked.

"He spent a lot of time in chat rooms—neo-Nazis, white power, all that bullshit. Of course, he wasn't just an internet warrior of hate; he also attended dozens of white supremacy rallies across the country. For a time he belonged to a group in Illinois that called itself the First Workers' Party. A straight-up hate group, according to the Southern Poverty Law Center. Walker was even recruited by a militia group in Kentucky to teach military tactics. He spent at least a half dozen weekends in the woods showing them everything he knew." Cahill paused.

"Frankly, Tom, I'm glad this asshole is dead. He was a disgrace to his jump wings. Too many men from the 82nd got killed fighting Nazis, and here's this moron teaching neo-Nazis modern shock-troop techniques."

"You said he fell off the radar at one point."

"That's where it gets interesting. The general who handpicked Walker to be his driver is a man named Graves."

Cahill opened another screen, replacing the images of Walker with a photograph of an older man.

It was a standard military portrait, with an American flag serving as the backdrop and the subject, in his dress uniform, facing the camera squarely. The man—midsixties, Tom guessed—wore a scowl on his weathered but taut face.

"One of the first things I learned when I enlisted was that the attainment of high rank was no guarantee of character and wisdom. In fact, in many cases, it was the exact opposite. We tend to want to think our generals are the cream of the crop, disciplined and honorable men, but more than a few of the ones I've crossed paths with over the years were useless—or worse, self-serving and arrogant pricks. It seems General Graves here was the latter. Five years ago he got caught up in a bribery scandal. Large sums of cash were exchanged for military contracts, and he was the intermediary, bringing the right Pentagon officials together with interested business leaders, all for a share of the profits. He was under investigation by the DOJ when he abruptly disappeared."

Cahill switched back to the two photos of Walker.

"About a month after Graves goes dark is when our man Walker here falls off the radar as well. And stays off for six months."

"He was somewhere being trained," Tom said.

"That would be my conclusion as well."

"But trained by whom?"

"No one we know," Cahill said.

"How can you be sure of that?"

"He exited the country on his passport, bound for Serbia. Raveis has no training compounds there. He's strictly US."

"You're positive about that."

"Yes." Cahill paused, looked at Tom. "You're thinking Raveis has something to do with the attack."

"I'm not sure what to think."

"I know the two of you have had your differences, but the close-protection agents escorting you were his men, Tom. You mentioned Lyman. I know him; he was a SEAL, decorated, four tours of duty. Raveis is an asshole, yes, no argument from me, but having his own men killed, that's a lot even for him. And sacrificing a Tier 1 asset like Lyman—I just don't see Raveis doing that. Plus, you said he gave you that vest before you left. Why would he do that if he was planning on having you killed?"

"The vest would only protect me from pistol-caliber rounds. It'd be useless against Walker's .308." Tom shrugged. "Who knows, maybe this conversation is the very reason he gave it to me."

"To raise doubts about his guilt."

"Get us to waste our time sorting through all the contradictions. Confuse us into inaction."

"Psy-ops," Cahill said.

Tom nodded. "There was a woman with Raveis. It was her meeting. All I got was a last name. Slattery. Ever hear of her?"

"No."

"She knew all about me—the Algerian, my father, what happened in Vermont. She knew about all of us. Her accent was predominantly southern, but it was a strange mix of southern."

"Like you hear from military brats? After a childhood spent moving post to post, picking up inflections from here and there?"

"Maybe."

"We should probably at least find out who she is. And sooner rather than later."

"I've got someone for that."

"Someone you can trust."

"Yes." Tom looked at the laptop. "How'd you get all this information on Walker so fast?"

"The Colonel has been interested in Graves for a while now, has teams of profilers gathering everything they can on the man and his associates."

"Why?"

"Because he suspects that Graves has done what disgraced generals sometimes do."

"Betray their country," Tom said.

Cahill nodded. "If Walker was sent by Graves to kill you, then that's the link the Colonel has been looking for."

"What link?"

"The one that connects Graves with the Benefactor."

"Graves is building his own private army," Tom concluded.

"And he's either subcontracting his men out to the Benefactor or worse—they're directly allied and pooling their resources."

"How many associates does Graves have?"

"We've accounted for close to fifty. All former military. But I've heard estimates of over a hundred. Our recruiters had actually looked at some of the same men after they separated from their respective branches, but in every case their social media activity was enough to rule them out as possible recruits."

"Neo-Nazis?"

"Not all, but enough. Every one of them, though, was either pissed off about something specific or disgruntled about everything in general. The classic loner-victim profile—the kind of person we know to avoid because they're often looking for an excuse to pull a trigger as opposed to dreading the day they might have to. So if the estimates are correct, that means Graves has at least a company of operators like that."

Tom thought about the implications. "His own zealots," he said finally, recalling Stella's observations about the men whose loyalty to Raveis was so apparent.

"Every authoritarian has them." Cahill continued. "You're not the only one of us to have a run-in with some of Graves's men. A three-man team was ambushed and killed in New Orleans six months ago. And a deep-cover operator in Miami—one of our best—was assassinated a few months after that. Both instances resulted in some of the attackers being killed. In New Orleans it was a mercenary from South Africa and an American. In Miami, it was two Americans. In both cases, the Americans fit the same pattern as Walker here. Former US military, angry, few prospects, and a sudden trip to Europe that lasted six months or more. The fact that the New Orleans team was comprised of a foreign-born merc and an American was what first raised the concerns that Graves was working with the Benefactor." Cahill stopped to give Tom time to take all that in, then said, "The prisoner you took, any idea what her nationality is?"

"She hasn't spoken."

"She was searched for intel?"

Tom nodded. "Yeah, nothing."

"Normally, we'd turn someone like that in for interrogation. It seems that option is out of the question for you."

"I'll see what I can get out of her when I get to the safe house." Tom paused. "There were certain lines I swore I'd never cross."

Cahill took a breath, let it out. "When it comes to loved ones, I don't think there is a line."

Two years ago, Cahill had hunted down and killed the man who had ordered the murder of the woman he loved.

A woman Cahill had done his best to keep hidden and safe.

Tom had been standing beside Cahill when Cahill had crossed the line separating justice and vengeance.

Cahill hadn't thought twice about it, and neither had Tom.

"It's not an easy thing to do right," Cahill said. "Interrogation, I mean. We're taught the techniques, we endure some of them as part of our training, that's one thing, but to actually apply them, that's something else. And it takes a certain kind of person to be on one of the Benefactor's hit teams. They make Raveis's zealots look like Boy Scouts. For them, there aren't any lines *to* cross."

"The thing is," Tom said, "I don't think that's what this was. I don't think the attack on me was just an assassination attempt."

"What do you mean?"

"The explosive that sent us off the road was only powerful enough to take off the front tire and disable the vehicle. If whoever put it there wanted me dead, they would have opted for something bigger, don't you think? Blow me into a few hundred pieces, do the job that way, eliminate the need to deploy a kill squad altogether."

"Maybe whoever planted it couldn't sneak in anything larger."

Tom nodded toward the flash drive. "Or maybe someone didn't want that destroyed."

Cahill looked at the device.

"The explosive had to have been put in place *before* Lyman left New York," Tom said. "I assume Lyman was as well hidden as the rest of the Colonel's assets, so that means the device had to have been put there by someone on the inside."

"We should keep in mind that Carrington was one of our best recruiters. He knows a lot of our people, and he'd know how to get to them. Where their families are, what their weaknesses may be. He could have coerced someone inside the organization into doing that for him."

Tom shook his head.

Cahill asked, "Why so certain?"

"We were heading home down Route 8," Tom said. "That's a wide and relatively flat highway. If the device had been detonated there, the SUV would have spun out or maybe rolled once, but either way, everyone inside would have been easy pickings. The kill squad would have overwhelmed us with immediate force on terrain like that, killed us while we were still in our seats, recovered the flash drive, then gotten back into their vehicle and taken off. A minute, tops, maybe less. But it didn't work out that way. We got . . . lucky."

Cahill said, "And since it was Carrington who gave you the flash drive in the first place, why would he want it back? And want it back intact? I see your point."

"It was someone inside the organization," Tom said. "Someone who knew what vehicle Lyman would be using to take my team and me back to New York. Someone who had access to Lyman's vehicle for the time it would take to attach a precision explosive device. That person not only had to know about the meeting with Carrington in advance but also the where and the when so his team could be waiting, ready to launch their attack."

Cahill looked at the flash drive again. "And that someone had to know the reason for the meeting," he added. "He had to know what Carrington was planning on giving you. Which is?" He looked at Tom.

"Instructions."

"Instructions for what?"

"Meeting with a man who has information about my father."

"What man?"

"Carrington didn't give me a name. But the man claims that he was in the hotel the night my father was killed. In the next room."

"Doing what?"

"Monitoring surveillance. Audio and visual. And apparently, he was supposed to be my father's backup, but something happened."

Cahill paused. "That sounds like an operation."

Tom nodded. "That's what Carrington seems to think."

"Did he tell you what information this man had?"

"No." Tom paused. "But it seems what we've all been told—that my father was driven to revenge and went rogue—isn't the whole story."

Cahill thought for a moment. "I had no idea, Tom. I would have told you if I'd known."

"I know."

"It makes you wonder what other lies we've been told."

Tom told him about the Colt that Carrington had left for him.

"You saw it," Cahill said. "It's definitely the same one?"

"The serial numbers were right," Tom said. "It looked like it had been preserved, too. So any fingerprints or DNA I left on it could be used against me."

"Shit."

"Exactly."

"If Carrington is right, Tom, if there is a shadow agent high up in the organization, then we're all pretty much fucked, no matter who it is."

"Yeah, pretty much."

Cahill let out a breath, studied Tom for a moment, then nodded and said, "I think I know what it is you really came all the way up here to ask for."

"Grunn's taking care of Hammerton," Tom said. "Torres and Lyman are in a safe house. Krista and Valena are off the radar, and Sandy is here with you. That leaves Stella. I can only guess where she is right now, and I have no way of reaching her. We set up a system before Raveis separated us, a way to communicate secretly via email, but she won't have online access for another three days. I can't wait that long."

"You want me to find out where she is."

"Yes," Tom said. "And I want you to go there. I want you to bust her out for me."

Cahill said nothing.

"I know it's a lot to ask, Charlie. But training is dangerous; accidents can happen. Or be made to happen. Right now, no one in the organization knows where I am. They can't get to me, they can't get to my friends, and they can't get to anyone on my team. But they can get to Stella. They could kill me without ever coming anywhere near me. I need to know that she's safe. I need all of us safe if I'm going to do what it looks like I need to do."

Cahill's silence lingered for a moment longer. "She must be in her final weeks by now," he said finally. "SERE training."

Tom nodded.

Cahill's statement was a reminder of what Stella was likely enduring.

It was clear to Tom that Cahill realized his words had generated unpleasant thoughts in Tom's mind.

"The good news is that it narrows down where she could be," Cahill offered. "One of two locations, actually. Neither is easy to get to, or away from."

"I'd owe you."

Cahill shrugged that off. "Listen, I don't want you doing what you're about to do alone. I have people I trust who can help you. Let me reach out to some of them, get some people here to at least shadow you—"

"No," Tom said. "Two people are dead already because of me. Everyone stays out of this, including you. I don't even want to know where you and Sandy take Stella once you get her. All I want is to know that she's out of harm's way."

Cahill thought about that, then said, "I've lost men under my command, too. I know what it's like; I know what that does. There isn't a day I don't think about them."

"So maybe don't fight me on this, then."

Cahill looked at Tom for a moment more. Finally, he said, "What was the name of your guy?"

"Garrick."

"Married?"

"Yeah."

"Family?"

"A kid, yeah."

Cahill took a breath, let it out. "He died doing what he wanted to do, Tom. He volunteered, wanted to make a difference. He could have gone into corporate security and been a bodyguard for some CEO, taken the safe route. For that matter, he could have been an insurance agent or bartender. But he chose a different way of making money for his family. He heard the call of duty, and he answered it."

Tom knew all this already, so he said nothing.

"Sandy and I will leave right away," Cahill said. "It might take me a few hours to find out which compound Stella is in, especially if I have to hide the reason why I want to know. And of course, depending on her location, it might take me a day or two to get there and get her out. The Colonel could help speed this process up, but I'm thinking the darker I keep this, the better."

"The Colonel was the one who assured me that the Colt had been disposed of."

"He could have been misinformed. A minor detail like that is way below his pay grade."

"Still," Tom said. "We need to be careful whom we trust. At least till you get Stella somewhere safe."

Cahill nodded. "Agreed." He pointed to the messenger bag. "I've got some gear for you. The mags you're carrying are for an HK45c. I don't have one of those here, but I'm thinking you'll be okay with what I've given you."

"I'll need something to open the flash drive with, too."

"There's a tablet in the bag. And a burner phone we'll use to communicate. Keys for that Ranger parked out back are in there, too. Maybe you've gone as far as you should in that Bronco."

"Thanks," Tom said. "Sorry about showing up like this."

"It could just as easily have been me showing up at your door. You wouldn't expect me to apologize if that were the case, would you?"

Tom shook his head.

Cahill looked around the unfinished space. "I'm in over my head here, you know that, right? I don't know the first thing about construction."

"I got that sense, yeah."

"Maybe we'll find our way back here when all this is done and you can give me a hand. It's a shame to leave a space like this unused."

"Sounds like a deal," Tom said.

Cahill clicked off the secure messaging program, then shut down his laptop, disconnected it from the router, and folded it closed.

"I'll go get Sandy ready," he said. "I don't think she'll mind a change of scenery. And if I get a hit on the facial recognition, I'll let you know."

Tom thanked him again.

Cahill closed the distance between them and extended his hand.

Tom took it, and they shook.

"Stay focused and watch your corners," Cahill said. "I'll let you know the minute Stella's safe."

Twenty-One

Tom was alone in the place that he and Stella had first called home.

The only time they'd ever spent in that unfinished retail space below her apartment was the hour prior to their leaving Canaan for good two years ago.

Not exactly a lifetime, but close, considering all the ground they'd covered in that time.

It was during that final hour at home that Stella had given Tom the Colt 1911 that her father had carried with him as a young marine.

Tom considered it fitting, then, that Cahill had passed on a similar gift in that same location.

The bag—a Direct Action Tactical Messenger Bag—was loaded with everything Tom might need.

That included a complete bleeder-blowout kit—RATS tourniquet, six-inch Israeli battle dressing, QuickClot sponge, Hyfin Vent Chest Seal for sucking chest wounds, emergency blanket, and trauma shears—as well as a course of antibiotics and a vial containing oral morphine.

This was everything needed to self-treat, should Tom be wounded, or for him to at least attempt to save the life of someone he had been given no choice but to shoot and from whom he needed information.

There was, of course, always the possibility that someone Tom cared about could get wounded or even shot down in front of him, but he couldn't think about that.

The messenger bag also contained the cell phone Cahill had promised, along with a wall charger and backup battery.

There were also several protein bars, two bottles of spring water, a seven-inch tablet in an OtterBox case, and a pair of black Mechanix gloves.

In a secret compartment behind the main one, covered by a flap so that its contents would be kept hidden from anyone casually inspecting the bag, was Tom's sidearm.

It's the Colt M45A1 close-quarter battle pistol, Cahill had said. *The marines commissioned a few thousand of these for their spec-ops units a few years back to replace the old rebuilt 1911s they'd been carrying for decades.*

A heavy pistol, all steel, just the way Tom liked them, the M45A1 CQBP was a modern 1911 in every respect and included a mil-spec Picatinny rail located under the dust cover to allow for the quick attachment of a light.

The added weight directly beneath the barrel would also minimize muzzle flip, allowing for faster follow-up shots.

The slide and frame were coated with a tan-colored Cerokote, making the weapon ideal for desert warfare, which Tom didn't see himself engaging in ever again.

The coating was faded and chipped in places, indicating hard use.

But the weapon's appearance didn't matter to Tom.

All that did matter was that the pistol was chambered in .45 ACP, his caliber of choice.

Tom had expressed concern over the weapon being traced back to Cahill, but Cahill had explained that he needn't worry about that.

It belonged to one of my marines, and after I was discharged, he was killed in an ambush. An insurgent stripped him of his gear, his weapons along with it, but a buddy of mine hunted the fucker down a few days later and got this back. He shipped it to me the next day. So as far as anyone knows, this was lost in Afghanistan.

Tom had told Cahill that he'd rather not be given something so meaningful, but Cahill shrugged his concerns off.

If I get it back, I get it back, he'd said. *If I don't, I don't. More important, if it saves your life or the life of someone we care about, then all the shit that went down before it was put into my hands wasn't in vain.*

The pistol was held in a carbon-fiber, inside-the-waistband holster, which was secured to the Velcro wall of the hidden compartment by a thick nylon strap.

Three backup Wilson Combat mags were held in a neat row by similar straps, as well as a Surefire X300U weapon light rated at 600 lumens.

I tuned the Colt up myself, Cahill had said. *It's kind of a Frankenstein's monster at this point. A Smith & Alexander mainspring housing with a magwell, an Ed Brown slide stop, lighter springs where it counts, better grips for concealed carry. I kept the trigger long, though, which is what you want in a combat pistol. And the white-dot stock night sights are good, but I switched out the low-profile rear sight for an angled one, in case you ever need to rack the slide with one hand. Oh, and the mags are loaded with those plus-P frangibles that you like. Nineteen hundred feet per second out the muzzle makes for quite the sonic boom. I wouldn't want to be stuck in a confined space when you shoot those things off. That's just asking for a concussion.*

Looking now at the paper-covered windows, Tom listened as the Mustang passed by the building, the sound of its performance exhaust fading as Cahill and Sandy headed north out of town.

Taking one last look around the place, Tom shouldered the messenger bag, then exited.

In the Ranger, he backtracked out of town, stopping at the McDonald's just a quarter mile past the railcar diner.

He parked in the lot and removed the tablet from the bag, powering it up.

Should he need internet access, he would simply log on to the free Wi-Fi that the restaurant provided, the signal of which, last he knew, was strong enough to cover at least sections of the surrounding lot.

But Tom knew that it was safer if the device he used to first open the flash drive was not connected to the web. If any illicit software had been installed on the drive it could make use of the internet to immediately determine—and broadcast—his location.

There'd be no reason for Carrington to do that, but if the drive had been given to him by someone else, that person may have had hidden motives.

This was the world Tom was in now—having to second-guess the actions and words of those who offered him assistance.

He would need to do this and more if he and Stella were to ever be together again.

Tom inserted the drive into the tablet's USB port, and instantly, a window opened, requesting entry of a four-digit security code.

There was a button at the bottom of the window labeled FORGOT YOUR PASSWORD? Tom touched it, and a smaller window opened, this one containing the password hint.

BIRTH DATE ON HEADSTONE.

Two years ago, Carrington had asked Tom to meet him in a cemetery in the town of Litchfield, roughly twenty miles south of Canaan.

The grave they had stood by was the resting place of Benjamin Tallmadge, George Washington's spymaster—and Carrington's childhood hero.

Tallmadge's birth year was 1754.

Tom entered those four digits, and the flash drive unlocked.

On it was a single document.

Opening it, Tom began to read.

It was predawn when he returned to New York City.

After the serpentine journey that Carrington had taken him on, Tom was expecting to be led to his next destination via a similarly complex path, but the steps he was to take were decidedly simple.

The document contained a list of locations Tom was to go to, along with the specific times he was to arrive.

Once in place, he was to wait for contact to be made. If no contact was initiated within fifteen minutes, Tom was to leave and try again at the next time and place on the schedule.

All the locations were in the Greater New York area, but the times were six hours apart.

The first meeting on the schedule was at six a.m., and Tom had every intention of making that.

In fact, he was parked three blocks away from that location with just minutes to spare. Twenty-four hours had passed since the call from Raveis had awakened Tom.

He recalled Sandy Montrose's warning about the effects of lack of sleep on the human mind, but there was nothing he could do about that.

There was truth to uncover, and everything—everyone he cared about—hung in the balance.

He wouldn't stop, nor would he let anyone get in his way.

Tom used his own burner phone to text Torres, instructing her to proceed with their original plan of using her trusted contact in the NYPD to attempt to identify Slattery via her motorcycle license plate.

Torres responded within a minute.

Leaving now.

Tom put on the gloves before removing the holstered Colt from the messenger bag.

Back in Canaan, Cahill had pointed out that he was handing Tom a "clean" weapon, meaning that it and all its components, including the mags and the ammo they carried, had been wiped of any trace evidence, after which Cahill had made a point of always wearing gloves whenever he had handled the weapon.

Tom intended to maintain that same diligence during the time the M45A1 was his.

Taking the pistol from its holster, he racked the slide, chambering a round. After completing a brass check to confirm the cartridge was properly seated, he engaged the thumb safety and returned the pistol to its holster, then slid the rig into his waistband at the four-o'clock position.

Two of the three backup mags went into his universal dual-mag holder on his left side. The third went into his left hip pocket.

On the passenger seat was a long-billed cap. Tom put that on to help obscure his face from the countless traffic and security cameras that blanketed the city.

He'd covered a half block when he received another text from Torres.

Interrogation begun.

This was contrary to the specific orders Tom had given Lyman back in Bridgeport, but there was nothing Tom could do about that now.

He didn't bother to reply, simply pocketed his phone and continued walking.

He had to remain focused, and any thoughts of the techniques likely being applied to their prisoner would only bring to mind the difficulties Stella was currently enduring.

All in the name of preparing her for the day when she might be captured.

Tom knew that distractions were deadly, so he pressed on, his mind on his surroundings, his eyes sharp and his body ready.

He and those he sought to protect would be better served if from now on he felt nothing, or at least as little as possible.

When it comes to loved ones, Cahill had said, *I don't think there is a line.*

Reaching his destination—the entrance to the Second Avenue subway station at Houston Street—Tom paused at the top of the steps to take one last look around before descending.

PART THREE

Twenty-Two

Naked in a dark closet, the makeshift hood covering her head, Esa breathed.

Her wrists, bound behind her back by mechanic's wire, were connected to a wall-mounted coat hook by another two-foot-long piece of the same sharp wire.

The deliberate shortness of the connecting wire forced her to both bend forward at the waist and stand on her toes. This was necessary to lessen the pain in her shoulders caused by the unnatural way her arms were being elevated behind her back.

Her legs trembling from both the cold and the strain, she did her best to keep her breathing slow and even as she eavesdropped on her captors.

She had been listening to them since her arrival hours before, when she'd first been placed in the closet.

The hood had been removed and her hands unbound then, but this was only so she could comply with the order to remove her clothing.

The order had been given by the male, who stood outside the closet and watched.

Esa recognized him from the files she'd been provided as Lyman, the former SEAL.

One of the two women who'd taken her to this place stood just beyond the SEAL—this was Durand.

The other woman, Torres, who had been part of Sexton's team, had been elsewhere in the safe house as Esa undressed.

Lyman had ordered Esa to gather her clothes and hand them to Durand, to whom he whispered something, after which Durand disappeared and Lyman and Esa stared at each other.

Esa heard cupboard doors opening and closing and then a faucet running, but she never broke her stare.

When Durand had reappeared, she was carrying a bucket of water, which Lyman told her to place on the floor. Handing Durand the roll of mechanic's wire, he instructed her to bind their prisoner's wrists together behind her back.

Durand had followed her orders.

Cutting from the roll a two-foot-long piece of wire, Lyman had first attached the wire to the coat hook mounted at head level on the wall. Stepping back, he picked up the bucket and, with one throw, doused Esa with cold tap water.

The makeshift hood was replaced over Esa's head, and the wire that was attached to the coat hook had been wrapped around the wire binding her wrists, then pulled taut, raising her arms behind her and forcing her to bend forward.

Esa had made no sound as the door was closed.

She'd spent the next few hours listening to her captors, keeping track of their movements. She couldn't hear their words when they spoke, but she could make out the tones in their voices, so she knew there was discord among them—specifically, between Lyman and Torres.

It was after several hours that Esa heard the chiming of a cell phone, which was followed by the most intense dispute yet.

This time, Esa could hear the words being spoken.

He told you to wait, Torres said.

Lyman replied, *I'm not waiting here and doing nothing.*

Their exchange went on, Torres insisting that Lyman follow orders, Lyman asserting his authority over the operation.

It was, essentially, a pissing match.

After a moment of this, Esa heard a door open and close, and then nothing more for several minutes.

In this silence, she felt her heart beating faster.

Finally, she detected activity beyond the closet—something heavy being dragged across a floor.

Her calves and lower back and shoulders were fatigued to the point of spasms, but she knew she needed to ignore that.

The dragging ceased just beyond the closet; another moment of silence fell, but this one was shorter and ended with the door being opened and the hood being pulled from Esa's head.

Though the room was dimly lit, she had been in total darkness so long that her eyes struggled to adjust to even the minimal light.

Once they did, she saw that Durand was standing in front of her, a pair of wire cutters in her hand.

Behind Durand, standing beside a heavy butcher-block table, was Lyman. He was holding the roll of mechanic's wire.

By his feet was another bucket of water, and on the floor behind him, plugged into a wall outlet via a heavy-duty extension cord, was a clothes iron.

Sharing the same electrical outlet was a small video recorder on a tripod, its recording indicator light glowing red.

Durand stepped aside, and Lyman picked up the bucket.

This time, ice cubes had been added to the tap water.

The forceful blast of icy water that struck Esa caused her heart to seize briefly, then beat even faster once it was able to resume.

But she refused the urge to gasp from the shock.

Goose bumps rose on her skin as the water poured off her and gathered into a shallow puddle around her bare feet.

Adding to her torment, the natural contraction of every muscle in her body caused by the cold also served to increase the power and frequency of her spasms.

Lyman put the bucket down, stepped behind the video camera, and removed his sidearm from its holster, placing the weapon on the windowsill.

Durand did the same—standard operating procedure when handling a dangerous prisoner.

Also on the windowsill was a single white sock, a roll of duct tape, and a plastic gallon-size gasoline container.

Esa understood what it was Lyman intended to do with those items.

After it was thoroughly soaked with gasoline, the sock would be stuffed into her mouth, which would then be covered by the tape.

Her inevitable screams would be significantly muffled, and over a period of time, as she alternated between gasping for air and biting down on the wadded sock, she would both inhale the gas vapor and swallow more and more of the acidic liquid.

And if needed, her tormentors could threaten to put a lit lighter to the sock, or worse.

Esa sized up the man who would take the lead in working her over.

Lyman's torso, as thick as a tree trunk, was covered by a plate carrier vest. Esa could tell by the thickness of the front and back panels that they contained steel plates. Attached to the face of the vest were several rifle-magazine holders, as well as a pistol-gripped knife in a Kydex holster and an IFAK—a small individual first aid kit.

Everything she already knew about him, combined with everything she was seeing now, told her that he was a man to be feared.

But she'd killed men like him before.

Lyman removed his vest and leaned it against the wall, then returned to where he had placed the empty bucket.

Durand joined him.

"Cut her down," Lyman said.

Twenty-Three

The Second Avenue subway station was empty.

It remained empty as Tom waited on the platform for the F local.

When the train pulled up, Tom boarded and, as instructed, walked back to the next-to-the-last car.

He saw only two people, an older man and a man in his late twenties. Seated apart, one was on the bank seat along the wall of the car, the other was across from him on the opposing bank seat but a few spots down.

The younger man was bearded and dressed in jeans, a sweatshirt, and a leather jacket, but his footwear—walnut-colored Merrell MOABS, the boot favored by a number of Special Forces units—told Tom what he needed to know about the man.

Whatever his specific background may have been, he was a close-protection agent now.

The younger man was watching Tom with a hardened yet indifferent stare. On the seat next to him was a messenger bag similar to Tom's, though larger.

The bag leaned against the man's left leg, the zipper to its main compartment open. The train moved with a lurch, but Tom kept his balance.

The younger man nodded to a seat near him, though not the one directly next to him. Tom sat where the man had indicated and was now facing the older man.

His head was bald, his face gaunt. The heavy overcoat he was wrapped in—heavier, Tom thought, than the chilly October morning called for—didn't hide a thinness that bordered on frailty.

A closer, second look at the man's face revealed that he had no eyebrows. And though he was seated, his breathing was labored.

Tom knew a terminal case when he saw one.

He knew, too, that the man was giving him the time needed to come to this very understanding.

To allow Tom to recognize what he was facing.

Finally, the man said, "You don't look like your father."

Tom ignored that. "What should I call you?"

"I'm known as the Engineer."

"Why is that?"

"There was a time when we chose to be identified by what we did. To protect ourselves as well as those we loved. When I first met the Colonel, I was a surveillance expert." He paused. "I've been hoping to meet you for a long time, Tom."

"How did you get my old Colt?"

The Engineer smiled. "You and I, we do our best to obey the orders we're given, like the good soldiers we have always striven to be. Well, good soldier in my case, good sailor in yours."

"Were you disobeying or obeying orders when you preserved that weapon?"

The Engineer shook his head, dismissing the question. "There are more important questions to ask than that."

Tom said, "I don't have time for games."

"On that we agree. But this entire business, what we do for a living, all of it in the name of serving our country—that's the game. I'm not surprised you haven't figured that out yet. It took me decades to recognize that fact. Or rather, it took me decades to stop ignoring what was right there in front of me and see the painful truth."

"Which is?"

"That I had given my life to a lie."

"What lie?"

"There isn't time for all that."

"I'm in no hurry."

"I am. Hunted men can't sit still for long. I'm afraid you may just understand what that means before this is over."

"Then why are we here? Why risk coming out into the open to meet me at all if there's no time to talk?"

"Because your father is dead and you have no idea why. And because I could have done something to save him but didn't. I would like to atone for certain things before my time comes. And I want that rarest of things for someone in our line of work. I want to die in my bed, with what family I have left at my side."

Tom glanced at the bodyguard, then looked back at the Engineer. "What happened that night?"

"Your father was a sacrificial lamb. And he was sent to his slaughter by his closest friend."

"What does that mean?"

"Carrington tells me that you shared with him a certain set of memories—memories of a man visiting your father during the two years following the murder of your mother and sister. This man came to your home always late at night, and from your bed you could hear him talking to your father down in his study."

"It was the detective in charge of the case, filling him in."

"Is that what your father told you?"

"Yes."

"That was no detective, Tom."

"Then who was it?"

"Your not recognizing the voice is understandable. It was decades ago, you were just a teenager, it was just the voice of a stranger in the night—"

"Who was it?"

"It was Sam Raveis."

Tom said nothing.

The Engineer gave Tom a moment before continuing. "It's amazing how that man has served as such a keystone in your life, and for as long as he has, all without your ever knowing it. You thought you first met him face-to-face two years ago. Later you find out that it was Raveis and the Colonel who sent Carrington to recruit you for his Seabee recon team. And now I'm telling you that two years before you even joined the navy, there he was in your own home, manipulating your father. He has guided your life, for better or for worse, for more than twenty years, and you hadn't a clue."

"How was he manipulating my father?"

"The night your father sought out the Algerian and his men—the night your father was killed in a fleabag hotel room—that was the event that made all this possible."

"All what?"

"The Colonel's great experiment. A private-sector spec ops group, ready to work for the highest bidder. A civilian organization but with a surprising number of government contracts, it turns out. I have given more than two decades of my life to this endeavor and only recently recognized it for the lie that it is. A lie that must be kept hidden, even if it means sacrificing you and your friends."

"How did my father's death make that possible?"

"He was the first sacrifice."

"What does that mean?"

The train slowed as it approached the station.

"This is your stop, Tom. Everything you want, everything you need to know, is waiting for you up top." He nodded toward the man seated to Tom's left. "Manning here will see you safely to your destination. After that you two will part ways. You'll want to go somewhere safe and review the material. I'd suggest you do that alone."

"No, we'll ride with you to the next stop," Tom said. "We can make our way back to our destination on foot after you've given me some answers."

"It's best to stay underground as much as possible."

"Then we'll take the subway back to this stop."

"Please, Tom, do as I ask."

"Then at least tell me why you had the Colt?"

"That's obvious, no? In case it became necessary to frame you. Just like it had become necessary to frame Carrington."

"You did that?"

"I played my part."

"Who ordered you to do it?"

"I think you know the answer to that."

Tom said nothing.

"Once you exit the station, you'll see a storage facility at the end of the block. Head up to the ninth floor, unit 955. Inside, you'll find a device. What it contains is for your eyes only. Understand?"

Tom glanced at Manning before looking back at the Engineer.

"Why the extra steps?" Tom said. "Why not bring the item with you, hand it to me yourself? For that matter, why didn't Carrington give it to me earlier?"

"The men sent to escort you home were Raveis's men. We couldn't risk the item ending up in his hands. Their orders were to bring you to him for debriefing, and he could have taken it from you then." The Engineer paused. "But I also wanted to meet you face-to-face. I wanted the chance to clear my conscience for this one matter, at least."

"You said you could have done something to save my father but didn't. What did you mean?"

"He was in the next room, fighting for his life."

"And you stayed where you were."

"We all have a job to do. I did mine."

Tom waited for more, but it became apparent that nothing else would be forthcoming.

He studied the man seated across from him for a moment, then asked, "How long have the doctors given you?"

"Not long. Not long enough, certainly. The device is encrypted. A seven-digit code is required to unlock it. A single failed attempt causes all that the device contains to be permanently deleted. Carrington assures me that the password prompt will lead you to the correct seven digits."

"And what do I do with the information?"

"What your heart tells you, Tom," he said. "Which is what I should have done a long time ago."

The train emerged from the tunnel and slowed for its stop at the platform.

Manning stood, and so did Tom.

"Good luck," the Engineer said.

Tom started for the still-closed doors, but he stopped when the Engineer spoke.

"The woman you took captive, the leader of the team that attacked you, her name is Esa Hirsh."

"How did you know about her? That we have her?"

"It is my job to know."

It took Tom only a second. "You had Cahill under surveillance."

The Engineer nodded. "It was put in place years ago as a precaution, in case you ever ended up back there. A complete workup—audio, cell, Ethernet. You'd be surprised how much of our resources are devoted to spying on our own people. The good news is I rerouted the signal before I pulled my disappearing act. I'm the only one who knows about it, so I'm the only one who knows what you and Cahill discussed."

Tom noted a discrepancy in something Carrington had told him earlier. "Carrington said he went looking for you after you disappeared."

"That is correct."

"So why did you divert the surveillance on my old place when you went black?"

"I knew that if you and I ever got here—if you and I ever got this far—there was a good chance you'd go to Cahill for help. He was already there with his doctor girlfriend. If you did end up going to him, I needed to know what he told you, if only to help keep you on the right track." He paused. "It was smart to ask of him what you did. Stella *is* vulnerable. But don't think you can protect everyone. It's already too late for that."

The doors opened. Manning moved through, but Tom waited.

He asked, "What can you tell me about the woman?"

"That your people will get nothing from her. No one has had the training she has had. No one has had the life she has had. She is a devil, Tom, from a long line of devils. If I were you, I would contact whoever is watching her and tell them to put a bullet in her head. Two, to be sure. And sooner rather than later. Trust me, the world would be just that much better off if she were no longer in it."

The doors began to close, and Tom slipped through just in time.

He watched as the train pulled away from the platform, picking up speed as it disappeared into the tunnel.

"We should get moving, sir," Manning said.

"I need to make a call."

"You won't get a signal down here. We'll head up."

They were midway up the exit's steep stairs when Tom saw enough bars on his burner phone to make a call.

He had no way of contacting Lyman and Durand directly—a failure of leadership on his part, no doubt about that, but there was nothing he could do about it now except learn from his mistake.

He had no intention of giving the order the Engineer had suggested—the summary execution of the prisoner—but considering Torres's last text, there was no way he wasn't going to warn what remained of his team of the danger they were in.

Moving just ahead of Tom, Manning watched their surroundings. They were at the top of the stairs and in the open dawn air by the time Tom reached Torres's voice mail.

As he and Manning hurried toward the end of the block, Tom spoke.

He could hear the urgency in his own voice as he explained that he needed Torres to get ahold of Grunn and inform her that she needed to send more security to the safe house right away.

He stressed that Torres wasn't to go back there herself, no matter what, and that he wanted her to text him once she had spoken to Grunn, then proceed with her own mission as planned.

Then he informed her he might be out of touch for a few hours but that he'd get back in touch with her when he could.

Ending the call, he pocketed the phone as they reached the end of the block.

The storage facility was a ten-story building, open twenty-four hours, seven days a week, and accessible by a security card, which Manning had ready in his hand as they approached the door.

Once inside the lobby, Tom instructed Manning to wait for him.

Manning suggested that he at least ride with Tom in the elevator, but Tom insisted that he go alone.

"Keep the lobby secure," Tom ordered.

He entered the elevator, pressed the button for the ninth floor, and waited till the doors closed.

The elevator, old and large, originally built for handling freight, was painstakingly slow, but Tom remained patient.

Opening his jacket, he reached for the Colt, adjusting the holster within his waistband so that it was properly canted for easy accessibility and rapid draw.

After roughly a minute, Tom noted that the elevator had passed only five floors.

Four more to go.

Twenty-Four

Stepping into the closet, Durand moved behind Esa and severed the wire connected to the coat hook, then took Esa by one arm and led her out into the room.

Esa sensed something akin to care in the woman's touch, but she wasn't sure what to make of that.

There was always the chance that Durand—early thirties, intelligent eyes, the quietest of her three captors—was in over her head, especially considering what Lyman clearly had in mind.

Kindness was a weakness that Esa had long ago learned to not only spot but to exploit as well.

Quickly surveying her surroundings, Esa determined that she was in a small apartment in an old building—a prewar building, as evidenced by the thick plaster walls and ornate molding that framed the two large windows.

The glass was covered with dark sheets of plastic, the edges of which were sealed with long strips of duct tape.

The floor, old linoleum, was cold, indicating to Esa that whatever was below this apartment was likely uninhabited.

As Esa was escorted from the closet, Lyman moved in behind her fast and wound a fresh piece of mechanic's wire around her left elbow, tightly. Holding the rest of the coil in his hand as though it were the end of a leash, he instructed Durand to cut the wire binding Esa's wrists.

Durand did so, and the instant Esa's hands were free, Lyman maneuvered in front of her, taking several rapid backward steps as he tugged on the wire and pulled her toward the butcher block.

Her slippery bare feet prevented her from resisting his sudden, violent action. She was slammed into the heavy butcher block, her pelvic bones against the hard wood edge, her lower abdomen nearly level with the surface of the block.

Lyman continued to step backward and pull Esa forcibly until she was bent over the table, at which point Durand grabbed Esa's right arm, holding it with one hand to keep Esa down as she passed the wire cutters to Lyman.

He took them and cut another two-foot-long piece from the coil.

The instant Durand had handed off the cutters, she grabbed onto Esa's right arm with her other hand.

Lyman knelt and pulled Esa's left arm straight down, and she knew then that he was intending to attach the other end of the wire to the leg of the table.

After that, he would do the same with her other arm, then secure her ankles, too, ensuring that her legs were spread as far apart as the width of the butcher block would allow.

Positioning her for maximum vulnerability.

But Lyman needed two hands to manipulate the wire and fully secure his prisoner's left arm, so he handed the cutters back to Durand. To accept them, Durand had to remove one hand from Esa's right arm.

In the process, Durand's remaining hand loosened slightly.

Lyman was focused on winding the stiff wire around the table leg, and this allowed Esa to turn her head and steal a glance at the younger woman.

Durand was holding the wire cutters with one hand, not by the grips but by the shears—a result of the way Lyman had hastily handed them back to her.

The grips, then, were right there for Esa to seize.

At best, wire cutters were not a weapon for killing, but maiming was a perfectly good place to start—the first step, at least, in what would no doubt be a race to get to one of the pistols on the windowsill.

But it was now or never.

The fact that Esa was slick from the recent dousing would mean she'd be difficult to hold on to, and this would work to her advantage.

Snapping her right arm back, sharply drawing her elbow toward her ribs, she slipped free of Durand's one-handed grasp, then immediately lunged for the tool in Durand's other hand.

Closing her fist around the metal grips, Esa saw her chance and took it.

Twenty-Five

Tom moved down the long corridor.

On either side were aluminum roll-up doors, each one roughly the size of a single-car garage door.

Mounted on the ceiling every twenty feet or so were security cameras, but there was nothing Tom could do about that except keep his chin down so that the long bill of Cahill's cap shielded his face.

Reaching the unit marked 955, Tom was confronted with his first problem.

As with all the doors he had passed, this one was secured by a padlock.

While the majority of the locks he had passed were the kind that needed a key, this particular unit, however, was secured by a combination lock. The Engineer, careful in all his details, had neglected to inform Tom of this.

Was it possible, as a precaution, he didn't want to state the combination in front of Manning?

Tom froze for a second, staring at the lock, but then he realized that locks such as these required three numbers in the proper sequence to open.

Each storage unit was identified by three numbers.

What did he have to lose for trying?

Holding the lock in his left hand, Tom spun the dial counterclockwise past zero, then turned it clockwise to nine, counterclockwise to five, and then clockwise again to five.

Yanking down on the housing, he opened the lock.

Tom removed it and, after setting it on the floor, grabbed the handle at the bottom of the door and lifted it up.

The aluminum was light, the rollers and casters well lubricated, so the door went up effortlessly and without too much noise.

With the SureFire weapon light from Cahill's messenger bag in his left hand, Tom searched the walls just inside the door for a light switch. Locating it, he flipped it up.

A single overhead bulb lit the five-by-eight space, which was empty save for a case made of protective plastic, similar to the one Carrington had left in the courtyard of the factory.

Stepping to it, Tom moved around it so he was facing the door, then knelt and opened the case.

Protected by the dense foam inserts was a tablet, which itself was housed inside an OtterBox case. Tom removed the tablet and stood.

He powered it up, and a few seconds later, the passcode request was displayed.

Below it was the option to view the password hint. Tom touched the icon, and a small window opened up on the display, overlaying the passcode keypad.

SERIAL NUMBER.

Tom was initially baffled. What serial number? The Engineer had told him it was a seven-digit number, but *what* seven-digit serial number?

That in itself had to be a clue, since most devices required even-numbered passcodes—four or six or eight.

A security program requiring seven digits was likely one that had been custom-made.

Tom's memory for numbers meant it could, technically, be any seven digits he'd ever seen, but he doubted Carrington would be so random, particularly since one failed attempt at unlocking the device would delete its contents.

It had to be something specific, then, maybe something Tom had recently seen.

Maybe something significant, if not positively then negatively.

And then Tom recalled the last seven digits he had viewed.

Seven digits that had caused him to feel deep concern.

The Colt that Carrington had left for him—that the Engineer had given to Carrington—was roll-stamped with a seven-digit serial number.

Tom returned to the passcode prompt and entered that series of numbers: 1096409.

The device instantly unlocked, and Tom was looking at a screen that displayed a half dozen video clips in a grid.

He touched the first clip with the tip of his finger; the media player opened, and the video began to play.

It was like looking back in time.

Tom saw his father's old study. The quality of the video indicated that this was a recording from a surveillance camera. By the camera's line of sight, Tom concluded that it had been hidden on his father's bookshelf.

The recording ran for a few seconds before a figure entered the frame.

That figure was George Sexton, Tom's father.

A second figure entered the frame a few seconds later.

Tom was now looking at a much younger Sam Raveis.

Tom heard his father tell Raveis that they had to keep their voices down because his son was asleep upstairs.

It was an odd thing to hear the man's voice again after all these years, and for him to refer to Tom as his son.

That role of son was from a lifetime ago.

Raveis asked how Tom was doing, and his father answered, *The boy lost his mother and sister.*

Tom considered ending the playback there, but he let it continue.

The bar at the bottom of the player indicated that this video was just under five minutes long.

Tom stood there and watched the whole thing.

And when it was done, he watched two more.

It took Tom a moment to come back from the memories that the videos had triggered.

There wasn't time to watch the rest, but the ones he had watched had shown him all he needed to know for now.

And anyway, watching the rest would only stir up even more memories, and he needed to keep his mind clear.

Putting the device into sleep mode, Tom awoke it again to confirm that the passcode needed to be reentered, then powered the device down and placed it inside the protective case.

He closed the lid, securing the two clasps. Grabbing the case, he exited the empty storage unit.

He didn't bother to close the door behind him as he headed back down the hallway. He reached the elevator, pressed the "Down" button, and was anticipating a long wait, since the car would have to make its way back up to the ninth floor.

To Tom's surprise, though, the doors opened immediately. The elevator hadn't moved since he had exited it moments ago.

Entering, Tom pressed the button marked LOBBY and waited for the doors to close. They did after a slight delay, and the elevator began its descent, which was as painfully slow as its ascent had been.

Tom was considering getting off and taking the stairs when the elevator stopped.

It had passed only the eighth floor and stopped at the seventh.

Tom had been holding the case with two hands but now let his right hand hang at his side, where it would be ready to initiate the well-drilled maneuver of drawing his sidearm from an open jacket—right hand cupping the bottom corner of the jacket, flipping it back and out of the way before reaching for the grip of his pistol and drawing.

There was a long pause before the doors parted. Waiting in the corridor were a man and a woman.

In their late twenties, their arms around each other, they smiled at Tom and boarded the elevator.

He stepped back to allow them room.

Turning their backs to him, they seemed to only have eyes for each other, though the male managed to press the already illuminated "Lobby" button without even looking at it.

Tom recalled the few close-protection details he and his team had worked in their first months together, and how on several of those jobs Torres and Garrick, for the sake of blending into their surroundings, had acted like a couple caught up in new love.

They had been wholly convincing, and Tom was wondering if the same act was being put on for him now.

The first detail that caught his eye was that the time of day—barely morning—was all wrong for a couple so passionate about each other, though of course they could have come here after a long night spent drinking.

Neither of them was carrying anything, so they had to have just dropped something off or, and this seemed a more likely possibility, used the storage room as a location for an illicit tryst.

Tom had seen stranger things.

But the detail that he focused on—the one that made clear to him the impending danger—was the presence of a smell.

It filled the elevator, blending with the woman's heavy perfume while remaining noticeable and distinctive.

It was a scent that was both natural and chemical, like pine mixed with alcohol, and Tom had smelled it as recently as the morning before.

Ballistol—the lubricant he and Torres and Garrick had used to prepare their firearms prior to Tom embarking on his journey to Connecticut.

And considering the fact that New York was a less-than-firearm-friendly city, the chances of Tom encountering even just one legally armed citizen were low at best.

No, Tom knew who was in the elevator with him.

His right hand still hanging at his side, he held the carrying case firmly with his left.

Lowering his eyes so he could examine the hands of the couple in front of him, he saw that they had one arm around the other's waist, leaving an arm free for each.

The elevator had passed the sixth floor and was approaching the fifth when Tom finally broke the silence.

"You cleaned your sidearms recently," he said.

The man and woman half turned their heads, listening to Tom without looking directly at him. They were still smiling, still caught up in each other.

The man feigned surprise. "What?"

"You're carrying firearms," Tom said. "You cleaned them recently. Ballistol, right? I can smell it."

The couple didn't reply, simply continued to face each other, holding the same smiles.

"You don't have to do this," Tom said. "You can just walk away. We can all just walk away."

The man looked forward, but the woman turned her head till she was looking at Tom.

Her now-frozen smile looked strained.

“Tell whoever sent you that I took the stairs,” Tom said to her.

She didn’t reply.

Finally, the man shook his head. “There’s a team watching the stairs, just in case.”

“Then tell them I didn’t let you onto the elevator.”

“The surveillance cameras are being monitored,” the man said.

Tom glanced up just far enough to glimpse the low-profile camera mounted in the right rear corner of the car.

“So I guess we’re fucked, then,” Tom said.

The woman turned forward. She and her partner remained that way, their eyes on the door.

Tom had flustered them, probably even embarrassed them, but he knew their hesitation wouldn’t last.

Chances were their intention wasn’t to strike while inside the elevator; confined spaces, as a rule, were more dangerous than open areas, which allowed an attacker to put just the right amount of distance between himself and his target.

There was also the chance that these two, and the team on the stairs, had come here to abduct Tom rather than to kill him.

After all, what good was the encrypted tablet without the passcode?

But by calling them out, Tom had forced their hand—it was either attack or be attacked.

In any conflict, victory tended to favor the aggressor, which was why Tom didn’t wait for them to make their move.

Sweeping back his jacket, he reached for the holstered Colt at his waist.

But the couple had had the same thought, because the instant Tom broke for his weapon, they abandoned their mutual embrace and reached for theirs.

In a split second, the three occupants of the elevator were in motion.

Outgunned and lacking the element of surprise, Tom improvised.

Twenty-Six

The first blow Esa landed was to the woman whose grasp she had just escaped.

Owing to her position in relation to Durand, as well as the manner in which she was holding the wire cutters, the best strike Esa could manage was a hammer blow—the weakest of all strikes.

But the ends of the tool's metal grips were jutting out from the bottom of her hand like a pummel, and this would significantly increase the potential for inflicting serious damage—not just to the soft tissue and bone in the area of direct impact, but to Durand's brain as the shock wave generated by the hit would send that vital organ slamming against the inner skull.

Esa aimed for Durand's temple but missed it by an inch, striking the woman's cheekbone just below her right eye.

Despite the fact that Esa had missed the optimal target, the blow was enough to send Durand straight to the floor.

And while the angle of attack on Durand had been limited, the options for striking Lyman, who was crouched down with his head bent as he worked to attach the stiff wire to the table's leg, were worse.

Esa could barely reach across the butcher block, never mind take a swing down its left side in an attempt to drive the sharp ends of the wire cutters into the back of Lyman's skull.

And such an attack in itself was likely to be less than effective.

The only real option was for Esa to once again make good use of the fact that her bare body was slick with water.

The instant Durand was struck, Lyman had been alerted to trouble, but before he had time to react, Esa pushed herself along the top of the butcher block.

Slipping across the wood, she slid off and threw her body onto Lyman's still-bent back.

Her hope was to line up a clear shot at his temple, where the skull was its thinnest, or maybe the side of his neck, where his carotid artery ran, or at worst, an ear.

The nose of the wire cutters was no more than two inches long, so a deep puncture was out of the question, but if serious injury couldn't be immediately inflicted, then excruciating pain was second best.

Lyman, however, had the situational awareness of a wrestler, because as soon as Esa landed on his back, he abandoned his attempt to stand and instead tucked into an even deeper crouch, simultaneously raising his right shoulder and easily rolling her off and onto the floor.

Landing on her back, Esa felt a sudden ache in her chest as the air was knocked out of her lungs, but she ignored that. She anticipated that Lyman's next move would be to mount her, so she was ready, countering him by thrusting the cutters into the nearest soft target—his groin—just as he climbed on top of her.

She followed the first jab with another, and then a third, all of them in rapid succession.

Instinctively, Lyman grabbed for her wrist with both hands, held it with all his considerable strength, but this meant her left arm was free.

The other end of the wire had been wound only once around the leg of the butcher block, and done so loosely, so Esa was free to reach up for Lyman's face.

Closing her hand into a fist but keeping her thumb extended, she lunged for his eye, jabbing into it deeply with her thumb.

But Lyman's grip on her wrist didn't lessen, and the triple jab to his groin, while undoubtedly painful, seemed to only anger him.

Abandoning his plan to mount Esa, he instead planted his feet firmly on the floor and stood, pulling her up by her one arm till she was standing, then grabbing her throat with his other hand.

Bracing himself, he lifted her until only her toes were touching the linoleum.

After taking several steps, Lyman stopped suddenly and flung her backward through the air.

Before she could even brace herself for the hard landing, Esa hit the floor on her left side.

To avoid sliding, she drew her knees to her chest, shaping herself into a ball. Coming to a stop after only a foot, she immediately looked at Lyman, who was obviously beginning to feel the effects of her attacks on his eye and groin.

He was bent forward slightly, standing on uncertain legs and covering his eye with one hand.

More than simply jabbing it, Esa had sliced open the thin tissue of his eyelid with her thumbnail.

Lyman's other eye was focused on the windowsill behind Esa, and it was in this moment that the two of them realized his mistake.

In his rage, he had thrown her across the room—and placed her closer by several precious feet to the firearms that he and Durand had laid there.

Lyman took a step, or tried to—he bent forward slightly, then stopped, a look of confusion on his face.

Only now was he beginning to recognize the damage Esa had done to him with the cutters.

Esa saw her chance and scrambled to her feet. Turning, she started toward the window, but she felt a shooting pain in her hip, which she must have injured when she landed.

The pain wasn't enough to stop her, though, and she continued on, only four strides from reaching the weapons.

What did stop her was Durand, who tackled Esa from the side, driving her off course and slamming her into the plaster wall.

Her previous estimation that Durand was likely the weaker member of the team had been unfounded, because the instant Durand had Esa pinned against the wall, she unleashed several skillful elbow strikes to Esa's face and head, each one landing exactly where she intended.

But Esa had managed to hang on to the wire cutters, and she didn't try to fight it when her knees buckled, knowing that by letting them give out she would slip beneath her attacker's fury.

Sliding down the wall and out of range, Esa drove the cutters into Durand's inner thigh, then repositioned herself so she could deliver a follow-up blow to Durand's lower abdomen.

Even an open-palm strike to the vulnerable area between the pelvic bones was enough to make the strongest person fold and drop.

Striking there with the sharp steel nose of the cutters would not only send Durand down again but also likely guarantee she wouldn't get back up, at least not quickly.

But Durand was full of surprises.

Though she went down as fast as Esa expected she would, she wasn't out of the fight.

As Esa rose from her crouch, sliding up the wall, Durand grabbed her ankle with one hand, preventing Esa from bolting immediately toward the windowsill. More than that, Durand delayed Esa's attempted escape long enough to fully embrace the same ankle with her other arm, effectively rooting Esa in place.

It was a temporary delay at best, but that was all Durand needed now that Lyman had recovered from his injuries enough to resume moving toward them.

He was lumbering, not covering ground with any kind of speed, but the man was a SEAL, had been trained to push through pain, and on top of that he was pissed, more so than when he had launched Esa across the room.

And she knew he wouldn't repeat that mistake.

His intention was to get ahold of her again and, once he did, rain down upon her everything he had.

A man like him—a man his size, with his power and hard-earned skills—could easily snap her neck, though she doubted he'd be that merciful.

So Esa did the only thing she could.

She balanced herself against the wall, lifted her free leg till her knee was almost level with her own chin, then drove downward with all her weight, stomping the back of Durand's head with her bare heel once.

And she did that a second time.

But Durand hung on, so Esa dropped down to one knee and grabbed Durand's arm, peeling back her embrace enough to slip her trapped foot free.

Lyman had closed the distance, was just an arm's length away, and Esa knew there was no way that she could turn and lunge for the windowsill before being grabbed.

And even if she did manage to reach the window first, Lyman would likely come crashing into her from behind, at which point a struggle for acquisition and control of the weapon would ensue.

It would be a struggle that played to all of Lyman's strengths.

Yet again, Esa saw only one option.

Twenty-Seven

Tom grasped the Colt, turning his torso as he drew the weapon so that his left shoulder was forward.

His position allowed him to keep his eye on the male as he shoulder-rammed the female in the middle of her back, driving her forward into the elevator door and pinning her there.

The male was carrying his pistol in an appendix holster, so he'd already had it drawn and was in the process of leveling it at Tom's center mass while Tom had yet to even disengage the Colt's thumb safety.

But Tom knew not to bet everything on being the faster draw, so his left hand had been put into action the very same moment he'd begun to reach for the Colt.

As a result, he was swinging the carrying case in an uppercut motion with all the speed he could muster just as the male was inserting his finger inside the trigger guard.

The case struck under the pistol's barrel, driving the weapon upward, but not so high that it had been driven completely off target.

In fact, instead of the muzzle being directed at Tom's chest, it was now aimed at his face.

Turning even farther so his back was now flat against the female's, Tom slipped out of the line of fire just as the male's trigger finger clenched, setting off a round.

The sound of the shot in the confined space was like an open-hand slap to both ears, and the concussive wave created by the nine-mil bullet breaking the sound barrier triggered a wave of nausea so powerful that all three occupants of the elevator grunted.

The ringing in their ears—like something metal had been shoved deep into the canal, then struck and left to reverberate—only served to sustain the sudden sick feeling.

Still, Tom and his opponents had no choice but to push through the overwhelming discomfort.

Not wanting to lose the initiative, Tom wasted no time and disengaged the Colt's safety as he brought the weapon to his right side, bracing his forearm just above his rib cage as he readied for his shot at the male.

But before Tom could even get his finger inside the trigger guard, the female pushed against the elevator doors with both hands, driving herself backward and sending Tom stumbling forward, taking away his clean shot.

She tried to continue to move Tom, clearly wanting to slam him into the back wall of the car, but he planted his feet firmly, setting his weight of 220 against her 130, creating a brief stalemate.

The male was bringing his pistol down, but Tom was ready with a backhand swing, this time striking the back of the male's hand with the corner of the hard plastic case, forcing him to drop his weapon.

The female turned then, bringing her own firearm to bear, but Tom stepped in close, positioning himself on the inside of her right arm and winding his left arm around her elbow, locking it down and temporarily immobilizing her.

He was free now to realign the Colt on the male, who was reaching for his secondary weapon—a fixed-blade knife holstered at the small of his back.

But that was a long way to reach, and Tom had the Colt lined up with the male's solar plexus and his finger inside the trigger guard. He was ready to fire despite the fact that the concussive wave generated by his lightweight, high-pressure round was going to be significantly greater than the wave they had just experienced.

He was bracing himself when the female reached out with her left hand and grabbed hold of his Colt by the barrel, then swept it off target.

The time she bought allowed her partner to remove his knife and swing at Tom, whose only recourse was to take a step away from his attacker while simultaneously leaning backward at the waist.

The razor-sharp tip of the five-inch serrated blade just missed Tom's face.

The female pressed down on Tom's pistol, driving it downward till it was pointed at the floor, as her partner stepped forward like a fencer pursuing an opponent in retreat.

As he moved, he began the return swing of his knife.

There was no way Tom could wrestle his pistol up in time, nor did he want to surrender his hold on the female's arm.

He had no other option except for a sacrifice play.

He pressed the trigger of the Colt, firing a round into the floor.

The blow that struck him as the shock wave tore through the elevator was like a sledgehammer to the chest.

And while the sound of the 9 mil going off had felt like an open-hand blow to his ears, the blast of the plus-P, 78-grain .45 round leaving the muzzle at nearly two thousand feet per second was like standing beside a cannon.

The shock was enough to cause everyone to drop to their knees.

Tom was immediately rendered deaf—even the ringing he'd been enduring since the shootout the night before was gone.

On his knees, he managed to hang on to the Colt, which the female had released. Because of the way they had fallen to the elevator floor, her right arm was still trapped by his left, though Tom had dropped the case.

Tom lost track of time, didn't know if one second had passed or more, but he could see that the male was on his hands and knees, vomiting. He figured it would have taken the man a few seconds to get into that position.

The woman was struggling to keep from throwing up, as was Tom, who at least had been expecting the violent assault on his senses. Still, he'd been rocked into utter stillness, as if paralyzed. But eventually that deep, sickening ringing returned to his ears, and the nausea's grip loosened just enough for him to gather himself and move.

He reached around with his left hand and pried the female's pistol from her, then took the knife from the male, tossing both weapons into the farthest corner so they'd be out of reach.

Rising from there to his feet, though still bent over and wavering, he swept the male's pistol with the heel of his boot into that same corner.

He'd stand between them and their weapons till the elevator door opened.

Finally, he grabbed the case off the floor with his left hand and forced himself upright, or close enough to it.

The wall helped him to remain that way. Glancing at the panel to the right of the door, he saw that they were passing the second floor.

It wasn't till they had reached the main floor and he was waiting for the doors to open that he realized he hadn't checked the condition of his Colt.

The female had been holding the barrel when Tom fired, which meant she more than likely hadn't allowed the slide to cycle properly, preventing the spent casing from being ejected as the slide kicked back and a fresh round from being chambered as it returned to battery position.

Tom confirmed this by glancing at the hammer and seeing that it hadn't been cocked back.

In effect, he was holding a dead pistol.

The elevator ceased moving and its doors began to part, so Tom positioned the hooked rear sight against the top of his rigger's belt and pressed downward on the grip, manually racking the slide and putting the Colt into condition 1—round chambered and hammer back.

Just as he completed the process, the doors opened and Tom saw the first man, standing twenty-five feet from the elevator door.

Armed with a carbine to which a suppressor was affixed, the man quickly raised the weapon to his shoulder.

In that same instant, Tom saw a second man, this one armed with a pistol, also equipped with a suppressor.

Lying facedown on the lobby floor, halfway between the elevator and the two men, was Manning, a pool of blood spreading from beneath his torso.

Tom ducked to the right as the man with the carbine fired. Finding cover by the panel, he dropped the case and shifted the Colt to his left hand, then pressed the button marked "Door Close" with his right as he extended the Colt around the corner.

He got off two rounds before drawing his arm back to allow the doors to close. But the doors moved slowly, giving the man with the carbine ample time to fire a half dozen rounds of 5.56 into the elevator's back wall.

Tom pressed the buttons for multiple floors, and once the doors finally closed, the elevator began to move in its slow-chugging way again.

Transferring the Colt back to his right hand, he bent down to pick up the case, but as he did, the female, still on her knees, suddenly scrambled for her partner's pistol in the far corner.

She reached it, dropping onto her side and leveling the weapon at Tom's chest.

He was swinging around to face her, just milliseconds from having the Colt pointed at her head, when she fired.

Twenty-Eight

Esa lunged toward Lyman, crossing the remaining two feet faster than he could have in his condition, making her the attacker and thereby taking the initiative away from him.

The man had two vulnerabilities—an eye that was tearing profusely and an injured groin.

These two areas were targets he'd be determined to protect from further attacks.

But Esa was just as determined to make her way to them again.

She passed through striking distance to trapping distance—the range in which fighters cannot throw effective punches and instinctively go for a clinch.

As Lyman did just that, closing his powerful arms around her, Esa jabbed him in the rib cage with the cutters, landing the steel points into a nerve cluster below his armpit.

He grunted, recoiling, but Esa wasn't done.

She drew her hand back and thrust outward again, this time straight into the unprotected bone of his sternum.

His arms, still closing around her, drooped slightly, and this allowed Esa to draw her hand back once more, then swing her arm out like a boxer throwing a high hook punch, finally delivering the blow she'd been working toward—his remaining good eye.

The cutters, coming in from the side, grazed his eye.

Lyman screamed, but he was still in the fight.

Despite the excruciating pain, he managed to clutch at Esa's throat with both hands.

He drove his thumbs into her windpipe, compressing it, and Esa instantly coughed.

His grip was well placed, with his index fingers pressing firmly along both sides of her neck, collapsing her carotid artery—the supplier of oxygenated blood to the brain.

Shutting that artery down for seven seconds was all it took to cause a blackout.

Esa could feel her eyes watering, and she could see the edges of her vision softening—the first sign of oxygen deprivation.

She could feel, too, the rage and relentless power in the hands grasping her neck.

Once she was unconscious, it was likely he would continue to squeeze and crush till her head hung limp from her dead body.

She was losing depth perception, everything blurring, when she reached for the back of his head, pulling it forward.

He resisted, but it was that very act—pushing back against her pull—that caused his chin to rise slightly, exposing the soft area between his jaw and Adam's apple.

She lost track of how many times she drove the tips of the cutters into him before his hands finally loosened, his thumbs slipping from her larynx.

Releasing her, Lyman dropped to the floor, blood gushing from his throat.

Esa, on the cusp of unconsciousness, dropped also.

For a moment she sat there and watched him, and then she found what it took to stand. Stepping over Durand, who was motionless, Esa reached the nearest window.

She was trembling from the cold and the adrenaline, her legs were like rubber, and if she wasn't gasping, she was coughing hard, but she managed to grab Lyman's sidearm, a SIG Sauer P226, and complete a brass check as she turned to face him.

Lyman was still seated, his chest rising and falling, his arms hanging at his sides.

Esa looked down at the carrier vest leaning against the wall and saw in one of its holders a suppressor.

She bent down and removed it; she almost couldn't stand up straight again but did, then attached the device to the threaded barrel of the SIG.

Through his left eye—the eye that was blinking and watering uncontrollably—he watched her.

Even if he were unable to see her, he'd still be able to hear the scraping of the two pieces of metal coming together.

Once the suppressor was firmly in place, Esa raised the pistol and aimed it at Lyman's forehead.

There was no point in dragging it out.

She pressed the trigger, killing him instantly.

Moving back to where Durand was lying, Esa stood over the woman, aiming down at her head.

Motionless and seemingly unconscious a moment ago, Durand was coming around.

Esa pressed the tip of the suppressor against Durand's skull and waited for her to open her eyes.

It took a moment for the woman's eyes to find Esa and focus.

Breaking her long morning of silence, Esa said, "Get up. You're getting me out of here."

Twenty-Nine

Tom felt the impact of the nine-mil round striking his chest, and though the hollow-point bullet mushroomed against his Kevlar vest without penetrating the densely woven material, the 400 ft-lbs of force generated by the fast-moving projectile instantly voided his lungs of air.

His legs buckling, Tom dropped down to one knee, but he managed somehow to keep himself from falling any farther.

More than that, he continued to bring the Colt to bear on the female, putting the white dot of the front sight on her as she was seeking to reacquire her aim and get off a follow-up shot.

There wasn't enough time for her to recognize that her first shot hadn't resulted in a mortal wound.

Her trigger had yet to even reset when Tom fired a single shot, the round striking her squarely in the forehead and, as it exited the back of her skull, spraying the corner of the elevator with blood and bits of bone and brain matter.

But the concussive blast, trapped within the confines of the elevator car, triggered in Tom the same violent reaction as before.

Temporarily deafened, with his wits scattered as though he had been hit in the head with a solid object, he struggled to remain focused on his surroundings.

His only consolation was that the male, still on the floor, was certainly suffering the same effects and therefore wasn't an immediate threat.

The utter and eerie silence continued as the elevator climbed toward the second floor. At one point Tom found the wits necessary to search the female for intel.

He found a smartphone and wallet, pocketing both as he moved to the male, who was barely conscious.

Searching the young man, Tom noted that there was blood trickling out of his ears, indicating, at the very least, that the man's eardrums had burst.

His search turned up the same items. Tom pocketed them as well, then stood and half stepped, half stumbled back to the control panel to the right of the door, leaning against it to help him stay upright.

The case was in his left hand, and the Colt was in his right.

The elevator stopped—something Tom didn't hear but felt. He used the now-familiar long pause that came prior to the doors parting to cross to the dead female and claim her pistol.

It was a Glock 17 with an extended baseplate on its magazine, which increased the standard capacity from seventeen rounds to twenty. The round the female had prechambered brought the capacity of that weapon up to twenty-one, but she had already fired that, so Tom had twenty rounds of 9 mil at his disposal—a caliber that better lent itself to single-handed shooting, but just as importantly, one that when fired in an enclosed space would be nowhere near as devastating.

His Colt holstered, the case in his left hand and the Glock in his right, Tom moved back to his position of cover by the control panel.

He removed the mag to check that it was, in fact, topped off, then reinserted the mag and executed a one-handed press check to confirm that a round was chambered—all with just the thumb and forefinger of his left hand.

With that done, he waited for the doors to open.

When they finally did, he checked that the long hallway beyond was clear. It was, but he didn't move.

The doors eventually closed again, the elevator rising to the next floor.

Tom needed every second of recovery time that he could get, so he was grateful for the crawl-like climb upward. Also, his only hope of getting out of there was to keep his enemy guessing.

And when possible, force the men seeking him to waste their time.

At the next floor, the doors opened, and Tom made certain the hallway beyond was empty before exiting.

The time he'd had between the second and third floors hadn't been nearly enough; he was staggering and his head was reeling and he was deaf, save for the ringing that had suddenly returned.

With every bit of concentration he could muster, he made a visual search of the long hallway to locate the door leading to the stairs.

He had to assume that the men who had fired upon him down in the lobby were on their way up those stairs, pausing to perform a quick search of each floor before moving to the next.

There was no way for Tom to know whether they were still on the floor below or had already reached this one and were waiting behind the door before one of them opened it and the other, likely armed with the carbine, peered out to scan the hall.

Tom spotted the illuminated EXIT sign at the far end of the hall on the right-hand side. He chose to skim that same side of the wall as he made his way toward it.

The aluminum storage locker doors were recessed slightly, and Tom made use of the concealment these narrow spaces offered by pressing his back flat against a door and pausing there before moving as swiftly and as quietly as possible to the next door, where he did the same before moving with the same speed to the next.

He was halfway down the hallway, caught in the open between two storage units, when a sudden box of light appeared at the end of the hall.

The door to the stairwell had been opened.

Rushing to the next unit, Tom reached it and pressed his back against the door, making himself as flat as possible and holding his breath.

Because the ringing was all he could hear, there was no way for him to ascertain what was happening at the far end of the hall.

Had the man with the carbine entered the hall, his weapon raised and ready as he scanned it? Had he spotted Tom and was now waiting for a clear shot? Or was he keeping his weapon trained in Tom's direction as his partner moved down the hall with the intention of flushing Tom out?

A moment passed with no indication of any of this.

Tom knew that if he leaned forward enough to view the end of the hall, he'd be offering his head as a target, but he couldn't stay where he was forever.

He could feel the pressure building in his lungs but didn't dare exhale. Finally, though, the need to breathe won out and Tom opened his mouth, exhaling as silently as he could. Then he drew in air with the same care.

He did that several more times before finally leaning forward just enough to take a quick look down the hall.

The light was gone.

And though his look had been barely more than a peek, he had been able to determine that the end of the hallway was empty.

Leaving the doorway, Tom hurried to the next unit, then to the unit after that.

One by one he made his way to the last unit, beyond which was the exit to the stairs.

The steel door had a narrow window of mesh-reinforced glass set roughly at eye level. Tom walked slowly forward, staying close to the wall, till his back was beside the door. Pausing, he leaned to see through the window.

Its narrowness meant his field of view was limited, requiring him to reposition his head frequently so he could glance through from several different angles and, in stages, see as much as possible of what was on the other side.

He focused on the top steps of one flight of stairs and the bottom steps of the next.

To further his view, Tom moved in front of the door, pressing his shoulder against it and peering through the glass. This angle allowed him to scan the landing and its corner.

He saw nothing—no shapes, no shadows, no movement—so he pushed down on the door lever with his left elbow and nudged the door with his shoulder. After opening it just enough to slip through, he eased it shut as he checked the stairs above. Then he stepped to the railing and looked down the stairwell.

Starting down the stairs, stepping as lightly as he could, Tom moved steadily except for when he stopped to clear a corner or blind spot.

By the time he reached the ground floor, the ringing in his ears was louder, but he could also hear ambient noises—the sound of his footsteps, his own breathing as he inhaled and exhaled through his nose, the faint echo of a door closing somewhere above him.

All those sounds, though, seemed to be coming from far off in the distance.

Opening the door, Tom paused to determine that the lobby was empty before rushing to Manning. He was still facedown on the floor, and the pool of red had spread, surrounding nearly his entire body. Careful not to tread in the blood, Tom got as close as he could, then laid the case down on the floor and reached out with his left hand to check the man's neck for a pulse.

The coldness that greeted Tom's fingertips the moment he touched the man's skin was indication enough that he was dead.

The absence of a pulse was merely a confirmation of that.

Tom's training told him to search Manning's pockets for intel as well, but there wasn't time for that. He was about to make a run for it when a sound penetrated the ringing in his ears and reached his damaged eardrums.

It was a voice, belonging to a male, urgently commanding him to freeze.

Tom looked for the source and couldn't find it at first because his sense of direction was askew, but then he saw the man with the carbine walking toward him.

The weapon was shouldered, and the man was hunched squarely behind it, walking with a soldier's glide.

Emerging right behind him through the stairwell door was the man with the pistol, who fanned out to the left, putting several feet between himself and his partner.

Both the lead man and his partner had Tom in their sights, but instead of opening fire, the lead man ordered Tom to place his weapon on the floor.

It was likely that the couple in the elevator had been put there to monitor Tom until they were reunited with their partners in the lobby, at which point they would, as a stronger force, compel Tom to surrender.

Abduction made sense—what good was the tablet without the passcode?

But if their orders were to take him alive, these men were at a disadvantage.

Tom laid the Glock on the floor, then raised both hands. Before the leader could give another order, Tom rose, keeping his hands slightly below shoulder level.

The Colt was holstered at his right hip, but these men didn't know that.

The leader ordered Tom to remove his messenger bag, but Tom didn't comply.

The man with the handgun ordered Tom to pick up the case.

Tom didn't do that, either.

The leader ceased his approach, maintaining a safe distance between himself and Tom, but the man with the handgun continued to move, completing a wide arc around to Tom's flank.

He was just three feet from Tom, his pistol aimed at Tom's head. "Pick up the case and start walking," he said.

Tom eyed the exit to the street, knew his best chance to make a move would come as they were moving through the door.

He reached down, picked up the case, and started forward, but at a steady, almost aggressive pace.

The man with the carbine remained standing between Tom and the exit, his weapon shouldered and aimed at Tom's chin. As Tom advanced and the man retreated, both he and his partner were forced to match Tom's speed.

The man with the pistol walked alongside Tom, just beyond arm's reach, his pistol level with Tom's head. When he wasn't looking at Tom, the man was glancing forward, monitoring his backward-moving partner's approach to the door.

Pressing his perceived advantage, Tom picked up his pace even more, requiring that both men do the same.

The protective vest that Raveis had given Tom would not stop a 5.56 round, so it didn't really matter where the man with the carbine aimed, but Tom noted that the man with the pistol kept his weapon trained at Tom's head.

Even at close range, the best target when covering a man in motion was the torso.

So was it possible that this man knew about the vest hidden beneath Tom's clothing?

Tom ignored the weapon in front of him and focused instead on the man's eyes, watching for any indication of a break in his concentration.

When they reached the door, however, the man with the carbine arced swiftly to his left, positioning himself on Tom's right, while the man who had occupied that position up till now moved behind Tom.

Their efficiency was a clear indication that they were experienced at handling a prisoner.

They had understood what Tom was hoping to force them into and negated that by shifting positions so Tom would move through the door first, with the man armed with the pistol following while his partner covered them from the rear.

This way, too, the man with the weapon that would be difficult to conceal would be the last one onto the open street.

Tom's only recourse was to continue to comply with their orders and look for another opportunity to escape.

He lowered his left hand to push the door open, then lowered his right to hold it, which allowed him to let his left arm drop and hang at his side, the case by his thigh.

The man with the pistol was directly behind Tom, but for the sake of discretion he had lowered his weapon.

It was now directed point-blank toward Tom's lower back—a place the vest did not cover.

Just as both men entered the doorway, however, Tom stopped abruptly.

The instant he felt the muzzle of the pistol touch his back, he made his move.

Spinning his torso counterclockwise and keeping his left arm hanging at his side, Tom reached for the Colt with his right hand, executing a fast-draw from concealment.

Shoving the man's pistol off its target with his left elbow as he continued his turn, Tom brought his weapon to bear, raising it and extending his right hand forward.

By the time Tom completed his turn he was facing the man directly behind him with less than a foot between them.

Placing the Colt above that man's left shoulder, Tom now had a clean shot at the man's partner.

That move also put the Colt an inch from the ear of the man with the pistol.

Reacting fast, the man with the carbine was taking a step back and raising his weapon, his eyes locked with Tom's.

But Tom had already found his target and fired, taking the man out with a single shot that struck squarely between his nose and upper lip.

That one shot, going off so close to the remaining man's ear, also served another purpose.

The man with the pistol, overwhelmed by the shock wave and deafening blast, screamed out as his legs immediately buckled.

Catching the man with his left hand, Tom kept him upright long enough to press the muzzle of the Colt to his temple and fire.

Then Tom let go of the now deadweight, allowing the man to drop.

Tom was the rest of the way through the door and onto the sidewalk before the lifeless body had completed its fall.

Thirty

Released at last from her confinement, Esa was in motion.

She grabbed Durand by the collar, pulling the woman to her feet, then held the SIG to Durand's head as she forced her down the narrow hallway to the kitchen.

There, on a table, was her clothing. On the floor beneath were her boots.

Esa pushed Durand down, forced the woman to lie on her stomach as she dressed.

She was still soaking wet, the dampness transferring immediately to her clothing. Even after she had her clothes on, she was still shivering, but then she saw Durand's leather jacket on a counter, hurried to it, and put it on.

All it really did at first was press her wet shirt against her skin.

A small plastic bag containing bottled water and snacks was on the table. Esa grabbed that, too, and began opening and searching drawers.

In the first drawer she found a box of matches and a container of lighter fluid, which she tossed into the bag. The second drawer contained a roll of duct tape, and she tossed that in as well. The third drawer was filled with items she had no use for, but the fourth one offered a selection of cutlery.

She claimed the sharpest knife—a steak knife—and slipped it blade-down into her right back pocket.

Pulling Durand to her feet again, Esa shoved the woman back into the living room, where she instructed Durand to remove the video camera from its tripod.

Esa also wanted Lyman's spare magazines, as well as Durand's sidearm.

Still injured and in shock, Durand did as she was told, though not as quickly as Esa preferred.

Following her as she performed every task, holding her by one arm, Esa several times pressed the suppressor to Durand's head and told her to move faster.

Once Durand was done, and all the items had been added to the bag, Esa bent Durand over the butcher's block and made quick work of binding her hands behind her back with the tape.

Leaving Durand there, she crossed the room to the container of gasoline, picked it up, and stepped to Lyman's body.

She doused it from head to toe with the gasoline, then tossed the empty container aside and removed the lighter fluid from the bag, making a thin trail with it from Lyman's body to the doorway.

Picking up the bag, she removed two of the magazines and placed them in her left back pocket, positioning them upside down and with the rounds facing forward.

Then she put her left hand through the handles of the bag, letting it dangle from her wrist.

Moving back to Durand, Esa grabbed her by the tape binding her hands, pulled her upright, and then pushed her to the doorway, where they stopped.

Esa took the box of matches from her bag, removed two, and placed one of them tip-up in the box before sliding it closed.

The upright match would serve as a makeshift fuse.

Striking the second match, she placed the box at the end of the trail of lighter fluid, then lit the standing match and stood up, blowing out the flame in her hand as she once again took hold of Durand.

Now she guided her captive toward the apartment door.

Opening it, she leaned out and looked in both directions to make certain no one was present, then said, "Which way?"

Durand replied, "To the right."

They moved down the corridor. Durand was walking with a limp, bent forward at the waist, but Esa showed neither sympathy nor patience.

At the end of the corridor was a window. As they got nearer to it, Esa could see the muted light of early morning beyond it.

The stairs were to the right of the window, but before entering the stairwell, Esa paused to survey what was visible from the window.

Though she'd estimated they were in the New York City area by the length of the drive in from Connecticut, along with the distinctive sound of car tires on a bridge roughly fifteen minutes prior to arriving at their destination, she had no way of knowing where exactly in the city she was.

An exfil was on her mind, and the faster she determined her location, the sooner she could send the coded text.

The view out the window was of a row of five-story brownstones, and their general design and condition, along with the presence of a convenience store on a nearby corner, told her that she was in Harlem.

Using Durand as a human shield, Esa pushed through the door and entered the stairwell, where she paused to listen, the SIG held up and ready right behind Durand's head. Hearing nothing, Esa guided Durand down the stairs using her bound hands as a means of controlling her.

On the ground floor, Esa moved them cautiously through the door and into the lobby. Spotting the exit, she pushed Durand toward it.

The door had a large window, and beyond it was a narrow foyer leading to another door, this one solid wood.

They were maybe ten strides away when the outer door swung open and two men entered, one right behind the other.

Esa stopped short, saw that the first man was talking on a cell phone and had a ring of keys in his hand.

His eyes were down as he sorted through the keys. The man behind him was pulling the outer door closed.

Neither had looked through the glass yet.

Holding the SIG with one hand, Esa lined up the pistol's front sight on the lead man as he unlocked and opened the second door.

The opening of the door allowed his side of the phone conversation to become audible, and Esa heard both urgency and confusion in the man's voice.

"I can see the flames from the street," he said. "Yes, I'm positive it's that apartment. Whatever they used to cover the windows is gone. It looks like the whole fucking room is engulfed."

He was stepping through the second door, telling whomever he was speaking to that he was on his way up, when he looked up and saw Esa.

Before he could do more than let his mouth drop open, Esa fired.

His head snapped back, and he dropped dead to the floor.

With that man out of the way, Esa had a clear shot of his backup, who was assuming a shooter's crouch as he reached with a well-practiced efficiency for his weapon.

A short-barreled pump-action shotgun was suspended by a bungee strap attached to his right shoulder.

The weapon hung between his arm and ribs, and while he was still in the process of clearing it from its place of concealment inside his jacket, Esa had already sighted the man and was easing the trigger rearward.

There was no panic, no thought, just years of training and decades of maintaining that training.

Sight, pause, trigger-press.

It was as the trigger was reaching its breaking point—that millisecond before the hammer is released and the trigger goes soft—that Esa realized her mistake.

A rookie's mistake, one not worthy of her.

Durand was standing between Esa and the man with the shotgun, but Esa was too focused on the imminent threat to guard herself from any action her captive might take, so she was taken by surprise when Durand ducked suddenly and spun to her right, breaking free of Esa's one-handed grip.

But Durand wasn't just looking to escape and get out of the line of fire.

Once free, she slipped under Esa's outstretched right arm, ramming her shoulder into Esa's exposed ribs and driving the woman sideways into the wall.

More important, she had disrupted Esa's careful aim at the second man just as the trigger broke and the pistol fired.

Esa missed her mark by inches, the stray shot shattering the glass of the partially open door.

The instant she had Esa against the wall, Durand launched a series of knee strikes to Esa's thighs, groin, lower abs—fast blows, some more effective than others; though as aggressive as the attack was, it wasn't enough to bring Esa down.

But it was enough to allow the second man, who had been driven down to a prone position by Esa's shot, to bring his weapon to bear.

Durand was brave, not ready to quit her mission—Esa gave her that much.

But her relentless attack had caused her to position herself once again between Esa and the man in the doorway.

The man was clearly part of a team sent to back her up.

What Durand wasn't expecting, however, was the man's panic, because once he had the shotgun pointed in the direction of the two women halfway down the hallway, he immediately fired.

Durand's back was to him, and she took the brunt of the double-aught buckshot—seven out of the nine .33-caliber pellets tore into her torso.

The remaining two pellets struck Esa side by side in her front deltoid.

Durand dropped to the floor, but Esa, thanks mainly to the presence of the wall, managed to remain standing.

The searing heat and the pain from the pellets lodged in her shoulder made her cry out, but there was no time for pain.

With Durand out of the way, the second man had a clear shot of Esa. He pumped the forend grip, exchanging the spent shell for a live one.

Esa wasn't going to let him do more than that, though.

Opting for point-and-shoot over pausing to take careful aim, she ducked and opened up with the SIG, firing nonstop.

Every round she unleashed hit the man, but it wasn't until the fourth or fifth that she landed an instantly fatal shot.

Somewhere in between those first rounds and the one that finally killed the man, however, he had pulled the trigger.

The buckshot flew high and landed in the wall above Esa's bowed head, bits of plaster raining down on her.

Esa crouched down, rolled Durand onto her side, saw closed eyes and an open mouth. She felt her neck for a pulse and detected one, but it was weak.

That and the blood flowing from the woman's multiple wounds told Esa that she'd be dead in minutes, if not sooner.

Esa searched Durand's clothing for a cell phone but found only a wallet containing ID and cash.

She took those, then realized she was wearing Durand's leather jacket. The first pocket she squeezed contained what she was seeking.

Taking the phone out, she touched the screen to confirm that it was unlocked and therefore usable before returning it to her pocket.

Standing, Esa hurried down the hallway, removing one of Lyman's spare mags from her back pocket as she went. She executed a tactical reload, switching the partially spent mag in the weapon for the fully loaded one in her hand. After a quick glance to determine how many rounds remained, she slipped the partially spent mag into her hip pocket in case at some point she needed those last shots.

Stepping over the first dead man to the second one, she tucked the SIG into her waistband at the small of her back, then took the steak knife from her right back pocket and cut the bungee strap, freeing the shortened shotgun.

She noticed that on the man's rigger belt was an individual first aid kit in a MOLLE pouch.

Using her left hand, Esa dumped the contents of the pouch onto the floor, finding right away what she was looking for—a QuickClot combat gauze.

Picking it up, she tore open the packaging with her teeth, then removed the dressing and placed it, still folded, inside the jacket, shoving it into the sleeve until it covered her shoulder wounds.

After gathering the remaining items from the emptied IFAK pouch and stuffing them into the plastic bag hanging from her wrist, Esa stood and, with the shotgun concealed inside the leather jacket, moved to the street door. She paused to survey the street before stepping through and moving down the half dozen steps.

She walked west along the sidewalk. Removing Durand's phone, she called an emergency number provided to her by the Benefactor and requested an immediate exfil.

Once she had been given the location of the extraction point, she ended the call.

At the corner ahead was a storm drain, and Esa casually tossed the phone into it as she passed.

Thirty-One

Tom walked toward the entrance to the York Street subway station located at the end of the block.

It took all he had not to run, though he did turn his head often as he scanned for any sign of other attackers.

This would be a clear indication of duress to any witnesses who should happen to be looking at him, but stealth was no longer his primary concern—survival was.

He saw no one rushing toward him, either head-on or from behind, and though he couldn't be certain, all the parked vehicles that lined both sides of the street appeared to be unoccupied.

Holstering the Colt, Tom pressed on, staggering several times, almost falling once, after which he had to stop and lean against a building before he found what it took to get moving again.

He was reminded by his condition of that eternity he'd spent inside the tumbling SUV back in Connecticut.

The violent rolling that seemingly wouldn't end and that had ultimately overwhelmed him and caused loss of consciousness.

Unconsciousness, however, needed to be avoided now at all costs.

What was it Cahill had said about Tom's preferred ammo?

I wouldn't want to be in a confined space when you shoot those things off. That's just asking for a concussion.

Tom had fired twice in the elevator, and then twice again in the open doorway.

And he knew the symptoms of a concussion even as he suffered from them.

He needed to keep his mind occupied so he would stay awake. To that end he asked himself how long ago the crash in Connecticut had occurred.

Had that been mere hours? Was it last night or the night before that?

The actual time mattered less than the fact that he couldn't recall.

Nor could he remember the walk from the storage facility to where he was now . . . wherever the hell that was.

There were moments when his vision was blurred at the edges, and then others when a floating black egg obscured the exact center of his line of sight.

He didn't have a lot of time, still needed to take the subway back to where he had parked Cahill's Ranger a few stops away.

He considered it a good sign that he was able to understand that much.

Another good sign was that, upon arriving at the subway entrance at the end of the block, Tom recognized that he needed to make sure that he boarded the Manhattan-bound train.

He was standing at the top of the stairs, fixated on that important detail, when he detected movement out of the corner of his eye.

Turning, he saw that someone was on the sidewalk, twenty feet away but coming behind him fast—someone who was seemingly as bad off as he was, staggering and yet moving with purpose, or trying to at least.

It took a few seconds for Tom to fully understand what was happening, but by then it was too late.

Ears bleeding, eyes glassy, the young man from the elevator closed in on Tom, his sidearm raised and leveled at his target.

Before Tom could even reach for his Colt, the young man, only steps away now, stopped and fired.

His first shot, aimed at Tom's head, missed, but the follow-up shot, executed quickly and pointed at Tom's torso, landed.

The force of the round impacting the Kevlar vest wasn't enough to drop Tom, but it caused him to stumble backward.

Twice his feet landed on solid pavement, but the third step he took was met only by open air, and he fell.

Hitting the concrete and steel stairs hard, he managed to keep his head up as he slid downward, fast at first but then slowing to a stop roughly halfway down the steep flight.

He also managed to keep his hold on the handle of the carrying case, and his long-billed cap stayed on.

The instant he stopped, even as the pain from the multiple injuries he had sustained began to register, Tom reached for his Colt.

But it was holstered at the four o'clock position on his belt, which meant the weapon was pinned between his back and the stairs.

He rolled his torso to the left so he could clutch the grip, rolled farther still so he could draw it from its holster.

It was as he was doing this—rolling onto his left shoulder, pulling at the pistol, his eyes on the top of the stairs—that he sensed a second wave of pain.

But he pushed through that, had his weapon finally free, and was rolling onto his back, when the young man appeared above him.

Not trusting his ability to aim, Tom simply pointed in the young man's direction and fired.

His opponent did the same, and both men missed.

Tom rode the recoil, then knew he had no choice; he needed to let go of the case so he could add his left hand to the grip.

He did that, and the case tumbled down to the bottom of the stairs.

Tom was looking for the front sight, but all he could see was that black floating egg in the center of his line of sight.

The young man fired a second time, missing. He, too, brought up his support hand, forming a two-handed grip.

Tom still couldn't see the white dot of the front sight, and he had lost count of how many rounds he had fired so far—and how many he had left.

And even if he could find the sight, his hands were shaking so much that hitting his target would be an issue of luck more than skill.

So he fired blind and then fired again, but the young man remained standing.

The slide of Tom's Colt sprang forward into battery, so it hadn't run dry yet, but he knew he had to be down to his last few rounds if not his last one.

The young man took the first step, moved down to the next step—to close the distance just that much more so he wouldn't miss.

His eyes, still glassy, were fluttering now.

Taking the steps in his condition required that he hold on to the railing with his left hand, so he was aiming one-handed again.

And that single hand was shaking as badly as Tom's joined hands were.

A shift in Tom's vision—the black egg disappearing as the edges turned hazy again—allowed Tom to find the front sight.

He willed his hands steady till the white dot obscured the circle of the man's face that contained his eyes, nose, and mouth.

Tom exhaled and eased back the trigger.

The young man dropped into a heap at the top of the stairs, his pistol falling from his hand and tumbling down several steps.

Tom didn't need to look at the Colt, could tell just by the feel of the weapon that its slide had locked open on the empty mag.

He grunted—a sound he could barely hear—as he rolled onto his left side, then reached for the railing and used it to pull himself to his feet.

Once standing, he released the empty mag, letting it, too, tumble down the stairs. Then he slapped in a full one, depressing the slide release with his left thumb and, once the slide slammed forward, engaged the safety with his right thumb before holstering the pistol.

Stooping, he grabbed the young man's weapon, which he unloaded as he hurried down the stairs.

At the bottom step he stooped again and picked up his case and the empty mag.

It took considerable concentration for him to stand up again.

As he approached the turnstile, he spotted a refuse container, dropped the mag inside, along with the single cartridge he had extracted from the chamber of the dead man's weapon.

Once through the turnstile, he saw that the train had already arrived, its doors opening.

There was no one on the platform waiting to board, and only four people had disembarked and were heading for the exit.

As he crossed the platform, he diverted to another refuse container, dumping the empty pistol into it.

He boarded the train, the doors closing behind him, sat with the carrying case on his lap, and scanned the faces of his fellow passengers.

There were only three, scattered throughout the car.

Not one of them even bothered to glance up from their respective devices.

Once the train was moving, Tom lowered his head and looked down at the carrying case.

His heart almost stopped when he saw, just off dead center, a hole in the case.

Tom laid the case flat on his lap to examine it, hoping his troubled eyes were playing tricks on him.

In a way they were, because upon closer inspection he saw two holes, not just one.

Two bullets—pistol-caliber bullets, by the size of the holes—had passed clean through the protective plastic.

Tom opened the case, already knowing what he'd find.

The tablet, its screen shattered, had been hit twice.

Tom just held it in his shaking hand and stared at it.

He didn't remember exiting the train or crossing the platform.

Nor did he remember climbing the stairs to the street.

But suddenly he was aboveground again, moving beneath an overcast morning sky, the smell of diesel fumes from idling delivery trucks nauseating him.

Over the ringing in his ears, he could hear the rattling of diesel engines.

He had parked the Ranger several blocks from the subway station, and it took at least another half block of walking before he was certain that he was heading in the right direction.

Though he was only two blocks away by that point, the sense of certainty came and went several more times.

His condition was deteriorating—labored breathing, rapid heart rate, moments of impaired balance so intense it was as if he were walking the deck of a ship afloat on rough seas.

He probably looked like a drunk or derelict to anyone who took notice of him, but he didn't care about that. He needed to get to the relative safety of his vehicle and, once there, contact Torres for assistance in getting somewhere safe.

There was no plan beyond that.

The sight of the Ranger gave him no sense of relief. The last few steps before he reached it were the most troublesome to make.

Suddenly his left foot was dragging as he walked.

But he made it into the driver's seat, shut and locked the door. He searched the messenger bag for his smartphone, but once he had it in his hand, he couldn't focus on the device long enough to make use of it.

The next thing Tom knew, someone was knocking on the driver's door window.

He had no idea how long he had been unconscious, but his smartphone must have slipped from his hand because it was now by his feet.

The key to the Ranger was beside it.

He was reaching down for the key, straining to grasp it, when someone arrived at the passenger door and started knocking on that window.

Voices were calling his name—a woman's and a man's.

"Tom. Tom! Unlock the door!" the woman urged.

"Let us in, mate!" the man called.

Tom must have slipped out of consciousness again, because suddenly the passenger door window was open, and there were bits of shattered safety glass on the seat.

Then the door was opened, and a pair of hands grabbed him.

He was upright, held that way by someone with unmistakable strength.

The man said, "Grab all his gear."

After that Tom was moving, guided forward by the same hands that were keeping him up.

Then he was overtaken by blackness again.

Tom was sitting still, but he also sensed that he was in motion.

At some point he realized that he was in the back seat of a car with someone beside him.

"I don't see a head wound, but it's obvious he has a concussion," a female said.

The voice sounded far away, but Tom recognized it.

It was Grunn, and she was turned sideways in her seat and facing him.

"Hand me my kit," she said to someone.

That someone—the driver—passed a MOLLE pouch between the two front seats and back to her.

Attached to it was a morale patch—a red cross on a field of black.

"He needs adrenaline," the driver said.

His voice, too, was familiar, his accent British.

Tom's head was lowered, his chin resting on his chest. It took all he had to raise his head a few inches, but it was enough for him to see that the driver was Hammerton.

Tom tried to say his friend's name but couldn't.

Grunn said, "We need to keep you awake. Do you understand?"

Tom nodded. Grunn had opened the pouch, was removing from it a six-inch-long tube—an auto-injector.

"I'm going to give you a shot of adrenaline," she said.

Tom nodded again.

Grunn readied the auto-injector, then held it above Tom's thigh as she made certain of her aim.

"How did you find me?" Tom asked, but as soon as he got the words out, Grunn brought her hand down, driving the injector into his leg.

Then she removed it and tossed it onto the floor.

Tom didn't feel anything at first, not even the prick of the needle, but after a moment the adrenaline made its way through his muscle and into his bloodstream.

What he finally felt was more of a steadily building surge than a sudden jolt of energy.

Within a few minutes he was awake, though barely.

At best he had entered into a twilight consciousness.

Grunn watched as the stimulant took effect. It wasn't till she was satisfied that Tom had stabilized that she answered his question.

"Cahill contacted Hammerton, asked him to keep an eye on you. There was a tracker in the Ranger. We got to it about a half hour ago."

Tom thought about that, still had more questions, but he only had the energy for a single word, so he spoke the one that mattered the most. "Stella?"

"Cahill's on his way to Montana. He won't be there for a few hours still. And then he has to scout out the best way to get to her."

This was for Tom confirmation that she was, in fact, at the final stage in her training.

He recalled the isolated compound where he had received his SERE training—the bare-bones barracks, the miles and miles of wilderness that surrounded the facility.

And yet what had occurred just minutes ago was significantly less clear in his mind.

It became clear to him the danger he was in.

From the front seat came Hammerton's voice. "Hang tough."

Tom looked at the rearview mirror. Hammerton was looking back at him.

Then Tom turned to Grunn. "Where are you taking me?"

"Hammerton has a safe house," she said. "No one knows about it."

"Leave me there; then you two go on out to Shelter Island like we planned."

"Not going to happen," Hammerton said flatly.

Tom looked at the rearview mirror again, but before he could respond, Grunn spoke.

"We tried it your way, Tom. You can't do this alone. You're going to need our help. We're staying with you. We're seeing this through to the end."

Thirty-Two

Esa was looking for the black Mercedes-Benz SUV with darkened windows.

According to protocol, the driver would keep the vehicle in motion, circling the block until Esa had reached a specific corner—the northwest corner, in this case.

As she made her way to the designated corner, she studied the vehicles parked along the residential street, looking for anything she didn't like.

Still cold and exhausted from the hours spent naked and drenched, she was trembling violently.

But when the Mercedes turned into her line of sight, she fought to suppress any sign of distress.

In her line of work, even long-proven allies could easily shift sides and become enemies.

So, then, no outward weakness, ever.

The vehicle headed down the street, picking up speed halfway down the block—an indication that its driver had seen her.

It pulled to a stop at the corner, its passenger window lowering to reveal the man behind the wheel.

It was Karl, the Benefactor's personal bodyguard—the last man she had expected to be part of her exfil team.

She had only ever seen Karl in the company of their employer, and the strangeness that came with his presence now reminded her of his behavior the night before at the East River State Park.

His proximity as she and the Benefactor spoke, which had put him within earshot, was unusual.

But so was the war footing that had been indicated by the armed men standing on the periphery.

In such an atmosphere, perhaps Karl's role in her rescue should have been expected.

"In the back," Karl said.

Esa opened the rear passenger-side door and immediately felt the inviting warmth of the cabin.

But that promise of relief was short-lived.

Seated inside the rear compartment were two men—one in the second-row seat behind the driver, the other in the row behind that.

The man in the second row gestured to the open seat beside him.

Both he and his partner had hardened faces and quarter-inch buzz cuts and were dressed in jeans and leather jackets.

Esa climbed in and pulled the door closed. The instant she sat, the man in the third row positioned himself directly behind her.

Leaning forward, he relieved her of the plastic bag hanging from her left wrist. Then he opened her jacket, revealing the short-barreled shotgun she had concealed there.

The man behind her took that as well, and the man beside her focused his attention on her breasts, braless beneath her still-damp shirt.

He searched her for other weapons with a complete disregard for her private areas.

Karl steered the Benz into traffic, waited till the search had been completed, then looked at Esa via the rearview mirror. "I'll take you to the surgeon. The Benefactor will want to debrief you after." He paused. "What we need to know right now is what you told your captors."

"Nothing," Esa said. "I have a tape to prove it."

Karl's eyes remained focused on her.

She met his glance, holding it till he looked forward again.

"Sorry about this, but these are his orders."

Before Esa could ask what Karl meant, the two men pounced, the one behind her grabbing her arms while the man beside her moved toward her with a syringe in his hand.

The drug took effect within seconds, and the last thing Esa saw was Karl's eyes framed in the rearview mirror.

PART FOUR

Thirty-Three

The barracks, a bare-minimum shelter, was really just a frame of two-by-fours with a floor, walls, and roof comprised of sheets of plywood and a half dozen narrow windows enclosed in semiclear plastic held in place by staples.

Lacking insulation and ventilation, the ten-by-fifteen room collected heat during the daytime as the sun arced across the open Montana sky. And while much of that heat was retained well into evening, every trace of it eventually bled out overnight, leaving behind by morning a damp chill.

There was just one barracks on the compound, and of the sixteen cots crammed into the open space, only six were occupied.

Stella was the solitary female currently enrolled in the program, which was overseen by six instructors, all of whom were former special operators and male.

Alpha males, she had concluded quickly enough.

Unlike the selection programs those men had endured prior to joining their respective spec ops units—programs that were designed to first eliminate the weak, then weed out the strong till only the soundest candidates remained—the training that Stella and her classmates had been undergoing was not intended to cull the ranks but rather to instruct and prepare.

That did not mean, of course, that the instructors—all hardened and highly intelligent men—took it easy on those who, for two hellish weeks, were in their charge.

The section of the program before SERE training, which had included skills such as evasive driving, marksmanship (both close-quarter and at long range), and hand-to-hand combat techniques, had been taught in a compound set on the edge of a Louisiana swamp.

The housing there had been slightly better—the barracks' windows could be opened to allow the air to circulate—but that improvement was probably as much a safety issue in light of the climate as it was another means of making these final two weeks seem in contrast just that much more miserable.

It was during the training in Louisiana that the instructors had begun to mention the horrors that awaited their students once they arrived in Montana.

It seemed, in fact, that instilling that sense of dread was an integral part of the Louisiana-based section.

It won't be easy, Tom had said to her in their New York hotel room. *And, frankly, I hate to think of you being put through that.* He had paused. *In fact, that might be all I'm able to think about.*

Stella had, of course, assured him that she could handle it.

Krista did it, she'd said. *Grunn, too. So, yes, I need to do it as well.*

The first week was devoted to ways of evading capture in a wilderness setting—all on less than four hours of sleep.

Every day Stella and her classmates were hooded, then driven to the scrub hills twenty miles to the south and given very basic supplies—and on one occasion, no supplies at all.

Then the hoods were removed and the six students, broken into cadres of two or three, were given a two-hour head start, at the end of which their instructors, skilled hunters with knowledge of the area, began to search for them.

In the hills, shallow holes called "hides" were dug, often by hand, and the cadres would lie inside them together, concealed under a cover of vegetation or, if they had been provided one, a single wool blanket, itself camouflaged with dirt and debris.

There, they would wait in silence as the former special operators tracked them down.

Never once did any of the cadres successfully evade capture, but that was the likelihood one faced in enemy territory.

As with everything that occurred at this final stage, the exercise was more about training the mind—preparing an operator for when the worst was inevitable—than building a skill set.

Each time, once they returned to the compound, five of the students spent the night posed outside their barracks in stress positions while one of them was taken away and subjected to waterboarding.

When the missing classmate was returned, they were allowed to move inside the barracks to sleep, but never for more than a few hours.

It was during the last two nights of the second week that the real work began.

After yet another failure at evasion, the cadres, their eyes covered with safety goggles spray-painted black, were transported back to the compound, where they were taken to a building they had not entered before—a metal-roofed shack known as the "resistance lab."

It was here that the true tests commenced.

For countless hours at a time, Stella and the others were subjected to the kind of treatment that was to be expected upon falling into the hands of an enemy.

Their wrists bound by plasticuffs, the students stood as their clothing—coveralls—was cut off them, leaving each participant clad only in his or her underwear.

Stella had lost track of how long she and her classmates were left to stand there in the stifling heat of the room.

Finally, they were required to kneel with their elbows and foreheads on the plywood floor as the instructors walked among them, gunning power drills and sawing through plastic jugs with serrated knives, speaking infrequently but disguising their voices when they did and always uttering threats.

Stella estimated this had gone on for hours. And she, like her classmates, knew what was awaiting each of them.

You will hate the box, one of the Louisiana instructors had liked to say.

One of the others would add, *Man, I hated that fucking box.*

The "box" was a plywood container barely bigger than a footlocker. There were two, actually, and one student was placed inside one, another student in the other, the lids closed and locked.

There they would be left for hours, while the others waited, kneeling on the plywood floor, for their turn.

To increase the sense of anticipation and fear, recordings were played—a crying baby on a loop, and after several hours of that, heavy metal rock, all of it loud enough to drown out most noises.

The enemy only did to one's mind what one's mind allowed to be done.

That was the essence of the "resistance" aspect of SERE training.

Stella hung on to that thought, even as she endured her times in the "box"—even as her legs fell asleep and the muscles in her lower back burned.

Once released from their initial confinement—no one quit during the first round—students were placed on their backs on the plywood floor as the instructors moved around, pouring buckets of ice-cold water onto their groins.

Stella heard the grunts of her male classmates, as if the ice water was intended as an agony that needed to be endured, but she knew that the water, although applied in a less than kindly manner, was to keep them from suffering heat stroke.

She gasped as the water hit her, yes, but as the men around her shivered and fussed, she did her best to breathe.

At some point after, the confinement in the boxes resumed—two classmates at a time, the others waiting on their knees for their turn.

Despite the prerecorded racket, Stella heard the men who couldn't take it anymore be escorted out.

One complained of muscle spasms and was freed from the box and taken outside. Another simply said that he'd had enough.

His body had held out, but not his mind.

Stella couldn't remember how many had quit. There had been the first two, those she definitely recalled hearing. But then came her turn, and everything after that, both inside and outside the box, was just pain and anguish and noise.

After a while, all she cared about was enduring each second.

And then the next.

And then the next . . .

At one point—Stella had lost all sense of time, her mind aware of only agony and boredom—two pairs of hands grasped her elbows and lifted her to her feet.

The instructors always handled their students with care because, unlike actual captors, injury wasn't their intent.

Considering the money being invested in them, even minor injuries were something to be avoided.

Stella was walked with the usual care across the plywood floor, then through a door and down three plank steps, after which she felt packed dirt beneath her bare feet.

Her escorts continued to lead her away from the resistance lab but didn't speak. Stella braced herself for what was next, felt fear—colder than ice water—in her stomach as she sensed that she was being taken somewhere else.

Somewhere far from her male classmates, someplace private.

In reality, if she were ever captured, sexual assault was all but guaranteed.

Was there another place that female students were brought to prepare them in some way for that inevitability?

Or worse, were these alpha males looking to have a little "fun" of their own?

She was mentally reciting the steps to break free of plasticuffs—a skill taught back in Louisiana—when the two men holding her arms stopped.

One of the men spoke, his voice no longer masked. "Congratulations, Number Five."

Neither she nor her classmates were ever called by name, and she often wondered if their instructors even possessed that information.

The other man said, "You spent the longest in the box. Twelve hours, total."

"That makes you the best in your class," the first man added.

A knife clicked open and the plasticuffs were cut.

Stella waited a moment, her ears still ringing from the loud playback. When no one said anything, she raised her hands toward her face, and when no one stopped her, she proceeded to remove the blacked-out safety goggles, seeing for the first time in more than twenty-four hours.

The two instructors were gone, and she was standing in front of the shower hut.

For the entire two weeks at this compound, Stella and her male classmates had shared the same shower. No stalls, just an open room, two dozen showerheads suspended from a pipe that ran along the center of the ceiling, and a single drain in the middle of the floor.

She'd had to wash herself along with—and in full view of—her classmates. Some had offered her privacy by looking away, at least initially, while others hadn't bothered with that courtesy at all and treated themselves to long looks each and every time they bathed.

But Stella had met every pair of staring and roaming eyes with a roaming stare of her own, half smirking as she watched five sets of male genitals reacting to the cold-water-only showers.

By the third or fourth day, those men had begun their showers by turning their backs to her so that she couldn't observe their shrinking manhood.

In the end Stella had outperformed them all, and in more than just the shower game. She had, in the eyes of her instructors, risen when it counted the most. And she was being rewarded now with a few moments of privacy.

It felt a little strange, once she was under the weak stream of frigid water, to be alone.

Despite the stiffness of her muscles—legs, lower back, abs—from clenching involuntarily as the icy water had been poured over her the night before, Stella knew that she needed to run.

It was late afternoon, an hour before sunset, and she was the first in the barracks to wake. They'd been allowed to sleep through the day, though that in itself wasn't necessarily an act of kindness, since the interior temperature had risen throughout the afternoon to a miserable ninety-something degrees.

There was no way of knowing whether or not their training had concluded. Stella couldn't imagine that there was anything left for them to endure. Or maybe she didn't want to imagine that there still could be more to come. Either way, she knew she needed to run, as much for her mind as for her legs.

She rose from her cot quietly, took a clean pair of coveralls from the assigned locker, and put them on over her sports bra and boy shorts. As she was lacing up her running shoes, Number Three sat up in his cot.

He was a runner, too, in his midthirties, so ten years younger than Stella, at least. The few times she had been able to work in a run, he had joined her.

Number Six rose as well. He was younger than Stella by twenty years, had the thick build of a powerlifter.

Both men announced that they would be running with her.

The path, heading west of the compound, was the same path along which their instructors made their daily predawn run.

Five miles out, five miles back.

Stella fought through leg cramps as she set the pace for the group.

She would have liked to think that the act of these men running with her now was a sign of their respect for her, and maybe it was to some degree, but she knew that alpha males were competitive by nature and that her having outperformed them in the resistance lab wasn't something that they could let stand.

This run was an opportunity for one of them to reclaim the spot as the dominant member of the class.

Reclaim it, too, from a woman, not to mention a woman pushing fifty years old.

It was a few miles into the run that Number Three suddenly dropped out. Stella glanced back to see him doubled over, his hands on his thighs—poised to vomit. She turned away before he did.

Number Six hung on for longer, matching Stella's pace till the five-mile mark, when he slowed to a stop as Stella kept going.

He watched her for a moment before calling out, "You're crazy."

Stella got the sense that it was not an insult but rather a statement of surrender.

Alone now, she could vary the pace, easing off for a stretch before pushing herself to maintain a semisprint for as long as her lungs would allow.

With no running path to follow past the five-mile mark, she was forced to cover rough terrain until she came across a two-lane road, which she followed, clocking maybe another two miles.

The twilight sky over the western edge of the Gallatin National Forest a mile away was the first hint of beauty she'd seen in two weeks.

She continued toward and was maybe a half mile from the tree line when she spotted a vehicle ahead.

A Range Rover, heading toward her, traveling from east to west.

Still a hundred feet or so away, the vehicle pulled over and came to a stop; its passenger door opened, and a figure climbed out.

Stella stopped, too, and recognized that the figure was a woman.

The driver emerged as well—a man, who left his door open as he moved around to the nose of the vehicle.

He remained there while the woman, waving broadly, started walking forward.

The tattoos visible on that waving arm—a contrast between colored ink and flesh more than discernible details—were what caught Stella's eye.

It didn't take long for her to recognize Krista MacManus.

And with that woman now identified, Stella took another look at the man waiting by the vehicle.

She had briefly considered that it might be Tom, but this was based more on hope than observation, because the figure one hundred feet away was clearly Charlie Cahill.

There could only be one reason why these two people were here.

Tom was in trouble.

Stella felt her gut tighten, but she ignored it.

Resuming her run, she moved in an all-out sprint toward her waiting friends.

Thirty-Four

Seated in an easy chair, naked but wrapped in a heavy blanket, Tom lingered on the edge of consciousness, held there by regular injections of adrenaline administered throughout the day.

Shortly after having been brought to this dark and quiet back room, Tom had heard Grunn and Hammerton talking through the closed door.

Equal to the sound of their voices was the steady ringing in his ears.

At one point Tom heard from somewhere deeper in the apartment the sound of a door opening and closing. This was followed by an enduring silence—save, of course, for the dull peal from which there was no relief.

Tom had no idea which of his friends had left; he was beginning to think that it might have been both of them, but then he heard Hammerton speaking on the phone.

Whatever the man had said eluded Tom, but he didn't really care.

All that mattered was shaking the effects of his multiple injuries and getting back on his feet.

Tom was left alone for no more than an hour at a time.

Hammerton would come in to administer more adrenaline, then would sit with Tom, neither man saying much.

The former SAS trooper knew enough about field medicine to recognize that while Tom needed to be kept awake, he also should be kept quiet.

The last time Tom had seen his friend was six months ago, when a new recruit had betrayed Hammerton. Shot and in hiding at an isolated location, Hammerton had self-treated his serious torso wound as best he could, after which all he could do was wait in his own blood to be found.

It was ten hours before Tom and Cahill located him.

Hammerton had been transported to a hospital, where he remained, recovering, for nearly three months.

Tom hadn't even been able to say goodbye to his friend before shipping out to begin his training.

Though Hammerton was easily the toughest man Tom had ever known, he was also in his sixties now. And even in Tom's current condition he could see that his friend had yet to fully recover from his near-lethal injuries.

The cruel truth of aging meant that Hammerton might never again be the man he used to be.

The man to whom both Tom and Stella owed their lives.

Tom was alone in the back room again when he heard the sound of the apartment door opening and closing a second time.

With the shades drawn to ease the strain on his eyes, there was no way for Tom to track the sun over the course of the day, so he had no sense of time.

And he had lost count of how many times Hammerton had come in to administer the hourly injections.

But shortly after the closing of the door, Tom heard another conversation—again, little more than indistinct words.

After a while the apartment door opened and closed again, and then Tom heard occasional footsteps but no voices.

Tom's mind, as well as his hearing, grew clearer as the hours passed, his inner thoughts becoming more complete.

There was darkness beyond the drawn shades—now he was ready, knew the questions he needed to ask.

The time to resume his mission had come.

He was rising from the chair that had held him all day when Hammerton reentered the room.

Standing, Tom faced his friend.

Hammerton moved stiffly, and Tom recognized that this was the effort of a man concerned with aggravating an injury.

Dealing with a discomfort not unlike that one, Tom didn't have to examine his own chest to know that the nine-mil slugs stopped by the Kevlar vest had left behind ghastly bruises the size of fists.

The similarity of their current conditions did not escape Hammerton and Tom.

Hammerton looked Tom up and down, then grinned and joked, "Ain't we a pair."

If Tom could smile he would have. Instead, he asked where Grunn had gone.

"You don't remember?"

"Remember what?"

"You wanted to know if the files on the tablet could be recovered. Grunn said she'd take it to a tech friend of hers."

"Oh. How long ago did she leave?"

"Nine hours, but it took her three just to contact her friend. Frankly, I thought she'd be back by now. I tried to call her a few times, but she doesn't answer."

"She's a capable person," Tom said. The statement of confidence, he realized, was more for his benefit than his friend's.

"Worse comes to worst, I have a resource who can try to track her phone," Hammerton said.

Tom thought about asking who that resource was but didn't. "I heard Torres out there at some point."

"She went to meet with some law enforcement associate. She said you'd know what that was about."

Tom nodded.

"Care to fill me in?" Hammerton said.

"There was a woman with Raveis. She seemed to know a lot about us. I asked Torres to find out what she can about her."

"How will she do that?"

"The woman's license plate. Torres used to be law enforcement, still has friends in the department."

"That's a handy person to have around."

Tom nodded. He needed to limit his thinking to what mattered at this moment.

"There were two other teammates," he said. "Lyman and Durand. They were about to interrogate a woman we had taken prisoner, but I'd contacted Torres and told her to get some extra hands to back them up. Did the backup get there? Are they all right?"

"Maybe we should take things slow, Tom."

"Are they all right?"

Hammerton let out a breath. "Your teammates are dead. And your prisoner is gone."

"How?"

"All I know is Lyman was killed in the safe house. His body—and the apartment it was in—was set on fire. Durand was found in the lobby of the building, as was the quick-response team that had been dispatched to back them up."

"How many in the QR team?"

"Two."

Tom was silent as he added to the list of the dead.

"None of that's your fault," Hammerton said. "At all."

"Fuck yeah, it is." Tom paused. "I'm starting to get very pissed."

Hammerton gave his friend a moment before continuing. "The reason Cahill contacted me this morning was because he'd run a photo of your prisoner through facial recognition and got a hit. Her name is—"

"Esa Hirsh," Tom said.

"How'd you find out?"

Tom shrugged off the question. "What do you know about her?"

"She's one of the Benefactor's top operatives. Third-generation killer, apparently. Her father and his father were nasty fucks, just like she is. Cahill was concerned, naturally, so he reached out, but he also wanted me to know that the two of you are starting to believe that Carrington is innocent."

"I don't think he's guilty of what he has been accused of," Tom said.

"You think he was framed."

"Yes."

Hammerton thought about that. "I've spent all these months thinking he was responsible for what happened to me. I wanted to kill him for it. That was all that mattered. In the hospital, that's what pushed me to get better, was my reason every day for getting up and fighting through the pain."

"I imagine that would be a hard thing to let go of."

Hammerton nodded. He watched Tom for a moment. "It's . . . disturbing to know that for all this time I wanted to kill the wrong man. And would have if I'd had the chance."

"The evidence looked solid."

"It didn't to you."

Tom shrugged. "Maybe that's only because I didn't want it to. I could just as easily have been deluding myself."

"So if not him, then who? Raveis?"

"One minute it looks that way, the next minute it doesn't."

"The woman you said was with him. What was her name?"

"Raveis called her Slattery."

"She rides a motorcycle?"

"A black BMW, yeah. You know her?"

"I've heard of her."

"Who is she?"

"An investigator. Some kind of whiz kid. Rumor is she spent ten years down in Washington, working for various senate committees, digging up dirt. She relocated up here a year or so ago."

"She had the kind of accent that military brats sometimes end up with. Any idea what her background is? Education?"

"No. She's a ghost. Whoever she was, wherever she came from, it's all been buried, which is no small feat these days. But with her Washington connections it makes sense that Raveis would hire her. You dig around enough down there, you end up knowing where the skeletons are."

"Why would Washington, DC, skeletons be of interest to Raveis?"

"Because DC is where the money comes from, Tom. The real money. It's always about the money, isn't it? The work we do—the plots we stop, the bad guys we expose or end—that's just our particular sausage, if you know what I mean. That's the product we make, that's what brings in the cash." Hammerton paused as if to decide whether or not to say what was now on his mind. "I've collected information over the years," he said finally. "I have detailed files on the key players, their ops, everything. I think when you're up to it, you should have a look."

"Where are they?"

"Here, locked up."

"They're actual files?"

"Paper is safe. It can't be hacked, then dispersed around the world in a second. And once you burn it, no one can retrieve it."

Tom looked around the room. "So where are we, exactly? Is this your apartment?"

"You don't remember getting here."

"No."

"It's a place for members of my old unit, somewhere we can go in times of trouble."

"Who else knows about it?"

"Just a handful of us. And the person who bought it."

"And who was that?"

"A grateful member of the royal family. We have a few of these around the world. London, Berlin, Buenos Aires—every one of them, like this one, purchased through a trust. They're just dives we can crash at, safe places where one of us can disappear or all of us can gather if it were to come to that."

"I guess you really didn't need me to send Grunn for you, did you?"

It was a rhetorical question, so Hammerton didn't respond.

"I'll need my clothes," Tom said. "I'll want to meet up with Torres. If she has anything to report, I don't want her to do it over the phone. And we shouldn't draw attention to this place with too many people coming and going all of the sudden."

"Yeah, well, there's a problem with that, Tom."

"With what?"

"With you going outside."

"What do you mean?"

"You were involved in a shootout in New York City. It's all over the news, and as of an hour ago, so is street-camera footage of you. It's grainy, and your cap helped hide your face, but right now the NYPD is canvassing all the shop owners and landlords in the area, looking for private security cameras that might offer a better angle. It's only a matter of time before they find footage of your face." Hammerton paused. "You're going to need to lay low for a while. At the very least, when you finally do leave here, you'll need to look different. Grunn had Torres pick up a change of clothes for you this morning. She got you a pair of clippers and a razor, too."

It wasn't the news he wanted to hear, but he nodded and said, "Okay."

Hammerton paused. "So what's this about, Tom? What's on the tablet?"

"Surveillance video of Raveis talking to my father."

"Talking about what?"

"Killing the man who killed my mother and sister."

"And you've seen that video."

"There were six on the device. I watched the first three. I need to see the others, though."

"Why?"

"Because it looks like over the course of a series of visits, Raveis went from sharing details of the murders with my father out of friendship to persuading him into going on an op he had no hope of completing. Watching the two of them talk, I got the sense that Raveis went there with no intention other than to exploit my father's grief. The story I'd been told was that my father had grown obsessed with the idea of getting revenge and hunted down the Algerian on his own. But these recordings tell a different truth. One that someone is desperate to keep hidden. And in the process, a lot of good people are dying."

"Why would Raveis do that? Why would he manipulate your father?"

"That's what I need to find out. The Engineer said that my father's death somehow benefited what he called 'the Colonel's great experiment,' which is the organization you and I and everyone we know works for."

"Hold on," Hammerton said. "You've met with the Engineer?"

"Yes."

"When?"

"This morning. He gave me the tablet. Why?"

"How did you two get together?"

"Carrington set it up."

Hammerton thought about that for a moment, then nodded toward the small table beside the easy chair.

His disposition had changed; he was now a man in a hurry.

"Your gear is in the drawer there," he said. "Phones and wallet, the Colt and mags. The new clothes we got for you are in the bathroom. Your vest is there, too."

"What's going on?"

"I'll be in the basement, getting the files together."

"John, what's going on?"

Hammerton nodded toward the table again. "Grab your gear, get dressed, meet me in the basement as soon as you can."

In the bathroom down the hall, stacked on the lid of the toilet tank, were a pair of jeans, underwear and socks, a black T-shirt, a button-down flannel shirt, a heavy canvas hooded jacket, and a baseball cap.

Beneath that stack of clothing was the Kevlar vest.

On the floor to the right of the toilet was a pair of work boots.

On the edge of the sink, still in their packaging, were the electric clippers and rotary-head rechargeable razor.

Tom removed the razor and plugged it into the wall socket, then picked up the vest and examined it.

There was no way of knowing whether the integrity of the densely woven material had been compromised by the two rounds it had already been required to stop. But Tom figured that limited protection would be better than none at all, so he pulled on his T-shirt and got into the vest, put the flannel shirt over it, and then pulled on the canvas jacket.

The cap went into one of the jacket's front pouch pockets.

Once he was dressed and geared up—the Colt tucked in at his right hip, the two spare mags in the carrier on his left with the third in his hip pocket—Tom found the stairs and headed down.

The room he'd spent the day in was on the top floor of a four-story building. Tom looked out the first window he came to and attempted to discern his location from the view, but he didn't see anything distinctive.

All he knew was that he was somewhere in one of the five boroughs of New York.

The next floor down had no back room, just several bunk beds along the wall.

The floor below that was a supply room, and the ground floor had a kitchen and dining area and second bathroom.

Tom came finally to the basement stairs and descended them. Hammerton was standing at a card table, a stack of folders in front of him and a cell phone to his ear.

He was sorting through the contents of one folder as he listened to whoever was on the other end of the call.

Nodding, he said, "Cheers," then ended the call and placed the phone on the table. He continued sorting through the contents of that same folder as Tom approached him.

Behind Hammerton was a large safe, its door opened. Inside was a mix of rifles and carbines standing side by side in a rack, as well as a half dozen pistols hanging on hooks mounted to the safe's wall.

Hammerton closed the file in his hand and laid it down on the table.

"We'll start with this one," Hammerton said.

Tom asked, "What is it?"

"Everything I could find on a man named Jack Emery."

"Who's Jack Emery?"

Hammerton looked up from his file. "That, Tom, is the Colonel."

Thirty-Five

Standing across the table from Hammerton, Tom opened the file and skimmed through the pages as his friend spoke.

"Emery was Tier 1 all the way. West Point, top of his class. Ranger School in '71, top of his class. Seventy-Fifth Ranger Regiment in Vietnam, running long-range patrols deep behind enemy lines. Three Purple Hearts, a Bronze Star, a Silver Star. He was eventually awarded the Congressional Medal of Honor for his defense of a downed Huey toward the end of the war. He single-handedly fought off an NVA patrol for more than eight hours, saving the badly injured crew and the passengers, all fellow Rangers. He was wounded three times during the night but kept fighting, which required constant repositioning on and around the copter so the enemy would think there was more than one shooter. He used every weapon on board—M16s, M14s, sidearms—and was down to his last few rounds when gunships finally swept in after dawn, followed by the evac team. In '77, with terrorism on the rise around the world, the Pentagon selected a Green Beret colonel named Beckwith to form the 1st Special Forces Operational Detachment, also known as Delta Force. Beckwith and another colonel named Henry chose Emery, then a major, as the unit's first commander. It took two years of training to get Delta fully operational. Emery didn't just oversee the training of his men; he went through it with them, every step. Four years later Emery, by then a colonel, left Delta for the CIA, where he was put in charge of the Special Activities Division. It was during his stint at the Agency that he met an ambitious young officer named Sam Raveis."

Hammerton laid another file next to the first one.

Tom opened the second folder, keeping it side by side with the first.

"Raveis was a first-class spook. He'd never held any other job in his life, didn't even flip burgers for a summer or mow lawns for cash as a teenager. Born into a wealthy family, he was a Yale man, like you. Tapped for Skull and Bones his first year, approached by the CIA during his third, graduated summa cum laude in '82 and went straight to the Farm, spent the usual eighteen months there, then served as a case officer in Lebanon, Somalia after that, and Iraq after that. Name a shitty part of the world, and Raveis was there when things were at their shittiest. Eventually, he became the station chief in Beirut, at which point he abruptly resigned to join the Colonel in the private sector. Every merit that the Agency gives out, Raveis earned it."

Tom alternated between the two files, flipping pages and stopping on photos of both men when they were younger.

He had often wondered about the man he knew only as the Colonel. There was no mistaking that the man had been a combat veteran—hardened, confident, fair-minded, but also no-nonsense.

And clearly intelligent.

Tom recalled the first time he had met the Colonel at the Cahill estate on Shelter Island.

Barrel-chested, bull-shouldered, six feet tall, salt-and-pepper hair buzzed close to the scalp.

Powerful and commanding, despite the fact that he was in his sixties.

Do you know who I am? the man had said.

Tom had replied that he didn't.

Good, let's keep it that way for now, okay? But you'll need to call me something, so why don't you call me what most people call me.

Tom had asked what that was.

Colonel.

After Tom's first assignment was completed, he had been allowed to leave, and that had been the Colonel's doing.

The act of letting Tom go—allowing Tom to wander with Stella, beholden to no one but himself and her—was the first indication that Tom had met a man he could trust.

A man as solid as James Carrington and Charlie Cahill and John Hammerton.

Tom's first encounter with Sam Raveis, on the other hand, had had the opposite effect on him.

Through an NSA analyst named Alexa Savelle, Raveis had intercepted multiple text exchanges between Tom and Stella, one of which had included a naked selfie that Stella had sent to Tom.

It was just one of many violations of Tom's privacy committed by Raveis that had led to conflict between the two.

As much as he sometimes disliked Raveis, however, Tom knew not to underestimate him.

Even when Tom had been informed that his father and Raveis had once been associates—close friends, even—he still couldn't shake that instinctive reflex of general opposition married with a wary respect.

If not for the Colonel, Tom would have never answered Carrington's second call—the call that had led to the violent end of the quiet life in Vermont that Tom and Stella had made together.

And that had led Tom to the truth about his father.

If not for the Colonel, Tom would have done whatever was necessary to avoid crossing paths with Raveis ever again.

Everything Tom saw in these two files, and everything Hammerton had stated, served only to cement Tom's already entrenched feelings about both men.

And yet, it didn't escape Tom's notice that Raveis had given him the Kevlar vest that had saved his life, not once but twice.

Nor did Tom fail to recognize the fact that the team sent to bring him back to New York had been comprised of Raveis's best.

Hammerton tossed another file onto the tabletop. Setting aside the first two, Tom opened the third, which contained copies of newspaper clippings.

Tom flipped through the clippings and noticed that the farther down the pile he went, the more aged the paper was.

This was a collection that spanned years.

Skipping to the last of the clippings, Tom saw a newspaper article dated nearly twenty years ago.

"What I'm about to tell you is classified," Hammerton said. "Some of it I'm not even supposed to know. But I think we're past that point now. We're through the looking glass, as they say."

Tom looked up from the pages before him, waiting.

"The organization Emery and Raveis founded was your standard private-military contractor at first," Hammerton explained. "Initial clients were corporations that wanted security for CEOs traveling overseas—Middle East, Africa, Central and South America—the usual close-protection gigs. But Raveis and Emery had a lot more than that in mind. That's when they brought on board a man named Smith, whom you know as the Engineer."

A fourth file landed on the tabletop. Tom opened that one as well.

It was, Tom noted, the thinnest of the folders he'd seen so far.

"As you can see, there isn't a lot of info about Smith, which makes sense, since that's not his real name. Everything I could get on him—everything you see there—dates from after his signing on with Emery and Raveis."

The files contained several surveillance-quality photos of the man Tom had spoken with in the subway car.

The differences between the man Tom had met and the younger—healthier—man in these few photos were significant.

As a young man in his twenties and early thirties, Smith had been muscular in that specific way of men who lift weights with the goal of building raw power: wide lats, rounded traps, delts like bowling balls, and thick limbs.

One of the photos showed Smith in black operator gear, leading a squad of similarly clad men down the street of a ruined city.

In another photo, Smith, dressed in a T-shirt and tactical pants, was seated at a table in a sidewalk café with another man and a woman.

Tom picked up that photo. In the background were two soldiers standing ready. Tom recognized them by their uniforms as members of the Israeli Defense Forces.

Another thing he recognized was the look that Smith and the woman in the photo were exchanging.

Tom asked when the photo had been taken.

"Nineteen ninety-nine," Hammerton answered. "That was in Jerusalem."

"So Smith has been in business with the Colonel and Raveis for thirty years?"

"Yes."

"The woman he's looking at, any idea who she is?"

"A Mossad agent named Yael Levy."

"They were involved," Tom observed.

Hammerton nodded. "Yes. She was killed in Iran five years later."

"How did you get this photo?"

"MI6, via an SAS brother of mine."

"Why was British Intelligence interested in an American?"

"They weren't. Beckwith, the founder of Delta, had served as an exchange officer with the SAS after Vietnam. So had Emery. The other man in that photo was the former commander of my regiment. Emery recruited him, and at first he was partnered with Smith. At the time this was taken, MI6 had the commander under surveillance."

"Why?"

"The SAS is the premier counterterrorism force in the world, with closely held techniques and tactics that our enemies would be interested in learning. Former commanders are often tailed after retirement, particularly when it's an early retirement."

"Where is your former commander now?"

"Dead. Killed in a late-night car crash on the New Jersey Turnpike."

Tom looked at Hammerton. "An accident?"

"That's how it looked."

"You don't buy that."

"He didn't drink. Ever. But there was alcohol in his blood. Three times the legal limit. Interestingly enough, he was killed a year after your father, and we all know that was no accident."

"You signed on with the Colonel to find out what happened," Tom said.

Hammerton nodded. "It was easy enough to get in. Back then, they were dying for someone with my credentials. I kept my head down, did my work, and collected every piece of information I could along the way. None of it has helped me, at least not yet, but maybe it can help you."

Tom thought about what it would take to maintain a deep cover for close to two decades.

He thought, too, of the secret the man he called a friend had been keeping.

"What was your commander's name?"

"Tuoghy."

Tom waited a moment out of reverence for the fallen, then said, "Smith said the organization was the Colonel's great experiment. What did he mean by that?"

"How the business looks from the outside—a private security firm led by former intelligence officers and staffed by former military and ex–law enforcement, engaged in bodyguard work, surveillance, and occasional corporate espionage, just like dozens of other companies like it—that's just the shell. The other work they're involved in is the work you and Cahill do. That was the brainchild of Emery and Raveis—a private-sector intelligence organization that certain agencies within the US government can turn to for off-the-books domestic ops."

Hammerton paused. "But there is a third level of operations, and it's at the secret heart of the organization. It involves work that's done by operators you and Cahill don't even know about. We're talking the blackest of black ops. Rendition, assassinations, cyber warfare. International operations that violate the sovereignty of enemy and ally nations alike. Someone high up at Langley or the Pentagon wants something done, or sees that something needs to be done, something the CIA or DIA can't touch, something maybe even the White House doesn't need to know about, so they send a communication down the line. Someone has lunch with someone who later that day has a drink with someone else who goes jogging that night and happens to run into someone walking his dog in the park. Multiple degrees of separation, many of them through attorneys, with the first person in the chain having no idea who anyone further down the chain is. All information and commands are relayed verbally and in person, so no paper trail. Within hours of that final meeting, the planning is underway. Before he disappeared, Smith worked on the operational details, side by side with Raveis, who reported everything to Emery. That was the fail-safe—they each had to agree to an op. Was it truly for the good of the country? Was the target a genuine clear and present danger? That way the organization couldn't be politicized. CIA directors, DNI directors, the Joint Chiefs of Staff—they are often career military people or career intelligence officers, but each one of them was put into their position by elected officials, whom Emery and Raveis had grown to distrust during their years of service, and for good reason. But my theory is that about a year or so ago, Smith learned that Raveis had been taking on operations in secret, giving them the go-ahead without doing his due diligence or putting them to a vote. I don't know if Smith brought this to Emery's attention. My guess is he didn't. My guess is he realized that he had to go dark immediately, so he disappeared—just like the man he'd been before he became Smith had disappeared. When a man like him goes into hiding, there's no finding him."

"Carrington did."

"All due respect to your former commander, Tom, but if Carrington found Smith, then Smith wanted Carrington to find him."

"To get to me without Raveis finding out."

Hammerton nodded. "To give you the surveillance video of Raveis and your father. Show you the truth that'd been hidden from you."

"Smith said my father's death put them on the map. Any idea what that means?"

"No. But what I do know is that it was shortly after your father was killed that the organization went from being just another private security firm to what it is now. That's when the third level of operations came into being."

"You know this for certain?"

"Yes."

"How?"

"Because I was one of those secret operators, Tom. For twenty years I was one of the men you and Cahill and everyone like you knew nothing about. I've been on rendition teams and kill squads. I've done the dirty work of unelected officials, men who had no right to give the orders they gave. And I followed every one of those orders to the letter."

Tom thought about that, the things that Hammerton had been required to do in the name of maintaining his cover.

It was the work they had been trained for—Tom, Stella, Cahill, Grunn, Torres, everyone.

Krista MacManus had maintained her deep cover as Tom and Stella's line cook for more than a year.

But Hammerton had continued his mission—his personal mission—for decades, hiding his true intention from everyone, including Tom.

All in the name of determining the real fate of his former commander.

These thoughts of loyalty and sacrifice and cunning brought to Tom's mind a question—the one question that mattered more than any of the others.

"When Raveis sent my father to that hotel room to meet the Algerian and his men," he said, "was he acting alone or on orders?"

"That's the million-dollar question, isn't it?"

"I'm guessing you don't know the answer."

"That was before my time, Tom. All I know is that Smith knew about it. He knew it was an op. He had gone in beforehand and set up the surveillance, then sat in the next room and let what happened happen. But that doesn't really tell us anything, does it?"

Tom said nothing.

Hammerton, it seemed, understood what Tom was thinking.

"It is likely Emery didn't know. That's my guess. Raveis has a history of overstepping his bounds. And of the two of them, who's the one you can imagine doing that? Who's the one who would sacrifice a close friend for gain?"

Again, Tom didn't reply.

Hammerton gave him a moment, then said, "If you want, you and I can leave here right now. What's left of my old unit is currently en route; the first of them should be here in six hours. We can get you anywhere you want to go. And we can escort Cahill and Stella there, too. We can disappear the both of you, keep you safe."

Tom shook his head. "I can't run without knowing what I'm running from."

"We'll bring Stella here, then. You're welcome to stay for as long as you want. It's not much, but it's secure."

"Hiding blind is no better than running blind."

"So what do you have in mind?"

"We need to find Grunn."

"I'll reach out to my contact. He has a back channel to someone in the NSA who can track her phone. It might take a few hours because of the time difference between here and the UK."

"Get that started," Tom said. "I'll text Torres, tell her to return here as soon as she can."

Hammerton nodded, looked Tom over, then said, "You should get yourself ready. In another twelve hours it should be safe for you to sleep for a bit. It's obvious you need it. You look like shite, Tom. I mean, if I'm not going to tell you, who will?"

"Thanks," Tom said.

"Seriously, you look like you're going to fall over."

Tom shrugged, said the only thing he could. "Ain't we a pair."

Tom barely looked at his reflection in the bathroom mirror before unplugging the charged electric clippers and going to work.

There was no reason to doubt Hammerton's observation, and there was no need to confirm it, either.

Tom knew better than anyone that he was in trouble—concussed, beyond exhausted, shot at countless times, struck twice.

Fourteen hours had passed since he'd left Cahill and Sandy in Canaan.

A part of him wanted to do the math, figure out how long it had been since he'd last slept, but it seemed beyond him at the moment, and in a way he was grateful for that.

He could think ahead, and that was what mattered.

Ten minutes later, his long hair and beard were gone. What remained was a quarter-inch burr.

The electric razor took care of removing that.

In the mirror now was a man he did not immediately recognize—a man with his face but a bald head and no beard or even stubble.

As he was leaving the bathroom, he checked his burner phone for a reply text from Torres, but none had come in.

He found Hammerton on the main floor. The door to the basement was locked, and Hammerton was looking at his phone as well.

There was an expression on the man's face that Tom had never before seen.

A look of both concern and confusion.

"What's up?" Tom said.

"I just got a text from Grunn." He turned the phone and showed the screen to Tom.

The message was comprised of two words that were familiar to Tom.

SEND TOM

Tom held out his hand, and Hammerton handed him the phone.

After keying in a one-word reply message with his thumbs—LOCATION—Tom sent it off.

Hammerton asked, "What's going on?"

Before Tom could respond, the phone in his hand buzzed.

He stared at the reply text.

Thirty-Six

It would take a little over an hour to reach their destination.

The two tolls that they had to pass through were under video surveillance, so as a precaution Tom tipped the bill of his cap low and kept his head down till Hammerton's vehicle was well clear.

Neither man spoke the entire journey, Tom opting to relax—every second he conserved energy was a second that he was healing.

And preparing for what awaited him.

Exiting I-95, they broke their silence, Tom instructing Hammerton what turns to make.

Within a minute they had navigated the streets of Bridgeport, Connecticut, to the old cab company's garage.

The gate was open, as was one of the bay doors of the garage.

Parked in the small lot was a black Jeep Cherokee. If anyone was inside the vehicle, its heavily tinted windows concealed them.

Rickerson, still in his barn coat, was waiting by the open gate.

Hammerton steered through, and Rickerson swung the gate closed behind him.

Tom told Hammerton not to pull into the waiting bay. Stopping the vehicle outside it, Hammerton killed the motor. He and Tom exited slowly, their jackets open.

From behind them, Rickerson said, "They're in the office."

Tom looked back and saw that Rickerson was on the street side of the gate. He nodded once at Tom, then walked to a utility van parked at the curb, got in, and drove away.

Hammerton and Tom glanced at each other before stepping through the open garage door.

The two bays were empty and unlit. The only light was coming from the small office to their left. Tom and Hammerton looked toward the open door.

No one was visible until Grunn appeared in the doorway.

Something about the expression on her face kept Tom standing where he was.

Tom was about to speak when a figure joined Grunn in the doorway. Hammerton, his right hand placed on the grip of his holstered SIG P229, moved to position himself between the figure and Tom.

Before Hammerton had fully covered him, Tom touched his shoulder, stopping him.

Tom looked at the figure, and the figure looked at him.

"C'mon in," the Colonel said. "We've got a lot of ground to cover, and not a lot of time."

Tom recognized that the expression on Grunn's face was regret.

A look of consternation must have been visible on his own, because the Colonel said, "Don't worry, Tom, she didn't betray you. And it had to be done this way. C'mon in and we'll talk."

Neither Tom nor Hammerton moved.

The Colonel smiled. "I'm afraid that's an order, son."

Tom started toward the room, Hammerton close behind him.

Grunn and the Colonel stepped back as Tom approached the door.

Reaching it, Tom glanced around the room, expecting to see armed guards within—either dressed in suits or clad in some degree of operator gear.

What he saw instead was a single person, whose presence only deepened his confusion and concern.

Standing in the office, dressed in her four-pocket motorcycle jacket, was Slattery.

On the desk beside her was a tablet. She picked it up and said, "Hello, Tom."

Tom simply looked at her.

The Colonel said to Grunn, "Would you excuse us?" Glancing at Hammerton, he added, "You, too, John."

Grunn started for the door. Hammerton didn't move until Tom looked at him and nodded. They closed the door behind them.

"You've already met Slattery," the Colonel said to Tom.

"I have. She works for Raveis."

"She does, Tom, but what Raveis doesn't know is she really works for me."

Stepping forward, Slattery offered her hand to Tom.

He eventually reached out and took it. Her grip was firm, the handshake brisk but friendly.

"I actually go by Angela," Slattery said. "It's good to see you again."

Tom said to the Colonel, "What the hell is going on?"

The Colonel smiled warmly, but then again, he had always treated Tom respectfully, showing a fondness for him that bordered on parental pride.

Tonight maybe even more so.

"We'll bring you up to date," the Colonel said. "And we'll figure out together what to do from there."

"I'll need some questions answered first," Tom said.

Thirty-Seven

"How did you find Grunn?" Tom said.

"The tech she approached for assistance alerted his handler, and his handler contacted me," the Colonel said. "The tech stalled her until Slattery and my people could get there."

"Why did the tech alert you?"

"The metadata on the files Grunn wanted recovered indicated that they were among hundreds of files that had been stolen from us—stolen and then wiped from our mainframe and backup systems."

"By Smith."

"The man you know as Smith, yes."

"What's his real name?"

"I made a promise that I'd never reveal his identity, and it's a promise I intend to keep. I'm sure you can appreciate that. What I can tell you is that Smith served as a Green Beret, specialized in communications. He was a computer whiz long before any of us had computers, which is why Raveis and I approached him when we left the government for the private sector. He quickly proved himself invaluable and became a full partner. We agreed to bury his past and create a new identity for him when he joined on with us."

"Why?"

"He said it was to protect the one person he had left."

"What did that mean?"

"I didn't pry." The Colonel shrugged. "It didn't matter."

"Does Raveis know his true identity?"

"Yes."

Tom thought about that, then said, "If your tech got into the metadata, that means the files were recovered, correct?"

Slattery answered. "Yes."

Tom faced her. "How?"

"The rounds went through the battery, missed the drive entirely."

Tom looked down at the tablet in her hands. "You have the videos there?"

"Yes."

"I want to see them."

"You will," the Colonel said. "If that's what you want. But I have a few questions of my own I'd like answered first."

Tom didn't give the Colonel a chance to ask. "Why the two-word text from Grunn? The whole 'Send Tom' thing. That was the same text Carrington had Grunn send to the cell she'd left behind."

"We thought it best, in case Raveis was monitoring her phone or yours. If he was, I wanted him to think it was Carrington reaching out to you again. It's vital that he doesn't know I'm onto him."

Tom thought to ask why that was so important, but there were more pressing questions on his mind at the moment.

"How long have you been carrying out foreign operations on behalf of unelected officials?" he said.

The Colonel glanced at Slattery before looking back at Tom. He smiled. Though he'd been visibly caught off guard by the question, there was no mistaking that he was impressed—impressed that Tom not only had come to possess this knowledge but also had no problem confronting his superior with it.

"It seems Smith has told you a lot."

It suited Tom that the Colonel had made this assumption, so he made no effort to correct the error.

"How long?" Tom repeated.

"The attempted assassination of your father—the attack that killed your mother and sister instead—was the incident that first sent us in that direction."

"Explain that."

"A kill squad had come after one of our operatives—attacked him on US soil, in his home. It was a matter of chance—a last-minute business trip—that was the only reason your father wasn't there that night. We saw the writing on the wall, Raveis and Smith and I. We recognized the message the Benefactor was sending, that there wasn't anywhere he couldn't go, anyone he couldn't reach. That there wasn't anything he wouldn't do to win the war we were engaged in. It was clear to us that we had a new enemy on our hands, that he was as vicious as he was smart, and with significant resources at his disposal. But our partners inside the government didn't see the same threat we saw."

"Your father's murder changed that," Slattery said.

The Colonel continued. "I had been told the same thing you've been told, Tom. The same thing Raveis told all of us. That your father acted alone, used his skills to track down the Algerian and his team. Raveis sold this story, said your father—his friend—was out of his mind with grief, had been driven by a desire for vengeance to do what law enforcement couldn't. More than that, your father wanted to look each of those killers in the face before he killed them."

Slattery said, "In reality, your father was sent on a suicide op by Raveis."

"In the two years between the attack on your home and your father's murder," the Colonel said, "we tried to alert our colleagues in the government to just how dangerous the Benefactor was. But it wasn't just the threat that he represented. We wanted them to know *what* he was."

"And what was that?"

Slattery answered. "The mercenary to end all mercenaries. The Benefactor doesn't fight for country or God. He doesn't even have an ideology. That's not to say he isn't political, because one thing we do know about him is that he's as Nazi as they come. His techniques are Nazi based, he studied at the feet of Nazis. But, really, he just wants the world in a constant state of chaos, because as long as one group wants to kill another group, he stands to profit. Arms sales and soldiers for hire when there are wars, and specialized assassins to tip the balance when those wars become intractable. That's not just his business, that's his purpose."

The Colonel interjected. "In a strange way, we are still fighting the Second World War. You're a student of history; no doubt you've heard the name Otto Skorzeny."

Tom nodded. "SS Lieutenant Colonel. Led the raid that freed Mussolini from an Italian prison in '43. Historians call him Hitler's favorite commando."

"The Mussolini raid was just one of many. Skorzeny was captured after the war but escaped, thanks to the unit of guerrilla fighters known as *Werwolves*—a unit he created and trained. Skorzeny ended up in Egypt in '52, served as a military adviser for President Nassar. Name a key player in terrorism during the past seventy-five years—Amin Al Husseni, Arafat, Saddam Hussein—they learned everything they knew from Skorzeny. By the end of his life, Skorzeny was in Argentina, where he served as an adviser to Juan Perón. He was even Eva Perón's personal bodyguard."

Slattery said, "Perón's atrocities against his own people are as well known as his Nazi sympathies."

"Here's another name for you, Tom," the Colonel said. "Walter Rauff."

"The inventor of the mobile gas chamber," Tom said.

Slattery nodded. "An ardent Nazi to the end. In the '70s he ran the DINA, Pinochet's secret police force in Chile. Nearly eight hundred detainment camps were scattered all over the country, practically one outside every town. Mini concentration camps where dissidents were taken to be tortured, killed, and buried in mass graves. Stripped of their names and issued a number upon arrival, never to be seen again, alive or dead. 'The Disappeared,' they were called. Survivors of the torture rooms report seeing two flags prominently displayed on the walls—the Chilean flag and the Nazi flag."

"The list goes on," the Colonel said. "Name a dictator or a mufti in the second half of the twentieth century, and one of Hitler's high-ranking henchmen had at some point served and advised him. There were dozens of escaped Nazis in Egypt alone, some with assumed names, others living right out in the open. The Middle East, South America—they were viper nests of Nazi war criminals."

"And these men weren't reenacting Nazi programs for their new employers," Slattery said. "They were extending them. The Nazi belief of state-sanctioned murder has continued unabated since 1945. And the Benefactor is the heir apparent."

The Colonel asked, "What's the definition of modern terrorism?"

"Small, autonomous cells that operate in isolation," Tom said. "No central command, so no upward trail to follow. Independent, self-reliant, self-funding, self-promoting."

"Otherwise known as the Skorzeny Syndrome. Modern terrorism was born in Nazi Germany and spread like a virus to the rest of the world." The Colonel paused before continuing. "Faced with this—with these enemies, these tactics, this cancer that can't ever be killed—how far is too far? How far would you go to fight such evil?"

Since that question was clearly rhetorical, Tom didn't answer. Instead, he focused on the conclusion—the only conclusion—he could reach.

"It took my father's murder to wake up your partners in our government."

The Colonel nodded. "The attack on your home was an attack on the United States, and yet that wasn't enough to convince them. So Raveis grew frustrated and acted on his own. It's clear to me now that he believed that the slaughter of a US citizen while seeking justice for his murdered family—the slaughter of a distinguished operative, one of their own—would provide the tipping point he needed to persuade our partners to act. And by 'act' I mean give us what we needed to fight the threat we were facing. Not just the funds but the green light to set up the organization within the organization."

The Colonel paused again. "Raveis sacrificed your father. He manipulated him to go after the Algerian. He *helped* him track the Algerian down and set up the meeting. He had Smith set up the surveillance cameras, told Smith to sit back and let your father die. Then he convinced Smith to conceal from me the true nature of those events. After his cancer diagnosis, Smith found God and went into hiding, but not without tipping me off first. We struck a deal and made a plan of our own. Smith would let Carrington find him, and together he and Carrington would bring you out into the open so you could be provided with the truth, which is what Raveis has feared all along."

"Feared why?"

"If you found out what he had done to your father, you would come after him yourself. All these years we kept our eye on you because we believed that the Benefactor saw you as a threat. But it turns out that he wasn't alone. Raveis saw you as a threat as well."

"But Raveis could have had me killed countless times in the past twenty years."

Slattery said, "Sam Raveis was never one to waste an asset, even an asset as potentially dangerous to him as you. If he could keep the truth from you, then he'd have nothing to worry about. More important, he could use you in our pursuit of the Benefactor."

The Colonel added, "And now that you know what really happened to your father, Raveis wants you dead."

Tom's mind was struggling with everything he'd been told. It was as if processing information was some kind of heavy lifting.

Finally, he said, "The team that came after me at the storage facility was sent by Raveis."

"Yes. An outside crew, so there'd be no trail back to him."

"How did they know I'd be there?"

"It's likely that Smith's close-protection agent, Manning, was loyal to Raveis. Overseeing the training of all our people gives Raveis a distinct advantage. He not only has access to them but also knows everything about them. He could have recruited Manning by labeling you a traitor who was conspiring with other traitors. Or he simply could have coerced Manning into betraying Smith by threatening Manning's loved ones."

"But they killed him," Tom said. "The team sent to the storage facility, they killed Manning."

Slattery said, "Of course they did. At some point Manning had to have contact with Raveis. Whatever it is Raveis said to him, it died with him."

Tom considered that, then looked at the Colonel. "The first hit team was led by a woman named Esa Hirsh. She works for the Benefactor, which means Raveis sold us out to him. But to do that Raveis would have to know how to contact the Benefactor, either directly or through back channels."

"We believe a former high-ranking officer has joined forces with the Benefactor."

"Graves," Tom said. "Disgraced general, has a fondness for neo-Nazis, building his own private army that he trains outside the US."

The Colonel was again caught off guard. Eventually, though, he smiled, showing the same pride that he had displayed moments earlier. "You're full of surprises, Tom."

"Are you thinking Raveis contacted the Benefactor through Graves?"

Slattery answered. "It's possible."

Tom thought about that, then said to the Colonel, "The first attack, the one led by Esa Hirsh, was a hit, there's no doubt about that. They wanted us dead, but they also wanted what Carrington had given me."

"Why do you say that?"

"They could have used a more powerful explosive device, killed us that way. Instead they disabled the vehicle and launched an attack with small arms. The second attack, at the storage facility, looked to me like an attempted abduction. That changed, though, when I forced that second team's hand."

Slattery asked, "What's your point, Tom?"

"Why would Raveis want me dead first and then want to abduct me second?"

"Because you had the files in your possession at that point."

"But why would he want them? It's not like destroying them would help him. They weren't the original surveillance tapes with no other copies in existence."

Slattery shrugged. "Maybe he had hopes of salvaging you as an asset. If he could keep you from seeing the files, he could continue to use you."

"Then why not attempt to abduct me first and then have me killed when the abduction failed? The way it played out is backward."

The Colonel said, "That might have been the Benefactor's terms. He'd only agree to the job if you were killed. But you survived, and Raveis had no choice but to take matters into his own hands, assemble a team of his own on short notice."

"It's also possible that they were taking you somewhere to kill you," Slattery added. "Somewhere more private, where they could dispose of your body in a way no one would ever find it. This way no one would ever know if you were actually killed. Knowing the Benefactor, he might have decided it would be useful to him if we were all left to wonder if you had defected. Misinformation to that effect could be leaked, rumors started. You know that he's done that kind of thing before, with Frank Ballantine."

Tom thought about that. It took work for him to clear from his mind the idea of Stella never knowing what had happened to him, left to wonder for the rest of her life if he might someday find his way back to her.

"But if Raveis is working with the Benefactor," he said, "then why groom me all these years to kill a man he's allied with?"

"All partnerships eventually come to an end," the Colonel said. "Particularly sordid ones. But that would be classic Raveis, wouldn't it? Use one threat to eliminate the other. And look like a patriot in the process."

Slattery said, "Remember, Tom, you aren't the only one Raveis needed to keep the truth from."

"He betrayed your father," the Colonel said. "But he betrayed me, too. He betrayed everything we stood for, everything we fought for."

Tom looked at the Colonel for a moment. "Raveis framed Carrington."

"Yes. He planted the evidence that made it look like Carrington led the Algerian to you and Stella."

"How do you know this?"

The Colonel nodded toward Slattery, and she said, "Smith provided Raveis with what he needed."

"The mirror copy of Hammerton's cell phone that was found in Carrington's apartment."

"Yes."

"How long have you known this?"

"Several months."

Tom turned back to the Colonel. "You had teams hunting him even though you knew he was innocent."

"It was necessary to maintain the illusion that I had full confidence in Raveis."

"What if Carrington had been found and killed?"

"It was my hope that wouldn't be the outcome. I suspect you were hoping for the same, Tom. That's why you never protested the kill order. Deep down you knew Carrington had what it took to keep eluding us. You knew that just like you knew he was innocent."

"And Raveis was prepared to frame me, too, if it came to that," Tom said. "Smith gave Carrington my old Colt. The one I'd been assured by you had been disposed of."

"Those were the orders I had given, and I'd been told they were carried out," the Colonel said. "And yes, if all else had failed, Raveis would have used that weapon to frame you. He wasn't the kind of man to let an opportunity pass him by. He collected opportunities. He saw them in everything. It was his gift."

"What about the kill squads assigned to Carrington?"

"We should assume they're still deployed, since they are Raveis's men. Your commanding officer isn't out of the woods yet."

Tom took one more moment, then said, "So what do we do?"

"You and your friends go into hiding. Someplace deep, someplace out of the way. It was smart of you to send Cahill to get Stella. Things might have been easier if you had involved me, but I understand why you didn't."

"He has her?"

The Colonel nodded. "Yes. She disappeared from the compound yesterday evening."

Tom let the wave of relief rush through him.

Then he said, "And while we're all tucked away somewhere, what happens?"

"Raveis has gone dark. We don't know exactly what caused him to do that—the first attack on you or maybe Stella's disappearance from SERE training—but he took a number of his best bodyguards. Another thing we don't know is how many; it could be a handful, it could be dozens. We're working on determining what it is we're up against. Is it a small rebellion or all-out civil war? I'm sorry, but at this point all we have to offer you is sanctuary. For you and your friends, for as long as it takes."

"We can take care of ourselves," Tom said.

"I don't doubt that, Tom, but you were involved in a shooting in New York City. As I am sure you know, the NYPD takes that kind of thing very seriously. Your shaved head and face and the change of clothes and boots are a good start, but until we know what evidence the police do and don't have, the best place for you is out of sight. We have to assume by now that the cops have at least tracked your movements from the scene of the shooting to the vehicle that Cahill had given you. They have fast access to subway station cameras and street cameras. If we're lucky, you were in a blind spot when Grunn and Hammerton got you into their vehicle, but I'm not much for counting on luck. And I think when it comes to your friends, you aren't, either. So Cahill has definitely been dragged into this, and Hammerton and Grunn will probably get dragged in, too. Everything I know about you—everything you've done since Carrington reached out to you, not to mention everything you did prior to that—tells me that your main concern is the welfare of those you care about. So the best place for all of you to be right now is a place where no one can find you. This way you can recover, maybe even get looked at by a doctor." The Colonel paused. "And you can decide what to do with the video files, because as someone who cares about you, I feel obliged to say that you might not want to see them all."

"What do you mean?"

Slattery replied, "The last of the six videos isn't of Raveis and your father talking in his office. It's the surveillance footage of the hotel room."

The Colonel said, "It shows your father killing three men before fighting hand to hand with the Algerian—a fight to the death that your father lost." The Colonel gave Tom a moment before continuing. "I'm not sure I'd need to see that. Or want to. But it's up to you what to do. Everything you know about me—everything I've done since we first met—should tell you that I take what is important to you very seriously. And I know what's important to you is your freedom to choose. Watch the video or don't. In the meantime, though, we need to get you out of here."

"Where will you be taking us?"

"I have a place," Slattery said. "About an hour from here."

Tom wasn't keen on trusting someone he barely knew, but he didn't see any better choice at this point.

The Colonel said, "I tried contacting Cahill to alert him that he and his team might need to reroute to a different location, but—"

"Team?" Tom said.

"He recruited Krista MacManus."

Tom found comfort in that piece of information.

Krista had more than once demonstrated her significant skills as a close-protection agent.

But more than that, she was the closest friend Stella had.

Tom understood the power of seeing a friendly face.

"Cahill has yet to reply," the Colonel said, "but I suspect he's maintaining radio silence. He may be waiting to hear of any alteration in plans directly from you."

"We'll leave things as they are for now."

"Whatever you think is best. In the meantime, I'll secure a more hardened location for all of you, one that Raveis doesn't know about. It may take a few days, but you'll be safe with Slattery until then. As a precaution, I don't even know where she's taking you."

Slattery stepped forward. "We should get moving." She offered Tom the tablet. He looked at the device for a moment before accepting it.

Then he took another moment to study her face.

There was something familiar about her now.

There hadn't been before, back when Tom had first met her in Raveis's Upper East Side parking garage, but now he couldn't shake the vague sense that he had seen her face before, or at least parts of it.

Or maybe this was just the concussion playing tricks on his exhausted mind.

He was reminded yet again of the words James Carrington had taught him a long time ago.

The only way out is through.

Finally, Tom said, "Yeah, okay. Take us to your safe house."

Thirty-Eight

Hammerton and Grunn exited the garage first, followed by Tom and the Colonel, Slattery behind them.

Waiting in the lot were Hammerton's vehicle and the black Cherokee.

The group hadn't taken more than a few steps when a caravan of three black SUVs—two Chevy Tahoes with a Mercedes between them—pulled to a stop outside the fence.

Tom recognized this formation as the Colonel's standard mode of transportation.

Several suited men exited the Chevys, some setting up a perimeter and scanning the area, others clustered together by the Mercedes's rear door, waiting for their charge to approach.

The Colonel extended his hand, and Tom took it.

"I'll see you in a few days," the Colonel said. "If you need anything, Slattery can reach me."

Tom nodded.

The Colonel's grip was as firm as ever, and he offered Tom the same smile of fondness and respect that he'd always shown him.

But he held Tom's hand slightly longer than usual.

Finally, though, the Colonel let go and started toward the gate. Four of his men converged there, waiting for him. After he reached them, they surrounded him, escorting him to the Mercedes.

Once the motorcade had driven from sight, Slattery said, "You'll need to leave your vehicle here. Like the Colonel said, we can't count on luck."

Tom nodded.

"Who does it belong to?" she said.

Hammerton answered, "It's mine."

"I'll arrange to have it towed and destroyed."

"I have people who can take care of that," Hammerton said.

Tom looked at him inquisitively.

Hammerton said to him, "The Redcoats have landed."

Slattery drove the Cherokee.

Hammerton was in the passenger seat, Grunn in the seat directly behind him. Tom was seated behind Slattery. From there he could see her eyes via the rearview mirror.

The more he looked at them, the more familiar she seemed.

A few minutes into the ride, Tom texted Torres again; he waited several moments for a reply but got none.

"I can maybe go look for her," Grunn said.

Tom shook his head.

"You okay?" she said.

Tom nodded and pocketed his phone.

After fifteen minutes on I-95, Slattery exited the highway. Through his window Tom saw a familiar sight—the outskirts of the city of New Haven.

Several turns later, they were just a few blocks west of Yale.

It wasn't, though, his one year of college there that was on Tom's mind. A few miles northeast of the campus was the neighborhood where he and Hammerton had gone to search for Cahill two years ago—a mission that Raveis had sent them on and that had nearly gotten them both killed.

If not for Hammerton, Tom would have died there, and Stella . . . well, Tom didn't want to think of the fate that would have befallen her.

It was obvious that Hammerton recognized the area as well, because several times he turned his head and glanced back at Tom.

Another thirty minutes passed before they reached their destination—the town of North Haven.

Deep within a few wooded acres was a secluded home of modern design. Unlike a traditional house, this structure was a series of rectangular shapes comprising a mix of building materials—wood and steel and glass. Two stories tall, the house had multiple wings and an attached three-car garage with a steel door.

As Slattery steered the Cherokee around the long circular driveway, Tom realized that this home was situated on a bluff. He knew the area well enough to understand that the bluff overlooked the Quinnipiac River.

Slattery pressed a button on the driver's console, and one of the garage doors began to rise. It was fully opened by the time the Cherokee reached it. She steered the vehicle inside, parked, and pressed the button again, lowering the door.

The interior of the garage was impeccably kept—orderly to the point of appearing sterile.

The cement floor was painted metallic gray, the whitewashed walls lined with chrome tool chests and a pegboard upon which hung a variety of hand tools.

In the next bay were two BMW motorcycles—matching K1200Rs. Hanging on the nearby wall were two helmets and a four-pocket jacket that was identical to the one Slattery was wearing, though larger.

His and hers bikes and gear, Tom thought.

The bay on the far left of the garage housed a Hummer H3T Alpha—midnight blue and rigged with over-cab lights, brush guards, and a low-profile roof rack containing a jack and a spare tire.

Getting out of the Cherokee, Hammerton took a look around, then said to Slattery, "Who are you, Bruce Wayne?"

"Yes," she answered. "I am."

Then she waved for her guests to follow her.

Once inside the house, Tom found his way to the large single-paned window in the main room. Standing by it with the lights still off, he looked down at the dark water.

Hammerton joined him there.

A few miles downriver, they had jumped from the second-floor window of a workshop and into that water, hitting it and plunging under its surface seconds before a timed explosive device was detonated.

Tom could still feel the brutal cold, as well as the strong current that had carried them underwater till his lungs ached for air.

He could also still feel the concussive blast that had hit him with enough force to cause his internal organs to shift.

After a moment, Hammerton said, "Full circle, huh? Or close enough to it."

Tom nodded. "Yeah." He turned his head and looked around for Slattery. He didn't see her but heard her talking to Grunn in another part of the house. In a low voice, Tom said, "How many from your old unit are here?"

"Three so far, more are on the way."

"They're in New York?"

"They've reached the safe house, yes. You want them here instead?"

"No. Torres might finally show up there. Or worse, if things went bad for her, she might lead someone there. Someone looking for me."

"I'll let them know. They'll handle it either way." Hammerton paused. "You know, the office door back at that garage wasn't very thick. We heard everything." He glanced at the tablet in Tom's hand. "You don't have to watch that alone. I'll watch it with you, if somehow that'll make it easier."

"Contact your men," Tom said. "Make sure they keep an eye out for Torres."

The sound of Slattery's voice grew louder as she and Grunn made their way toward the main room.

"I'm going to want to talk to Slattery alone for a few minutes."

"Sure, Tom."

Hammerton left the room, following the sound of Slattery's voice.

Tom looked at the mantel above the large fieldstone fireplace, upon which more than a dozen framed photos stood in a row.

Walking toward the mantel, he paused at a doorway leading to a sunroom.

The only furniture in it was a hospital bed, beside which were several monitors.

The bed was made, the equipment turned off.

Tom got the sense that this room was waiting to be used.

Continuing to the mantel, he studied the various photos of Slattery. In some of them she was with a man and a woman Tom did not recognize, and in others she was alone, dressed in a Girl Scout's uniform or a prom dress or a graduation gown.

The majority of the photos showed Slattery posing in what appeared to be a living room, and the fact that each living room was different indicated to Tom that each occasion had likely occurred in a different home.

Of the dozen-plus photos, two interested Tom the most.

The first was of Slattery as a young girl, maybe five.

That early face looked the most familiar to him.

The eyes, the mouth, the shape of her cheeks—so close to the features he'd seen in another photo recently.

The second photo was of a thirteen-year-old lighting a row of candles with that same man and woman at her side—Slattery's bat mitzvah, no doubt.

Tom was staring at that photo when Slattery entered the room. "You wanted me," she said.

Tom turned to face her. "I have some questions I think you can answer."

"Of course."

"Am I right to assume you know a lot about the Benefactor?"

"I've been investigating the man and his network for most of my adult life. It's actually the only job I've ever had."

"Do you know his identity?"

"I believe so."

"How long have you known?"

"That information was only revealed recently."

"How was it revealed?"

She paused. "Someone inside his operation approached us."

"Who is 'us'?"

Tom waited for her to say more, but when she didn't, he said, "I need you to tell me everything you can about the Benefactor."

"Is there anything specific you want to know?"

"Stella's on her way," Tom said. "Sooner or later, she'll be part of this again. The consensus seems to be that the Benefactor is . . ."

Tom was searching for the word when Slattery jumped in.

"Vicious," she said.

Tom nodded. "I want to know what we're up against. I want to know what to expect. So exactly how vicious is he?"

Thirty-Nine

In a darkened room, Esa struggled for consciousness.

Whenever she approached the edges of wakefulness, the only sensation she was aware of was a weight pressing down on her body, and the only movement she could make for a long time was to open her eyes.

But at best her lids would flutter to the halfway point before blinking closed again.

Those brief moments of semiconsciousness, though, grew more frequent, each one lasting just a little bit longer.

Finally, she sensed more than the heaviness of her limbs and head.

Someone was nearby.

At some point this presence spoke, and she recognized Karl's voice.

"Just take it easy," he said. "Rest up; you're going to need your strength."

It was only then that she realized she was trying to sit up—and fighting him as he attempted to subdue her.

His hands around her wrists, he eased her back down onto the cot, then picked up the thin wool blanket she had flung off and covered her with it.

"You're my nurse?" she muttered.

"Something like that."

"Where am I?"

"That doesn't matter now. He wants to see you once you're ready."

"I'm ready."

"No, you need to rest more. He wants you fully conscious."

She became aware of something else—a throbbing, searing pain in her shoulder. "When will I see a doctor?"

"He already came and went—took the pellets out and stitched you up this morning. He sedated you before he left. Pretty major stuff. It'll take a while more for you to shake it off."

"Where am I?" she repeated.

"You'll see soon enough. Right now you need to get better. He won't see you till you're better."

Esa was drifting back toward unconsciousness, but she felt the cot shift as Karl stood.

A door opened and closed, and she heard nothing after that.

Esa woke with a start, opening her eyes to a bright light that caused her to turn her head to one side and squint.

The blanket was gone, and she was dressed—jeans and a black sweater, socks but no shoes.

She tried to raise her arm to shield her eyes but felt the same heaviness she had felt before, or at least thought she did.

There was something different, though. What was stopping her from moving her arms this time wasn't a uniform weight pressing down but rather something specific, something localized.

Her wrists were tied to the cot by plastic zip ties.

Attempting to move her legs, she felt the same restraints around her ankles.

When her eyes could tolerate the harsh light, she assessed her surroundings.

The room was small. Brick walls, cement floors, no windows. Maybe a storage area, but her cot was the only item in it.

The ceiling was crisscrossed with pipes of varying thickness. An exposed steel crossbeam was coated with flame-retardant foam that had been painted over, seemingly a long time ago.

Restricted by her restraints, she'd only made a few movements so far, yet every one of them had caused a pinching sensation in her shoulder, where her torn flesh just hours ago had been sewn closed.

At one point she heard the sound of footsteps approaching and determined as they got closer that they belonged to two men.

The door to her small room was unlocked and opened, and the two men who had been part of her exfil team—who had disarmed and drugged her earlier—entered the room.

Their hands were free of weapons, but their MA-1–style nylon flight jackets hung open, offering Esa glimpses of holstered sidearms.

In the pockets of their jeans, held in a quick-draw position by clips, were folding knives.

It looked to Esa as if these men had recently trimmed their buzz cuts, because the fine hairs covering their scalps shimmered under the bright overhead light.

One man was blond, the other had darker roots. Both had complex tattoos on their necks and hands.

Esa had seen their type many times before—angry, restless, and ready for violence.

Her exiled grandfather had attracted men just like these, and there hadn't been a month during her long years as his caretaker when some misfit hadn't shown up at the door of his cottage, drawn to him like flies to waste.

She'd hated those men then, and she felt an instinctual hatred for these men now.

The blond stepped into the room, removed and opened his pocketknife, cut her ankle ties followed by the ties around her wrists, then stood beside the cot.

Esa sat up, placing her feet on the floor. Even with socks on she felt the coldness of the cement. Immediately, her head throbbed and a wave of nausea gripped her, but she ignored both issues and stood, facing the blond.

She asked for shoes, but the man in the doorway told her she wouldn't need any.

Esa didn't bother to ask what he meant by that, because the reason for withholding footwear was clear to her—it was unlikely that she could fight well with just socks on, and it was also unlikely that she would get far, should she somehow escape.

The blond man nodded toward the doorway. The dark-haired man gestured for her to follow him. She did, with the blond walking close behind her.

Beyond that small storage room was a larger one. This space was vast but empty, its tall windows—four walls of them—painted over with thick paint.

Much of the far end of that room was lost to darkness.

A chair and a short stool were located to the right of the door behind Esa. The dark-haired man picked up both, handed the stool to his partner, and placed the chair next to Esa, positioning it so it was facing the room.

The blond man carried the stool to the center and set it down.

The man next to Esa told her to sit in the chair. She hesitated before following his orders.

It was then that Esa saw something suspended from the ceiling.

A long piece of wire, connected to a crossbeam, hung directly above the short stool.

The end of the wire, roughly seven feet above the floor, had been fashioned into a noose.

The dark-haired man removed a walkie-talkie from his pocket, clicked the "Transmit" button, and said, "She's up."

Karl's voice came back right away. "On our way."

Forty

"We believe the Benefactor is a man named Pascal Henkel," Slattery said. "Born in Munich in 1950, university educated, he worked as a mercenary following his discharge from the KSK, but it was really just a means for him to meet and, in many cases, serve under the men he admired, all those dictators who employed escaped Nazis after the war. Legend has it Henkel even worked in Saddam Hussein's notorious torture room. It was through Skorzeny that Henkel was told of a man named Ernst Schmidt living in exile in Argentina. In 1944 Schmidt had been recruited out of the Hitler Youth to be one of Skorzeny's guerrillas, the *Werwolves*. Schmidt quickly proved himself, even accompanied Skorzeny on the mission to liberate Mussolini from an Italian prison. Another *Werwolf* was a woman named Ilsa Hirsh. She and Schmidt married and had two sons, one of whom had a daughter in 1962."

"Let me guess," Tom said. "Esa Hirsh."

Slattery nodded. "She assumed her grandmother's surname at some point. Esa first met Henkel when she was a teenager. Later, when he consolidated power and became the Benefactor, Henkel employed her grandfather and father, and when she was old enough, he employed her as well."

"Why is he known as 'the Benefactor'?"

"The literal definition of *benefactor* is one who provides help to a cause, and that's what he did—for a price. 'The Benefactor' was his code name during his time in Chile, and from there, as he took the steps necessary to bury his name and personal history, it became his only identity."

"Other than his time working as a torturer for Hussein, what has he done to earn his reputation for viciousness?"

"When he was a merc in Africa he was known for flaying prisoners." She paused. "He'd skin them alive, starting at their ankles. It often would take all night to complete, and the only parts of his victims where any skin remained were their feet. In Chile he perfected torture by electricity. I won't even tell you the things he mastered under Hussein. He was promoted from torturer to state assassin, which he also excelled at. But he learned the hard way that all regimes fall, so he went freelance, training terrorist groups throughout the world, passing on to them what he'd learned from the men who had mentored him. Later, those groups became the pool he would draw from to build his own stateless terror organization. Just like Skorzeny, Henkel had a collection of hyperloyal operatives he controlled and directed, but the fact that he lacked any ideology allowed him to make his terror units available to anyone willing to pay. Any sides, all sides. In the '70s terrorism was on the rise all over the world, and terroristic acts provided the perfect cover for what in reality was a targeted assassination."

"Henkel would direct an operative in a particular terrorist cell to carry out an assassination and disguise it as terrorism," Tom said.

"That was part of what he did, yes. Another service he provided was to create or increase tensions in any given region through propaganda. He would sustain that tension for as long as it was profitable, then once he'd milked it for all it was worth—once he'd made everything he could from selling arms and providing mercs—he'd tip the scales just enough to trigger an all-out war. Somalia is the best example of what he did. By supplying arms to opposing warlords and sending in small units of his own operatives to stir up the shit when necessary, he added to the chaos and escalated the violence, which resulted in more arms sales and more opportunities for his own guerrillas to create havoc."

Slattery paused before continuing. "There was one man who studied everything Henkel did, who observed what small-scale guerrilla units and the terrorist techniques first envisioned by Skorzeny could achieve. This man saw what happened in Somalia in 1989, when the mighty United States of America—a mixed force of Army Rangers and Delta—were driven out of a black hole they should have easily dominated. Our best-trained fighters, with the benefit of uncontested air superiority, were essentially defeated by a poorly led militia of drug-addicted insurgents armed with AKs and Soviet-era RPGs."

"You're talking about the Battle of Mogadishu," Tom said. "The events of *Black Hawk Down*."

Slattery nodded. "And for one man, that confirmed what he had experienced fighting the Soviets in Afghanistan. All it took was a ten percent loss of personnel and a prolonged fight with no clear win in sight to drain a superpower of its will to fight. The same thing happened to the US in Vietnam. Mogadishu was a bad day for a lot of good fighters, but in terms of losses it was, at best, a bloody nose. And yet within weeks the Rangers and Delta were pulled out by an administration that was more concerned with bad headlines back home than achieving its objective. The man who saw this—who lived it firsthand fighting the Soviets in Afghanistan, who celebrated as the US recoiled after *Black Hawk Down*—was Osama Bin Laden. All Bin Laden wanted was to defeat the 'great Western Satan that is the United States of America,' and all he needed to achieve that was to drag the US into a war in Afghanistan—the graveyard of empires. He set off a truck bomb in the World Trade Center back in '93 and attacked the USS *Cole* in 2000, but it took 9/11 for him to finally achieve his goal, which was the realization of Skorzeny's theory that acts of terrorism—small, independent cells working toward a shared goal—could not only affect policy but also dictate it. Nineteen men hijacked four commercial airliners, and eighteen years later the US is still fighting a war that can't ever be won, because the enemy isn't a place that can be bombed or a division of fighters that can be overrun. It isn't even an idea. It's an emotion, a gut feeling. You can kill people, you can flatten entire cities and regions, but you can't kill the irrational hatred of 'the other' that's in all of us. I've read your psych reports; I know your personal history—you seem to be a decent man, defined by your deep sense of loyalty and high intelligence. And yet I know there are 'others' in your life—men and women who oppose you in one way or another or whose values are in direct conflict with yours and who therefore can be viewed, when push comes to shove, as less worthy of living. It's human nature to feel hatred for those who are in opposition to us. Not to get all *Jedi Knight* on you, but hatred rises from only one place: fear. Fear of losing to the other, fear of having what's ours taken by the other—that's the engine that has driven human history. The ideological children of Skorzeny know this. As long as there is that innate fear and hatred, there will be wars. And asymmetrical wars cannot be won by the side with the most power, not anymore. The philosophical children of Skorzeny bet their lives on that understanding, and the smart ones, well, they find every and any way to profit from it."

Tom took a moment, then said, "You said someone inside Henkel's operation approached us recently. That's how you now know who Henkel is, where he came from, the men he studied under."

"That's correct. For the first time, we have an agent on the inside. Negotiations are ongoing, but the plan is that when the time is right, he will act."

"Act how?"

"Take out Henkel for us."

"You trust this man."

"It's not about trust. Everyone has a price."

"And the Colonel knows about this."

"He handled the negotiations."

"Why didn't he say anything about this to me?"

"He wanted you to stay focused on what you needed to do."

"So why are you telling me?"

"Because like you, I know what it's like to have vital information withheld, and for far too long." She paused. "And before this is over, we may need to depend on each other. To stay alive—to keep those we care about alive—we have to trust each other fully. I'll keep nothing from you if you keep nothing from me. Deal?"

Tom nodded. "Deal."

Slattery extended her hand, and Tom took it.

"So who is your man on the inside?" he said.

Forty-One

It took close to a minute before Esa heard another set of approaching footsteps.

These took much longer to reach her, and they were echoing loudly by the time they had arrived at the door at the far end of the large room.

Karl opened that door and started to cross the empty space, followed by a man Esa had never seen before.

An older man, maybe in his sixties.

The two men reached the wire noose and stood on either side of the stool beneath it.

Karl was dressed in the usual expensive, well-fitting suit that showed off his powerful build, but over his right shoulder was a medium-size backpack made of ballistic nylon.

The tailored suit and tactical bag struck Esa as being at odds with each other.

Another moment passed before Esa heard one more set of footsteps approaching—but this time a single set.

Finally, those steps reached the door. It opened, and the Benefactor entered. He was talking on a cell phone, but ended the call once he reached Karl and the unknown man.

The Benefactor looked at Esa for a moment before saying to the unknown man, "Would you hand me that stool, General?"

The man picked up the stool and handed it to the Benefactor, who walked toward Esa.

Setting the stool in front of her, he sat down, facing her.

"I hope you're not in too much discomfort, Esa," he said. "Unfortunately, I instructed our doctor not to administer any pain medication after your surgery. It is essential that you feel what is about to happen to you, and, of course, any medication that would ease the pain caused by your wound would also numb you. I need you fully aware, able to sense everything—every sensation and emotion. Otherwise, there'd be no point in doing what now must be done."

Esa glanced briefly at Karl and the unknown man.

"And what now must be done?" she said to the Benefactor.

"Address your betrayal."

"The video proves that I gave them nothing."

"Yes, that much is clear." He nodded to the two thugs behind him. "Our friends here enjoyed that show quite a bit, by the way. In fact, they reminded me just moments ago that, despite your age, you'd bring a fair price, should the decision be made to sell you instead." He smiled. "Our partners in that trade are skilled at confinement, but you'd likely escape nonetheless, so that isn't an option I'm willing to consider. Can't risk the possibility of you—with all your skills and training, and with the blood that runs through your veins—getting free and coming after me for revenge."

"How exactly is a failed operation a betrayal?"

"The failure to carry out your mission is a separate matter, Esa. It was a colossal failure, don't get me wrong. And that will need to be addressed. What I am talking about right now are the actions you took prior to that."

"What actions?"

The Benefactor raised his hand, and Karl approached him, reaching into his jacket and removing an envelope.

Pulling out the contents of the envelope—a stack of five-by-seven photos—he placed them into his employer's waiting hand.

The Benefactor raised the first photo and held it up for Esa to see.

It was a screen capture of surveillance footage taken by a camera that had been mounted high on the wall of her grandfather's bedroom.

Esa saw herself seated at his bedside, preparing the syringe of fentanyl.

The Benefactor offered her the next photo from the stack.

This one showed her injecting the fatal dose into her grandfather.

"The murder itself is perhaps defensible, but the desecration is not."

He held up another photo, this one showing Esa in her grandfather's secret study, an upended gasoline container in her hand.

"He deserved a grave, and one with a monument to his incredible life, for the world we inherited from him and men and women like him." He paused. "And on a personal note, I would have preferred that his cherished belongings had been preserved."

Esa said nothing.

The next photo shown to her wasn't a screen capture from surveillance footage but instead an actual photograph.

In it was a hanged man.

Esa looked at it long enough to recognize that the dead man was the doctor who had provided her with the drug.

And around his neck—cutting deep into it—was a noose of thin wire.

Esa locked eyes with the Benefactor.

"A traitor's death should never be an easy one," he said. "Admiral Wilhelm Canaris was a traitor to his own cause. He played a role in the attempted assassination of his leader. Do you know how he died?"

Esa nodded.

"Tell me."

"He was hanged by piano wire, cut down when he lost consciousness, and revived. Then he was strung up and hanged all over again."

"And why was that done?"

"So he would taste death twice."

"Your grandfather taught you well." He gestured to the two thugs in nylon jackets. "You may be interested to know that our friends here currently hold the record. At their hands a traitor tasted death five times before the attempt at resuscitation failed. It's a terrible thing, being hanged by wire. A noose of thick-enough rope, properly placed, compresses the carotid artery, cutting off the supply of oxygen to the brain and causing a loss of consciousness in seven seconds or so. A noose of wire, however, offers no such mercy. It is death by strangulation, which can take minutes. Meanwhile, your feet are flailing, and the wire is cutting into flesh and tendons, and your tongue protrudes from your mouth. It's agony, and it's ugly."

Esa scanned the placement of the men in the room, and her muscles tensed.

The Benefactor smiled at that. "You have him in you," he said. "Your grandfather. You have your father in you, too. I owe both men very much, and because of that you will be given a chance to make up for your lapse in judgment. A plan is in the works, and should it come to fruition, you will have another opportunity at your original target. Do you understand?"

She nodded.

"Speak, please."

"I do."

The Benefactor removed another photo, but this time he handed it to Esa. She took it and looked at it.

"You live a rich life, Esa. I envy the freedom you enjoy."

The photo in Esa's hand was of her and the McQueen twins in her hotel room.

Captured by a hidden camera, it showed them engaged in a sexual act by the window.

He handed her another photo, and then a third.

Each one had been taken at different moments in their hour-long encounter.

"I understand that you are a deeply troubled woman," the Benefactor said. "And I understand why. As your grandfather's only companion, you were saddled with a particular . . . burden, one that no child should have to bear. But the greater the man, the deeper his darkness, wouldn't you agree? Your grandfather was a brutal man. He was brutal by nature and made even more so by the times he had been born into and lived through. The things that he did to you were an extension of that nature, I suspect. That's the thing about brutality. Once one has acquired a taste for it, going without it is all but impossible. So I understand why you are the way you are. Why you use others for pleasure, then leave them behind. And I understand why you did what you did in Bariloche. Maybe it was mercy, maybe it wasn't. If I were you, I'd want to kill my abuser, too. And I'd likely want to burn to ash everything that might one day remind me of him. But the man was like a father to me, Esa, and what son wouldn't want to avenge his father's murder?"

Esa had never told a soul about her grandfather's unwanted attention, which had begun when she was a teenager—well, had begun in earnest then.

That the Benefactor knew this secret, closely guarded for decades, meant that he held a power over her that she could not allow.

No man would have such power again.

It was this realization, more even than the threats he had spoken of, that formed in her mind the conviction to see him dead, and sooner rather than later. The Benefactor stood, picked up the stool, and started back toward Karl and the other man, speaking as he walked.

"You will kill your target this time. And there is a business arrangement I entered into decades ago that has become more trouble than it's worth. You will take care of that as well at no extra cost to me. To ensure your success, you will be teaming up with our two friends." He gestured toward the thugs. "Karl will command this operation. He will bring you up to speed once you're underway."

The Benefactor returned the stool to its place directly beneath the wire noose.

"Success will forgive your betrayal. The desecration is, I'm afraid, another problem for another time. A penalty of some kind should be paid, I think. We will come to our own arrangement, once your mission has been completed. But fail me again, Esa, and there is no place you can go where I won't find you, nothing you can do to keep you from a traitor's fate."

But his threats no longer mattered to her. She would see him dead.

The Benefactor turned to Karl. "Our contact assures us that our window should open within the next twenty-four hours. Be ready."

Karl nodded.

The Benefactor and the man he had called General started for the door, but it wasn't until they had exited the room that Karl or the two thugs moved.

Karl told them to take down the noose as he walked toward Esa.

She was on her feet before he had closed half the distance.

"I'll need shoes," she said.

"You'll be provided with everything you need. In the meantime, I have to prep you for travel. For obvious reasons, you can't know where we are."

"Cover my eyes or my head."

"I'm afraid I have to insist," Karl said.

He nodded toward the room behind her.

Esa glanced at the men working to disconnect the wire from the crossbeam before returning her eyes to the closet-size room.

Karl instructed her to sit on the cot, then swung the backpack from his shoulder and knelt down. Reaching into the pack, he removed a small plastic carrying case, laid it on the cot beside Esa, and opened it.

The case contained a clear glass vial and syringe.

Karl prepared the syringe, looked through the door at the two men in the center of the room. Seeing that they were occupied with their task, he said to Esa in a quiet voice, "He's going to kill you whether you succeed or not."

Esa said nothing.

His voice still low, Karl added, "But his two animals get to have their fun with you first."

He took hold of her right upper arm with his left hand, turning it to expose the underside of her forearm.

In his normal speaking voice he said, "You have good veins."

Karl found the same vein in her forearm as before and cleaned the area surrounding it with an antiseptic swab.

His voice quiet again, he said, "I've made a deal. Money and safe passage. But I could use your help. And it's clear to both of us now that you could use mine."

It took Esa a moment to speak. "What good am I if I'm unconscious?"

"This is just something for the pain. You'll have to convince Frick and Frack out there that you've been sedated. Can you do that?"

Esa nodded.

The dark-haired thug was on the top rung of a stepladder, a pair of wire cutters in his hand. His partner was standing beside the ladder, holding it steady.

He looked at Karl and Esa through the open door.

Karl eased the tip of the syringe into Esa's arm and slid the plunger forward slowly.

Esa waited until the blond thug looked away. "Tell me what you need me to do," she said.

Forty-Two

Tom asked, "Do you know what it is the bodyguard wants?"

"Money, a new identity, and a safe place to live."

"That's all."

"What more would he need?"

Tom didn't answer. He looked around the room. "Would you mind if I asked you a few questions?"

"No."

"Whose place is this?"

"It belonged to my uncle and aunt. They raised me."

"Where are they?"

"Dead," Slattery said. "A plane crash while I was in college."

"Is this place in your name?"

"What do you mean?"

"Their estate must have gone through probate. Is your name on the deed?"

"A trust owns it. My uncle set it up. I can assure you, Tom, no one knows about this place, not the Colonel, not Raveis."

"Your father knows, though, right?"

Slattery smiled, but it was the kind of gradual, perplexed smile that portends an uneasy denial.

"What are you talking about?" she said.

"You don't seem to have a history, beyond your work as an investigator in DC. That's what you did prior to your coming up here and working for Raveis, correct?"

"Yes."

"You're a military brat, aren't you? The people who raised you, they were military, moved around a lot."

"My uncle was an army officer, yes. But I don't see—"

"It isn't an easy thing to completely bury a past and become someone new. Trust me, I know because I tried once."

Slattery paused for a long moment. Finally, she said, "How did you know?"

"I was shown a photo of your mother and father at a Jerusalem café. You have your mother's face, even more so back when you were younger."

Slattery glanced at the photos on the mantel, then looked back at Tom.

"Hammerton," she said.

Tom didn't confirm or deny that.

"Is he British Intelligence?"

"No," Tom said. "He's exactly what he has said he is. So you're the only loved one Smith has left. That hospital bed in the other room, that's waiting for him, right?"

She nodded.

"What's Smith's real name?"

"Pintauro. Joseph Pintauro."

"And is Pintauro your real name?"

"No. My real name is Sheehan. That's what's on my birth certificate, that's who I was until after college. My mother and father hid my identity from the start, even from me. I didn't know that the people who raised me weren't my actual parents until after they died." She paused. "Like you, a lot was kept from me by the people around me."

"Why did your mother and father do that?"

"They were both operatives. There isn't much room in that kind of life for a child." She thought for a moment, then added, "If no one knew I was theirs, I'd never be put in harm's way." She shrugged. "Maybe they learned a lesson from what happened to your family."

Tom took a breath, let it out. "You said Angela was your first name. Is that Sheehan's first name, too?"

"No, Sheehan's first name is Colleen."

"How did Angela Slattery come about?"

"My father revealed himself after my aunt and uncle were killed. Creating Slattery was his idea. He obtained the documents necessary, got me my first job working for a senator he'd served with, so that solved the problem of there being no background to check. Every person who hired me after that did so based on Slattery's track record, as well as the recommendation from the one powerful senator."

"You've been building your cover for ten years," Tom said. "Your father has been grooming you for that long."

"Just like the Colonel has been grooming you since you enlisted in the navy."

"Your father got Raveis to hire you. That was part of his plan. So you could spy on him."

Slattery said, "Technically, the senator I was working for at the time recommended me to Raveis. Raveis needed an outside investigator, started asking his contacts in DC. It was the opportunity we'd been looking for."

"But the Colonel said you worked for him."

"That's what the Colonel thinks. I was working for Raveis for a week when the Colonel approached me."

"He doesn't know who you are."

"No."

"Why would your father keep that from him?"

"Because at the time he didn't know who he could trust. He had sacrificed so much to keep me safe up to that point, he wasn't going to take unnecessary risks."

"And now?"

"What do you mean?"

"He didn't know who to trust at the time. Does he now?"

"All evidence points to Raveis as the shadow agent, doesn't it?"

"Every piece," Tom said. "Is there any way you can contact Raveis? A back channel, a burner phone, a coded communication, anything?"

"No. Why? You want to draw him into a trap? We're supposed to sit tight, wait for the Colonel to find you a more secure location."

Tom said, "I just want to know all our options."

"Something's on your mind."

Tom shook his head. "How will the Colonel contact you? I mean, if he can reach you, then he can also find out where you are, no?"

"I have a burner phone that's turned off. Twice a day I'll drive to a random location five miles from here and turn the phone on and wait thirty minutes. If the Colonel doesn't call during that window, I turn the phone off and remove the battery and drive back." She paused. "Just like the system you and Carrington had in place back when you and Stella lived in Vermont."

Tom nodded. "You know a lot."

"It's my job to."

"What time will you make the first drive?"

"First thing in the morning."

"What time is it now?"

"It's almost midnight."

"And what about your father? Can you reach him if we need to?"

"We have no contact at all."

"You must have some kind of plan to communicate."

"Not until this is over."

Tom considered what it must be like to discover one's real father after the death of the man who had acted the part diligently—if those photos on the mantel were any indication.

He considered, too, what it would be like to then have to table getting to know that newly found man because of a long game that had to play out first—only to learn that the time to reunite and reconcile once the job was finally done would be limited to months or weeks or maybe even days.

The long list of people whose sense of duty had made it necessary for them to sacrifice time with a loved one had now increased by two.

"I'm sorry your father is sick," he said.

Slattery said, "Me, too." Then she glanced down at the tablet still in Tom's hand. "I'll take you and your friends to your rooms now, if you want. Is it safe for you to sleep yet?"

"Almost."

"I'll sit up with you until it is. We can talk."

"I'll be fine."

Slattery looked again at the tablet. "I'll be honest, Tom. I'm surprised my father included the surveillance video of your father's murder. I don't see why he would think you'd need to see that."

"My father died alone, surrounded by enemies," Tom said. "I couldn't be there then, but I can be his witness now. I owe him at least that."

The rooms were upstairs—Tom's at the end of the hallway, Grunn's before that, Hammerton's across from hers.

As they were heading to their separate quarters, Tom pulled Grunn aside and quietly told her that Krista was with Cahill, and that they and Stella were en route to an unknown but safe place.

He wanted her to know that the prolonged separation she and Krista had been enduring on his behalf would be over, maybe even soon.

There was little doubt in his mind that she was as eager to see the woman she loved as he was to see Stella.

Moments later, in his room, Tom sat on the edge of the bed and powered up the tablet.

The device wasn't encrypted, so he didn't need to enter a code.

Right there on the display was the folder icon marked VIDEO.

Tom opened it and selected the fourth of six files—where he had left off.

Adjusting the volume till he could hear his father's voice clearly, he once again watched the man he hadn't seen in more than twenty years.

As George Sexton had done in the previous videos, he spoke the same words of warning to Sam Raveis as Raveis entered the dimly lit office and came within the camera frame.

"My son's asleep upstairs, so we need to keep our voices down."

Forty-Three

Esa was hooded but fully conscious as the two thugs lifted her off the bed and carried her from the room.

She heard one of them ask Karl why the hood was necessary if he had sedated her, and Karl answered that it would take a few minutes before the drug would take full effect.

There was, he stressed, no point in taking the risk of her being able to identify their location.

Esa knew that the hood would also serve to spare her having to act as if she were succumbing to the sedation.

Any fault in her performance might raise suspicion in the minds of those two dangerous men, and it was crucial that they had no reason to be wary.

She could feel the painkiller Karl had administered in place of sedation starting to do its work—dulling her nerves and causing a lightness in her chest—but she wasn't so inured to pain yet that she didn't flinch whenever the rough way in which she was being carried caused a sharp tugging sensation inside her freshly sewn tissue.

It took a few minutes for them to carry her through the building—a journey that required they move through several doorways and down multiple flights of stairs.

Finally, she was put in a seated position inside a vehicle. A door immediately to her right opened and someone sat beside her, pulling that door closed. This was followed by two doors in front of her opening and the car swaying as two people took their seats.

She knew by this that she was in the seat behind the driver, placing the man beside her, who she believed was Karl, behind the front passenger.

The front doors closed, and the engine was started. By the sharp echo of the exhaust, she concluded that, given the industrial nature of the two rooms she had seen, the vehicle was inside what was likely a loading dock area.

It accelerated forward; within seconds the sound of the exhaust changed, and Esa knew they were outside. After several minutes of turns and stops, the vehicle entered a long straightaway and picked up speed rapidly.

Merging to the left, the vehicle increased its speed, then maintained it.

They were on some highway.

Esa did the only thing she could do: focus on her breathing, the sound of which was the loudest noise in her ears.

She did that until the painkiller took root and she felt adrift, as though she were floating effortlessly in warm, still water.

Regaining consciousness abruptly, Esa at first didn't understand the complete darkness surrounding her, but she fought back the urge to panic and soon enough remembered that she was hooded.

The next thing she realized was that the vehicle she was in had come to a stop, its engine no longer running.

The two doors in front of her opened.

This was immediately followed by the sound of a pistol fitted with a suppressor being fired.

One of the thugs, the blond, Esa thought, exclaimed, "What the—" but was cut off by a repeat of the same sound.

A quick follow-up, a brief pause, and then a fourth and final shot, and it was done.

Even with the hood still on, Esa understood what those shots had meant—a single round to the man in the passenger seat directly ahead of Karl, then a double-tap to the back, right quarter of the driver's head, then back to the first man for another round, just to be certain.

The hood was pulled from Esa's head, and there in front of her were the two dead thugs.

A burst of blood and tissue spatter covered the passenger-side windshield; a similar mosaic was visible on the driver's door window.

"Let's go," Karl said.

They exited the vehicle, an older-model sedan with heavily tinted windows. Esa looked around and saw that they were in an open-air parking garage.

By the look of the buildings beyond, it was obvious they were in New York City. Esa guessed they were on the west side of Midtown and at least seven or eight floors up.

Karl tossed the suppressed subcompact pistol onto the back seat, then peeled off his gloves and tossed them over the rail and into the air.

He closed both his door and the still-open front passenger door. Esa did the same with her door and the driver's door.

With the four doors closed, the only indication of the carnage inside the sedan was the bloodied front windshield, which faced the rail.

If no one took notice of that, it would be a day or two, maybe more, before the rotting bodies inside would smell enough to catch the attention of a passerby and cause them to alert the authorities.

Karl walked around the rear of the sedan, gesturing to the SUV in the next spot.

Still under the effects of the painkiller, Esa didn't move, just stared at the sedan.

Karl stopped midstride. "What's wrong?"

She shrugged and stared at the car for a moment more before turning her head and saying, "Shooting was too good for them."

Karl nodded in agreement. "We're on a schedule, Esa," he said. "We need to move."

The parking garage was located above the Port Authority Bus Terminal on Eighth Avenue and Forty-Eighth Street.

Ten minutes after leaving the structure, they were driving northbound on the West Side Highway.

Karl opened the compartment between them and removed two baseball caps, handing one to Esa and keeping the other one.

The long bills obscured their faces from the security cameras as they passed through the tollbooth at the Henry Hudson Bridge.

Thirty minutes later, the SUV crossed from New York State into Connecticut, and another thirty minutes after that, Karl steered off I-95 at a city called Bridgeport.

A few turns and they were approaching what looked to be an abandoned garage situated in a small, fenced-in lot.

Rolling through the open gate, Karl parked the vehicle and killed the motor.

Esa followed him through the open bay door, to the left of which was another bay. Beyond that was the entrance to an office.

Stepping through the next bay, Esa saw a man appear in that doorway.

He was in his sixties but powerfully built. His salt-and-pepper hair was buzzed close to his scalp.

Karl stopped a few feet from the man, waited for Esa to reach his side, then said to him, "I got her."

Looking at Esa, the man smiled. His expression struck her as both welcoming and fond.

"Do you know who I am?" the man said.

Esa shook her head. "No."

The man nodded. "Good. I can call you Esa, correct?"

"Yes. And what should I call you?"

"Why don't you call me what everyone else calls me."

"And what's that?"

"Colonel."

Even in her semiaddled state of mind, Esa understood whom it was she was standing before.

This man was the sworn enemy of the man for whom she had worked for four-plus decades.

As one of the Benefactor's best, she had hunted and killed numerous operatives of the man now smiling at her.

And it was impossible that this man didn't know that.

Esa looked at Karl before facing the Colonel again. "You've brought me here to see if you can turn me. You want my help killing the Benefactor."

The Colonel shook his head. "I'm seeking something simpler than that."

"What?"

"I need you to confess to something, in front of someone."

Esa once again looked at Karl.

The Colonel gestured toward the office behind him. "C'mon inside, the two of you; we'll talk."

Forty-Four

Tom powered down the tablet but remained seated on the edge of the bed.

It had taken nearly an hour for him to view all three videos. The two remaining videos of Raveis talking to Tom's father in his study were much longer than the previous three had been. Each nearly twenty-five minutes in length, they were more involved than the others, concerned with logistics as well as Raveis's continuing efforts at manipulation.

The unedited surveillance video of Tom's father meeting and ultimately fighting with the Algerian and his three men was the shortest of the three videos, running just ten minutes.

That time was broken into roughly eight minutes of tense conversation and two minutes of sudden and shockingly brutal violence.

Tom knew it would take a while before he could do anything more than sit still and relive what he had witnessed.

He knew no other way to process it.

Finally, though, he rose and stepped into the bathroom, running the sink faucet and splashing water on his face with trembling hands.

After that he took a moment to look at his reflection in the mirror.

He'd been exposed to violence many times before—more than he could remember right now, for which he was grateful.

And he'd also been forced to engage in life-and-death, hand-to-hand struggles of his own, the kind of intensely chaotic brawls during which he was close enough to the man who wanted to kill him to feel every one of his exhalations.

But viewing his father killing three men before he himself was killed—that was something else.

Maybe it was the fact that Tom could only watch, rendered helpless by time. Or maybe it was that he was viewing something that up till this point had been left to his imagination, only to discover that the actual events of that long-ago night were far, far worse than anything his mind could have manifested.

The hotel room had been small, that much he'd known, but just how small had stunned him.

At first this confinement had worked to his father's advantage, putting two of his enemies within easy reach. Making use of the other thing he had going for him—the element of surprise—he'd cut open the throat of the nearest man with a single sweep of the long-bladed knife that he had suddenly, expertly produced.

Then immediately altering the swinging motion, George Sexton had repositioned his hand so he could drive that same blade into the open mouth of the next man just as that man had moved to begin his attack.

Positioned as close as they were, these first two men had been easy kills, but Tom's father had been unable to remove the knife from the second man's skull with any semblance of speed, so he'd abandoned that weapon and reached for the small of his back, where a backup weapon—a spring-assisted folding knife with a four-inch serrated blade—had been hidden.

The third man had closed the distance and grabbed the collar of George Sexton's overcoat, but this had been, it turned out, a mistake, because George Sexton then ducked and spun out of his coat, showing an agility and level of skill that Tom had had no idea his father had possessed.

More than that, his father's actions had exhibited a cool that bordered on serenity, which was the opposite of what Tom had always seen whenever he imagined that night.

Tainted by the stories of a man driven to madness by grief, Tom had been expecting to see a fighter who reflected that—someone who screamed from the gut as he attacked, and whose reckless violence rose from a deep rage.

But the expression on his father's face was virtually blank, and his eyes were fixed on each of his targets in the manner of a craftsman carefully eyeing his work.

The third man had been stunned into a sudden halt by an upward slash to the groin, which had been followed by a thrust into the solar plexus.

He had dropped instantly, as though a trapdoor had opened beneath him, the knife still lodged in his heart.

And then it was just George Sexton and the Algerian, who had produced his own knife.

Tom had paused the playback there, to allow himself to prepare for what was to come.

When he was as ready as he was going to be, he resumed watching the two men engage in their fight to the death.

Tom's father had grabbed a lamp to use as a weapon, but as the struggle progressed, each combatant had effectively disarmed the other.

It was bare hands, then—vicious, close-in fighting.

The two men were evenly matched for a good minute, grappling on their feet before going to the floor.

One applied a hold, and the other escaped from it, applying a counter hold that was itself countered and escaped from.

In the end, though, the Algerian had gained the advantage, pinning Tom's father in a corner, allowing the man no route of escape.

Pressing his forearm down on the side of George Sexton's neck and crushing the carotid artery, the Algerian had waited till the lack of oxygenated blood had caused George Sexton to lose consciousness.

Their faces were bloodied, their eyes locked.

Then George Sexton's eyelids fluttered, his eyes suddenly glassy.

The Algerian had continued pressing his forearm down, holding it in place a long time, ensuring that the man beneath him was dead.

Tom looked down from the bathroom mirror, splashed more water on his face, then reached for a towel and dried himself.

He took one last look in the mirror before leaving the bathroom.

He heard a phone vibrating on his nightstand, where he'd put his few things.

Next to his Colt and burner phone was the smartphone Cahill had given to him.

Tom picked it up and looked at the incoming text message.

ARRIVED LOCATION, ALL SAFE, AWAITING INSTRUCTIONS.

Tom was tempted to instruct Cahill to bring Stella and Krista to Slattery's place, but that temptation was brief.

As desperate as he was to reunite with Stella, he knew he would need to wait.

He composed a reply and hit "Send."

HOLD POSITION.

A reply came through a few seconds later. U R SAFE?

Tom knew by the abbreviation and the phrasing—the awkward "you are" instead of the more common "are you"—who was texting him now.

He replied, YES.

This was his and Stella's first communication, albeit an indirect one, since their emails to each other nearly a week ago, which had been monitored and therefore didn't qualify as a free and intimate exchange.

They'd had no such exchange since parting ways months ago.

Still, knowing that Stella was standing beside Cahill and reading Tom's texts as they came in, then dictating her own, gave Tom a much-needed sense of connection, as well as a sliver of hope.

He had come far, but there was still an unknown distance yet to go before the goal they had both set out to accomplish would be complete.

For a moment he allowed himself to envision what it was they both wanted—to live quietly somewhere, free of the looming threat of the Benefactor and any and all obligations to shadowy men, free to make a living in whatever way suited them, spend their nights together, and wake next to each other every morning for the rest of their lives.

This was all that mattered, and Tom was resolved to do whatever it took to get to that world beyond the one in which they now dwelled.

Grunn and Hammerton took turns checking on Tom every hour to make sure he hadn't fallen into a deep sleep.

As each one entered, they glanced at the tablet but didn't ask the obvious question.

It was five a.m. when Tom heard the sound of one of the garage doors opening. Looking out his window, he saw Slattery driving off on her BMW motorcycle to await contact from the Colonel.

Tom took note of the time, calculated that she should return within forty minutes—ten minutes, at the most, to get five miles out; thirty minutes for her to wait; then another ten minutes, max, to return.

Barely fifteen minutes had passed when Hammerton came to Tom's door. "We've gotta roll."

"What's up?"

"Slattery said the Colonel wants to see us. Right away. She texted me the address where to meet them. You won't believe it."

Hammerton held up his cell phone so the display was facing Tom.

Tom read the address, and then he and Hammerton looked at each other.

"Full circle yet again," Hammerton said.

Grunn was behind the wheel of the Cherokee, Hammerton was in the passenger seat, and Tom was in the seat behind Grunn.

Once they were a few miles from Slattery's house, Tom used his burner phone to send another text to Torres, requesting that she check in.

He kept the text open and watched the display as he waited for a reply. After a few seconds an ellipsis appeared directly below his message, indicating that Torres—or someone—was replying to his text.

But almost as soon as the ellipsis had appeared, it disappeared, and when a minute passed without any reply, Tom pocketed the phone.

If it were Torres reading his request, why hadn't she replied?

It took forty-five minutes to reach their destination—a small farm atop a hill in a town called Watertown.

Tom and Hammerton had made this exact journey two years before, following their jump into the Quinnipiac River.

It was at this farm, owned by Sandy Montrose and her then-husband, a veterinarian, that Tom had found Charlie Cahill.

And it was also here that the Algerian had met his end at Grunn's hands.

Now the three of them were being brought back to this place for a meeting with the man whose "great experiment," as Smith had called it, had brought them all together.

Tom understood the likely reason for the Colonel having chosen this location—after the murder of her husband, Sandy Montrose had closed up the place, unable to bear the painful memories that now lived there.

Currently unoccupied, it would provide the privacy they needed, and its isolation atop a hill would make it easy enough for the small army of men with whom the Colonel always traveled to secure it.

As Grunn steered the Cherokee into the driveway, Tom was greeted by more or less the very scene he had been expecting.

The motorcade of four black SUVs—three Chevys and a Mercedes—was parked nose to bumper along the edge of the long dirt driveway, and two-man teams of suited bodyguards were positioned throughout the property.

Facing each other just outside the renovated three-story barn at the end of the driveway were the Colonel and Slattery, but there were two other people Tom didn't immediately recognize standing shoulder to shoulder a few feet behind the Colonel.

"Is that Cahill and Stella?" Grunn said.

There was a hint of excitement in Grunn's voice, and Tom understood why.

If this were Cahill and Stella, then Krista should be here as well.

Even at this distance, though, Tom knew that those two people weren't who Grunn had hoped, despite the fact that the woman bore a resemblance to Stella.

Tom would know the woman he loved from a mile away.

Grunn parked the Cherokee behind Slattery's motorcycle, shifted into park, and shut off the engine and lights.

It was not yet dawn, and though the sky was a patchwork of dark clouds, there were enough gaps between them for some starlight to show through.

This light was just enough for Tom to confirm the identity of the woman who was standing behind the Colonel.

His gut tightened as he felt rage rising like a fire in his heart.

Forty-Five

Esa watched as the occupants of the Cherokee exited the vehicle.

The first out was the front-seat passenger, and she recognized him from the files she'd been provided as being John Hammerton, former SAS.

Next was the driver, Sarah Grunn, one of the two women a surveillance camera had captured sharing an intimate moment on a back porch. Grunn was, of course, also part of the team that had taken Esa captive.

The third man was, of course, Sexton, the target of her failed assassination attempt.

Like the two before him, Sexton's eyes locked on Esa, but she saw in his stare the hard look of a man who was ready to kill—maybe even looking for an excuse to kill.

Esa noted that as the trio walked forward, the two-man teams standing guard on the perimeter adjusted their positions to prevent setting themselves up in a cross fire.

Any one of them—or all of them—could open up on Sexton and his friends without the risk of taking friendly fire.

Sexton's efforts to contain his anger were evident as he spoke to his commander. "What is she doing here?"

The Colonel raised his hand in a calming gesture, but Sexton ignored it and kept approaching steadily.

"She killed Garrick," Sexton said. "And Lyman and Durand."

"Things have shifted, Tom." The Colonel positioned himself between Sexton and Esa. "Lyman gave her no choice. I've seen video proving that. What was it your favorite philosopher said? The first law of nature is self-defense. As for Durand, a surveillance camera in the lobby of that safe house shows that she was killed by our own security team."

Sexton stopped several feet short of the Colonel. Esa got the sense that the two friends flanking him were prepared to grab him should he suddenly charge.

"I've always counted on your levelheadedness, Tom," the Colonel said. "You have never let me down once. I need to ask right now if you can ally with a former enemy, because that's what you'll be required to do if we're going to do what needs to be done."

Sexton's eyes remained fixed on Esa for a long moment. No one spoke. Eventually, Sexton broke his stare and looked at the man standing in front of him. "What's going on?"

The Colonel gestured to Slattery, who was holding a large folder, which she handed to Sexton.

He took it but didn't open it. "What is this?"

The Colonel answered. "That is definitive proof that Raveis is the shadow agent."

Sexton still didn't open the folder.

"Inside are the dossiers provided to our new friend here by the Benefactor prior to her op," the Colonel said. "Detailed files, Tom, on you and everyone you care about, complete with still photos, a number of which were taken by a surveillance team outside the Cahill estate on Shelter Island, a place very few know about. Even fewer knew you and your friends were there. The file on Stella includes a printout of a private cell phone photograph that she sent to you two years ago and that had been intercepted, along with all your text exchanges, by

Savelle, Raveis's contact at the NSA. You were promised that photo would be deleted, but it clearly wasn't."

Sexton glanced down at the folder in his hand before looking back at the Colonel.

"I told you, Tom," the Colonel said, "Raveis collects opportunities. He sees them in everything. It's his particular genius." He paused. "Raveis conspired with the Benefactor to have you killed—you and whoever happened to be next to you at the time. That included the men he'd sent to bring you back to him."

"Why?"

"Raveis lived for twenty years with the awareness that one day you might learn that he sent your father to his death. But there were purposes you could serve in the meantime, things you could do for us. Raveis was never one to squander an asset. Six months ago, though, he decided for whatever reason that he had pushed his luck and needed you dead. You were guarding the Nakash girl, Valena, and maybe he saw that as his best opportunity to get rid of you. He, as we've now learned"—he gestured to Esa and Karl—"was how the Algerian found you in Vermont, Tom. He leaked your location to the Benefactor and framed Carrington for it, then sent kill squads to silence him. But Carrington started digging and ended up joining forces with the one man who knew Raveis's secret, a man who is now motivated to clear his conscience. Raveis suspected that the information Carrington wanted to give to you was directions on how to meet Smith, so he made yet another deal with the Benefactor that was beneficial to both of them: he provided the Benefactor with the location of the meeting and the route you'd be taking back to New York. He had the explosive device planted on the vehicle. And the team the Benefactor sent to kill you would retrieve the information Carrington had provided, which Raveis would use to take out Smith."

"But the drive Carrington gave me was encrypted."

"Encryption only slows access, it doesn't prevent it. In the meantime, you'd be out of the way and your friends would believe that the Benefactor alone had had you killed. Raveis would be in the clear, and perhaps more importantly, he would be in the position to use your friends' grief and anger to manipulate them into doing whatever it was he wanted them to do. My guess is he'd peg Smith as the shadow agent and send your friends to hunt him down and extract him." The Colonel nodded toward the pair flanking Sexton. "Hammerton and Grunn here, as well as Stella and Cahill and the MacManus girl—they'd be unwitting pawns in Raveis's game. And if the op he sent them on didn't kill them, then once they served their purpose, whoever was left would be eliminated, too, because there'd always be the threat in Raveis's mind of one of them getting wise and coming after him."

Sexton remained silent. His only movement that Esa could see was the rising and falling of his chest as he breathed in and out.

Finally, he said, "How long has Raveis been making deals with the Benefactor?"

"From the start."

"Was the Benefactor behind the attack on my mother and sister? Did he play a part in the Algerian's hit team coming to my home?"

The Colonel nodded. "If your father hadn't been called away on a business trip at the last minute, he would have been killed that night. A decorated career operative murdered, along with his wife and daughter, in their home—assassinated by foreign agents—the outrage triggered by that would have opened the DOD coffers. Instead, Raveis had to wait another two years for his second chance. And when one didn't present itself, he decided to create it."

The Colonel paused before continuing. "I'm afraid your father wasn't the only one of us that Raveis betrayed over the years." He glanced at Hammerton. "Your former commanding officer, Tuoghy, was a friend of mine. I recruited him. Raveis conspired with the Benefactor to have him killed."

"How do you know this?" Hammerton said.

Esa answered that. "Because it was my op. The Benefactor sent me to kill him."

She watched as the physically imposing Brit hardened, his eyes locked on her.

The Colonel said, "It's time to end this, once and for all. This is what you've been waiting for, Tom. This is what you and Stella have trained for. I'm activating you. Unlimited budget, everything you need, anyone and everyone you want on your team, starting right now." He reached into his jacket and removed an envelope, offering it to Tom. "Cash, prepaid credit cards, and a series of phone numbers that will connect you with support personnel. Any tech or gear you might need, these people will get it for you."

Sexton looked at the envelope, then took it.

The Colonel said, "I've been informed by Karl that General Graves has taken over the Benefactor's security detail. His private army is made up of former US military. That's what we're up against, Tom. Fighting our very own." The Colonel stepped closer to Sexton. "I founded this organization to keep Americans safe. A system free of the whims of poll-obsessed politicians and the interference of bureaucrats. For every operation you know about, there are dozens you don't. Operations that took out imminent threats, hard missions carried out by dedicated men and women, some of whom paid the highest price in the performance of their duties. To continue doing what we do—what is necessary in these dangerous times—I need you to cut out the tumor at the heart of what I have given my life to. I need you, when the time comes, to hunt and kill Sam Raveis. With Raveis and the Benefactor gone, there'll be no reason for you to spend your life in hiding. I know that's what you want. That's the deal we made, and that's what I want for you, too. But we have to act fast, or we will lose this moment. We have a plan to take out the Benefactor tonight, and once that's done, your hunt for Raveis begins. We have to do what needs to be done, Tom, without hesitation or remorse. We have to be as ruthless as our enemy. I need to know if you can do that. I need to know that I can count on you to do what needs to be done when the time comes."

Sexton was staring at Esa when he answered the Colonel. "What's your plan?"

"I'll need to borrow Hammerton."

Sexton turned and looked at the Brit, who was also staring at Esa.

Finally, Hammerton glanced at Sexton and nodded.

Forty-Six

Grunn drove the Cherokee.

Ahead of them was Slattery on her BMW, leading them along back roads to her secluded home.

In the passenger seat, Tom was holding the cell phone that Hammerton had passed to him discreetly prior to their parting ways.

The Redcoats will answer this, Hammerton had said. *If there's trouble, any trouble, they'll be there for you.*

Back in his room in Slattery's house, Tom stretched out on the bed.

Though it was now safe for him to sleep, he was too restless to do more than lie still and stare out the only window, beyond which was a sky cluttered with black clouds that threatened rain.

The morning, as dark as dusk, seemed to only grow darker as the hours progressed.

On the table next to the bed were Tom's three phones—his burner phone, as well as the phones Cahill and Hammerton had given him.

Stella was reachable by one; Torres—if she was still alive—by another; and a contingent of former SAS was waiting on the other end of the third.

The SAS were a legendary counterterrorism group, and Hammerton, in Tom's eyes, had never once fallen short of that status.

Tom recalled the first time he had seen Hammerton—that night two years ago when a coded distress call had lured Tom into New York City to meet with Carrington.

That meeting had been brief—Carrington had simply needed to inform Tom that a man named Sam Raveis wanted to talk to him.

As Tom was driven away in an SUV sent to transport him to where Raveis was waiting, another man had joined Carrington, who was watching Tom from the sidewalk.

He had a shaved head, like Tom's was now, but a scarred, scowling face, and he was dressed in the manner of a private military contractor—black jacket, khaki pants, black boots.

Less than twenty-four hours later, Hammerton had saved not just Tom's life but also Stella's.

And it wouldn't be the only time.

Next to the phones on the nightstand was the envelope the Colonel had provided, along with Tom's sidearm and spare mags.

It was hard to avoid the fact that his life had been reduced to so little, but he didn't really care about that. If anything, the life he'd been forced to live these past months—moving from safe house to safe house, waiting to be activated, clinging to his memories of Stella during his long hours and days of inactivity—served to both reaffirm what mattered and allow him to let go of what didn't.

Stripped of excessive possessions and any semblance of a daily routine, Tom had been made free to focus on his one and only goal.

All that was required of him, in fact, was the patience necessary to wait for the day when he would be set loose.

He had thought of little more than that very moment of action, and it was, it seemed, finally at hand.

And yet the goalposts had been moved.

The man he had believed was his target—the Benefactor—was no longer his primary target, and the man who had provided him with every assignment, not to mention his training—Raveis—was now the obstacle standing between Tom and the life he desperately wanted.

I can see why you finally settled down, Raveis had said during their first meeting, letting him know that Stella's cell phone had been hacked and that all the communications between them—including the private pics she would occasionally send Tom while he was at work—had been intercepted. *She's a very attractive woman. In great shape for her age. And the pearls are a nice touch.*

Tom had almost bolted from that meeting, and a part of him wondered now what would have happened had he listened to his gut that long-ago night.

Would he and Stella still be in her apartment in Canaan, working long shifts, spending their nights together, waking beside each other at the crack of dawn every morning?

But there was a more pressing question on his mind: Of those who were dead, who might now be alive?

And another question: Of those still alive, who would be dead?

Tom realized quickly enough that there was no point in asking such unanswerable questions, but that didn't stop him from thinking of the peaceful existence he and Stella had made for themselves—the life they'd been living right up to the moment when Sam Raveis had entered it and forever altered their future.

He was still thinking of that life when, around noon, he unwound enough to drift into a heavy sleep.

Tom hears a sound from downstairs and sits up.

He is surrounded by darkness.

Reaching for the table beside his bed, he finds nothing but empty space.

No weapon, no cell phones, no light to switch on.

Rising from the bed, he crosses the room and opens the door.

The hallway is empty, but the sound—a door closing, coming from below—repeats.

Barefooted, Tom makes his way along the hall to the stairs, and then down those to the living room with the large fieldstone fireplace and stone mantel.

The house is utterly still in that way unoccupied spaces can be—dormant and lifeless, and eerie, like a museum after closing.

Tom hears the sound again, closer this time, and follows it to a room in Slattery's house that he has so far not yet seen.

The room is long and contains no furniture, but here the air is stagnant and cool, like the air inside a cavern. The only source of the noise that stirred him can be the closed door at the far end of that room.

Tom approaches it, feels no fear as he opens it, sees only an even deeper darkness within, and steps through anyway—only to find himself back in the storage facility's slow-moving elevator.

To his right is the young man, who says to Tom, "I told you, the surveillance cameras are being monitored." He pauses. "He's watching you."

The man is smiling in a friendly way, but Tom doesn't understand what his comment means.

Before Tom can say anything, though, a woman's voice comes from his left.

"Hey, Tom."

He turns and sees the young woman, the muzzle of a nine-mil Glock leveled at his chest.

The weapon is just inches away.

The woman says, "We gotcha," and fires.

Tom woke with a gasp, sat up, and moved to the edge of the bed to wait for his racing heart to slow.

Eventually he looked for the alarm clock on the nightstand and saw that it was four p.m.

He had slept for four hours.

If anything, though, this sleep had only made him more tired.

His heart was just calming down when one of the three cell phones on the nightstand vibrated.

It was the phone that Cahill had given him. Grasping it quickly, he looked at the display.

U R OKAY?

He thumbed the keys and sent his reply: YES.

Another message came through, and this one told him that Stella was the sender.

MISS YOU.

He replied that he missed her, too.

A half minute passed with no other message. Tom was returning the phone to the table when it vibrated in his hand.

He looked at the display.

HAVEN'T SEEN YOUR FACE IN SIX MONTHS. DO YOU LOOK DIFFERENT?

Tom smiled and replied, MORE HANDSOME THAN EVER.

Stella's reply was a pair of emojis—a smiley face and a red heart. This was followed by: SEE YOU SOON.

Tom keyed in YES and sent the message.

He was still smiling when he returned the phone to the tabletop, but the smile faded as he was struck by a sudden realization.

At first he wasn't certain what to make of it, but after a half minute he understood what it was he would have to do.

Forty-Seven

Tom gathered his belongings, pausing to check the phone that Cahill had given him.

Its call log contained only one incoming number. A single glance at the ten digits was all Tom needed to memorize it.

Exiting the room, he moved down the hallway to Grunn's room one door away. He opened it quietly and slipped inside, closing the door carefully behind him.

Facedown on her bed, Grunn was asleep, but she woke as Tom stepped toward her.

Reflexively, she reached for the weapon on the nightstand, but Tom placed his hand gently on hers and whispered, "It's okay, it's me."

Still on her stomach with her head raised, Grunn said, "What's going on?"

"I need to check something out." Tom placed one of his phones on the nightstand. "I want you to keep this for me."

Grunn turned onto her side, sat up, and looked at the device. "That's the phone Cahill gave you."

"Yeah."

"You'll need that to reach Stella."

"If things go bad for me, it's better if I don't have that on me. Someone could use it to get to her." Tom turned and started toward the door.

"Hang on," Grunn said. She got to her feet, dressed only in her underwear and a tank top. Tom turned and faced her. "Where exactly are you going?"

"The Colonel said something to me back at the garage. I didn't think anything of it then."

"What?"

"He knew that I had shaved my face and head."

Grunn nodded, still a bit groggy. "Yeah, Hammerton and I were right outside the door. I heard him say that. What of it?"

"The last time I saw him was more than six months ago. So how did he know that I had changed my appearance right before meeting with him yesterday?"

"I can think of a couple of reasons. He had a team watching your team. Maybe he saw the street-camera footage of you the New York cops have. He has connections in law enforcement."

"Maybe," Tom said. "But that young couple who tried to kill me in the storage facility—I was giving them the chance to walk away when the guy said something."

"What?"

"That the surveillance cameras were being monitored. He said it like he and his partner had no choice but to do what they'd been sent to do because someone was watching."

"And if the Colonel was the one watching, that's how he would have known that you had shaved off your hair and beard."

Tom nodded. "I'm tired, Grunn, and maybe my head is still all fucked up from the concussion, so I need you to tell me if I sound crazy. All the evidence points to Raveis and has from the start. And maybe all the evidence is right. But what if he's being framed? Just like Carrington was framed. Just like I would have been framed, if that's what it came to. What if I'm being manipulated to kill Raveis just like Raveis manipulated my father to go after the Algerian?"

"But that's the thing, Tom. Raveis *did* that. You saw the videos, right?"

"Videos don't always tell the whole story. And the tech you went to for help recovering the data works for the Colonel."

"You think they switched or altered the videos or something?"

"Just the last video."

"What makes you think that?"

Tom recalled Slattery expressing surprise that her father had included the video of George Sexton fighting for his life and losing.

Of course, he couldn't explain that to Grunn without revealing Slattery's secret.

Tom shrugged. "It doesn't matter. But every attack on me—whether the intention was to kill or to abduct me—was an attempt at keeping me from learning the truth. The hit as we were heading back to New York, and the hit as I was leaving the storage facility—they shared the same goal. They just looked different enough to confuse me into thinking it was possible they were ordered by two different people for two different reasons."

"But you're talking about the Colonel, Tom. You're saying he is somehow allied with the Benefactor. Why would he do that? Why build an organization and then secretly work against it? Why recruit and train the best people, only to sacrifice them—"

Grunn stopped short as she and Tom came to the same realization. "Hammerton is with the Colonel right now," she said.

Tom stepped forward and handed her another cell phone. "There's only one number programmed into this phone," he said. "Call it and tell whoever answers to stand by. Tell them I told you to call."

"Who am I calling?"

"Some of Hammerton's SAS buddies are waiting in his safe house. More are on the way. After I leave, wake up Slattery and tell her we need her to find out where the Colonel is and if Hammerton is with him. If Hammerton isn't, then we need to know where he is."

"And if she can't find out?"

"Then it's up to me."

"I can do more than that, Tom. Let me come with you."

"No, we can't risk the two of us. You're my liaison. If Slattery can't find Hammerton's location, but I do, I'll relay it to you, and you'll inform Hammerton's men. And if something does happen to me after that, at least you'll still be in the fight."

"So where are you going?"

"To talk to Raveis."

"I'm not sure that's a good idea. He's taken a lot of men with him. They might just shoot you on sight. And anyway, no one knows where he is. How will you even find him?"

"I'm pretty sure I know someone who knows where he is. Or at least how to reach him."

"Who?"

Tom ignored the question. "Getting Hammerton's men to him, that's your job, Grunn. That's what I need you to do. Once you've done that, get Krista and go somewhere no one can find you. Make sure everyone else scatters, too. Because if I'm right, if the Colonel is behind all this, then none of us is safe. I need you to promise me you'll do that, okay? Save Hammerton, then disappear."

Grunn nodded.

Tom started toward the door again.

"At least tell me where you're going," Grunn said.

"My guess is Raveis is somewhere in New York City still. If I can't reach him, then there's somewhere I can go where he might come looking for me."

"Tom, what if someone sees you there? The NYPD is looking for you. I think that's the last place you should go."

Tom exited the room without replying.

As he was moving down the hallway, the bedroom door across from Hammerton's room opened. Slattery was standing in it as Tom passed it.

It was obvious that she, too, had just woken up.

"What's up, Tom?"

"I'm borrowing a vehicle," he said.

"Okay. But, wait, where are you going?"

Tom didn't answer her, either. Nor did he wait. Reaching the stairs, he removed his last remaining cell phone and opened up his text conversation with Torres.

He recalled the night he was considering whether or not he wanted her on his team.

Initially, he had thought he'd be better off with someone who had a military background—and who wasn't so young. But Raveis had insisted that Tom look over her files carefully before reaching his final decision.

You'd be lucky to have her, Raveis had said.

He recalled, too, the unanswered text message, as well as the ellipsis he had seen shortly after sending his most recent communication.

Tom keyed in a message as he made his way down the stairs and was heading through the kitchen when he sent it.

CAN U ARRANGE MEETING WITH RAVEIS?

Entering the garage, Tom hurried toward the center bay and took the large four-pocket jacket and helmet off the wall.

Inside the helmet was a pair of insulated leather gloves.

The motorcycle nearest to the door was the one that Slattery had used this morning, so Tom went straight to the other one. The key was in the ignition. Gripping both handlebars, he leaned the bike upright and shook it twice.

The top-heavy feel of the bike, along with the lack of echo to the sloshing sound he heard, told him that its gas tank was full.

Tom was leaning the bike back down onto its kickstand when he felt the phone in his pocket buzz. Taking it out, he looked at Torres's reply on the display.

YES.

A second text came in almost immediately: WHEN?

Tom replied: ASAP.

He put the jacket on as he waited for her response, zipping it closed and fastening the waist belt.

He had balanced the helmet on the seat and was removing the gloves stuffed inside when her reply came through: WHERE?

Tom could think of only one place where both he and Raveis would feel safe.

He replied: HOTEL.

Then he sent a quick follow-up: TWO HOURS.

A few seconds passed, then her reply: ALREADY HERE. SEE YOU THEN.

Tom slipped the phone inside the top left pocket of the weather-resistant jacket and pulled on the full-face helmet.

Connecting the chin strap, he put on the gloves and mounted the bike.

An EZ-Pass transponder and an automatic garage door opener were attached to the inside of the windscreen.

Below the tachometer was a sticker that read: PROTECTED BY LOJACK.

Tom pressed the door opener. Pulling back on the clutch, he started the engine, dropped the shifter into first gear with his right foot, then eased out the clutch with his left hand and twisted the throttle with his right.

The door was not yet fully open, so he had to duck down as he sped out of the garage.

He followed the long driveway to the two-lane back road, and from there, reversing the circuitous route Slattery had taken when she brought them to her house, he drove south toward I-95.

Grunn was dressed and geared up when she heard the motorcycle exit the garage below and speed down the driveway.

Slattery entered, and Grunn passed on to her everything that Tom had wanted her to.

"But he wouldn't tell you exactly where he was going," Slattery said.

"No."

Slattery said, "Hang on," and left the bedroom in a hurry.

Grunn called the only number programmed into the second cell that Tom had given her. The male with a British accent who answered sounded guarded. Grunn stated what she'd been instructed to say—*Tom needs you to stand by.* The man's tone changed.

"Will do," he said.

Grunn ended the call, but with no other task to occupy her now, she felt a sense of helplessness.

In her other hand was the phone Tom had placed on her nightstand.

The one that Cahill had given Tom and that was Tom's only direct connection to Stella.

Grunn looked at the device for a long time before opening it and finding the only text conversation it contained.

Scrolling backward through it, she saw a mix of texts—some that were obviously from Stella, others that were from Cahill. She skimmed each one before composing her own message.

She sent it off just as Slattery returned to the room with a notebook computer balanced on her left hand.

Grunn saw that a program was up and running on the display.

The program showed an interactive map of Connecticut—its highways and streets.

Slattery was focused on a single dot in motion along a winding road as thin as a thread.

Forty-Eight

Tom was still a few blocks from the abandoned hotel in Brooklyn when the rain began.

Though it was a light, misty rain, the legs of his jeans were soaked through by the time he turned the corner onto the desolate street.

Parked outside the hotel was a fleet of vehicles, but it wasn't comprised of the Town Car and multiple black support SUVs Tom was expecting to see.

Raveis was on the run now, and those vehicles he typically traveled in, being company property or leases, were likely equipped with trackers.

The vehicles that Tom spotted were a mix of crew cab pickup trucks and Jeep Wranglers—the personal transportation of choice for the kind of former special operators who Raveis always kept close to him.

Tom circled the block several times, viewing as best he could all visible sides of the hotel while he made his first run, then studying the buildings immediately surrounding it as he made the following runs.

He hadn't seen anything he didn't like, but, really, would he have?

And, of course, one side of the hotel wasn't visible from the street at all.

Blocked from view by an adjoining building with just a narrow alleyway between them, it was that side of the hotel Tom had chosen to occupy during his stay, in a room with nothing but brick for a view.

Finally, Tom parked the motorcycle halfway down the block, killed the engine, and dismounted.

He unfastened the belt and unzipped the jacket so he could access his sidearm, then removed the helmet, revealing his face for the first time since he'd left Slattery's.

The anonymity with which he had made his way into and through the city had provided Tom with a real sense of comfort, but that was gone now.

This street, prior to Tom's taking up residence several days ago, had been assessed as being safe—meaning there were no city traffic cameras or business cameras that he was in view of now.

Still, he was exposed, but there was no avoiding that.

He tucked the gloves into the helmet, which he carried in his left hand as he approached the entrance to the hotel. He kept his right hand free.

The last time he'd been on this street was just shy of forty-eight hours ago, and he had been with his team, whom he had trusted with his life and who had trusted him with theirs.

But Garrick was dead, and Torres had turned out to be, at the very least, a Raveis plant.

Tom was alone, but he'd been alone before, and there was solace in that, because only his life was on the line.

Reaching the main door, he opened it and slipped inside.

Torres was waiting in the lobby, two men behind her.

Raveis's security detail was usually comprised of neatly trimmed men dressed in dark suits, but the two men flanking Torres were in civilian clothes—jeans, dark shirts, nylon jackets, and operator caps. One of them was wearing Merrell sneakers, the other 5.11 tactical boots.

Both were armed with HK416s—short-barreled carbines chambered in 5.56 that were the primary weapon of choice for elite special operation units, both in the US military and the militaries of numerous allies.

Equipped with Aimpoint Red Dot optics and SureFire weapon lights, the 416s were suspended via two-point VTAC Slings lying diagonally across the chests of their operators.

Suppressors extended the ten-and-a-half-inch barrels out to fourteen and a half inches.

Only the best for Sam Raveis.

Tom approached Torres and, anticipating that he would be required to surrender his Colt, he extended his arms out to the side.

"You can keep your sidearm," Torres said.

Tom lowered his arms as Torres turned and started toward the stairs.

The two men behind her parted, letting her through. Tom walked between them as he followed her. They held their positions by the entrance.

As he passed the door to the bar, Tom glanced into that room. Six more men, similarly dressed and equally geared up, were waiting inside. They watched Tom with stoic faces as he passed.

Climbing the first flight of stairs, Torres was ahead of Tom by a few steps. "I'm curious," she said. "When did you know?"

"That you could get me to Raveis?"

"Yes."

"Not until just before I texted you."

Torres smiled. "Raveis always bragged about how smart you are. Smarter than the smartest man he's ever known, which, of course, was your father. He was confident you'd figure it out sooner or later."

"I had help," Tom said.

They were close to the top of that first flight when Torres stopped and pointed at the step ahead. "This plank's rotted," she said. "Be careful."

She stepped over it to the next step. When he reached it, Tom did the same.

They were on the second flight when Tom said, "How long has he been here?"

"Since dawn. We were getting ready to bug out, so you contacted me just in time. If you thought to look for us here, then so might the Colonel, but that was a risk Raveis said we needed to take for as long as we could take it."

They climbed the remaining flights in silence. Every time they came to a questionable step, Torres warned Tom of it.

Eventually they reached the top floor. Another two-man security team was waiting halfway down the hall.

Torres stopped at the top of the stairs and gestured toward the room where the two men were standing.

The room Tom had occupied two nights ago.

"He's in there," she said.

Tom paused, not because he was wary of proceeding down the hallway but because he was impressed that Torres had at no point offered him an apology.

Nothing in her manner indicated discomfort, awkwardness, or regret.

She'd been given a job to do—keep tabs on her team leader for their employer—and had done it.

But she had also fought to keep her teammates alive, and had done so effectively and with courage.

Tom looked at her for a moment and said, "It's good to know you're not dead." Then he walked toward the door with the two men standing outside it.

They watched him carefully as he approached.

Reaching the door, Tom opened it and entered.

Forty-Nine

Raveis was standing in the center of the small room.

Tom closed the door. To his right was a broken-down dresser, and to his left was the bed where he had gotten his last real sleep.

A sound-enough sleep during which vivid dreams of Stella had flowed.

Though currently only occupied by two pieces of furniture and two grown men, the room felt crowded, and this reminded Tom of the confined space in which his father had fought for—and lost—his life.

Having seen the surveillance video, it was now clear to Tom that this space wasn't that much different from the room his father had been sent to by the man now standing five feet away.

Tom noted that like his security detail, Raveis had also given up his expensive suits for more durable and nondescript gear.

Another notable change Tom saw right away was that Raveis was armed.

A leather paddle holster at the two o'clock position on his belt held a Smith & Wesson M&P.

Raveis's leather jacket was open, allowing him easy and fast access to his weapon.

Neither man did anything other than look at each other for a moment.

"It's good to see you, son," Raveis said finally.

Tom wasn't interested in pleasantries. "I need to know where the Colonel is," he said.

"I'm afraid I won't be able to help you with that."

"Why not?"

"The man has been thinking moves ahead of all of us for two decades. You really believe he doesn't have an undisclosed location somewhere that he has managed to keep from us?"

"He tried to have me killed. Twice."

"I know."

"And now he has Hammerton."

"Of course he does."

"What does that mean?"

"You were always the ideal operative, Tom, as far as the Colonel was concerned, and for a number of reasons. He could dangle the chance of killing the Benefactor in front of you for as long as he wanted. What man wouldn't want to avenge his murdered family? And if you didn't want the Benefactor dead, if you didn't take that particular bait, then you'd definitely want the Benefactor dead because he was, as we have been telling you for two years, actively seeking to kill you and everyone you care about. This meant that in you the Colonel had someone he could use as he saw fit. More important, he'd be keeping a close eye on what he knew was a potential threat. As long as you didn't learn the truth, you were an asset. And if and when that changed, or if it even just looked like it was about to change, then he'd have you right there within easy striking distance. Of course, that's where it would end for you. An op would go bad, and you'd be killed in the line of duty, mourned by all who care about you. And then, lo and behold, your friends are now the ideal operatives. Their grief makes them easy to manipulate into accomplishing whatever suited the Colonel. False intel—so easy to manufacture—is all he'd need to have them eager to do his bidding."

"Carrington was set up, wasn't he?"

Raveis nodded. "The Colonel is very good at covering his tracks. And there's always somebody nearby to take the fall for him. Carrington took the fall for the Algerian finding you in Vermont. And I was to take the fall for your father walking into that hotel room."

"You talked him into it. I saw the videos."

"And yet you're here," Raveis said. "Nice to know that your tendency to give others the benefit of the doubt isn't just reserved for your friends."

"The tapes aren't the whole story, are they?"

"Far from it."

"So enlighten me."

"The truth is, as much as I'd like to claim innocence, it's the opposite. I manipulated your father into taking on a suicide mission. I instructed Smith to remain in the next room, no matter what happened. I betrayed my friend knowingly, all in the name of procuring DOD black-budget money. It was a sacrifice we had to make. The decision was ours—the Colonel's and mine, that is. We kept Smith in the dark on this one. Like you, he was burdened with a conscience. But he did what he was ordered to do—sit tight while your father was killed."

"You said the Colonel was responsible for the Algerian finding us in Vermont. Why did he do that?"

"To kill the Nakash girl, in part to cover up the fact that Ballantine wasn't a defector."

"If he wasn't a defector, what was he?"

"Part of an exchange program."

"Between the Benefactor and the Colonel."

"Yes. They realized at one point they could go on fighting each other—his people killing ours, our people killing his—or they could negotiate a détente that was beneficial to both parties. In exchange for the Benefactor staying out of the US, the Colonel would hunt and kill the Benefactor's rivals. If for some reason an operation had to be conducted on US soil, it had to be cleared through the Colonel and involve what he liked to call an adviser. Ballantine was one such adviser. With us eliminating his rivals, who just happened to be our enemies, the Benefactor faced limited competition abroad. He would rake in the money, and as long as the Colonel's organization was taking out terrorists and those who support them, we'd continue to receive DOD funding."

"The Colonel is his own shadow agent," Tom said.

"Exactly. Ballantine was in danger of being exposed, so the Colonel tipped off the Benefactor, and a ten-man team led by the Algerian came to your place. If the Colonel had to lose you, so be it. Business is sacrifice. But you beat those odds, you fought your way out, saved Stella and the Nakash girl, and to the Colonel's relief, one night later, you put a bullet into Ballantine's head. Evidence implicating Carrington was planted—evidence that turned Hammerton against Carrington." Raveis paused. "Division is useful; it's one of the Colonel's favorite tactics. In this game it was especially useful because it drove apart the two men the Colonel feared the most."

"Esa Hirsh claims she killed Hammerton's former CO. A year after my father was killed."

Raveis nodded. "Which meant you and Hammerton posed the same threat to the Colonel—you each would have a reason to come after him should the truth get out. It's interesting, Tom, that everything the Colonel ascribed to the Benefactor—that the Benefactor wanted you dead because you might one day come after him for killing your family—was also his fear. The fact that the Colonel had you trained to do the very things he feared you might one day do to him is a testament to what a gambler the man is. It's his pathology. And I'm confident it's what will one day lead him to his ugly end."

"How long has the Colonel had this understanding with the Benefactor?"

"It came about after your father's death. The attack on your mother and sister, that was real. That was an attack on all of us. That was a defining moment, and it brought all of us together for a time, at least. But then the Colonel made his deal—a deal that required the occasional sacrifice of our own people."

"Why, though?" Tom said. "Why sacrifice our own assets?"

"Our funding was dependent on fear. Absent a clear and present danger, our leaders tend toward complacency. A frightened government is one that pays. So when it became necessary, when all that we built was on the line, another tragedy involving one of our own was orchestrated."

"Hammerton's former commander," Tom said.

"Yes. Your death up in Vermont would have helped the cause as well. After all, what's an organization tasked with staving off chaos without chaos? What's a fire department without fire?"

Tom looked around the room. "And now you're on the run, just like Carrington."

"If only you'd had the good sense to die, Tom," Raveis mused. "Things would have been very different indeed. But you didn't, and the Colonel played the only hand he could—turning you against me so you'd kill me for him. I'm curious, what did he use to frame me?"

"Two years ago he told me that the Colt I'd used during my first op had been destroyed. But Smith had it, and he gave it to Carrington to give to me."

Raveis thought about that. "That was it?"

"No. The cell phone pic of Stella that your NSA friend intercepted. It was in a file that was given to Esa Hirsh by the Benefactor. The file also contained dossiers and photographs of everyone I know. Some of the photos had been taken outside the Cahill estate on Shelter Island by a surveillance team. No one but you and the Colonel knew we were there."

Raveis smiled. "And of the two of us, who was the bigger asshole?"

Tom understood that to be a rhetorical question, so he didn't answer it. "If my getting killed was better for you, then why did you give me the vest?"

Raveis smiled again, knowingly this time. "A lapse in judgment," he joked.

Tom thought about that for a moment, remembered his conversation with Torres after she had looked over the blueprints to the factory. "Before I left to meet Carrington, Torres tried to talk me out of going. You sent her to do that."

Raveis nodded. "Yeah. I knew something more was going on. If this was the Colonel making his play against you, I couldn't stop you from going, not directly, not in front of Slattery. But I could do whatever it took to give you a fighting chance at getting back alive. The vest, some of my best men to escort you back, Torres next to you to keep an eye on you for me—whatever I could think to do, I did."

"Why couldn't you say anything in front of Slattery?"

"Let me put it this way: you weren't the first one to try to find out what you could about her. If Torres had run the plates like you'd asked, she would have hit the same roadblock I hit, which is that Slattery's vehicles are all registered to a limited-liability corporation out of New Haven created by an attorney over a decade ago. She—Angela Slattery, that is—owned nothing, had no history that went back further than ten years. People with no past have no past for a reason, Tom. I decided to work with her under the assumption that she was working for the Colonel. I said nothing in front of her that I didn't want the Colonel to know. There were even occasions when I intentionally offered her misinformation. This is the life we live."

"But you and I were alone in your garage after she left. You could have said something then."

"Have we ever really trusted each other, Tom? And what if the Colonel had gotten to you already? What if he had turned you against me? That was always part of his plan—just one of his many possible uses for you, and one of the many possible outcomes for me." He paused. "The problem with making a devil's bargain is you're bound to the devil for the rest of your life. And if, like me, you know things that the devil doesn't want anyone to know, then he sees you as a problem that he will someday have to deal with. Two mornings ago, riding with you and Slattery, I was wondering if that day had finally come. By later that night, when you were attacked by one of the Benefactor's best—an attack that killed some of my best—I knew that day had arrived."

"The Colonel is cleaning house."

"Yes."

"Why now, though?"

"Carrington got his hands on the evidence Smith had stolen before he disappeared. It wasn't just the videos, it was documents, too. The genie was out of the bottle, and the Colonel knew there was no putting it back, which meant he'd have to kill everyone who knew about it. You, me, Smith. It was smart for you to get Stella out when you did. If Cahill had gotten there an hour later, she'd be in the Colonel's hands now, too."

Tom didn't want to imagine that. He took a breath, let it out.

"It's difficult to control a man who has nothing you can take away from him," Raveis said. "After your discharge you roamed around alone for five years. The Colonel just waited that out, knew it would change sooner or later. And then Stella came along. Obviously there is nothing you wouldn't do to keep her safe. The Colonel knew then that he could use you. And as time went on, the list of pressure points grew. Cahill, Hammerton, Grunn, MacManus, Montrose, Garrick, Torres—an embarrassment of riches for a man like the Colonel. And if there's one thing we've learned about you over these past two years, Tom, it's that the scars you carry because of what happened to you—not the physical scars on your chest from Afghanistan but the emotional scars because you were unable to save your family—those very scars are what make you vulnerable to that exact kind of manipulation we're experts at applying. I'm sorry to say it, Tom, but it's that very weakness in you that the Colonel is banking on now."

"Hammerton is bait."

"The Colonel knows you won't run and leave Hammerton for dead, though you should. He knows he can use Hammerton to draw you back out into the open if he needs to. He would want to cover every contingency, which includes the possibility of you and me doing what we're doing right now. Another contingency he would prepare for is the possibility of your friends learning the truth at some point as well. Grunn, Cahill, Stella—every one of them will die. He'll use them for a while if he can, send them on ops until he doesn't trust them anymore, at which point he'll send them on a suicide mission. Just like your father. Or maybe he'll just play it safe from the start, lure them out as soon as possible, using you or a video recording he made of you before he killed you or cryptic texts asking for help that your friends think are from you. Either way, he'll get them to come to him, and one way or another, when it suits him, he will kill them."

No one spoke for a moment.

Finally, Raveis said, "I won't insult you by saying that I could always use more people on my team. We're both hunted men. Strength in numbers and all that. But there's no time to go back for Hammerton. We leave the city tonight."

Tom shook his head.

"You won't ever find me once I disappear. There won't be any codes or ciphers, no secret back-channel communications like you and Carrington had. I can't risk the chance of someone using you to draw me out into the open."

"I understand," Tom said.

"I'm sorry I can't help you. But I can tell you this: if things go south for him, and he wants you to find him, like I wanted you to find me, then he left you a way. What's the point of him taking Hammerton as insurance if he can't bait you with him? Did the Colonel give you a cell phone, or maybe a number to call in case you got into trouble, anything like that?"

"No. But Slattery has a cell he calls at certain times during the day. She drives to a safe location to take the calls, keeps the phone shut down the rest of the time."

"Then that's how he'll get you. When the time is right for him. Unfortunately, that puts Slattery on the kill list, too."

"There has to be a way to reach him."

"This is the Colonel, Tom. This is what he does, who he is. Like I said, unless he wanted you to find him—"

"Cahill," Tom said.

"What about him?"

"The Colonel called Cahill. He made a point of telling me he had called him."

"Then that's how you can reach him. But it also means it's possible that he knows where they are."

Tom turned, exited the room, and headed toward the stairs. The cell phone was in his hand as he took the first flight.

The phone's signal was weak, and what Tom had to communicate was too much for a text anyway, so he focused on getting down to the lobby as fast as he could so he could call.

He remembered where the rotted steps were, slowed as much as he dared as he approached them, then skipped them and resumed his quick descent.

Reaching the lobby, he bolted for the door. Torres was on her cell phone—Raveis had likely called her to instruct his bodyguards to stand down.

Baffled but motionless, the men watched as Tom moved past them and exited the hotel.

It was raining harder now, but Tom didn't care. Entering Cahill's number, he pressed the "Talk" button and brought the phone to his ear.

As it rang he saw three of Raveis's men step out onto the sidewalk, positioning themselves like sentries—one looking east, another looking west, the third scanning the buildings across the street.

Torres stepped into the hotel doorway and watched Tom.

The phone rang three times before it was answered. Tom heard Cahill's voice and felt a wave of relief.

"It's me," Tom said. "You need to relocate."

"What's going on?"

"I don't have a lot of time. Go somewhere else, don't tell me where. And after we hang up, ditch this phone."

"We won't be able to reach you."

"Tell Stella we'll use the system we put in place the last time we were together. She'll know what that means. I'll use it to reach out when I can."

"Tom, what's going on?"

Tom didn't respond at first. He considered the possibility that this call was being monitored. The Colonel had the resources for such a thing. And if the Colonel or someone working for the Colonel was listening in, then this was Tom's chance to prove that Cahill and those with him didn't know the truth.

But Tom knew that was a foolish hope, and anyway, Cahill needed to know, just like Tom had, exactly what it was he would be running from.

"The Colonel has betrayed us," Tom said. "The Colonel is the shadow agent."

There was a moment of silence. Finally, Cahill spoke, his tone grave. "What else do you need from me?"

"The Colonel called you last night. I need the number he called you from."

Fifty

Soaked through, Tom was in the hotel bar, facing Raveis and Torres.

Raveis said to one of his men, "Get him some clothes."

That man passed the order on to another, who left the room.

Tom heard the hotel door open, the sound of the driving rain echoing down the entranceway. The door was closed again, and the sound diminished sharply.

"So what's the plan, Tom?" Raveis said.

"The Colonel likes to make deals. So I'll make him one."

Torres asked, "What deal?"

"Me for all of them. In exchange for my life, he forgets about the others. He can kill me or employ me, but they go free."

"That won't be enough," Raveis said.

"It's all I have."

Raveis glanced at Torres. She watched him, waiting. Finally, he nodded, and she stepped to the bar, opened a small backpack laid upon it, and removed her tablet.

As far as Tom could tell, it was the same tablet she had used to show him the blueprints of the abandoned factory in Ansonia.

Walking back toward him, she began touching the display with her index finger, navigating an app.

"Smith wasn't the only computer whiz we employed," Raveis said. "And he wasn't the only one to collect evidence."

Torres reached Tom and pressed the display with her finger a few more times before handing him the device.

Tom saw a list of documents contained in a secure cloud backup system.

Among the Excel and Word documents was a mix of audio and video files.

"My insurance policy," Raveis said. "All the evidence needed to bring the Colonel's world crashing down around him."

"You hacked him."

"Some of those are his private documents, yes. Correspondence, bank records. The audio recordings are of conversations between him and me that I'd made without his knowledge. The videos are surveillance clips documenting his travel over the years, one of which is of particular interest."

Torres reached over, located the video file Raveis was referring to, and touched it with her fingertip. After a short lag, a media player opened up and the video played.

There was no audio, and it was obvious that the camera was handheld.

The camera operator was inside a vehicle, shooting through the driver's door window. For a few seconds the screen went dark as the camera was lowered behind the door.

When the camera was raised again, it was aimed at a doorway located directly across a city street.

Tom noted that the signs above the stores, as well as the traffic signs along the street, were in Spanish.

The newer-looking vehicles visible in frame—some parked, others passing between the camera and the doorway—were at least twenty years old.

Several men entered the picture, and the camera operator zoomed in on them, revealing the Colonel and his security detail.

They moved through the doorway, and the camera zoomed out again.

The playback continued for another half minute before another group of men entered the frame. Torres waited until the camera zoomed in on the man in the center of that group before reaching across the screen again and pressing "Pause."

Tom was looking at a man in his forties. Dark hair, handsome, well dressed.

"That's the Benefactor," Raveis said.

It was the first time Tom had seen the man's face.

There was nothing about it to indicate that he was a mass murderer capable of unspeakable cruelty, the ideological child of the twentieth century's vilest monsters.

Tom handed the tablet back to Torres and said to Raveis, "So why are you running if you have this?"

"Because what brings him down also brings me down."

"You could cut a deal with the prosecutor, turn state's evidence."

"We're guilty of treason, Tom. I'm talking about the literal, constitutional definition of treason. We aided the enemy in a time of war. There is no deal I'd get that wouldn't include prison time, and I'm not going to prison."

"What good do these files do me?"

Raveis nodded to Torres, who once again navigated the open app on her device.

After a moment she looked up and said, "It's on its way."

A few seconds later, the cell in Tom's pocket vibrated.

He took it out and looked at the display.

Torres had sent a copy of that video via text.

"That should get his attention," Raveis said. "At least he'll know you have something more than your life to negotiate with."

"I need to do more than just get his attention."

Again, Raveis looked at Torres, and again she went to work on the device.

Tom's phone buzzed again. The text she had sent him included a link to the cloud storage as well as the username and password Tom would need to log in. He allowed himself the seconds it took to memorize the information.

"It's yours to use," Raveis said. "If you use it right, maybe you and Hammerton can get out of this alive."

"You said this evidence incriminates you, too. What if I have to turn it over to the feds? They'll be after you."

"By the time that happens, I'll be long gone. They won't find me. No one will." He paused. "Anyway, I let my friend die. The least I can do is to give his son a shot at avoiding the same fate."

It took Tom a moment, but finally he said, "Thanks."

The door to the hotel opened and closed again. The bodyguard returned with a duffel bag. He handed it to the man who had ordered him to retrieve it.

That man placed it on top of the bar and unzipped it.

He removed a pair of tactical pants, a T-shirt, and a light jacket, all of which were black, as well as a pair of socks and boots. He stacked the clothing and carried the pile to Raveis, handed it to him, then went back for the boots.

Raveis held the pile out for Tom, who began to undress, first by removing his sweatshirt, which revealed the Kevlar vest he was wearing beneath.

Raveis's eyes went to the marks in the material left by the two rounds that had struck Tom.

"He'll need a new vest, too," Raveis announced.

His men moved to carry out that order as Tom continued to undress.

"It's not just the Colonel and his men you'll have to contend with," Raveis said. "He made a deal with the Benefactor's bodyguard. A man named Karl Weber. Remember, the Colonel's housecleaning includes the Benefactor, too."

"Esa Hirsh is with them," Tom said. "I saw her with the Colonel this morning at Cahill's old safe house."

Raveis nodded. "The Colonel doesn't miss a trick."

"What does the bodyguard stand to gain for his betrayal?"

"Once the Benefactor is eliminated, the bodyguard replaces him. The détente continues, except this time with more favorable terms for the Colonel. They have been working on this for a while. The bodyguard knows everything the Benefactor knows. He has been watching the man for over a decade. It will be a seamless transition."

Tom had removed all his clothing. The cold, dormant air rushed across his still-damp skin as he reached for the pants atop the pile Raveis was holding.

Torres was looking at the scars on Tom's torso, but there wasn't anything he could do about that.

"Why didn't the bodyguard just assassinate the Benefactor instead of defecting?"

"Without the Benefactor, there was no keeping you in line. Maybe you'd find out, maybe you wouldn't, but the Colonel didn't want to take that risk. He needed you where he could get to you when the time came. But that doesn't matter anymore. Now the Colonel needs you both dead. Here's the ironic thing, Tom: you've only lived this long because the Benefactor was alive. You were trained to kill him, and it's the job you were waiting all these months for, but killing the Benefactor wouldn't have set you free. It would have marked you for death. You would have remained a hunted man, only this time you'd be sought by the men and women who've had the same training as you, who may have even worked beside you at some point. You wouldn't have known who to trust. And I'm sorry to say, you wouldn't have lasted very long."

Tom didn't see any point in dwelling on that fact.

"Anything else you can tell me?" he said.

He had pulled the pants and T-shirt on, and then was handed a new Kevlar vest. As he put that on, Torres moved behind him to help him adjust the fit.

"You'll need to pick the right location for the meeting," Raveis said.

Tom nodded. "I know."

"You'd better have a good plan. And help."

"I'll have both," Tom said.

It was at best a half truth.

He had a plan, and only time would tell how good it was.

As for help, Tom was determined to put no one but himself at risk.

He finished dressing, then transferred his holster and mag carrier to his new belt and removed his belongings from the pockets of his jeans, placing them into the pockets of the tactical pants.

Raveis watched him, waited till he was done and ready before saying, "Keys."

The man who had jumped at all his orders so far stepped to Raveis and handed him a set of keys.

Raveis held them up for Tom to take. "There's a black Rubicon parked outside. This rain is only going to get worse, and in a few hours the winds will be gusting at up to fifty miles an hour, so that bike isn't going to cut it for you. You'd be in a pretty sorry state by the time you got back to Connecticut."

"What makes you think I'm going to Connecticut?"

"You were a Seabee, Tom. You not only constructed bases but also protected them. There's only one location that offers the advantages you'll need."

Tom said nothing.

"The Rubicon has a dashboard-mounted computer. Torres will email the blueprints to it. You'll need them. That factory is a maze."

Tom looked at Raveis's men one by one. Then he faced Raveis and Torres again.

“Thanks,” he said.

It was more than the comfort and safety the Jeep would afford that Tom appreciated.

Slattery’s motorcycle was equipped with LoJack, and Tom had no doubt that she and Grunn had tracked his movements to his current location.

Leaving the motorcycle where it was eliminated the possibility of their following him to his next destination.

Raveis wished Tom luck.

Torres said nothing, simply looked at Tom, smiled, and nodded.

Tom turned and exited the room.

One of the men guarding the doorway held up a black duffel bag as Tom passed him.

Tom stopped, then took the bag from the man.

By its weight Tom knew what the bag contained.

Fifty-One

The Rubicon limited-edition Jeep Wrangler was the last in the line of a half dozen vehicles parked on the street.

Behind the wheel, Tom started the engine and touched the computer's keyboard to wake the system. The blueprints were already there. He clicked on the file and waited as it opened.

On top of the shifter knob was an operator's cap. Tom put it on. The duffel was on the passenger seat, and Tom unzipped it and looked inside.

It contained a suppressed HK416 and a battle belt with three double-decker mag holders attached. In each holder was a thirty-round mag. The belt also held several other carriers, one containing a bleed-out kit, another, a multitool.

The last items in the duffel were two mags joined together by a coupler.

There was for Tom no avoiding the fact that a short-barreled carbine equipped with a suppressor and capable of automatic fire was prohibited under federal law, and that magazines with capacities greater than ten rounds were illegal in both New York State and Connecticut.

There was also no doubt that the credentials Tom was carrying, which had been provided by the Colonel, were no longer valid.

But there was nothing he could do about that.

What he needed to do would require more firepower than the Colt M45A1 holstered on his right side afforded him.

Tom zipped the bag closed and laid it on the floor in front of the passenger seat.

Once the file was opened, Tom scrolled through it fast to make certain the document was complete.

The plans for all four wings and the courtyard, as well as for all four floors and the basement, were there for him to study.

Shifting into gear, he pulled away from the curb.

Ansonia should have been a ninety-minute ride, but there was rush-hour traffic.

And just as Raveis had said, the rain grew heavier and the winds stronger, sometimes gusting with such force that the Jeep veered in its lane.

Added to that was the fact that the last thing Tom needed was to get pulled over for speeding or find himself party to a fender-bender—or worse.

As a result, it was three hours before Tom steered off the Merritt Parkway and onto Route 8 northbound.

With Ansonia just fifteen minutes away, he pulled over and took out his cell phone, entering the number that Cahill had sent him into the message app and attaching the video file that Torres had provided.

He thumbed in a four-word message—SEND THE COLONEL. TOM—and sent the text.

As he waited for a reply, he went ahead and composed a follow-up text.

This one contained the coordinates he'd been shown by Slattery two mornings ago.

41° 20′40.7″ N, 73° 04′42.9″ W

He was entering the last few numbers when a reply came in.

LOCATION?

Tom keyed in the final number and pressed "Send."

There was just one more instruction he needed to pass along.

BRING HAMMERTON.

Then Tom shut down the phone, lowered the window, and tossed the device as far out into the darkness as he could.

Pulling back onto the highway, he resumed his journey northward.

Tom circled the block occupied by the abandoned factory several times.

The small city had appeared desolate when Tom had stepped off the train just minutes before midnight two nights ago.

Now it was even more so, but the pounding rain and monsoon-like winds did that.

As Tom scanned the building, he saw nothing different about it.

The same number of windowpanes was smashed out, and through them he could see an interior faintly illuminated by the streetlights, though as he studied the upper-floor windows, he noticed that his view was limited to the ceilings.

Just like Carrington had, Tom would choose the upper floor for his meeting place, if only to keep himself and the Colonel out of the view of anyone passing by on the street below.

It was possible that the Colonel would arrive with some degree of security in tow, which was why Tom hadn't bothered to include in his instructions the demand that the Colonel come alone.

And it was just as possible that Tom would be disarmed by whomever was accompanying the Colonel.

But Tom had a plan for that.

He continued to circle the block, this time scanning the windows of the apartments across from the factory.

In one dark window he saw what looked like the silhouette of a seated man looking out. The figure didn't move as the Jeep passed. Tom made one more revolution—his fourth—but this time the figure was gone.

He parked the Jeep a block away, then grabbed the duffel bag and got out.

Moving around to the rear bumper, he opened the hatch and searched through the gear stored in the back compartment. The elevated hatch protected him from the hard-hitting rain.

Tom found a rolled-up military-surplus wool blanket, put it into the duffel, then closed the back hatch and headed toward the entrance he had used two nights ago.

The building was unheated and exposed to the elements, and Tom might need the blanket to keep warm as he waited.

The jacket and hat protected him from the downpour, but the wind blew the rain sideways at times, spraying his pants legs with sheets of cold water.

He'd anticipated having to overcome a locked door, had learned during the first weeks at Raveis's compound how to do that, but as he approached the entrance, he saw that it was slightly ajar.

Slowing almost to a stop, he considered what that could mean, but then he resumed his steady stride.

There was no turning back.

Reaching the door, he laid the duffel down and opened it, removing the HK416 and slipping it into its sling. He grabbed the coupled mags, inserting the right-side mag into the mag well, then drew back and released the charging handle, chambering a round.

Thumbing the safety on, he shouldered the duffel bag, then stood ready.

A light was attached to the front end of the Picatinny rail, its activation pad taped to the right side of the foregrip. Tom knew not to switch on the light until he was inside.

As he had done before, Tom pulled the door open just enough to slip through. Balancing on his right foot, he eased the door closed behind him with his left foot.

Facing forward, he shouldered the carbine as he lowered his left foot to the floor. He was about to take a step into the vast room when he heard a sound and froze.

Someone was to his immediate left and moving toward him.

He heard the sound of fabric swishing and heavy feet on the rotting floor directly ahead of him.

Out of these vague sounds came a specific one: the click of a safety being disengaged.

It was immediately followed by a man saying, "Don't move, partner."

Tom ignored his words, dropping into a crouch and activating the rail-mounted light with his right hand as he thumbed the safety to the "Fire" position with his left.

In this dimly lit space, the 600-lumen light was as bright as a camera flash.

Tom saw a man standing just a few feet in front of him—a man with a surprised look on his face who yelled, "Shit!" when he saw that Tom was armed with more than just a pistol.

Before the man could do anything more than that, Tom put two rounds into his chest, dropping him.

The man to Tom's left, holding a Beretta 92, had aimed the weapon at the side of Tom's head—or rather, where he had estimated in the dark that Tom's head would be.

Tom turned, lay on his back on the floor, and aimed his carbine up at the second man.

He looked just as surprised as his associate, but he was adjusting and bringing his pistol to bear when Tom fired two rounds into his torso.

That man fell, and Tom scrambled back to his feet, stood over the second man, and fired a single round into his head, then quickly did the same to the first man.

Without hesitating, Tom displaced, scanning the room with his light as he moved from position to position.

Only when he was certain there were no more men on that floor did he allow himself a moment to gather his thoughts and catch his breath.

Raveis had anticipated that Tom might come looking for him at the hotel, and it was clear that the Colonel had had the same idea about this location.

No doubt the Colonel, after receiving Tom's texts, had alerted his men that Tom was on his way.

Had Tom not been better armed than they . . . Well, he didn't want to think about that.

It took Tom fifteen minutes to clear the rest of the building—all four floors of all four wings as well as the basement. He kept his light off as much as possible.

With that done, he began his preparations.

His first stop was the fourth floor, where his Colt 1911A1 was hidden.

Reaching through the hole in the wall and grabbing the leather bag, he removed and opened it, took out the pistol, and freed it from the baggie. As he returned to the third floor, he removed the magazine, which was empty, and inserted one of the Wilson Combat mags that Cahill had given him.

Chambering a round and engaging the safety, he searched for a loose-enough floorboard, finding one and prying it free with his knife, then placing the weapon in the dark crevice and laying the board back in place, being careful not to fully seat it.

He was facing the same row of windows overlooking the courtyard that he'd faced during his meeting with Carrington.

It was here that he would make his stand.

Moving into the dark corner to his right, he switched from the semidepleted mag to the full one, then unslung the carbine and leaned it against the wall. He removed the battle belt from the duffel and placed it on the floor next to the weapon before walking to the dark corner to the left.

There he drove the tip of his knife into the floorboard, leaving it standing grip-up and ready for him to grab.

A weapon of last resort.

Removing the blanket from the duffel and tossing the bag aside, he returned to his last-stand position by the center of the five large windows.

He performed a brass check on the M45A1 before returning it to its holster.

The SureFire light Cahill had also provided was in Tom's left pocket. He removed it, checked that it was in working order, and tucked it into his waistband right behind his belt buckle.

He unfolded the wool blanket, wrapped it around his shoulders, and waited.

Twenty minutes later Tom heard the sound of the door below opening, followed by footsteps that stopped abruptly. He knew this meant that the Colonel's advance security team had encountered the two dead men.

The hesitation didn't last for long, though, and Tom dropped the blanket from his shoulders as he listened to the men make their way upward, floor by floor.

It was when those men were on the floor below that Tom heard another noise, this one from the wing on the other side of the courtyard.

He looked toward the broken window across the way, and for a second he thought he saw someone move into a dark shadow.

Tom watched that same space for more movement but saw nothing.

He was forced to look away when the Colonel's three-man team entered and fanned out.

Converging on him, they stopped just a few feet away, their suppressed M4 carbines trained on him.

Tom raised his hands.

The center man stepped forward, reached for Tom's waist, and pulled his sidearm from its holster. The man passed the weapon to one of his partners before cautiously patting Tom down from ankles to collar.

In his search for a backup weapon, the man missed the SureFire light hidden behind Tom's belt buckle.

Rejoining his men, the center man clicked a walkie-talkie attached to the shoulder strap of his carrier vest and said, "Secure in here. Proceed."

A reply came through: "Roger that."

A moment passed before Tom heard the ground-floor door open again.

He listened to the footsteps on the stairs, but even as they drew closer, he was unable to determine exactly how many people were advancing.

All he knew was that it was a group.

But that changed when he suddenly heard footsteps shuffling beneath him, and voices, too, echoing in the empty space below.

A part of the group had peeled off and was moving through the second floor.

The footsteps that continued on the stairs were now easily discernible as belonging to two people.

Heavy, moving steadily upward.

Tom waited, looking past the three men before him to the door at the far end of the room.

It wasn't long before the two men reached the doorway.

PART FIVE

Fifty-Two

The Colonel entered the dark room, followed by another man.

It wasn't until these two men were halfway across the dark room that Tom recognized the second man as Karl.

His presence made Tom wonder where Esa Hirsh was.

The leader of the three-man advance team waited till the Colonel had reached them, then handed over Tom's sidearm. Holding it with gloved hands, the Colonel studied it for a moment before returning it to the leader.

"The men downstairs weren't killed with a .45," the Colonel said. "Their entry wounds are too small. Tom has a primary weapon here somewhere. A carbine or rifle in 5.56. Find it."

The men fanned out, leaving Tom and the Colonel standing face-to-face. Tom's back was to the broken window; the Colonel and Karl faced it.

Karl remained a few feet behind and to the right of the Colonel—the traditional position of a bodyguard.

There wasn't anywhere else in the empty room for the Colonel's men to search, so they went straight into the darkened corners, starting with the nearest ones first.

They returned almost immediately, the leader holding the HK416, and his partner the battle belt. The third man emerged from the opposite corner with Tom's pocketknife.

The Colonel visually inspected the carbine. He looked at Tom. "Raveis provided you with this?" He seemed genuinely surprised, even a little perplexed.

Tom didn't reply.

"Did he warn you that I had a scout team here?"

Again, Tom gave him nothing.

"A trickster to the end, that one," the Colonel said.

Tom wasn't certain what that meant, but he also didn't care. "Where's Hammerton?" he demanded.

The Colonel nodded to the leader, who gestured to his team. The three men backed away, positioning themselves in a half circle roughly twenty feet from Tom and the Colonel, their weapons ready, their eyes fixed on Tom.

"This isn't going to go the way you thought it would go," the Colonel said. "You know, I never took you for a gambling man. Just the opposite, in fact. But here you are. Like the man said, 'Desperate times call for desperate measures.'"

"Where is Hammerton?" Tom repeated.

"He's right below us. They're getting things ready." He paused. "A Paine quote comes to mind right now: 'These are the times that try men's souls.'"

"I have more than just the video of you meeting the Benefactor," Tom said. "I have it all. The documents, the audio and video files, everything."

"Of course you do. How else were we to get you here?"

Tom heard the street door open and close again, followed by more footsteps.

"To be completely honest, Tom, I didn't think this would work," the Colonel said. "I thought you would see right through the ploy. But Raveis believed otherwise. He knew you'd take the bait. He knew he could get you here, and that you'd come alone."

Another armed man entered the room, carrying a tablet. He walked to Karl and handed the device to him, then took position with the other men in the half-circle perimeter.

Karl was looking down at the device, navigating its display with his index finger.

"How are we doing?" the Colonel said.

"Almost ready," Karl answered.

The Colonel looked at Tom. "It's beginning to dawn on you, isn't it? You're beginning to piece it together. You really think Raveis would hand over information that would implicate him? I have never met a man with a stronger survival instinct than Sam Raveis. Whatever it takes to stay alive, he'll do it. Those same instincts are what made him a valuable business partner—well, until recently. Until our misunderstanding."

"What misunderstanding?"

"Carrington's reaching out to you—we knew Smith was behind that. But Raveis is the kind of man who sees opportunity in a crisis. He thought he saw a chance to get rid of me. Ambition, after all, is just survival dressed up. And Raveis is very ambitious. He put his thumb on the scale when the attack on you was planned. He wanted you to live, knew if you did that there was the chance you would come after me. With me gone, the organization would be his to run. It was a brilliant play on his part, I have to admit. And when the second attack on you failed, I knew I had to get to you somehow. I knew that if I could turn you against him, I'd have a motivated killer hunting him. After all, he had betrayed your father, the videos proved that, and he had betrayed you."

He paused before continuing. "Replacing the sixth video Smith had provided with the video of your father's death would do the trick, or so I thought. But you didn't take the bait—any of it, Raveis's or mine, for that matter—so we called a truce and struck up a last-minute deal. Just like Raveis had sent your father to meet the Algerian, he would send you to meet with me here. The evidence he showed you is real, but what Raveis kept from you, Tom, is that I have an identical collection myself. Everything Raveis has I also possess, including Stella's . . . self-portrait, let's call it. Mutually assured destruction was what kept the Cold War from becoming World War III, and these duplicate collections are what will keep Raveis from betraying me and me from betraying him, even now that our partnership has been dissolved."

"Why did he send me here? Why didn't he just kill me at the hotel?"

"You'll understand in a few minutes."

Tom glanced at the four bodyguards, then at Karl, who was still watching the tablet. Finally he looked back at the Colonel.

The loose floorboard was to Tom's left, three strides away. He located it in his peripheral vision, made certain to keep it there.

"Just so you know, Tom, I'm sorry it turned out this way. I was genuinely fond of you. Maybe there was even a part of me that hoped it wouldn't come to this, that you would actually kill the Benefactor when the time came, Smith would succumb to his cancer and take his secret with him, and there'd be no reason that you and Stella couldn't go on your merry way. After all that had been taken from you, I'd hoped we wouldn't have to take more. I had once said that I looked forward to a day when you could meet my family and sit down for a meal with us. Nothing would have made me happier."

"They're ready," Karl said.

The Colonel nodded. "Show him."

Karl stepped forward and turned the tablet so it was facing Tom.

On the display was a video feed showing Hammerton.

It took Tom a moment to understand what precisely he was seeing.

The first thing he noted was that Hammerton was standing on a stool.

His face was bruised, and that angered Tom, but the anger gave way to fear when Tom realized that something was around Hammerton's neck.

It looked to be razor-thin wire.

Surrounding Hammerton were several armed men, but Tom also glimpsed Esa Hirsh.

"You have one last purpose to serve, Tom," the Colonel said. "We need your help bringing in the others. Cahill, Stella, Slattery, Grunn, everyone. If you refuse, Hammerton dies a slow and agonizing death. If you cooperate, he dies quickly, as will you, as will everyone. That's the best I can offer, but it's a simple choice for you. Actually, there really is no choice, is there? I know you well enough to know you aren't going to let the man who saved your life, and Stella's life, suffer needlessly. And suffer he will, Tom. I understand there are ways to prolong the agony. Ways to revive Hammerton after he loses consciousness and start the process all over again. I think you know me well enough to know that I will do whatever it takes to protect my business—the business of protecting our country from all enemies, including those within. Even if what it takes is brutalizing a man I admire and respect. I faced the same choice with your father, and you know I did what I needed to do then."

"I have no way of reaching any of them," Tom said.

"I suspect there are phone numbers in that memory of yours."

"None that is current. All burner phones have been ditched."

"You're a clever man, Tom. You spent eight years serving under James Carrington. You know all about codes and ciphers. I made certain he taught you all about them. There's a way for you to reach Stella at least. All you need to do is bring her in for us, along with the rest of them; otherwise, we'll need to use her to bring them in, too, and you don't want that."

Tom looked at the display before shifting his eyes back to the Colonel.

The loose floorboard remained in his peripheral vision at all times.

"It doesn't have to go this way," the Colonel said. "I don't have to tell Karl here to give the word and start the demonstration. I'm guessing the system you have with Stella is similar to the one you and Carrington had. Every time she had internet access, she checked out the same book on Amazon, skimming its recent reviews, so that tells me I'm right in my thinking. We'll provide you with a computer and a place to sit to compose your review. I'm curious what it is she will be looking for. A simple progression—the first word of the first sentence, second word of the second, and so on? Or maybe another combination of numbers? Her birthday or yours. Or the date of the signing of the Declaration of Independence, or of the first shot of the Revolutionary War, or something like that?"

Tom remained stoic. He knew he had one advantage—the Colonel needed him alive.

If he lunged for the hiding place, it was likely that the Colonel's men would swarm him, not immediately open fire.

It took the average person one and a half seconds to cross twenty feet, and in that time maybe Tom could get the plank free and the weapon in his hand, and maybe as they scrambled to control him, he could start to take them out, one by one, then get a clear shot at Karl and kill him before he could give the order.

That would leave Tom and the Colonel, with three rounds to spare.

It was a foolish thought, Tom knew that, but his heart was pounding and his blood was filled with adrenaline and his mind was racing.

He was seconds from blindly bolting for the hidden weapon when his eye caught something that didn't make sense at first.

There was a dot on Karl's head, a green pinpoint of light, wavering just slightly, but otherwise holding steadily at the dead center of the man's forehead.

It was a laser sight, and the instant Tom realized this—the instant his rushing and exhausted mind reached that startling conclusion—he heard the *clack* of the first suppressed shot being fired behind him.

Not directly behind him but from across the courtyard, from the window through which he had seen someone move.

Fifty-Three

Tom dropped down to a crouch and turned, seeking and finding the source of the green light—a figure kneeling and using the window frame as a brace for his rifle.

A flash of light from the window below that one drew Tom's attention.

There was a second shooter on the floor beneath the first shooter, and he had fired almost simultaneously into the floor below Tom's.

Tom saw his chance and spun around, diving from his crouch for the loose floorboard and hitting the rotted planks at the same moment that Karl, head shot, landed in a heap of lifeless limbs just behind the Colonel.

The four armed men reacted fast, training their weapons on the window across the courtyard, but the shooter got off two more shots in rapid succession.

One man went down, then another.

The fact that each torso shot had been fatal despite the plate carriers both men wore meant that the shooter was armed with something heavier than an AR-15–type rifle.

The Colonel dropped to the floor as well, not hit but taking cover.

Tom was on his stomach, pulling up the loose floorboard with his left hand and reaching into the hiding place beneath with his right.

Scrambling to his knees but careful to remain below the window, the Colonel reached for his own sidearm.

But Tom had already rolled onto his back and planted his feet flat on the floor. He was bringing the Colt to bear, raising his head and extending the weapon between his bent knees as he took aim.

Tom fired but knew right away that he had jerked the trigger instead of pressing it.

That first shot pulled to the left, the round grazing the side of the Colonel's head and taking a chunk of scalp with it.

The wound had no visible effect on the man. Grasping his weapon, he removed it from its holster, extending his arm—but still a second from taking aim.

There was a moment of cognition between the Colonel and Tom—each man looking stoically at the other's face.

And there was a microsecond at the end of that moment during which the Colonel's attention shifted to the weapon in Tom's hand.

The look in the man's eyes told Tom that the Colonel was confused by the sudden presence of a weapon.

Or perhaps, in that last instant, the Colonel had recognized it and understood the chain of events that had led to it being here.

Tom allowed the weapon to settle back down by its own weight, finding its target again.

But this time he took his time.

Aim, exhale, pull.

He fired, and the shot struck the triangle between the Colonel's nose and chin, passing through teeth and bone to his medulla oblongata, destroying it and killing him instantly.

Still on his back, Tom shifted and aimed the Colt at the man farthest from him, taking the same care before pulling the trigger and bringing him down with a head shot.

The last remaining man—nearly standing over Tom—spun and lowered his M4, but Tom was ready for him, firing a round between his eyes, striking him as a rifle round from across the courtyard took off the left side of his head.

Tom scrambled to his feet, holstering the Colt and picking up the HK416.

He paused to complete a brass check, after which he shouldered the carbine and aimed it across the courtyard. But instead of activating the rail-mounted light, he removed the SureFire light from behind his belt buckle with his left hand and, with his arm extended as far out to the side as it could reach, he pressed and released the switch with his thumb, flashing the light once.

If whoever was across the courtyard fired on the light, he would miss Tom.

But the shooter didn't do that, and the flash of light was enough for Tom to see the face of the man who had saved him.

It was James Carrington, armed with a suppressed SR-25—a long-barreled semiautomatic DMR chambered in the .308 round.

But his former CO, just a figure in the darkness again now that the flash had ended, didn't linger. He turned and moved, displacing, Tom knew, to the floor below to assist whoever was down there.

Carrington's echoing footsteps reminded Tom of the second set of footsteps he'd heard as his former CO had made his escape two nights before.

Turning, Tom tossed the light aside and slipped the sling over the right side of his head, then under his left arm.

He ran for the stairs, too, and with everything he had.

Fifty-Four

His weapon shouldered, Tom moved down the stairs, his right eye fixed on what he could see through the AimPoint optic and his left eye open to detect what was beyond it.

He was halfway down the stairs when a backward-moving man passed the doorway below, firing into the room as he exited it.

The man must have also been maintaining his situational awareness, however, because he instantly turned in Tom's direction.

But Tom had already sighted the man and dropped him with a controlled pair to the head before the man could even elevate his weapon.

Cautiously, Tom continued down the stairs, stepping over the fallen man when he reached the bottom step and taking cover to the left of the door.

From the room came continuous clacking sounds, as well as flashes of light—indications of an ongoing firefight.

Before Tom could peer around the doorframe and into the room, another man was driven backward through the door, firing as he went.

Instantly aware of Tom, he pivoted just enough to direct his M4 at his new, closer target.

Tom and the man fired at the same time—Tom's shots finding their mark, the man's striking the wall just inches to the left of Tom's head.

Tom had no idea how many of the Colonel's men remained in the room, but the flashes and sounds were an indication that a force of some size was present and fighting.

Peering fast around the corner, Tom glimpsed a scene of chaos before pulling back behind cover.

Despite the smokeless cartridges, the dark room was filled with a shifting haze of gun smoke, but through it Tom had counted a half dozen shooters, all of whom were facing the window and returning the fire coming from across the courtyard.

Tom had also seen Hammerton, still on his stool, his hands bound behind him.

Stealing a quick look again, Tom witnessed one shooter on the left side of the room go down, followed by another shooter on the right.

The danger of Tom surrendering his cover was that he might take friendly fire, but the sight of his friend balanced on a stool with a wire around his neck—and helpless in the middle of a firefight—was too much to bear.

Tom entered the room, assuming a kneeling position and firing at the man who was nearest to Hammerton.

That man was leaning forward, offering no clear shot at his head, so Tom opened up with automatic fire, putting a burst of three into the man's back, followed by another burst, and yet another—intentional overkill that pushed the steel plate of the man's body armor beyond the point of failure.

At some point between the second and third burst, the weaker 5.56 rounds penetrated, severing the man's spine and bringing him down.

The bodyguard to his right pivoted to face Tom, displacing as he fired, his movement causing him to miss, but before Tom could even track him, the man reeled and dropped, struck down by either Carrington or his bodyguard.

The left side of the room was clear, so Tom moved into one of the shadowed corners as he circled for a clearer view of the right side.

Three of the Colonel's men remained, two of whom were engaged with the shooters across the courtyard, but it was the actions of the third one that caught Tom's attention.

Kneeling so he was below the window line, he was making his way toward Hammerton. When he was close enough, he kicked at one of the stool legs with the heel of his boot, but Hammerton's weight kept the stool in place.

The man kicked it again.

Tom needed to reposition to get a clean shot at the man—three long strides to the left were all he needed.

He was making his second stride when the man kicked the stool again, knocking it free.

Hammerton was dangling, his feet kicking, when Tom abandoned his third stride to the left for a quick step forward, followed by another.

The man who had kicked the stool out saw Tom coming and raised his weapon, but before he could even shoulder it, someone appeared behind him—someone who'd also been kneeling and who had risen suddenly.

It was Esa Hirsh, a knife in her hand.

She threw herself onto the man's back, wrapping her left arm around his head, thereby obscuring his sight and holding him steady as she drove the knife into the back of his head, twisting it once.

Then she was up on her feet, doing the last thing Tom had expected.

Risking making herself a target to the shooters across the courtyard, she rushed to Hammerton, bending slightly and wrapping her arms around his legs, then thrusting her hips forward till she was standing up straight.

She supported him as Tom resumed his maneuver to the left, clearing the way for a clean shot at the last two men.

Instead of bursts of three, Tom pressed the trigger and held it down, spraying rounds at one man, then the other, then back, and then back again.

Each man remained standing as his body armor absorbed the rounds—until the moment the body armor failed and he went down.

Tom felt the bolt carrier lock back on the empty mag, switched it for the other mag connected by the coupler, and slapped the bolt release as he ran toward his friend.

Though Hammerton's weight was no longer a factor, the wire noose was still tight around his throat.

Tom had no knife, but there wasn't time to waste.

He knelt over the man Esa had killed, removed the knife from his neck, and pushed the stool closer to Hammerton with his foot. Stepping onto the stool, he dragged the serrated blade across the wire, severing it.

Hammerton dropped to the floor, knocking over the stool as he landed and taking Tom and Esa down with him.

In a heap together, Tom and Esa were face-to-face.

The fire from across the courtyard ceased immediately.

Esa moved first, scrambling to her knees and climbing over Tom to reach Hammerton.

The wire had cut into him, and she had to slide her fingers between it and his skin to loosen the noose.

Hammerton was coughing as Tom joined Esa, the two of them examining him for any serious lacerations.

To Tom's relief, his friend's wounds were only superficial.

He looked at Esa, was about to thank her when she spoke.

"We're not out of this yet," she said.

Tom heard footsteps moving below as Esa used the knife to cut the plastic ties securing Hammerton's wrists.

They helped Hammerton to his feet. Standing on either side of him and holding him up, they faced the courtyard.

Tom saw Carrington standing beside a man in his twenties. Though Tom didn't recognize him, he knew this similarly armed individual was Carrington's bodyguard.

“We’re coming around to the door,” Carrington called. “White panel van.”

Tom nodded, and he and Esa turned and started toward the door, Hammerton between them.

The man was stunned but still had the presence of mind to stop as they passed the first of the fallen men and say, “Grab his weapon.”

Esa did as ordered, also grabbing two spare magazines from the man’s carrier vest.

She handed the items to Hammerton, repeating the process when they reached the next fallen man.

That weapon and spare mags she kept for herself.

Hammerton was able to walk on his own—or so he insisted.

Together, the trio readied their weapons as they approached the door.

Fifty-Five

The last flight of stairs was clear, but Tom remained cautious as he took point.

Esa followed Tom, Hammerton behind her.

When Tom glanced back to check on his friend, he noted that Hammerton seemed just as concerned with the woman in front of him as he was with the remaining men in the building.

She had, after all, saved Hammerton's life, but she had also killed the man whose murder Hammerton had spent the past two decades seeking to avenge.

Even under the best conditions, such conflicting information would be difficult to process.

Tom paused at the bottom of the stairs, listening for the activity he had heard before—footsteps and hushed voices coming from the street-level room, all of it hurried and urgent.

But there was none of that now, and just feet from where he stood was the exit, the two fallen scouts not far from it.

Still, men could be waiting to ambush them from the rear as they exited, so Tom positioned himself by the doorframe and peered into the room.

He saw no figures in the dim light, but there was something in the middle of the empty room.

The shape of it was familiar, and Tom recognized it immediately.

Three fifty-five-gallon drums joined together by wires, all of which fed into a single control panel mounted to the top of the center drum.

On the panel was a blinking light, either indicating that the incendiary device had been armed or signifying the ticking down of a digital timer.

Either way, it was time to leave.

Tom turned to Esa for answers.

Anticipating his questions, she said, "It was set for a two-minute countdown, but there's no knowing when it was started."

Hammerton had gathered enough of his wits to say to Tom, "Jesus, full circle again."

Tom started a countdown in his head as he led them past the two fallen men to the main door, which was ajar again.

He gave them thirty seconds to get clear.

Beyond the door was a downpour that sounded like the steady roar of crashing waves.

Here, though, Tom and the others faced a similar problem: men were likely waiting outside to ambush them as they fled.

Tom knew from his study of the blueprints that there were other exits, but none was near enough that they would reach it in time.

The only way of escape was the door in front of them.

The only way out is through.

Tom once again took point position, standing to the side of the door and opening it halfway. Ten seconds had passed. When the movement of the door didn't draw any fire, Tom peered around and scanned the street beyond.

He saw nothing—no armed men, no indications of movement, and no vehicles, including the white panel van Carrington had promised.

But the lack of an enemy out in the open didn't mean no enemy was present.

Ten more seconds had passed—so ten more were all that was left.

Drawing back behind cover, Tom took a breath before risking another look, this time scouting the Jeep Rubicon parked at the far end of the block.

More than one hundred yards away.

It was a long haul to make, and they'd be out in the open for a good minute, maybe more, but it was the only option he saw.

To make matters worse, they would need to cross the wide street not once but twice—first to get clear of the building, and then again to reach the vehicle once they were down the block.

Tom turned to the others and said, "Straight out the door; stay close."

Then he exited, Esa behind him, Hammerton behind her. Crouching low and moving as a phalanx, they sprinted, crossing the street at an angle, Tom scanning ahead, Esa looking to the right, Hammerton to the left.

Tom's thirty seconds ended as they reached the other side of the street, so as they continued toward the Jeep, he began to count forward.

Maybe—maybe—they had another thirty seconds, but he couldn't imagine it would be more than that.

Tom was thinking this when a vehicle rounded the corner where the Jeep was parked.

But it wasn't the white panel van he'd been on the lookout for.

It was a black SUV, shiny and ominous, and bearing down on them.

Just seconds after it turned the corner, another SUV appeared, following the first.

Passing the Rubicon, the lead vehicle locked its brakes and slid sideways to a stop. The second SUV did the same.

Obviously, the drivers of both vehicles didn't want to be near the factory when the device detonated, but they also weren't about to let Tom and the others get clear.

The instant the SUVs stopped and the barricade was complete, the doors opened, and men scrambled out.

Six in all, including the drivers.

With no cover or concealment immediately available, Tom dropped to his knees, Esa and Hammerton following his lead. All three opened fire just as the last of the Colonel's men, still fanning out, did the same.

The men being in motion, as well as under steady and more accurate fire, meant that their shots were less than precise, but Tom knew it was only a matter of time before those men took position behind their vehicles.

And once they did that, Tom, Esa, and Hammerton, pinned down with nowhere to go, would be easily picked off.

Another vehicle appeared at the corner.

The white panel van.

Instead of turning, however, the van continued straight before skidding to a stop in the middle of the street, its right side facing the barricade of SUVs.

Even before the vehicle had come to its stop, the panel door slid back, revealing a kneeling shooter inside—Carrington's bodyguard.

His SR-25 shouldered, he began firing immediately.

Four of the six men turned to face the new threat, so Tom and his team focused on the two still firing at them.

At this distance, roughly seventy-five yards, precise head shots would be difficult, and the body armor would stand up to the 5.56 rounds, at least initially.

So Tom went for the two-foot-by-two-foot target that started at the abdomen and extended down to midthigh—the generally unprotected part of the human body that kept it upright. He dropped one man with a pelvic shot, and either Esa or Hammerton followed suit, dropping the other man with a shot to the lower abdomen.

With no more enemy fire coming at them, Tom said, "Move." He stood and pressed forward, the others behind him.

The running count in his head was approaching twenty, and they still had twenty-five yards to go before they'd be clear of the building.

Even then there was no guarantee that they'd be safe from the effects of the IED inside.

His eyes forward, Tom saw that one of the Colonel's men was turning around to face the running trio. Tom was slowing and taking aim at the threat when a bright flash of light all but blinded him.

Then a gust of heated air hit him like a speeding bus.

The last thing Tom felt was the sensation of his feet losing contact with the pavement as the violent blast cast him airborne.

Fifty-Six

Tom heard ringing, and when he opened his eyes, he was in a dark room.

It took a moment for him to understand that he was in a warm bed, stretched out between clean sheets and beneath a heavy comforter.

Stella was there, leaning over him, smiling and saying in a soft, teasing voice, "Get up, Tom. Get up."

Tom looked up at her, wanted to reach out for her but couldn't. He needed just a little more rest before he could move his arms, so he closed his eyes, and when he opened them again, the dark and serene room had been replaced with a raining nighttime street, and the woman leaning over him wasn't Stella but Esa.

And though she was telling him to get up, she wasn't smiling, and there was nothing playful about her manner.

Tom knew by the look on her face that she wasn't speaking softly.

She was, in fact, yelling loud enough to pierce the sickening ringing in his ears.

"Get up, Tom! Get up!"

He was flat on his back, and there was debris around him—glass, pieces of brick, thick dust that had yet to absorb the rain.

Placing his left hand on the sidewalk, Tom pushed himself into a seated position. Two pairs of hands grabbed him and pulled him the rest of the way to his feet, then proceeded to half carry, half drag him forward.

He looked to the left. The incendiary device on the ground floor had been powerful enough to blow out the factory's remaining windows, but the only damage to the structure was a missing chunk barely big enough for a vehicle to drive through.

The heart of the long-abandoned building, however, was ablaze, and the fire was spreading fast.

The panel van had maneuvered between the two sideways SUVs and around the downed men scattered on the pavement. Tom was uncertain if they, too, had been knocked unconscious by the blast or had been shot dead by Carrington's bodyguard.

Even in his current state—ears aching, senses overloaded to the point of numbness, mind rattled—Tom concluded that since they'd been farther from the explosion than he and his friends, it was unlikely that they were simply unconscious.

Still, he kept an eye on them as the van approached, almost willing them not to get up.

The van came to a stop, and Hammerton and Esa helped Tom inside. Carrington's bodyguard—young, with a middleweight boxer's build, blond hair, and beard trimmed close—was helping Tom sit on a tool bench as Esa entered, followed by Hammerton, who swung the door closed and called to the driver, "Go!"

Carrington flattened the accelerator, steering the van past the burning factory and turning right onto Kingston Drive.

Tom looked at the rearview mirror until Carrington glanced at it and met his stare.

"That was you in the apartment window," Tom said.

Carrington nodded.

Tom said, "What were you doing there—"

He was cut off by the sound of gunfire, which was followed by the shattering of glass as rounds penetrated the rear door windows.

That was followed by the whizzing of rounds flying past Tom like angry bees.

The shots were coming from the passenger side of an SUV on their tail.

Tom rose, firing his HK416 as he moved toward the back door, but the small 5.56 rounds did little to the SUV's windshield of reinforced glass.

But the cluster of starlike fractures forming in front of the driver was rendering the clear glass opaque, so once Tom reached the back door he kept firing through the window till the bolt locked on an empty mag.

He had no spare on him, but before he could say anything, Esa was beside him, handing her spare mag to him.

Then she raised her M4, aimed through the other window, and fired at the windshield.

The SUV was falling back, but its passenger was still firing.

Tom inserted the mag and slapped the bolt release, was ready to rejoin the fight when Carrington called out.

"Contact left!"

The van was passing another of the Colonel's men, this one standing on the sidewalk and taking aim at the side of the speeding van.

He opened up with a burst of automatic fire, the rounds penetrating the sheet metal panel and filling the rear compartment.

The man was just coming into Tom's view when he felt Esa slam against him as if shoved. His legs buckled and he fell, too, hitting the floor hard, Esa landing beside him.

Tom was immediately overwhelmed by a burning sensation deep inside his torso.

He tried to breathe but couldn't draw in air, was lying there stunned and gasping as Carrington's bodyguard appeared by the van's back door, firing through one of the windows at the lone gunman on the sidewalk and dropping him with a single shot.

Then the bodyguard acquired the SUV still falling back behind them and put a round through its radiator, incapacitating the vehicle.

Tom was still struggling to breathe when Hammerton leaned over him, saying something Tom couldn't hear.

Carrington's bodyguard appeared beside Hammerton, opening a bleeder-blowout kit and calmly giving instructions to Hammerton.

The van was still moving, and as it rounded a corner, gravity turned Tom's head.

He saw Esa beside him, saw her eyes find his.

Looking down, he could see blood flowing from her wound, the location of which was nearly identical to his own.

Hammerton had one hand on Tom's wound and the other on Esa's, applying pressure.

Through the ringing in his ears, Tom heard Carrington's bodyguard speak.

"We only have one bleeder kit."

His tone was both calm and grave.

Tom felt himself drifting—a tranquil sensation at first, but then it suddenly shifted into a sense of rapid sinking.

It was as if he were being swallowed by a vast ocean of cold, swirling water.

The last thing he remembered was the face of the woman beside him.

A woman who vaguely resembled Stella.

Tom slipped in and out of consciousness.

At one point he was in the van, Hammerton and Carrington's bodyguard standing over him and working frantically. He felt no pain but could sense the speed at which they were traveling. As he drove, Carrington was on a cell phone, giving orders.

The next thing Tom knew, he was on a stretcher, being carried by men who were running. He didn't recognize them, but he knew by their uniforms that they were some kind of med-evac team.

Tom wondered whether he was back in Afghanistan, being transported by medics to a waiting Huey, the grenade fragments that had entered his torso—after first passing through Cahill's—moving deeper into his flesh with each step the rushing men took.

He wondered, too, if it were possible that everything he had experienced since that night had been some kind of trick of the mind, the reverse of seeing one's life parade by in a flash when near death.

Maybe everything—Stella and Canaan and all that had followed—had been nothing more than a dream of the mind unfolding in milliseconds, utterly unreal despite having been vividly felt, and despite the lingering memories of the woman—the only woman—he had loved.

But the sky that had spread out above him back in Afghanistan was different—a desert sky, full of stars and vast.

Above him now were only dark clouds from which fell a cold and bracing autumn rain.

Tom's vision darkened, and the ringing in his ears faded. He could sense motion every now and then, but nothing more.

When he finally could open his eyes, once he had sensed that all that motion had finally ceased, the face above him, though not Stella's, was one that he welcomed the sight of.

"We're going to take care of you, Tom," Sandy Montrose said. "You're going to be okay."

Tom spoke the only word that mattered. "Stella."

His voice was more of a gasp than a whisper.

"She's on her way. They'll all be here soon."

Tom sensed that there were people around him, maybe even a crowd, but the only other person he could see was Carrington's bodyguard.

He was standing next to Sandy, as if preparing to work alongside her.

Tom closed his eyes, and the last thing he heard was Sandy saying, "Okay, let's put him under . . ."

Fifty-Seven

Semiconscious and adrift, Tom hears voices.

Stella's first, asking, What happened?

Sandy answers. A round penetrated the van wall and struck the person next to Tom, passing through her and into him. He was wearing a Kevlar vest, but it was only rated for pistol calibers. Fortunately, the round had lost a lot of its energy by the time it reached him. As badly wounded as he is, if it weren't for the woman next to him, things would have been a lot worse.

What woman? *Stella asks.*

Carrington answers, Her name is Esa Hirsh. She works for the Benefactor.

To Tom the voices sound distant, as if his drifting has carried him away from where they are—wherever it is they are.

Stella wants to know where Esa is now.

Hammerton's voice cuts in: She's not going to make it.

We only had one bleeder-blowout kit, *Carrington explains.*

But the Benefactor is still out there? *Stella asks.*

Tom can barely hear her. He wants to reverse his drifting, get back to where she is. To have come this far and waited so long, only to lose her again, angers him.

He wants to call to her, tries to scream, but has no voice of his own.

He is even farther away than he was a moment ago.

He remembers the concerns he had about Stella undergoing the training that Raveis offered at his compounds.

She would not be the same after it.

No one was.

He wants to see, wants to detect the changes in her.

Who she is now, as seen by who he is now.

But he is carried farther and farther away, her voice and the other voices fading to almost nothing.

Tom hears Hammerton answer, Yes, he's still out there.

Carrington says, That's what we need to talk to you about.

Then Stella replies, So let's talk.

Tom can hear only murmurs that grow fainter and fainter.

It isn't long before he hears nothing at all.

Lost, he succumbs to the emptiness that surrounds him.

Tom is walking along a tree-lined street covered with brittle, colorful leaves.

The air is chilly, the blue sky clear.

Among his favorite memories are those of returning home from military school for Thanksgiving break.

An early indication of his natural tendency toward self-reliance was the fact that Tom had opted every year to make his own way back.

That journey required that he take an hour-long bus ride—the 370—from Troy to Schenectady, then Amtrak from there to the Lake Champlain ferry at Essex, New York. Once across and into Vermont, he would hitch a ride the rest of the way.

Dressed as he was in his school uniform, a duffel bag over his shoulder, it didn't take long before one of the cars disembarking the ferry stopped for him.

Though the various drivers always offered to take him to his front door, he preferred to be let out on the edge of town and walk the rest of the way.

He is aware that he is dreaming, so he goes with it, relives those long-ago sojourns, which were precursors to the five years of wandering that he would embark upon after his discharge.

These were the first of an uncountable number of steps in an odyssey that would eventually bring him to that railcar diner in Canaan, Connecticut, where Stella worked.

As he walks old and familiar streets, he chooses to savor the sights and sounds and smells his unconscious mind is re-creating.

He passes the homes of his neighbors—childhood playmates and family friends he sought out during the long holiday weekends.

But it is his own family right now that he wants to see.

The first he should spot is his kid sister, who watched for him from her bedroom window, waving as he came into her view.

Then the next he would encounter is his mother, who would greet him at the door with a warm embrace that, after she was lost to him, he would never again know.

And finally he would see his father, emerging from his study, smiling proudly, eager to shake his only son's hand.

With all this in mind, Tom turns onto his street, sees his childhood home ahead, hurries toward it till he is running, kicking leaves, and pulling the sharp autumn air into his uninjured lungs.

But as he approaches the home, he does not see his kid sister in the upper-floor window.

No one is there to open the door as he reaches it.

And once inside, he is alone in a place that has clearly been abandoned—a place too much like the spaces in which he has dwelled these past few months as he waited for his chance at claiming justice for those who were taken from him.

He hears a voice behind him, thinks it's Stella's.

He turns, desperate to finally see her, but the woman he is facing isn't her.

It's Esa Hirsh.

Tom sees the lacerations on her face, looks down at the fatal wound in her torso spilling blood.

Tom asks what she said.

Esa approaches him and extends her hand.

In it is a cell phone smeared with blood.

She places the phone into his hand.

Her skin is ice-cold.

She will kill him, *Esa says.* She will kill him for you. She will kill him for all of us.

Fifty-Eight

Tom woke in a bed, not flat on his back but slightly upright.

It was a hospital bed, but even in the darkness, he knew he wasn't in a hospital room.

There was furniture—sofas and easy chairs—and the walls were covered with floor-to-ceiling built-in bookcases.

On one end of the room was an ornately carved door, and on the other, a set of French doors, beyond which was a body of water, its smooth surface twinkling under moonlight.

Even in his condition, Tom recognized that he was at the Cahill estate on Shelter Island.

This room was the study in which he had first met the Colonel just shy of two years ago.

It was shortly after that meeting that Tom and Stella had slipped away with the intention of roaming free, only to end up not far from Tom's hometown, which Stella had wanted to see so she could know him better, and where they had spotted as they were leaving a small and secluded roadside diner for sale.

It took a minute before Tom was able to do anything more than look around the dimly lit room.

He was alone, and the stillness he sensed told him that it was likely late at night and possibly everyone was asleep.

Eventually, he looked down at his arms. An IV was feeding a Ringer's lactate solution into his bloodstream via the antecubital vein in the crook of his right arm. A cuff around his upper-left arm monitored his cardiac telemetry and oxygen saturation, as well as his blood pressure.

He removed the cuff first, then withdrew the 18-gauge needle from his vein and sat up.

If he had forgotten about his gunshot wound, he was reminded of it by the sudden wave of pain that almost sent him back down onto his back.

But he pushed his way through it, remaining upright and catching his breath before swinging his feet off the bed and onto the floor.

It took all he had to get that far, had to summon more just to stand.

His legs were less than steady as he searched the drawers of a nearby wheeled cart for gauze and tape, which he found and attempted to place over his vein.

The overall lack of dexterity he displayed made it clear to him that he had been administered some form of pain medication.

It was by sheer will alone that he managed to complete his task and head for the door.

Once through it, he followed the long hallway till he was standing in the main entranceway. There he heard voices, coming from the kitchen.

Quiet talk, female voices.

He turned down the narrower hallway and pushed open the swinging door at its end.

He saw Sarah Grunn and Krista MacManus seated side by side at the island counter. Someone was standing at the open refrigerator door.

It was Slattery.

They all had their backs to Tom, but Slattery caught the open door behind her in the corner of her eye and turned. "Jesus, Tom," she said.

Leaving the refrigerator open, she hurried across the room to him.

Grunn and Krista looked back.

Tom said, "Where is everyone?"

The painkillers made his mind work slowly, and he slurred his words.

It seemed for a moment that none of the women knew what to say.

Tom looked at each one of them before asking, "Where is Stella?"

Fifty-Nine

Six hours earlier, at sunset, Stella was standing on the back lawn.

Carrington and Hammerton were facing her.

White gauze was wrapped around the wounds on Hammerton's neck.

Positioned behind Stella at the water's edge were two men, and a second pair was on the back porch.

Former members of Hammerton's SAS unit, each man studied the surroundings carefully.

"Cahill has retrieved the cell phone from Esa's hotel room in the city," Carrington said. "He and Grunn and Krista are on their way back."

Stella nodded. "How long does the woman have?"

Hammerton answered. "Sandy doesn't think she will last much longer. Just too much blood was lost."

"What are the chances of her regaining consciousness?"

"Not good."

"But she gave us a lot of information while she could," Carrington said. "We should be able to use it to get the Benefactor to a meeting place once Cahill returns with her cell phone."

"And why would the Benefactor show up?"

"His longtime bodyguard defected before being killed. He'll want a report."

Stella thought about that. "So why is she helping us? What does she want in exchange?"

"Mercy," Hammerton said. "When the time comes."

Stella remembered her father's death. Unlike her mother, who had passed relatively quickly, her father had lingered for weeks, drifting in and out of consciousness, though after a point he was never fully conscious again, never really the man she had known and loved her entire life.

There were times as she'd sat by his hospice bed when she wished she could help speed up his passing.

He likely had wanted that as well.

Stella said to Carrington, "Do you think the plan will work?"

"Slattery is already back. She found clothes that are close to what Esa was wearing when the Benefactor last saw her."

"And there is a resemblance," Hammerton said. "From a distance, at least," he added. "And that's all we'll need."

Stella nodded, glanced out at the water.

Moored to a small dock was a rowboat, rocking silently on the gentle tide.

She and Tom had once used that very rowboat to slip quietly away in the middle of the night—to make their own way, for a while at least.

When she turned back to face the two men, she saw that Carrington's bodyguard had joined the former SAS troopers on the back porch.

The contrast between Carrington's bodyguard and Hammerton's friends couldn't be greater.

The bodyguard was young, handsome, and lean, while Hammerton's compatriots were well into their sixties, menacing, and powerfully built.

Still looking toward the porch, Stella said to Carrington, "And what's your friend's name again?"

"He goes by J. D."

"Do you know what 'J. D.' stands for?"

Carrington shrugged, as if any answer he gave would be at best a guess. "John Doe," he said.

"How old is he? He looks like a kid."

"He's twenty-five. But I've never seen a more talented shooter. Or a better field medic. And he has access to certain critical resources that made it possible for me to do what I needed to do."

"Your own zealot," Stella observed.

He smiled. "Something like that."

Stella faced the two men. "I'll need to leave now, though, right?"

Carrington nodded. "Soon, yeah. Esa and the Benefactor last met in the East River State Park in Brooklyn. She said he's likely to suggest the meeting take place there, without actually mentioning it by name, as a way of confirming that it's really her sending the texts. You'll need to be able to get there at a moment's notice. If he even senses that something's not right, it's unlikely he'll take the bait."

"General Graves has filled the role as his security chief, so chances are good that he'll be there, too," Hammerton said. "We won't ever get an opportunity like this again. The Benefactor will replace the Colonel's organization with Graves's. It's obvious that's been his plan all along. Graves doesn't have the government connections that the Colonel had, but he brings something else to the table."

"What?"

"He shares the same ideology as the Benefactor. It won't just be a business arrangement this time. They'll combine their army of supporters, and with the Benefactor's rivals gone, thanks to our efforts under the Colonel, there'll be nothing to hold them back. It will be as if everything Tom did—everything we've all sacrificed—was for nothing. The only thing we can do is wait for the next big attack, helpless to stop it or do anything about it once it does happen."

But standing by wasn't an option. Stella had formed that conviction fighting by Tom's side. And her time at Raveis's compounds had only deepened her resolve.

She hadn't endured all that she had only to sit on the sidelines as others suffered and died.

This wasn't about just Tom and herself anymore.

This wasn't about finding a way to safe ground so they could live out the rest of their lives as they saw fit and in peace.

Tom had been right when he'd warned her that her exposure to Raveis's training would change her.

She'd learned what men like the Benefactor were capable of doing, and she would do whatever it took to end him.

"Hammerton and his men will get you and J. D. there," Carrington said. "J. D. will take him out. They've used satellite photos to map a number of good roosts to shoot from. All you have to do is be what draws the Benefactor out into the open. If you're afraid—"

"I'm not," Stella said.

Carrington and Hammerton waited.

Stella turned and started toward the house. "Tell everyone to get ready," she said. "And have Slattery meet me with the change of clothes."

Hammerton asked where she was going.

"I'll be with Tom."

Stella was dressed in jeans, a black sweater, and boots.

She sat alone with Tom for a few moments, holding his hand, saying nothing.

When she wasn't looking at his face, she was watching the rise and fall of his chest as he breathed.

The sun was down, the early moon lighting the water outside the French doors.

Hammerton entered the dark study and said, "We should get going."

Stella nodded, leaned forward, and kissed Tom's cheek, then she stood, facing Hammerton.

"I want to see her first," she said.

"Who?"

"Esa."

"There's not much to see."

"If I'm supposed to pass for her, then I should at least take a look at her."

The state-of-the-art med bay was located in the basement.

An oversize elevator, large enough to transport a full-size hospital bed, carried Stella and Hammerton down one floor.

Stella tried to imagine the difficulties of retrofitting the generations-old house to accommodate such a system, but she supposed that with the kind of money the Cahill family had, anything and everything was possible.

An enclosed surgical theater with an observation window occupied one half of the facility, and three hospital beds, with a space for a fourth, took up the other half.

A woman was in one of the beds. Hammerton stayed back as Stella approached and stood at her bedside.

An endotracheal tube was in Esa's mouth, held there by sterile tape, and this obscured part of her face, but Stella had been told that wasn't where the resemblance was.

Their hair was the same color and cut, and they were the same height with similar builds, though Stella was leaner.

Cahill had reported finding an empty box of hair dye in the woman's hotel bathroom.

Looking at her, Stella saw nothing that would help her become this woman, but despite what she had said to Hammerton, that wasn't why she was there.

Tom would be dead if not for Esa—a woman who two nights before had tried to kill him.

How could Stella not be curious about a paradox such as this?

Sandy entered and walked to Hammerton's side.

Hammerton asked if Cahill and the others were back yet.

"He just texted," Sandy said. "They're almost at the ferry."

Still looking at Esa, Stella said, "What's her condition?"

"The blood loss was just too catastrophic, and the bullet punctured a lung and shredded her diaphragm on its way through. The hemorrhagic shock caused kidney failure. She could go an hour from now, or it could take days."

"But she was able to communicate," Stella said.

Sandy nodded. "She was determined. When speaking became impossible, she wrote things down."

Hammerton said, "The last thing she wrote was, 'This ends.'" He paused. "It was her idea. The Colonel had given her a dossier on you—dossiers on all of us. She knew what you looked like."

Stella watched Esa, her breathing regulated by the mechanical ventilator.

"Any idea why the change of heart?"

"No."

"And she saved your life, too."

"Yes."

Stella turned to Sandy. "There was a deal made," she said. "A promise in exchange for information."

"I know," Sandy said. "But I can't do that to a patient. I took an oath. I can't kill someone under my care."

Hammerton said flatly, "I can."

Stella detected no pleasure in Hammerton's voice.

He turned to Sandy. "At least help me do it right."

Sandy looked at Hammerton, then back at Stella. Stepping away, she walked to a stainless-steel cabinet, opening its glass door.

From a top shelf she removed a syringe still in its white paper wrapper, and from two shelves below that, she removed a glass vial.

She placed the items on the foot of Esa's bed and stepped back.

"Thanks," Hammerton said.

Sandy nodded. "I'll stay and see you through it."

Hammerton moved to the bed and reached for the syringe.

Stella picked up the vial, glancing at the label.

FENTANYL CITRATE, .50 MG.

She handed the vial to Hammerton.

"I'll stay, too," she said.

Hammerton removed the syringe from its packaging, inserted the needle through the vial's rubber stopper, and drew the plunger all the way back, filling it.

It was obvious by Hammerton's manner that he'd had some degree of medical training.

This was even more evident when he inserted the needle into the IV port and steadily eased the plunger forward, emptying the syringe.

Then he stood back with the others and watched.

In less than a minute, Esa was lifeless.

They stayed with her for another minute, and then Hammerton said, "We should go."

Stella nodded and turned away.

Sandy was shutting down the telemetry monitors as Stella and Hammerton exited.

The helicopter, an EC-135, was warming up on the north lawn, not far from the stables and the five-bay garage.

Stella and Hammerton hurried across still-damp grass toward it.

The side door was open, and already on board were Hammerton's four SAS brothers, Carrington, and J. D.

The men were in street clothes, but at their feet were gear bags that no doubt contained the tools of their trade.

"Watch your head," Hammerton said. He had to raise his voice to be heard over the rotor wash.

Stella had no doubt that it caused him pain to do that.

They boarded, took the last two seats, and buckled in. Thirty seconds later, the EC-135 was airborne, banking to the west.

From her window Stella could see the gatehouse at the end of the long gravel driveway, a team of four armed men standing outside it.

Similar teams, unseen to her at the moment, were walking the perimeter of the property.

The helicopter straightened and continued west, passing over the water. A few hundred feet below was the ferry landing at North Haven.

The dock and sloping road leading to it were empty, but as the helicopter continued westward, Stella spotted the ferry midway in its crossing.

Cahill's Mustang was the only vehicle on board.

A half hour into the flight, with New York City just minutes away, a text came to Carrington's phone.

He looked at the display. "We're on. One hour. But he changed the location."

Hammerton asked, "To where?"

"Madison Square Park."

"That isn't exactly secluded. And it's small, isn't it?"

Carrington said to J. D., "Can you make it work?"

J. D. removed a tablet from his bag, navigated to Google Earth, and proceeded to search for the park.

Even before consulting the satellite footage, he said, "I know that park. There's not a lot of cover. There's a statute of William Seward at the southwest entrance. It's on a pedestal in a fenced-in, circular garden; there might be cover to be found there, but getting in without being seen by his men if they're staking the place out, or even by random passersby, for that matter, will be a problem. And there's no guarantee I'll have a shot if I do get in."

Hammerton said to Carrington, "The Cahill family has a lot of real estate holdings in New York. Hotels, apartment and office buildings. Maybe they have something that would provide a position."

"There are no hotels or apartments that overlook the park, just office buildings. Even if they were connected to one of them, there's not enough time to get J. D. in place."

J. D. zoomed in on an overhead, high-definition view of the park, studying it quickly. "It's not a good location for us. Four entrances on each corner, no border trees, no cover or concealment. Which I'm sure is why he chose it."

Hammerton said, "We have to abort."

"With a vehicle, we could circle the park with me in the back. We might get a shot that way."

"We can't push an op. I'm calling it—"

"No," Stella said. "We're doing this."

"It's too dangerous."

"You said it yourself; it's our only chance."

Carrington said, "He'll have men, Stella."

"And I have all of you. The fact that the park is likely to have people passing through can work to our advantage. I'll arrive alone, but I won't stand still and wait, I'll walk the perimeter. Esa turned on him, and there had to be a reason for that, so it would make sense that she'd take precautions of her own, too. Any men he has in the park will be watching me; I'll make sure of it. Then you can approach the park from all four sides, one at a time, maybe mix in with other people passing through if you can. I mean, we're all deep-cover agents, aren't we?"

"We wouldn't be able to conceal our long guns," Hammerton said. "We'd only have sidearms, which means we can't provide effective cover for you at range."

"Then I'll take him out myself. If we're lucky, he won't realize his mistake until he's a few feet from me."

"We can't let you do that," Carrington said.

"That's not your call to make. It's mine."

None of the men spoke.

"I'm our only chance," Stella said. "I'm doing this."

Again, the men said nothing.

Finally, J. D. said, "She's right. How many more people will that fucker torture and kill? We all know who he is. We all know we're on the top of his kill list, and with no organization anymore to count on. We can spend the rest of our lives running and hiding, squandering whatever resources we have, or we can put a stop to this right now—for us, for everyone. Just get me a vehicle and someone to drive it. I'll get him. And if I don't, Stella will do what she has been trained to do. And so will all of you." He paused. "Either he goes down or we all do. And if only one of us is left standing, that person makes sure the Benefactor doesn't leave that park alive."

Carrington and Hammerton looked at each other.

"Cahill has a garage in the city," Carrington said. "Where he keeps cover vehicles."

Hammerton nodded. "Call him."

As Carrington placed the call, Hammerton's men leaned forward and opened the duffels at their feet, gathering and prepping their gear.

Pistols affixed with suppressors, spare mags, vests, and gloves.

One of the men—the smallest of them—offered Stella a Kevlar vest.

She took it, thanked him, and without hesitation pulled the black sweater over her head, placing it on her lap.

Caught off guard, the men glanced at her briefly before looking away.

Stella tightened the Velcro straps on the vest till it was fitted to her torso, then put her sweater back on.

"She'll need a sidearm," Hammerton said to the men.

The man next to her removed from his kit a SIG 320 fitted with a suppressor.

The weapon was empty, its slide in the locked-back position.

Stella took the weapon from him, and he reached into his bag and grabbed two mags along with a leather inside-the-waistband holster, offering her those as well.

Stella thanked him and took the mags, loading the weapon with one and placing the other in the back pocket of her jeans.

She holstered the weapon and laid it on her lap.

Leaning back in her seat, she took a breath and let it out, then settled into a calm stillness.

She noticed that J. D. was still as well. He sat straight in his seat, and the gear bag at his feet remained closed.

Unlike the others, he was in no rush to prepare.

He and Stella stared at each other for a moment. Then he nodded once.

She returned the gesture before leaning her head back and closing her eyes.

She stayed that way till the helicopter touched down on the West Thirtieth Street Heliport.

Sixty

At nine p.m. Stella approached the park from the southwest.

Passing the Seward monument as she entered, she turned right and headed east, walking at a fast pace.

One of Hammerton's men had given her an operator's cap, which she wore with the bill pulled low, making sure that as much of her dark hair was visible as possible.

Another had given her a windbreaker, which she carried, folded in half, in one hand.

She scanned her surroundings as she moved, taking in both the small park itself and the streets beyond it.

Reaching the southeast corner of the park, Stella turned north, walking parallel to Madison Avenue, where there were several parked cars but currently no vehicle traffic.

A minute later, at the northeast corner, she turned left, heading west along Twenty-Sixth Street—less well lit than Madison and just as quiet, but lined with parked cars.

It was here that she removed the SIG from its holster with her right hand and handed it off to her left, gripping it by the barrel and draping the windbreaker over her hand to conceal the weapon.

The transfer, completed with just a few smooth motions, took all of two seconds.

Hidden as she was in the shadows on the park's darker side, she was confident that no one had witnessed the act.

The busier and brightest-lit part of the park was the northwest corner—at Twenty-Sixth and Fifth Avenue. Two blocks south of there Broadway and Fifth converged, crossing like the two lines of an *X*.

Traffic was heavier, mostly speeding taxis and buses—Fifth heading uptown, Broadway heading downtown.

Turning south at that corner of the park, Stella was now walking toward the spot where she had entered. That entrance was another minute away, give or take, and when she reached it, she had circled the entire park.

Now she began another circuit.

This time as she walked, though, she concentrated on the pedestrians inside the park.

An art installation—a towering Buddha head—occupied the center of the space, and there were three people standing before it.

Others were passing through—a man and woman holding hands, a chattering group of four hipsters walking shoulder to shoulder, and the occasional individual—but none of these people paid any attention to the woman walking at a brisk pace, though that was to be expected.

New Yorkers were experts at ignoring the seemingly odd.

The men she was expecting—the men she wanted to be puzzled by her actions and choice of pace—would make no effort to conceal themselves or their interest in her.

Their presence would be obvious, as both a general deterrent and a specific tactic of intimidation.

Stella was halfway through her second trip around the park when she saw what she knew was the first of the Benefactor's men.

They appeared in the northeast corner, entering from Madison, watching her intently as she passed. Once she had and was heading west again along the park's north perimeter—the darker side—they followed her, but they did so without making an effort to match her pace.

They sauntered, walking side by side.

Toward the west, at the corner of Broadway and Twenty-Third Street, two of Hammerton's men, one following the other, appeared.

With strides not unlike the men behind her, they made their way toward the park.

Looking straight ahead to the southwest entrance, Stella saw that two more men had arrived and were standing beside the Seward monument.

They, too, stared at her, their gloved hands hanging at their sides.

Stella shifted her focus beyond them, taking solace in the fact that Hammerton's remaining two men were already in position across Twenty-Third. Standing by the prow of the Flatiron Building, they faced each other as if in conversation, smoking cigarettes.

She wondered if the Benefactor's men would even take note of any man over a certain age.

Would men in their sixties even be visible?

As she walked parallel to Fifth, Stella kept an eye out for the vehicle that Carrington and J. D. had rushed to retrieve.

It was a battered Ford Econoline van that Cahill had purchased from an out-of-business general contractor, complete with a collapsible aluminum ladder attached to a roof rack and the contractor's license number still stenciled on the driver's door.

The company's name and logo were on the right side panel, though the letters and image were faded by exposure to two decades of New York City summers and winters.

A vehicle like that would be easy to pick out among the typical nighttime traffic, but she saw no sign of it yet.

She saw no sign of Hammerton, either, but she trusted he would be where she needed him, when she needed him.

He was the only man other than Tom whom she implicitly trusted.

Reaching the southwest corner, Stella turned left, passing the two men, who had moved away from the monument to assume a blocking position at the entrance.

No doubt her two circuits had worn down their patience.

It was time.

She walked a dozen or so steps past a row of benches, then sat facing the park, laying the jacket and the firearm it hid on her lap.

Behind her, beyond the wrought-iron fence and the border of trees, was the point on Twenty-Third Street that was roughly halfway between Fifth and Madison.

The two men back by the southwest entrance held their position, and the two who had entered in the northeast corner by Madison had made their way to the southeast entrance, blocking it after the last of the civilians had left the park.

Like their partners to Stella's left, this pair alternated between watching her and scanning the park and the streets surrounding it.

These men were dressed in either sweatshirts or short jackets, and the absence of longer coats was an indication that they, too, had likely left behind any long gun in favor of more concealable firearms, though that didn't necessarily rule out the possibility that one or more of them was armed with some kind of submachine gun—an Uzi or MP5 or KRISS Vector with its shoulder stock in the folded position.

If things went as planned, these men wouldn't even get the chance to reach for their weapons.

Of course, Stella knew that things seldom went the way they were supposed to go.

No plan ever survives first contact.

For a minute or so, nothing changed.

A mix of concerns raced through Stella's mind.

First among them was the possibility that the Benefactor wouldn't show, that he had simply sent his men to kill Esa or had recognized the trap and sent his men to kill whomever had come to bait him.

But wouldn't his men have made their move by now?

Unless someone was in one of the vehicles parked along Twenty-Sixth Street—a sniper making use of the relative darkness there to conceal himself as he took his time to zero his target.

Her second concern was that she had made a mistake by pushing for this mission, that she was in over her head.

The first concern she could do nothing about, but the second was within her control.

She knew that doubt was the mistake, not her decision, not the unassailable conviction to do whatever it took to save Tom.

Just like he would do whatever it took to save her.

Stella remembered the first time they had left Shelter Island in that rowboat, Tom keeping them on a straight line as they crossed to the mainland despite a broken forearm.

A year and a half later, they had found themselves back on Shelter Island, and once again they had planned a similar late-night escape, only to change their minds at the last minute and commit to the world that Tom had tried so hard to avoid.

The world he didn't want for either of them, and that she was in the heart of right now.

Her mind clear, her heart rate and breathing steady, Stella slipped her right hand under the jacket on her lap till she found the grip of the SIG.

Holding it, she waited.

Another minute passed before two men entered the park via the northwest corner.

Both were dressed in suits and wearing leather shoes that gleamed in the bright lights. Starting across the park, following one of the diagonal paths that crisscrossed its center, they headed straight for the solitary woman in the black sweater and jeans seated on the wrought-iron bench.

Stella knew by their bearing alone that this was the Benefactor and General Graves.

Cruel and entitled men carried themselves in a specific and unmistakable way.

Tucking her chin to her chest as if looking down at her feet, Stella was counting on the long bill of her cap to keep her face hidden for as long as possible.

The lowered bill, however, also prevented her from seeing the men, but she knew she would hear their footsteps on the stone path.

Once she did, she would be able to gauge their distance from her as they closed it.

As she listened, she caught something from the corner of her left eye.

A white van—or the roof of it, at least, appearing just over the top of the fence.

The vehicle, with a ladder mounted to its roof, was coming down Broadway, racing for the turn onto Twenty-Third.

The glimpse was only fleeting, the vehicle passing from her peripheral vision nearly as soon as she saw it, but this seconds-long distraction was enough for her to have missed the initial audible steps of the two men closing in.

By the time she shifted her focus back to them, their shoes were in her line of sight.

After a few more steps, both men stopped.

"Esa," one of the men said.

Stella didn't lift her head.

"Esa," the man repeated.

There was a touch of German in his accent, but it was the authority in the man's voice that caught Stella's attention.

It carried the weight of a command, and she felt an instant desire to resist that authority.

"Look at me, Esa," the Benefactor said.

Stella knew now which feet belonged to whom.

The Benefactor was the man on her left.

"Is she deaf?" the man on the right said.

"Esa, look at me," the Benefactor barked.

Stella waited, keeping her grip on the SIG hidden beneath the windbreaker firm but relaxed.

A few more seconds at the most was all she had—all that she could give J. D.

If he was in position on the south side of Twenty-Third, then he was no more than two hundred feet behind her, and the *clack* of his suppressed SR-25 would cross that distance and reach her ears nearly instantly.

If he failed to get into position, or was in the only position available but couldn't get a clear shot for some reason, then it was up to her.

From the corner of her eye she detected the two bodyguards to her left. Drawn by the unusual activity as well as the sound of their employer's angry voice, they began walking in her direction.

A quick glance to her right revealed that the two men by that entrance had stopped scanning and were fixed on her.

Stella had only seconds to decide, so she started a countdown in her head.

Three.

No *clack*ing sound.

Two.

Still no *clack*ing sound.

One.

Time was up, and Stella made her move.

Sixty-One

Raising her head, Stella lifted her right hand off her lap just enough to turn the SIG so it was pointed at the man on the left.

Squaring the weapon with her body so that it was aligned with her target, she saw the Benefactor's face, and he saw hers.

His look of annoyed disdain was replaced by angry confusion, the shift occurring in less than a second.

That was all the time Stella needed to make sure the pistol was centered on the torso of the powerful man standing ten feet away.

She put two nine-mil rounds into his center, and he staggered back but remained upright, his look of anger and confusion deepening.

The man beside him took a step to the side, flinging his suit jacket open as he reached for a pistol in a brown leather shoulder rig.

Stella raised the SIG, allowing the windbreaker to drop away and placing the weapon between her eye and the target.

She put two rounds into that man's chest as well, but like the Benefactor had, he, too, merely staggered backward.

More than that, the impact of the rounds did not slow his effort to reach across his stomach for his firearm.

Stella's eyes went to the two points in his suit where her rounds had struck the man, and the lack of blood made it clear to her that he was wearing a protective vest.

It was then that she glanced at the Benefactor and saw the same lack of blood where he had been struck.

And he was reaching for a weapon as well.

Stella shifted her focus back to the second man—Graves—as he was fast-drawing his sidearm. Even at close range, and especially while under duress, shooting a handgun accurately was no easy thing.

All it took was an improper trigger technique or faulty grip to guarantee a clean miss, even at ten feet away.

And Stella now needed to pull off not one but two head shots, so inches counted more than ever.

Graves, his suppressed pistol in his hand, was maybe a second ahead of the Benefactor, who was still reaching to the small of his back for his weapon. If Stella fired at Graves, the Benefactor would have time to remove his weapon and fire on her, and if she fired on the Benefactor first, taking the time necessary for a clean head shot, then Graves, already bringing his weapon to bear on her, would easily take her out.

There really wasn't a choice.

She had to kill the Benefactor.

Shifting her focus to him, she positioned the night sights of the SIG between her eyes and the man's face, adding her left hand to her grip.

The Benefactor, his look of anger solidified into rage, had removed his weapon and was swinging his arm around.

It was a move he was not to complete.

Stella laid the pad of her right index finger on the trigger and, letting out a slight sigh, eased it back in a straight line.

Before she even felt the recoil, the hollow-point 9 mil had passed through the Benefactor's right eye.

With no heavy bone or tissue to resist the bullet, its serrated tip failed to mushroom, so it lost little of its velocity as it sliced through his brain and pierced the back of his skull, exiting with a burst of blood and brain matter that formed a brief halo of red mist above his head.

The dead man had not yet hit the pavement when Graves fired at Stella, striking her directly in the sternum.

It felt to her like someone had taken a sledgehammer to her chest, knocking the air out of her lungs.

Stunned, she dropped her left hand but managed to hang on to her pistol with her right.

The agony was unbearable, the shock overwhelming, but she couldn't give up.

She started raising the SIG, ready to unload it into Graves, but he had closed the distance between them fast, parrying her right hand away and pressing the still-hot muzzle of his Walther PPQ against her head.

Owing to the bruised sternum, she could barely register the burning sensation.

Graves paused to say, "Look at me, bitch."

More out of defiance than compliance, Stella met his stare.

He pressed the muzzle even harder, and Stella closed her eyes.

Then, from behind her: *clack*.

She opened her eyes in time to see the general's head fly backward violently, a cloud of red greater than the Benefactor's halo bursting into the air behind him.

His feet came out from under him, and he dropped to a seated position before slumping to one side and falling the rest of the way to the ground.

Stella slid off the bench and landed on the pavement.

She couldn't do more than that. Her voided lungs were aching, yet she was unable to draw in air.

She faced west and saw the two men rushing toward her, their weapons on her, but Hammerton's men appeared directly behind them, each firing their suppressed pistols, putting two rounds into the backs of their heads.

The men from the east began firing at Hammerton's men out in the open.

The first got off only two shots before a mist sprayed from his head as he, too, was felled by J. D. from his position in the van parked on Twenty-Third.

The last remaining man, his eyes fixed on Stella, had removed an Uzi from under his jacket and pulled back the bolt, but that was as far as he got.

Hammerton's other two men brought him down with head shots, though Stella observed that through fading eyes.

On the hard pavement, with two dead men just feet away, she struggled to breathe.

The next thing she knew, she was being lifted.

She wondered if she were a child being carried in the arms of her father.

Maybe she was dreaming this. She couldn't tell, though.

It took a moment for her to open her eyes and realize that she was in the cabin of the EC-135, flat on her back on the floor.

The lifting she had felt was the helicopter rising off the helipad.

She was breathing now, though she could fill her lungs only partially before a wave of pain nearly knocked the air out of her again.

She saw Hammerton's face above her, J. D. beside him. Both men were kneeling.

Her sweater and Kevlar vest had been removed, and a blanket had been placed over her.

J. D. was prepping a syringe. He said to Stella, "It's for the pain. Your sternum is cracked, and this will help you breathe. We're taking you back to Shelter Island. We'll be there before you know it."

He pulled the blanket back, exposing her shoulder, then wiped the skin clean with an antiseptic swab and injected her with morphine.

She felt the warmth moving through her almost immediately.

J. D. covered her up again and moved back to his seat. Hammerton adjusted the blanket, like he was tucking in a daughter, and then did the same.

Stella looked at them for a bit before she realized that the four former SAS men were staring at her.

Seated in a row, their gear bags closed and stowed at their feet, they each had an open can of Guinness in hand.

They nodded at Stella, a clear gesture of recognition and respect, then one by one, raised their drinks in salute and collectively said, "Cheers, mate."

Together they took long sips.

Then everyone in the cabin sat still and silent, to allow Stella to rest.

While she did, they would bring her back home.

The men remained quiet even after Stella had fallen asleep.

She dreamed of Tom.

PART SIX

Sixty-Two

The departures began three days later.

The first to leave were Hammerton and his SAS men, while Tom was still bedridden and passing in and out of consciousness, and Stella had only just started to move around.

Before leaving, Hammerton's men gave Stella a business card with a phone number on it.

If she were ever in trouble—any kind of trouble anywhere in the world, she was told—all she had to do was call that number, and someone would be there to help within twenty-four hours.

This promise of aid and support was a long-standing code among all former SAS, and as far as Hammerton's men were concerned, Stella was an honorary member of their brotherhood now.

One by one, the four men shook her hand and left the room, and finally only Stella and Hammerton remained.

They were quiet for a moment, and then Stella asked him where he was going.

"Home," Hammerton said.

"How long since you've been there?"

"A long time."

"Do you have family, John?"

He nodded. "A sister. It'll be good to see her again."

Stella smiled, but tears welled in her eyes. It took another moment before she could speak. "We owe you everything," she said. The tears fell then, spilling down her face.

Hammerton took her hand, held it gently. "No debts between friends," he said.

Stella embraced him. She didn't let go till she was ready, which took a long time.

Grunn and Krista left a few days later, bound for Krista's adoptive father's farm in Northern Vermont.

Tom was able to sit up for short periods by then. Stella brought the two women into the study to say their goodbyes.

"You guys are welcome at the farm anytime," Krista said. "It's a big house, lots of rooms. We'll always have one ready for you."

Stella asked them if they had thought about what they were going to do.

Grunn said, "Sleep. After that, who knows."

Krista asked, "What about you guys?"

"We're still figuring that out," Stella answered.

But she said it with a smile, as though, at least for now, the fact that the future was finally theirs to choose mattered more than the actual future itself.

It was another week before Tom was able to get out of bed for more than a few minutes at a time.

Another week passed before he left the study and began spending his nights with Stella in the room they had occupied during their two previous stays.

As pleased as he was to be in that room again—to be beyond mere convalescence and on his way to full recovery—he grew eager to leave it after a few nights.

During bouts of sleeplessness caused by the termination of pain medication, Tom would plan their own departure—he and Stella leaving quietly and disappearing, just as they had done once before.

For the longest time, Tom had desired that—wanted nothing more—and he wasn't about to settle for anything less.

On one particularly bad night, as Stella slept beside him, Tom got up and removed a pad of paper and pen from the drawer of his nightstand.

He had once, as a child, asked his father what their last name meant.

A sexton used to be an officer of the church, George Sexton had explained. *He was the caretaker for church grounds. My grandfather told me that the word was derived from the Old French word* sacristan, *which means "sacred." Part of a sexton's duties was to dig graves, and eventually the word came to be used as the title of someone who is the caretaker of a cemetery. Someone who tends to the grounds, buries the dead, keeps a list of their names and where exactly they are interred.*

Tom placed the notebook on his thigh. The night beyond his window was clear, so there was enough light for him to see by as he began to list the names of the dead—those who had died because of him.

The last name on that list belonged to the only person whose resting place he was currently aware of.

The woman interred illegally on the Cahill property, which, should she ever be discovered, would bring nothing but trouble to the family to whom everyone—not just Tom and Stella and the others, but also the entire citizenry of the country Charlie Cahill had loyally served—owed so much.

There was no point, though, in keeping Esa's name off the list of the dead.

A list that, for Tom, would be too long if it contained only one name.

He would keep that paper with him always, and he would never allow anyone but Stella to see it.

Others had left Shelter Island without Tom's knowledge, some departing while he had been unconscious, some slipping away without saying goodbye to anyone.

Tom learned that Slattery had left not long after Hammerton and his men, and he wondered how long she would have to wait before being reunited with the father she barely knew.

Were they together now, the two of them, in that secluded and secret house? Tom remembered the empty hospital bed waiting in the room off the living room. He hoped she and her father would have time together before he was confined to that bed.

Tom tried not to imagine her tending to the man in his final days, being required to watch him slowly die.

Tom had had to endure the loss of only one father, but Slattery was now facing the loss of a second.

But if anyone was strong enough to survive that, it was she.

J. D.'s departure had also occurred while Tom was unconscious, and he'd left in a manner that, when described to Tom by Stella, pleased them both.

One morning, J. D.'s room was empty, his bed made and his gear gone.

Not even Carrington knew when his onetime bodyguard had left or where the young man might be headed.

But Carrington did point out that if the need ever arose, there was a system in place that would allow him to reach J. D.

Stella expressed regret that she hadn't been able to say goodbye, though she understood the desire to just disappear.

"I think he was a lot like us in that regard," she said to Tom.

Carrington and Cahill came and went during those three weeks, sometimes for hours at a time, other times for days.

As Tom became more aware of the happenings in the house, he mentioned the activity to Stella.

"I think they're tying up loose ends," she said.

Tom thought about that for a moment, then said, "Raveis."

Stella nodded. "He's still out there, right? He all but hand-delivered you to the Colonel."

A full month passed before Sandy Montrose released Tom from her care.

"You're Stella's problem now," she teased.

Tom would need to take it easy for a while, but he and Stella were free to go.

Tom thanked her and made his way from the med bay to the back porch where Stella was waiting for him.

It was a brisk day in early November, the sky cloudy and the water the color of steel. Stella was wearing one of Cahill's coats. She and Tom owned nothing more than the clothes on their backs, carried with them only what could fit in their pockets.

"Well?" Stella said.

Tom's response was a smile.

It was later that day that Cahill's Mustang turned onto the property, passed the manned gatehouse, and headed down the long gravel drive toward the house.

Tom and Stella were asleep in their bedroom. Hearing the noise, Tom got up and stepped to the window.

Something told him to get dressed and go downstairs.

His jeans and sweatshirt and boots on, he left the room. Stella, naked under the tangle of sheets and blankets, was still asleep.

Downstairs, Tom opened the front door as Cahill's vehicle came to a stop in the wide circle at the driveway's end.

Cahill and Carrington emerged, and Tom knew by the looks on their faces that something was up.

He stepped onto the front porch and asked what was going on.

Cahill said, "We need to talk."

They gathered in the study with the door closed.

The hospital bed had been moved back to the med bay in the basement a week ago.

Everything in this room was as it had been when Tom and the Colonel had first met here.

"What's up?" Tom said.

"A month ago, after we got you here, we checked the cloud account that Raveis gave you the access info for," Carrington said. "He never changed the username and password. We immediately downloaded the documentation, made hard copies and digital backups, and stored them in a number of locations, real world and online."

Cahill said, "It's unlikely that Raveis would forget to change the log-in info, so it's possible that he's dead. He tended to make enemies."

Tom nodded. "That he did."

"But I keep thinking about how he gave you a Kevlar vest, not once but twice," Cahill said. "And yes, he sent you to that factory, where he knew the Colonel had a recon team waiting, but he also gave you a better weapon. In fact, it seems that he did everything he could to help you without tipping off the Colonel."

"It's even possible that he knew I was there," Carrington said, "in an overwatch position right across the street, in case you did come back. He had sent a recon team to Ansonia prior to sending you in. I may have been spotted by them. For that matter, Raveis may have known all along that I was there. One of his kill teams might have found me, but he held back the execute order."

"Why would he do that?" Tom said.

Carrington answered. "The Colonel always said that Raveis saw opportunities in everything, that he collected them. Maybe his sparing me was another way of possibly helping you."

Tom said nothing.

"The documents and audio files and videos, they served as a form of détente between Raveis and the Colonel," Cahill said. "Maybe by letting you gain access to them after the Colonel's death, Raveis was making the same deal with you. Maybe he's telling you that he'll grant you the professional courtesy of leaving you alone if you grant him the same courtesy."

Carrington said, "Raveis didn't show it because he couldn't—it was his job to be an asshole—but he had a lot of respect for you. I'm thinking he knows you'd be smart enough to recognize a peace offering when you see one. You could destroy him, just like he could destroy you. If neither of you does a thing, then everyone gets to live the rest of their lives in peace."

Tom thought about that, then said to Carrington, "No one knows where he went, right?"

"He could be anywhere in the world," Carrington said. "If you prefer, if it will make you sleep easier, we can turn everything we have over to the feds. Raveis wasn't the man who killed your father, but he did put him in the room with his killer."

Tom shook his head. "No," he said. "Raveis knows we're here. He's had an entire month to come after us, if that was what he wanted." Tom took a breath, let it out. "I'll take the peace offering, for everyone's sake."

Cahill and Carrington nodded in agreement.

"There's something else," Cahill said. "With Slattery's help, we checked into whether or not the NYPD were looking for you. And for Stella, too, considering what she did in Madison Square Park. I even had one of my family's attorneys standing by to get involved, just in case."

"And?"

"It turns out someone with influence made it clear to the police commissioner that you and Stella were operatives of the United States government, and that any and all courtesies that could be afforded to you both should be afforded."

Carrington said, "Someone's looking out for you, it seems."

"Raveis?" Tom said.

"Maybe. Or maybe it was someone else. Someone you haven't even met and who might one day want to cash in on the favor he or she did you."

Tom felt as if a cloud had suddenly moved in over him.

But his freedom wasn't his only concern.

"What about Hammerton and his men?"

Cahill smiled and said, "It turns out they were security personnel attached to the British embassy in New York. Or at least that's the word that came from London a week after their return to the UK. It looks like they have friends, too."

Tom nodded, looked at both men. "Thanks for all this."

"It's time for you to go now, Tom," Carrington said. "You can go anywhere you want without having to look over your shoulder. You can start over again, as yourself or as someone else, whichever you choose."

Tom thought about the possibilities.

Then Carrington added, "Maybe this time don't answer your phone, no matter who's calling, stranger or friend."

Carrington left that evening.

Tom and Stella and Cahill and Sandy Montrose were the only remaining occupants of the house.

After dinner, Stella and Sandy went out to sit on the back porch, and as Tom and Cahill were cleaning up, Cahill made Tom an offer.

Later that night, in their room, Tom passed the offer on to Stella.

She thought about it for a few moments. "It's funny," she said finally. "My father was a marine and then a state cop. My mother was a doctor, back in the days when most towns only had one. So it kind of feels right, doesn't it? Cahill and Sandy moving in. I mean, Sandy's a damn good doctor, and Cahill was a marine and is what he is now, you know, this . . . protector."

"He's willing to pay whatever you want for the property."

"Fair-market value is fine with me."

"He asked me to help him get the downstairs space ready. It would probably take two weeks for us to do that."

Stella looked at Tom. "You joined the Seabees because you wanted to build things. I can't think of a better use of those skills now."

"So it's a yes."

Stella nodded, leaned in, and kissed Tom.

Leaning back, she said, "Yes, it's a yes."

The renovations ended up taking ten days.

Cahill was clueless, like he'd once said he was, but he caught on fast, and as the project moved along, he and Tom picked up momentum to the point where they were taking breaks only for meals and to sleep for a few hours.

While they transformed the unused ground-floor retail space into a physician's office, Stella and Sandy painted the apartment above, finishing their work just as Tom and Cahill had completed putting the wall frames and Sheetrock in place.

Once the downstairs painting was done, they put down floor tiles and carpeting and then brought in the furnishings and equipment.

It was eight in the evening on November 15 when they finished.

They shared a meal of Chinese takeout, toasted their efforts with glasses of red wine, and in the morning, an hour before dawn, Tom and Stella were ready.

Cahill had given them both backpacks, each one loaded with everything they might need—emergency medical equipment, survival gear, burner phones with a single number programmed into them.

"I'll see you around," he said to Tom. Then he smiled. "Or maybe not. It's all up to you."

He and Tom shook hands.

Sandy and Stella embraced.

Sandy kissed Tom; Stella kissed Cahill.

It was a cold morning in Canaan, and it was time for Tom and Stella to go.

The pickup truck was a ten-year-old Chevy Colorado, a gift from Cahill and Sandy for all the work Tom and Stella had done on the property.

At first Tom had refused the vehicle, said they could get their own, but Cahill had insisted.

Tom was steering the pickup north on Route 7, taking the same two-lane road out of town that he had taken into it two and a half years ago, on that chilly spring day when he had stopped for an early lunch at a converted railcar diner and found the reason to cease his five years of wandering.

But that hadn't been the end of his wandering; he knew this now. It was merely a stopover to pick up a passenger who would one day travel on with him.

Someone to watch over, and to watch over him.

"So where are we going?" Tom said.

Stella waited a while before answering.

"We're coming from where I grew up, and we've been to where you grew up, so how about someplace neither of us has been before? What do you think of that? Someplace in the middle of nowhere."

Tom smiled and reached over to touch the side of her face, his eyes on the open road ahead.

It was good, he thought, to be moving again, and to be free.

"Nowhere sounds perfect," he said.

Acknowledgments

Much appreciation for the hard work (and patience) of the following kind souls, in order of appearance:

Scott Miller, Alison Dasho, Gracie Doyle, Liz Pearsons, Caitlin Alexander, Sarah Shaw, and Sarah Simone, RN.

Thanks also to:

Lenora Martorelli, Theresa Schwegel, Audrey Terry, Brian Dewey, and Janet and Chris Antilla.

About the Author

Photo © 2012 Tracy Deer-Mirek

Daniel Judson is the Shamus Award–winning (and four-time finalist) author of *The Temporary Agent*, *The Rogue Agent*, and *The Shadow Agent* in the Agent Series, as well as *Avenged*, *The Poisoned Rose*, *The Bone Orchard*, *The Gin Palace*, *The Darkest Place*, *The Betrayer*, *The Water's Edge*, *The Violet Hour*, and *Voyeur*. Judson's immersive research method lends his work a distinctive authenticity and has fostered an ever-expanding eclectic skill set that includes Vipassana medicine, Filipino knife-fighting, and urban-evasion techniques. A Son of the American Revolution, former gravedigger, and self-described onetime drifter, Judson currently lives in Connecticut with his fiancée and their rescued cats. For more information, visit Daniel at www.danieljudsonbooks.com.

About the Author